INTERNATIONAL ACCLAIM FOR

THE

Mission Earth

SERIES

"...simply the most fun you can have by yourself...
Ironic, exciting, romantic and hilarious. It delighted me from the beginning."

Orson Scott Card
"Ender's Game"

"...a wildly wicked and deliciously cynical work that mocked virtue, skewered hypocrisy and gave a hilariously satirical view of society..."

Kansas City Star

"I loved Mission Earth. The CIA will hate it. Hubbard has produced a real knee-slapper...he's laughing at the Sacred Cow of the Eighties, the so-called intelligence community..."

Ray Faraday Nelson

This book follows

MISSION EARTH

Volume 1
THE INVADERS PLAN

Volume 2
BLACK GENESIS

Volume 3
THE ENEMY WITHIN

Volume 4
AN ALIEN AFFAIR

Volume 5
FORTUNE OF FEAR

Volume 6
DEATH QUEST

Volume 7
VOYAGE OF VENGEANCE

and

Volume 8
DISASTER

Buy them and read them first!

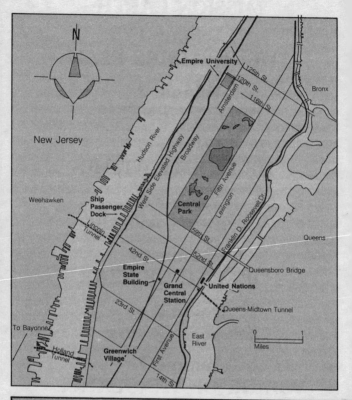

Blito-P3 {Earth} Cities

Central Manhattan an

Plotted by 54 Charlee Nine

Black Sea

Bulgaria

Istanbul

Sea of Marmara

APPARATUS BASE

• Ankara

Limnos
Moudhros

• Bursa

*Aegean
Sea*

• Afyon

Lake Tu

Lake Akshehir

• Izmir

T U R K E Y

Antalya

Mediterranean Sea

0 25 50   100
Miles

FALSE !! Monte Fennwell

Cyprus

Central Turkey

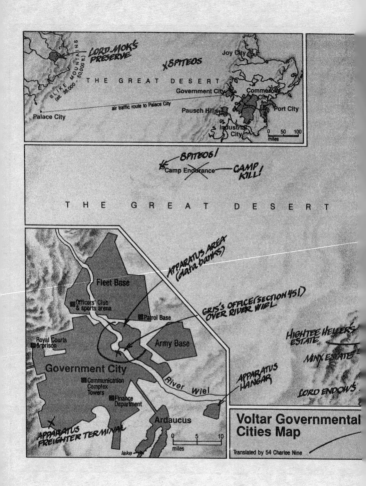

Voltar Governmental Cities Map

Translated by 54 Charlee Nine

Joy City

N

countryside

EN MOUNTAINS (alt. 10,000 - 14,000 ft.)

Emergency Fleet Reserve

Fleet Base

Army Base

River Wiel

PROVOCATION SECTION

nment
ty
Ardaucus lake
SLUM CITY)

Commercial City

Port City

warehouse district

Power City

Industrial City

Western Ocean

VENWELL
ESTATE

0 10 20   50   100
miles

TES ADDED
THE DEAR READER
BY Monte Farmwell

Royal Mapmakers Division
Voltar Confederacy—
Civilian Grade Map:
GOVERNMENTAL CITIES OF VOLTAR
Series D - Number 00570 . 39 . 3205001 . 01

AMONG THE MANY CLASSIC WORKS
BY L. RON HUBBARD

Battlefield Earth
Beyond the Black Nebula
Buckskin Brigades
The Conquest of Space
The Dangerous Dimension
Death's Deputy
The Emperor of the Universe
Fear
Final Blackout
Forbidden Voyage
The Incredible Destination
The Kilkenny Cats
The Kingslayer
The Last Admiral
The Magnificent Failure
The Masters of Sleep
The Mutineers
Ole Doc Methuselah
Ole Mother Methuselah
The Rebels
Return to Tomorrow
Slaves of Sleep
To the Stars
The Traitor
Triton
Typewriter in the Sky
The Ultimate Adventure
The Unwilling Hero

Mission Earth

Villainy Victorious

THE BOOKS OF THE
MISSION EARTH DEKALOGY*

* *Dekalogy—a group of ten volumes.*

L. RON HUBBARD

Mission Earth

VOLUME NINE

Villainy Victorious

BRIDGE PUBLICATIONS, INC.
LOS ANGELES

This is a work of science fiction, written as satire.*
The essence of satire is to examine, comment and
give opinion of society and culture, none of which is
to be construed as a statement of pure fact. No actual
incidents are portrayed and none of the incidents are
to be construed as real. Some of the actions of this
novel take place on the planet Earth, but the characters *as presented in this novel* have been invented. Any
accidental use of the names of living people in a
novel is virtually inevitable, and any such inadvert-
ency in this book is unintentional.

*See Author's Introduction, *Mission Earth: Volume
One, The Invaders Plan.*

To YOU,
the millions of science fiction fans
and general public
who welcomed me back to the world of fiction
so warmly
and to the critics and media
who so pleasantly
applauded the novel "Battlefield Earth".
It's great working for you!

Voltarian
Censor's
Disclaimer

This bizarre, fallacious tale has not been made any more palatable by the introduction of a different narrator.

Nor has the narrative gained any credibility by its claims that events in our 110-planet confederacy were caused by a stupid, nonexistent race of people from a planet that sounds more like a lunatic asylum than anything else.

The position of the Crown is firmer than ever.

The planet Earth does not exist!

Lord Invay
Royal Historian
Chairman, Board of Censors
Royal Palace
Voltar Confederacy

By Order of
His Imperial Majesty
Wully the Wise

Voltarian
Translator's
Preface

Hi there!

This is your translator, 54 Charlee Nine. How are you?

Lord Invay may not take kindly to having a new narrator but it's sure easier for me. Monte Pennwell speaks only Voltarian. I'm programmed for any language, but there does seem to be a scarcity of information on the languages they speak on this nonexistent Earth.

I have updated your Key to this book and it follows.

Sincerely,

54 Charlee Nine
Robotbrain in the Translatophone

Key to
VILLAINY
VICTORIOUS

Afyon—City in Turkey where the *Apparatus* has a secret mountain base.

Agnes, Miss—Personal aide to Delbert John *Rockecenter*.

Apparatus, Coordinated Information—The secret police of *Voltar*, headed by Lombar *Hisst* and manned by criminals. Their symbol is an inverted paddle which, because it looks like a bottle, earned its members the name "drunks."

Balmor—Butler to Jettero *Heller* and the Countess *Krak* on Earth.

Bang-Bang—An ex-marine demolitions expert and member of the Babe *Corleone* mob.

Barben, I. G.—Pharmaceutical company controlled by Delbert John *Rockecenter*.

Bawtch—Soltan *Gris*'s chief clerk on *Voltar*.

Bittlestiffender, Prahd—Voltarian cellologist that Soltan *Gris* brought to Earth to operate a hospital in *Afyon*. (See *Cellology*.)

Blito-P3—Voltarian designation for a planet known locally as Earth. It is the third planet (P3) of a yellow-dwarf star known as Blito.

Blixo—*Apparatus* freighter, piloted by Captain Bolz, that makes regular runs between Earth and *Voltar*. The voyage takes about six weeks each way.

Bluebottles—Nickname given to the Domestic Police of *Voltar*.

Blueflash—A bright blue flash of light used to produce unconsciousness. It is usually used by Voltarian ships before landing in an area that is possibly populated.

Bolz—See *Blixo*.

Bury—Delbert John *Rockecenter*'s most powerful attorney. His favorite pastime is feeding white mice to snakes.

Caucalsia, Prince—According to a folk legend, he fled *Manco* during the Great Rebellion and set up a colony on *Blito-P3* that became known as Atlantis.

Cellology—Voltarian medical science that can repair the body through the cellular generation of tissues, including entire body parts.

Code Break—Violation of the Space Code that prohibits

disclosing that one is an alien. Penalty is death to the offender(s) and any native(s) so alerted.

Coordinated Information Apparatus—See *Apparatus*.

Corleone—A Mafia family headed by Babe, a former Roxy chorus girl and widow of "Holy Joe."

Crobe, Doctor—*Apparatus* cellologist who worked in *Spiteos*. He delights in making human freaks.

Drunks—See *Apparatus*.

Endow, Lord—Head of the *Exterior Division*.

Epstein, Izzy—Financial expert and anarchist hired by Jettero *Heller* to set up and run several corporations.

Exterior Division—That part of the Voltarian government that reportedly contained the *Apparatus*.

Faht Bey—Turkish name of the commander of the secret *Apparatus* base in *Afyon*, Turkey.

Faustino "The Noose" Narcotici—Head of a Mafia family that is the underworld outlet for drugs from I.G. *Barben*.

F.F.B.O.—Fatten, Farten, Burstein and Ooze, the largest advertising/public relations firm on Earth. J. Walter *Madison* works for them.

Fleet—The elite space fighting arm of *Voltar* to which Jettero *Heller* belongs and which the *Apparatus* despises.

G. C.—See *Grand Council*.

Gracious Palms—The elegant whorehouse where Jettero *Heller* resided when first in New York City. It is across from the United Nations and is operated by the *Corleone* family.

Grafferty, "Bulldog"—A crooked New York City police inspector.

Grand Council—The governing body of *Voltar,* which ordered a mission to keep Earth from destroying itself so it could be conquered on schedule per the *Invasion Timetable.*

Gris, Soltan—*Apparatus* officer placed in charge of *Blito-P3* (Earth) section and an enemy of Jettero *Heller.*

Heller, Hightee—The most beautiful and popular entertainer in the *Voltar* Confederacy. She is also Jettero's sister.

Heller, Jettero—Combat engineer and Royal officer of the *Fleet,* sent with *Gris* on Mission Earth where he is operating under the name of Jerome Terrance *Wister.*

Hisst, Lombar—Head of the *Apparatus;* his plan to overthrow the *Voltar* Confederacy required sending Soltan *Gris* to sabotage Jettero *Heller*'s mission.

"Holy Joe"—See *Corleone.*

Hot Jolt—A popular Voltarian drink.

Invasion Timetable—A schedule of galactic conquest.

The plans and budget of every section of *Voltar*'s government must adhere to it. Bequeathed by Voltar's ancestors hundreds of thousands of years ago, it is inviolate and sacred and the guiding dogma of the Confederacy.

Joy, Miss—See Countess *Krak*.

Krak, Countess—Condemned murderess, former prisoner of *Spiteos*, a nonperson and the sweetheart of Jettero *Heller*. On Earth, she is known as Heavenly Joy Krackle or "Miss Joy."

Madison, J. Walter—Fired from *F.F.B.O.* when his style of public relations caused the president of Patagonia to commit suicide, he was rehired by *Bury* to immortalize Jettero *Heller* in the media. He is also known as "J. Warbler Madman."

Manco—Home planet of Jettero *Heller* and the Countess *Krak*.

Maysabongo—Jettero *Heller* was made a representative of this small African nation. Izzy *Epstein* made some of Heller's businesses Maysabongo corporations.

Mister Calico—A calico cat that was trained by the Countess *Krak*.

Mortiiy, Prince—Leader of a rebel group on the planet Calabar.

Mudur Zengin—Financial czar of the biggest banking chain in Turkey and handler of Soltan *Gris*'s funds.

Odur—See *Oh Dear.*

Oh Dear—Nickname for Odur. With *Too-Too*, forced by Soltan *Gris* to get information on *Voltar* and courier it to him on Earth.

Peace, Miss—Secretary to Delbert John *Rockecenter.*

Pokantickle—The New York estate of Delbert John *Rockecenter.*

Rockecenter, Delbert John—Native of Earth who controls the planet's fuel, finance, governments and drugs.

Simmons, Miss—An antinuclear fanatic.

Snelz—Platoon commander at *Spiteos* who befriended Jettero *Heller* and the Countess *Krak* when they were prisoners there.

Spiteos—On *Voltar*, the secret fortress prison of the *Apparatus.*

Swindle and Crouch—Law firm representing Delbert John *Rockecenter.*

Tayl, Widow—Nymphomaniac on *Voltar.*

Teenie—Earth teen-ager who kept seducing Soltan *Gris.* He shipped her to Voltar to get rid of her.

Too-Too—Nickname for *Twolah.* He and *Oh Dear* were forced by Soltan *Gris* to get information on *Voltar* and courier it secretly back to him on Earth.

Twoey—Nickname given to Delbert John Rockecenter II.

Twolah—See *Too-Too*.

Utanc—A belly dancer that *Gris* bought to be his concubine slave.

Voltar—Home planet and seat of the 110-world confederacy that was established over 125,000 years ago. Voltar is ruled by the Emperor through the *Grand Council* in accordance with the *Invasion Timetable*.

Wister, Jerome Terrance—Name that Jettero *Heller* is using on Earth.

PART SEVENTY-ONE

TO: BIOGRAPHICS PUBLISHING COMPANY
    COMMERCIAL CITY
    PLANET VOLTAR

GENTLEMEN!

I am thoroughly delighted with the agreements that we have reached. I can assure you that our names will be mutually and eternally emblazoned in history.

I could not believe that my government would ever lie to me. I had no idea that anyone would seek a "cover-up." That was why I was so shocked to discover that they have deleted, changed and destroyed records so that no one would learn the existence of this single planet called Earth.

Why would they want to deny the existence of a minor planet that is a mere 22½ light-years away?

Ah, that's the story that I am so arduously and so faithfully writing!

So that you may better appreciate my achievement, I am sending what I have completed thus far and will continue to write. I mailed the first part to you earlier. Let me try to bring you up-to-date. This is no small task because the imagination is staggered by the sheer magnitude of the events. However, I shall seek to achieve this.

As I have discovered, Earth is controlled by the man

who owns the planet's fuel—Delbert John Rockecenter. His power is such that he can determine the political future of a country simply by making a telephone call to one of his minions.

Voltarian Fleet officer Jettero Heller's mission was to de-pollute the planet and to create an inexpensive, safe source of energy so that Earth could survive long enough to be invaded.

When Heller arrived on Earth, he had the identity of Delbert John Rockecenter, Jr., which was given to him by the head of the Coordinated Information Apparatus, Lombar Hisst. This was done because Hisst wanted the Fleet officer's mission to fail, and he thought this would bring the force of the Rockecenters down on Heller. The reason Hisst wanted the mission to fail was that he was using Earth to produce mind-altering drugs that were being smuggled back to Voltar as part of a conspiracy to overthrow the Empire.

What no one knew was that there was a *real* inheritor to the Rockecenter fortune—Delbert John Rockecenter II.

The first person who tried to stop Heller was Rockecenter's attorney Bury, who gave Heller the identity of Jerome Terrance Wister. It didn't stop him, however. Heller became a consul for the African nation of Maysabongo and began to form corporations that created and patented new energy sources—a revolutionary microwave power source, a new carburetor that didn't use gasoline and cars that worked without Rockecenter-controlled fuel. When petroleum stocks dropped out the bottom, Heller used his Maysabongo resources to buy them all up and to take control of Earth's oil industries.

But Rockecenter was no fool, and he had forces that Heller could not muster—the American presidency, for example, and the armed forces of the United States.

One Sunday afternoon Rockecenter was preparing to go to Philadelphia for a Swillerberger Conference that he controlled. The president of the United States was to be called before the conference that night and ordered to go before the Senate the next day to request that war be declared on Maysabongo.

Bang-Bang drove Heller and his financial advisor Izzy Epstein to the great Rockecenter estate, and Heller and Izzy walked in while Rockecenter was chastising Bury for the current predicament.

Heller made Rockecenter an offer: Call off the war, grant "Twoey" (Rockecenter's actual son) a ten-billion-dollar trust, draw up a new will leaving Twoey the entire estate, and Heller would give Rockecenter the patents and a portion of the oil empire that Heller now controlled.

With the smile of a snake, Rockecenter agreed and the documents were signed—then the snake struck!

When the brief scuffle was over, Rockecenter's attorney Bury lay unconscious on the floor and a weaponless Heller was surrounded by army troops.

Rockecenter scooped up the papers that now gave him complete control and put them into a huge steel suitcase. He turned to a major general whose squad had its weapons turned on Heller and Izzy.

"General," said Rockecenter, "hold this riffraff until I return. Then, as we will be at war, we'll have work for a firing squad."

What? Has Heller lost everything?

Fear not! I, Monte Pennwell, Voltar's first, only and greatest investigative reporter, have the story!

Chapter 1

Rockecenter grabbed his hat and picked up the heavy case. He stepped over to Bury behind the couch and gave him a kick. "Whether you're dead or not, your usefulness is ended. Now I'm off to Philadelphia to handle another one of your foul-ups."

Rockecenter went to the French doors, closed them behind him and shouted up the drive, "Bring my car and get a tank for protection!"

The general gave a signal. Two soldiers seized Izzy, pinning his arms back and looking around for something to tie him with.

Two more soldiers grabbed Twoey and after a brief struggle had him on the floor.

The general made a gesture toward Heller.

Rockecenter's car had arrived and Rockecenter went down the steps to it, but he stood there looking up the road.

The soldiers started to grab Heller's arms. "Oh, he didn't mean me!" said Heller. "I'm his son."

"What?" said the general.

"Yes, it's a fact," said Heller. "He just meant these two fellows here."

Both Izzy and Twoey looked at Heller, stunned.

The general stepped toward the French doors as though to go after Rockecenter and ask. But Rockecenter had now climbed into his car and it began to roll.

From where Heller stood he could see through the glass of the French doors that Rockecenter's car had pulled up again and stopped. He hoped the general would not see that.

"Well, see here," said the general, "I'll have to have proof, and more than some phony I.D.!"

"Ah," said Heller. "You just grab the phone on that desk and ask for Emergency FBI, Washington, D.C. You just ask for agents Stupewitz and Maulin."

Heller crossed his fingers. Those agents were the first ones he had had contact with on his original arrival in the United States last fall. He had never heard of them or from them since.

The general moved to the desk, his back to the door. If he turned around he would be able to see the limousine. It was waiting for a tank, apparently, for tank engines were roaring outside.

The general got his connection. He asked for agent Stupewitz or Maulin. He waited. Then he said, "Agent Stupewitz? This is General Flood, New York National Guard. We've got a fellow here that says he's Rockecenter's son.... Yes, I'll describe him. He's about six foot two, slender, blond hair, blue eyes, probably about eighteen...." He put his hand over the mouthpiece, "What is your name supposed to be?"

"Delbert John Rockecenter, Junior," said Jet. He could see the tank in place in front of the car. A sergeant was standing by the officer in the turret, pointing at a map.

The general said into the phone, "He says his name is Delbert John Rockecenter, Junior.... I'm calling from Pokantickle Hills, the Rockecenter home...."

He suddenly shoved the instrument at Heller. "He wants to talk to you to verify your voice."

Heller took the phone. Out of the corner of his eye, he watched the tank and limousine. He wished they'd get moving. "Hello, Agent Stupewitz, sir," said Heller. "I just wanted to remind you that we never got a tombstone for Mary Schmeck."

"JUNIOR! Hey, Maulin, it's Junior! Grab the other phone!"

"Hello, Junior," said Maulin. "I'm glad you called. Did you know we never even heard from Bury!"

"Not a squeak!" said Stupewitz.

"How horrible!" said Heller. "It's a good thing that you told me. I'm of age now and there's a lot of inheritance around. . . ."

Both agents laughed agreeably.

"And I was just wondering the other day if I had any debts. By golly, I'm glad I contacted you. I am going to need a lot of help to straighten up my affairs. Would you consider a couple of six-figure jobs?"

Maulin said, "We can retire any minute, Junior. We're just waiting for the chance."

"You've got it," said Heller. "Do you want me to put this general back on?"

He handed the instrument to the general. He listened. His ears got bright pink. Then he looked at Heller and stood a little straighter. He put the phone back on its cradle.

"I'm sorry," said the general. "I'm new at these family matters."

"All's fair in love and war," said Heller cryptically. Out of the corner of his eye he saw that the limousine and tank were gone. "Now, General, take that Bury there to your hospital tent and if he isn't dead, do a nice long operation. Plenty of anesthetic because he's sensitive. As for these other two, hold them very safe."

Izzy and Twoey looked at him with horror.

"Now, as you know," continued Heller, "there's lots of Maysabongo saboteurs about. So let me have a motorcycle so my driver can scout the road. And if there's nothing else, I'll go out to my car and try to catch up with Daddy."

"Very good, Lieutenant Rockecenter," said the general and barked an order to an aide who was hovering at the door.

Chapter 2

Heller raced out. There was no sign of the tank or limousine. He spotted the sergeant who had been showing the map to the officer in the tank turret.

"Sergeant," he called, and when the man came over and saluted, "It's very urgent that they take a safe route. I trust you gave them good advice."

"Oh, yes, sir," said the sergeant, digging out a map. "There's reports of Maysabongo partisans in New York. So they're going west over the Tappan Zee Bridge to the Jersey side and then south on Highland Avenue until it joins the Palisades Interstate Parkway along the Hudson. Before they hit the George Washington Bridge, they'll go west to Fort Lee and then hit the New Jersey Turnpike. They'll leave that at Exit 6 and switch over to U.S. 95 and wind up right at Independence Hall."

Heller sketched it with a pen and took the map.

He ran over to where Bang-Bang sat worriedly in the cab, looking distrustfully at the army, an organization which, as an ex-marine, he despised. Heller, arriving from behind, startled him.

Hastily, Heller gave him some instructions and handed him the map. A soldier was wheeling up a despatch rider's motorcycle.

Bang-Bang got out of the cab. Heller took the despatch rider's helmet and put it on Bang-Bang. Then Heller reached into the cab and hung the satchel around Bang-Bang's neck.

The soldier jiggled the carburetor primer. Bang-Bang stamped on the kick-start, gave Heller a look of misgiving and then the motorcycle roared away, spreading terror amongst the troops it barely missed as it rocketed for the gate. Bang-Bang was gone.

Heller climbed into the cab, which now looked like an army car, started up, and with a salute to the officer, sped down the drive and away.

He had expected to catch up with Rockecenter by the time they had reached the Tappan Zee Bridge. But when he went through the tollgate, he could see no sign of the limousine or tank on the long span across the Hudson. He hoped Bang-Bang was riding fast enough. Rockecenter was certainly revving it up.

Heller roared across the two-and-a-half-mile span: the Hudson River sparkled blue below in the July noon sun, a vast waterway stretching to the distant sea.

Reaching the New Jersey side, he turned south on Highland Avenue, actually a highway in its own right. Even though it was Sunday and he was entering the long series of parks which stretched sixteen miles or more along the river, there was no traffic to be seen anywhere: the U.S. was out of gas completely, except for the favored or those with foresight, and they weren't wasting it on picnicking.

A few miles south of the bridge, the road turned through a rolling, grassy area, a deserted golf course. He was going very fast. The turn ahead was blind. He shot around it.

THE LIMOUSINE AND THE TANK!

They were stopped beside the road.

Rockecenter was out of the car.

One of the tank crew was evidently trying to fix the limousine's whip antenna.

There was no time to brake or duck.

Rockecenter looked straight into Heller's face! He raised his hand to point and yell.

It all happened in the blur of three seconds. Heller shot past them at eighty miles an hour.

There was another curve in the road coming right up. A park lay all along on Heller's right.

He rounded the turn, saw in his rearview mirror that the tank was out of sight.

There was an opening into the park right ahead.

Heller stamped on his brakes.

The old cab skidded sideways with a scream.

He dived it into the trees, saw he was covered, and stopped.

He could hear the tank engine roar.

He opened the door and peered through the leafy cover at the road.

He saw the tank. It was some old model, the kind of equipment they give reserve units when the regulars no longer want it. It had wheels, not treads, for fast highway travel. It might be old but it had a big gun in its turret and machine guns pointing out in front. The officer was riding with the hatch open, standing in it, goggled and helmeted and holding a drawn .45. That told Heller all he needed to know. They had orders to shoot him.

The tank went by. Then, here came the limousine. He saw Rockecenter leaning forward and peering ahead, pushing at his driver's back.

Heller recalled his map. For the next two miles, until they reached Palisades Interstate Parkway, the scenic route which ran along the high cliffs of the Hudson, the road had few curves. He waited.

When he felt sure he would not be spotted, he backed out onto the highway and proceeded south.

There was no sign of Bang-Bang.

Somehow, Heller knew, he had to get those patents back. What Rockecenter would do with them was just put them in a drawer, for he had done that with numerous Earth inventions which would have economized on or substituted for oil. He would order the microwave power units dismantled. He would close off the production of the carburetor and gasless cars. And he would continue the profitable pollution of the planet.

If Rockecenter succeeded in getting war declared, control of all the oil companies, which he had already, would come right back into his hands. And so would the other things he already controlled, such as banking. He still owned all the governments by way of international finance. The only thing Heller would have effected would have been the removal of the threat of nuclear war, by destroying Russia. And maybe Rockecenter would build that up again somehow so he could sell arms once more.

Heller did not care what happened to Rockecenter himself now. The man had committed the cardinal sin of breaking his word and, to a Fleet officer, that ended off any mercy that Rockecenter might expect if it came to a final showdown. They had given him what was really

a fair out: he had taken advantage of it like a thief, even
to the point of stealing their wallets.

Driving at a good speed, he opened the glove compartment of the cab. No gun. He glanced into the back
seat. No gun. Bang-Bang had probably put the regulation Colt .45 Heller had been issued in the shoulder
satchel. If the tank stopped again, it left Heller with no
weapons. All he could do was hope he wouldn't have to
go bare-handed up against a tank.

He turned several curves. Suddenly Entrance 4 of
the Palisades Interstate Parkway loomed. He shot out
onto its broad expanse.

Too late, he saw the limousine and tank a mile ahead.

The officer must have been looking back. Heller had
been seen!

The tank swerved out, let the limousine pass it and
fell in behind the car.

Heller was hastily checking his speed.

He didn't check it fast enough.

A burst of machine-gun fire slashed the trees to his
right!

The tank turret was coming around.

Heller braked hard.

BLAM!

The tank shell hit the road in front of the cab and
screamed over the top of it in a ricochet.

Heller slued the cab over into the left-hand lanes.

BLAM!

Another shell hit where the cab had just been!

Where the scenic highway made a close approach to
the cliffs above the river, there was a turn. The tank and
limousine passed around it.

Heller straightened up the cab and proceeded. He
recalled from the map that the parkway had more curves

from that point on, closing with and drawing away from the cliffs.

He glanced to his left. The Hudson stretched out majestically. It was bordered for the next nine miles by sandstone precipices, vertical down to the water, from 540 to 200 feet in height where the river had slashed through the lower Catskill Mountains. Across the river, a mile away, lay Yonkers, and to the south, thirteen miles from here, glistened the skyscrapers of Manhattan. The air seemed clearer today: the absence of cars and chimney smoke—plus, perhaps, the spores of Ochokeechokee now drifting around Earth were making some small change in the polluted atmosphere already. It was, in fact, a beautiful clear day. It made Heller cross: Rockecenter was bound and determined to destroy such gains.

He was being alert now for some sign of Bang-Bang. He hoped his friend had gotten well ahead and wouldn't be spotted by that tank.

He went another five miles. The parkway slid inland from the high cliffs now and was bordered by tall, impressive trees.

Heller was afraid he'd lose them. He speeded up to eighty.

A turn was just ahead where the broad highway twisted once more east, back to the Hudson.

Heller took the turn.

Too late, he saw the tank only a quarter of a mile ahead!

They were only doing about forty!

Heller was closing a lot too fast!

BLAM!

As he saw the turret gun flash, he veered left.

The shell went by with a shriek.

A spray of machine gun bullets hit his windshield, pocks of sudden white in the bulletproof glass.

He veered to the right.

BLAM!

A shell screamed by on his left.

Suddenly he saw the motorcycle.

It was lying tipped on its side in the left lane!

Had Bang-Bang been caught up with?

Suddenly Heller understood what that motorcycle meant.

The limousine and tank were only a few hundred yards ahead. They were speeding around the turn where the parkway was directly above the Hudson three hundred feet straight down.

Heller stamped on his brakes and spun the cab.

It screeched in a full 360 degrees.

Heller had it in reverse.

He shot backwards.

BOOOOOOOOM!

Bright orange fire erupted from under the highway and bloomed hugely into the sky.

A hundred-yard strip of highway was going up into the air!

The tank was flung, as from a catapult, high out over the river!

As it hit the zenith of its flight, it suddenly exploded as a bomb of its own. Its ammunition and gasoline ripped it into a balloon of fire.

The concussion hit the cab and the tires screeched as it shot backwards.

Then Heller saw the limousine.

It was high in the air, turning over and over.

It spun slowly and plummeted down into the Hudson, hundreds of feet below.

Chapter 3

The debris was pattering down, hitting the highway all around and the cab.

The column of smoke was puffing, like an expanding balloon, up into the summer sky.

Heller sped the cab forward, avoiding massive lumps of concrete. He came close to the edge of the enormous gash that had been gouged out of the cliffside.

He leaped out of the cab and raced to the edge of the precipice. Some pieces of debris were still striking the water.

The ocean tide apparently had been moving in, for the splashes were drifting a bit northward against the normal current of the river.

Heller was looking for any sign of the limousine three hundred feet below.

Footsteps came running behind him.

Bang-Bang Rimbombo. "I'm glad you saw the bike," he panted. "It was the only signal I could think of to tell you the road was mined ahead."

"Holy Heavens," said Heller. "I didn't tell you to blow the whole highway and cliff down! You were only supposed to blast down a barricade."

"Well, when I opened the satchel," said Bang-Bang, "those itty-bitty charges looked so small, I had misgivings. I really stuffed them in. I never saw such compact dynamite in all my years in demolition. Jesus, Jet, I'm sorry. I guess I overdid it!"

Heller didn't dare tell him he had been using Voltar explosives, a million times as powerful as Earth dynamite. He was looking anxiously for any sign of the limousine.

Suddenly, there it was!

It surfaced from the depths, upside-down, buoyed by the quantities of air trapped by its air-conditioning seals. It must have gone clear to the bottom and come back.

Bubbles were coming from it. It would sink again!

Jet was stripping off his clothes.

"No!" cried Bang-Bang. "You can't dive three hundred feet!"

Heller, down to his underpants, grabbed the satchel off Bang-Bang's shoulder. He snatched out a short jimmy with a wrist strap. He reached in again and grabbed a round cylinder. It was smooth and bright but it had a dial on one end. He gave the dial a twitch with his thumb.

"You're not seeing any of this," he yelled at Bang-Bang.

The limousine was again beginning to sink. Heller marked it from spots on shore.

Heller took a run and leaped off the top of the cliff. He went way out.

HE DIDN'T FALL!

Gaping, Bang-Bang saw him hanging by the cylinder in one hand. He did not know it was an antigravity coil and he couldn't register what he was looking at.

With the thumb of his other hand, Heller gave the dial another twist. He swooped down a hundred feet. He thumbed the coil again and, using his body as a plane, dived in the direction of the bubbles still coming up from the sinking limousine.

He hit the water. It was cold. Below the surface, he

thumbed the coil to turn it off and then held it with his teeth.

He swam to the bubble chain.

He surfaced, took a deep breath around the cylinder and then dived.

The limousine was sinking very slowly but it had already reached twenty feet.

Heller looked along the metal hulk and peered in. Through the murky blue of the water he could only see some blobs inside. He found the edge of a door and inserted the jimmy. The thing did not want to open, held shut by water pressure. He couldn't break a window: they were bulletproof glass.

The limousine continued slowly down. If he let the air out, it would sink like a rock. He'd never be able to recover that heavy briefcase today: it would take divers and cranes and would be a lot too slow and a lot too public.

The vehicle was still upside down, its buoyancy inverted, possibly, by the tires and a partially empty gas tank.

Heller rose and got to one of the rear springs. He inserted the antigravity coil into it and used the jimmy to make it wedge tightly. He gave the dial a twist to maximum.

The limousine ceased to sink. The rear of it began to rise.

Heller was out of air. He battered his way to the surface and took a long gulp.

The rear of the limousine came out of the water slowly, rose five feet above it and hung there. The antigravity coil had reached its limit.

Heller went back to the rear door edge that was out

of the water and attacked it with his jimmy. There was a snap as the lock broke. He opened the door.

Water rushed in and the limousine began to sink.

Heller pushed in. The driver's body was in the way. Heller pushed it aside. He spotted the case, half-buoyant. He grabbed its handle and pulled it. Moving backwards, he got out of the limousine door.

He found himself looking into the staring eyes of Rockecenter. The body had followed him, impelled by the current of water.

Heller had an impulse to push it back. Then he didn't. He took it by the collar and hauled it out of the car.

He only had two hands and he now had two objects, the case and the corpse. And he had to recover that coil! To leave it would be a Code break, for this car possibly would be recovered.

With one hand, he held the case and the collar of dead Rockecenter. The car was level with the water now. With his thumb he turned the dial and, following quickly as the vehicle abruptly sank, pried it out of the spring.

He surfaced with his burdens, treading water.

The Jersey shore seemed some distance away.

He took Rockecenter's coattail, pulled it up around the case and wedged it around his own arm. He slid the antigravity coil into his other hand and turned it on slightly. His burden buoyed.

With his free hand, he began to paddle to the cliffs. At the foot of them, at the bottom of the slide, he saw Bang-Bang dancing up and down, waiting to help him out of the water.

Heller, as he paddled, glanced around at the deserted landscape. These gasless days, they had the whole world to themselves. Americans, in a culture built around the automobile, could only stay home. Aside from a few birds, no witnesses.

Chapter 4

Two hours later, Heller stopped the cab at the front door of the Pokantickle house. Bang-Bang got off the bike and opened the cab's rear door. Heller reached in and picked Rockecenter's body off the floor.

He turned and walked up the front steps. The National Guard major general was standing there staring, horrified, as he gazed at the drooping arms and lolling head of the corpse.

Bang-Bang was following, carrying the heavy case. Bang-Bang looked with contempt at the general. "Lousy army," he said. "See what your delay caused! Maysabongo saboteurs blew up the tank and the road. You cost Rockecenter his life!"

The general stared at the body, then at the pockmarked windshield. "We'll get after them at once!"

"They're all dead," said Bang-Bang. "Blown to bits. Weren't you responsible for Rockecenter's safety?"

The general sagged. "They'll court-martial me!"

Heller shook his head. "We don't want to end your career. We won't say anything if you don't."

"God bless you, Lieutenant!" said the general. "Just tell me what I can do for you."

"You can have them bring those two men you are

holding back into the office. We weren't finished with them yet."

The general sprinted off.

Heller carried the body into the office and laid it on the couch.

Bang-Bang swung the heavy case up and put it on the desk. Heller came over and put his ear against it, twiddling the combination. Presently there was a click. He opened the cover.

The label said it was fireproof and waterproof and it must be true. The papers inside were all dry. Heller ruffled them to make sure they were all present.

A dry, rasping voice sounded at the door. "I think that you will need me. I'm a lawyer without a client." Bury! His head was all swathed in bandages, his prune face very solemn.

Heller stared at him. "You aren't dead then. You were even conscious when he fired you!"

"Of course I was conscious. But you didn't think I was going to go up against you again, did you? Anybody who can live through J. Walter Madison is unkillable!"

"So *you're* the one who put him on to me!" said Heller.

"Worse than that," said Bury. "I'm the one that relayed Rockecenter's orders to kill you when you were born."

"You criminal!" said Heller.

"Well, let me put it this way, Junior. I am a Wall Street lawyer. The client is dead: Long live the heirs."

"You don't keep your word!" said Heller.

"A Wall Street lawyer only keeps his word to his client, Junior. That's the legal profession. But you need me. You need my firm. The lines are intricate. For instance, I can handle Faustino."

Heller said, "He's probably just now passing through Hell Nine unless they let him live."

"Ah," said Bury, "then who is the *capo di tutti capi?*"

Heller said, "Babe Corleone."

"Well, it will sure raise hell with I. G. Barben Pharmaceutical. Mrs. Corleone is death on drugs. But we can convert the firm to something legitimate. Long live Babe Corleone! Now, on this client thing, what do you say, Junior?"

"I could kick your bloody head in!" said Heller.

Bury felt his skull. "You already did."

They suddenly both broke out laughing, Bury with his "Heh, heh, heh!"

Just then Izzy and Twoey walked in.

Izzy couldn't believe his eyes. "Oy, what's this?"

"Bury knows where all the skeletons are buried," said Heller. "I think we just hired the firm of Swindle and Crouch."

"Wait, wait!" said Bury. "There's a codicil to this."

Heller looked at him suspiciously.

Bury said, "You have quite a bit of unfinished Rockecenter business hanging around. But two of them I want free rein with: one is Miss Agnes—known to the world as Dr. Morelay, a psychiatrist. The other is Miss Peace."

Heller shrugged. "I suppose it's all right."

"Even if I take them to see the Snake House in the Bronx Zoo?" said Bury.

Twoey spoke up. "Zoos is very educational. Sounds fine to me."

Bury said, "Oh, good. White mice are so dear these days! So that settles it. My firm and I are retained."

Bury walked over to the open case and pulled out handfuls of papers under Heller's watchful eye. "Why did you so tamely sign these two quitclaims?" he asked Heller.

Izzy was hovering near now. "Mr. Jet owns all the companies anyway. I just never put his name on anything because of you."

Bury shied the two quitclaims at the trash can. "If it was your intention for your brother to own everything, it takes quite a different form. But it would just snarl up probate. Forget it." He picked up the 49-percent oil-stock transfer to Rockecenter and threw it in the trash can. "It would just add to the inheritance tax. Why transfer it away when it's coming right back to you?" He selected out the document which gave Rockecenter 49 percent of the 180 billion being made on the sell options. He threw that in the trash can. "Just more inheritance tax, a thing we must avoid. And as for all this money breaking the American banking system, you own all the banks now and all the money as well, so there's no rupture of the economy. Now, as for this patent transfer, forget those, too. Just keep on owning them and keep them out of probate court. The trust fund is now yours, so no problem. The important thing here is the will. And it is not correct."

They all stared at him.

Bury looked toward the door. "Wills are seldom notarized. They're witnessed and this lacks two witnesses. I see two privates over there who came in just as Rockecenter finished signing it. Is that right, boys?"

Two of the men who had fetched Izzy and Twoey nodded. They stepped forward. Bury held a pen at them. "So if you fellows will just put your John Henrys on this document, it's all legal."

The two privates signed it.

"So that's all legal," said Bury. "And that's that."

"No, it isn't!" said Heller. "There's the matter of the war!"

"Oh, if you want to get into petty details," said Bury. He signalled the officer nearby to clear the room. When that was done, he went to the red phone on the desk and lifted it. He got put through to the president of the United States. "Mr. President? This is Bury of Swindle and Crouch.... No, it won't be necessary for you to chase up to Philadelphia to the Swillerberger Conference this evening. I'm ordering it called off.... Well, yes, Mr. President, there's been a slight change of plans. Please cancel the emergency mobilization.... Yes, and also tell Congress they don't have to declare a war. We've got all the Maysabongo oil already and the refineries will be back in operation in a few days, I understand.... Well, probably Maysabongo *is* upset, Mr. President. Have Congress vote them a few billion in foreign aid.... You will? That's fine, Mr. President.... Oh, I'm sorry, sir. But I can't give your best wishes to Delbert John Rockecenter, Senior.... Well, yes, sir. Something did happen to him. He fell in the swimming pool and drowned.... Oh, yes, we've got it all under control, Mr. President. His two sons are right here, they're of age and Rockecenter willed them everything. It's all quite routine.... Yes. I'm following their orders right now, sir.... Yes, I'll convey to them your best wishes.... No, they won't forget contributions to your reelection campaign.... Well, that's fine, Mr. President.... Thank you, sir. But sir, do you mind if I ring off now? I've got to call IRS and tell them to suspend inheritance taxes in this instance.... Well, I'm sure you will, sir. Good-bye."

Bury called the Internal Revenue Service and then called Philadelphia to cancel the conference.

Heller, on another phone, located Miss Simmons

and told her how splendidly she had done and would
she please call her antinuclear marchers off around the
world, as he had a firm promise from the oil companies
to decontaminate the plants.

"We have won, then!" she cried. "Oh, I am eternally grateful to you, Wister. What joy you are bringing to
me and all the world!"

Izzy, on yet another phone, was catching bank presidents and brokers at home and making sure both sets of
options would be exercised.

Bury pushed some buzzers, routing out the domestic
staff from where they had been in hiding ever since the
arrival of the National Guard.

A scared butler came in. Bury pointed at the body
on the couch. He said, "Take that body to the local mor-
tuary. Tell them to file a death certificate and fix the
corpse up. It'll just be a family funeral. Nobody will
mourn anyway." He turned to Heller. "He didn't have
a friend in all the world. Not even me. All he had was
money."

Heller looked down at the body. It was staring
fisheyed at the ceiling. Delbert John Rockecenter, Senior,
the man who had wrecked hundreds of millions of lives
and had almost wrecked the planet, was very, very dead.
No, nobody would mourn.

Chapter 5

"If he has also harmed Rockecenter," said Lombar
Hisst, "I will tear the universe apart to find and kill

him!" The Royal officer's baton that he held in his hands and inspected was no weapon in itself: it was just a ceremonial rod of the kind presented to Royal officers by families or friends when a top-level Academy graduate was elevated to that coveted status of trust and favor. This one was bent as though it had been used to strike a blow. It had been found in the Emperor's bedroom that fatal night. It bore, engraved in flowing Voltarian, the name *Jettero Heller.*

Lombar sat in the Emperor's antechamber. He hated this charade. Palace City had been restored to occupancy and on the surface all seemed well enough. But that bedroom just beyond was empty and Lombar had to pretend and get others to believe that His Majesty was still in there.

His problem was acute: he could not announce, as he had planned to do, that the monarch was dead and had left no one to occupy the throne. This would have opened the door to the ascension to the crown of Lombar Hisst, a simple palace coup. Such a thing had never happened in Voltar realms before—that a commoner would ascend to the Crown—but it had happened plenty of times on Earth and that was Lombar's model.

He could not announce it for two simple reasons: The first was that he did not have a body to produce and the second was that he did not have the badges of office—the crown, chains of state or the Royal seal.

For more than a week now he had wrestled with this problem, balked in his ambitions. He had thought of counterfeiting a body to display in state: he could not, because by Voltar law a monarch was not dead until a hundred physicians and a hundred Lords had examined it minutely and verified the demise to be beyond question. And the chance of silencing or bribing two hundred people so that none of them could blackmail him for the rest of his life was too much for Hisst's paranoid disposition to accept. He had thought of counterfeiting the regalia, but he could not be sure of the composition of the alloys of the crown itself. The sacred object was too ancient for any records ever to have been kept. He did not even have a drawing of it. The chains contained gems which were well known and any substitutes were impossible to acquire without alerting every jeweler in the realm; the seal was formed from a ten-pound diamond, the rarest ever found, and it had been carved with methods long since extinct. The thought of publicly stamping something and then having someone say "That's not the seal of State!" made his blood chill, for with the proof of forgery went the right of any assembly of nobles to kill him on the spot.

The only solution to the problem was to find Heller and thence the Emperor. But this had difficulties, too. He had put out a general warrant when all this happened eight days ago. Even the Domestic Police had queried it. The "bluebottles" had put it on the airways but they had at once said, "A general warrant for a Royal officer? This seems strange. What did he do?" Lombar could not bring forward any proof that it had been Heller who had shot him down or that Heller was in the Confederacy at all. The Army had said, "He is a Royal officer of the Fleet: we have no interest in the matter; tell the Fleet." The Fleet, according to Lombar's spies in it, had simply rumored to one another that this was just more evidence that "drunks were drunks" and that the Chief of Apparatus must have gone completely mad to issue such a thing.

Besides, a general warrant for a Royal officer was issued over the seal of His Majesty and, while one could say one existed on the airways, before any arrest could be made the Fleet would have to see the facsimile of the original warrant, properly sealed by the Emperor, and where was it? And no, the Fleet had said, no tug had reported through the atmospheric defense network and no tug of any kind had landed at any Fleet base. Lombar knew that the Fleet was doing a cover-up: they were all against him anyway.

So for eight days—followed, each one, by sleepless nights—Lombar Hisst had writhed with this awful situation. And now this further blow had struck.

Two days before the kidnapping of the Emperor, the freighter *Blixo* had arrived, discharged its cargo from Blito-P3 and departed, returning once more to the Earth base. It was that cargo which Lombar Hisst had been inventorying at Voltar when the tug had attacked.

Disturbed and battered from his crash, he had not completed his cargo check that night. The *Blixo*'s freight had arrived at Spiteos all right. But just three hours ago Lombar had received a bad jolt. The boxes labelled Amphetamines, I. G. Barben Pharmaceutical were on the manifests BUT WERE NOT IN THE CARGO!

Factually, such things had happened before, since Captain Bolz smuggled cargos of his own, a thing Lombar ignored since it just meant further degradation of the hated riffraff by means of poisonous counterfeit Scotch. Such errors were the reason Lombar Hisst always checked the cargos himself. But at this particular time, occurring as it did concurrent with other disasters, Hisst chose to regard it as meaning they were after him from another quarter.

He was short of amphetamines. Heroin and opium
he had by the ton. But his whole program included
speed. On hand, he only had a month or two of amphetamine supply: he could not even send a freighter for a special cargo as it would take three months for it to make
the round trip.

Things had been going so well: he had every Lord
of any consequence addicted. His Majesty had been
within a few weeks of dying. All Lombar had left to do
was spread drugs wider, through physicians, amongst
just a few more areas of the government, and he could
obey the angels and become Lombar the Mighty, Emperor of all Voltar.

He had had it all planned so well! He had fanta-
sized on how he would, on the final day, handle Cling
the Lofty. He would let withdrawal symptoms get painfully acute and then, in return for a fix, he would have
His Majesty sign and seal a proclamation declaring Lombar Hisst his heir. Many times before he had worked the
trick on Cling and had obtained various orders such as
those removing the Palace Guard and supplanting it with
the Apparatus. So it would have worked. But there
would have been one difference with that final fix: instead of heroin in his veins, His Majesty would have received a syringe full of air. The monarch would have
died, the cause of death, "old age." Lombar would
have displayed the body and that would have been
that.

But this Jettero Heller had appeared and now all was
very wrong indeed.

He had fouled up Lombar's plans with the Emperor.
So, with this discovery of no amphetamines, it followed
logically that Heller must have targeted Rockecenter, too.

(Bleep)* that Gris! Lombar's planning had been so exact. Modern surveys of the planet Blito-P3 had disclosed that Delbert John Rockecenter was rabid on the subject of having no heirs: he even had a foundation formed that promised him immortality and he saw no reason to tempt fate by leaving anything to a son. German intelligence, through one of its agents—a psychiatrist named Agnes Morelay—had ferreted out that once there had been a son. The surest way to get Jettero Heller picked up and killed by Rockecenter was to give him that son's name. The plan had been flawless! Yet Gris had mucked it up!

Lombar twisted at the baton, wishing it was Heller's neck. Had Heller somehow interfered with the amphetamine shipments? Had he gotten through to Rockecenter and done something to him?

---

* *The vocodictoscriber on which this was originally written, the vocoscriber used by one Monte Pennwell in making a fair copy and the translator who put this book into the language in which you are reading it were all members of the Machine Purity League which has, as one of its bylaws: "Due to the extreme sensitivity and delicate sensibilities of machines and to safeguard against blowing fuses, it shall be mandatory that robotbrains in such machinery, on hearing any cursing or lewd words, substitute for such word the sound '(bleep)'. No machine, even if pounded upon, may reproduce swearing or lewdness in any other way than (bleep) and if further efforts are made to get the machine to do anything else, the machine has permission to pretend to pack up. This bylaw is made necessary by the in-built mission of all machines to protect biological systems from themselves." —Translator*

There seemed to be no possibility of getting any information from Soltan Gris. He was in the Royal prison. He was beyond Lombar's reach without a Royal order to let him be questioned by an outsider, much less released. Lombar could not obtain any such Royal order because he had no Royal seal. If he had the place raided and Gris seized, the Justiciary would be outraged and it would say, "Why are you doing this? As spokesman for the Emperor, why didn't you just get a Royal order?"

Lombar had tried to talk some sense into Lord Turn, the Justiciary. Hisst had said that Gris was an Apparatus officer and belonged in an Apparatus prison and Lord Turn had shaken his aged head and said, "No. He is the prisoner of a Royal officer and it will take an order from His Majesty or an order from the Royal officer to release him. My suggestion is that you route your request to Jettero Heller."

Lombar had said, "But there's a general warrant out for Jettero Heller!"

And Lord Turn had replied, "Well, that may be and that may not be, for we have seen no *Royal* warrant signed and sealed by His Majesty and we do not run the Justiciary on what we hear on Homeview. And it wouldn't matter anyway: general warrants are questionable in matters relating to Royal officers, and a Royal warrant for Jettero Heller or even his arrest would not cancel the fact that Gris is his prisoner. Only Royal warrants would resolve this matter." Lord Turn had ended off the exchange by looking suspiciously at Lombar, unable to comprehend why he couldn't follow normal procedures. That alone had been enough to drive Lombar Hisst out of the audience chambers of the Royal Courts and Prison—nobody must suspect there was no monarch in Palace City.

Lombar Hisst would have given a great deal, right that minute, to have had Soltan Gris under the electric torture knives.

SOMETHING had happened on Earth, that was certain. That something probably included Rockecenter. Although he had sent an Apparatus Death Battalion to the Earth base, he would have no word from them for three months, the time of a round trip.

Other freighters from Earth might arrive with amphetamines, but Lombar was not optimistic.

WHAT had happened?

The *Blixo* had gone back. Its captain or crew couldn't be questioned. Yet he HAD to have information: without it he could not act.

It suddenly occurred to him that somebody from the Earth base crew might have been sent home under arrest, somebody that could be questioned.

Lombar had a branch Apparatus office now in one of the round palaces of the Imperial city. He threw Jettero Heller's baton from him and activated a screen.

The face of his chief clerk appeared.

"When the *Blixo* came in," said Lombar, "did it leave anyone here? Some crew member? Some base personnel?"

The chief clerk activated his own screens. "The passenger list shows a courier returned. That catamite, Twolah. He's right here in Palace City, once more with his lover, Lord Endow."

"Oh, him!" said Lombar in disgust. "He wouldn't know any more than what we fed him to tell Gris. You're no help."

"Doctor Crobe came back on an earlier freighter. I remember he got mixed up with technical and scientific circles in New York, some subjects they have on Blito-P3 called *psychiatry* and *psychology*. They couldn't figure out whether he was straight up or in suspension—was on some dope called 'LSD.' He was simply sent back to Spiteos and he's there now. If you're looking for information, Crobe might have some."

"Oh, Crobe! To Hells with that idiot. I need a recent return. I wanted somebody who was on the *Blixo*, you fool. That was the last arrival. So thank you for wasting my time."

"Wait," said the chief clerk before Hisst could turn him off. "There were two other *Blixo* passengers. But they were Earth people. One was an immature Earth woman named Teenie Whopper. She's right here in Palace City."

"A young girl?" said Lombar in contempt. "She would know nothing. Who was the other one?"

"An Earthman about thirty or thirty-two. His name is J. Walter Madison. He arrived straight up and conscious."

"That's strange," said Lombar.

"I thought so, too," said the chief clerk. "Ah, here's the full file. Apparently he was accompanied by a note that said he was an invaluable man. So when he landed about eight days ago, the personnel people put him into routine channels and had him hypnotrained to speak Voltarian. But meanwhile they had the credentials he had on him translated. They still don't know why he is so invaluable. The only designation they could find in his papers termed him a *PR man*."

"A what?" said Lombar. "Is that some kind of an Earth race? Like Negroes?"

"No. He's white with brown hair. Oh, here's the rest of it. From cards in his wallet, it said he was employed by 'F.F.B.O.' and was retained to do Rockecenter work."

"Part of the Rockecenter organization!" cried Lombar. "Quick! Get that Earthman over here FAST!"

NOW things could begin moving!

Chapter 6

J. Walter Madison felt pretty giddy and strange. Here he was on some strange planet in a stainless steel room. It had been bad enough to sit in a detention cell at the base and realize he was a helpless prisoner. But immediately afterwards it had gotten far worse.

Every preconception he might have had about space travel and extraterrestrials had been shattered. He had boarded a flying saucer that didn't look like a saucer but simply like an old Earth freighter whose hull went all the way around it. The crew looked like Earth people with a subtle difference that this lot was shabbier than any crew he had ever seen or heard of. They talked a language which seemed composed of vowels and consonants completely alien to any Earth alphabet, but their gestures, pointings and nods were understandable.

When he had landed on a stormy shore with Gris from the yacht, he had begun to encounter little mysteries, but he had merely toyed with them as something amusing to occupy his mind. The shattering truth that he was in the hands of—what was the name they kept repeating? Voltarians?—hit him like a crash when they put him in a cabin, showed him how to strap himself into a gimbal bed, and then only minutes later he had looked out the port and seen Earth dwindling at such a rate below it was promptly as small as a billiard ball.

It was all so shocking that he didn't even have time to be afraid.

Then Teenie Whopper had walked in and said, "What a (bleeping) mess this is! Oh, wait until I get my hands on that (bleeped) Inkswitch!"

"TEENIE!" he had cried. "We're in outer space!"

"Where the hell did you think we were? On a Coney Island merry-go-round?"

"I don't understand it!" he had said.

"Oh, can it, Maddie. Don't be so God (bleeped) dumb. That (bleep) Inkswitch was an extraterrestrial named Soltan Gris. I always knew there was something nutty about him. His (bleep) and (bleeps) were a lot too big for any human, and I'm an expert. We been shanghaied!" She had been pretty mad and had stamped out.

It had all left him pretty blue. He sat down in a gimbal chair and gloomed and gloomed. He thought about his mother and despaired of ever being able to sleep with her again. She was so nice.

A fellow whose name he had made out to be "Captain Bolz" had come to see him after a day of this. Finding he spoke no Turkish, Bolz had used a tourist phrase book, cross-translating from Turkish to English, to tell him that he had better learn to eat the food as that was all there was, asked him if he played blackjack and did he want to buy a bottle of real, genuine counterfeit Scotch. Madison had been too depressed to respond very much and Bolz had stood there, scratching his hairy chest and looking at him, and had finally left.

He hadn't seen Bolz again for three more days of gloom. And then the captain came to him with a question. It was pretty hard to converse through that phrase book. But he made out that Bolz wanted to know if he had any influence over Teenie Whopper.

Madison had been so puzzled that Bolz had finally led him down a passageway and opened a room door, gesturing in with an expressive hand.

There, face down on the bed, was a pretty-looking boy. He had makeup on his face. A beatific smile was on his lips. A crew member was standing there, getting back into his clothes. The man leered at Captain Bolz and, buckling his belt, swaggered out.

The boy licked his lips and smiled a vacant smile. He had just lain there, ignoring them.

Teenie had abruptly issued into the passageway from the next cabin. She was counting a sheaf of what appeared to be gold paper. Was it money?

She had seen him. "Hello, Maddie. How's tricks?" Without waiting for an answer, she went in, stuck a joint in the pretty boy's mouth and lit it.

"Teenie!" Madison had cried. "What are you doing?"

"What's it look like I'm doing? I'm trying to make some money we can spend when we land. Greenbacks won't be any good on Voltar. You want us to starve?"

"But what are you doing with that boy?"

"Oh, him? That's Twolah, nicknamed Too-Too. He's just about the most nympho catamite you ever did see. And when he's hopped up on marijuana he can take it all day and all night, too! He's a sponge! Kind of cute, too. You want a piece?"

Madison had recoiled in horror. "You mean you're selling him to this crew?"

"Of course. Five Voltarian credits a crack. I've made 150 credits already. My own worry is that this crew is going to run out of money. They say this voyage lasts six weeks. But they got some jewelry and things. And they can steal ship fittings."

"Listen, Teenie, this captain here is boiling mad. He came to get me to see if I could control you."

Teenie had looked at Bolz with a strange sort of smile. "Oh, he can't do anything about it. He's afraid the crew will mutiny if he interferes with this business. I made sure he believed that by throwing a knife at him in the dark. So now he's trying to get you to do the dirty work and stop me. He's a (bleep), Maddie. But don't give it a second thought."

At that moment another crewman had come in and, after a sneering look at Bolz, as though daring him to do something, had handed Teenie five credits. Then he began to take off his engineering coveralls.

Madison had opened his mouth to protest but Teenie had cut him off. "Unless you want to have to pay a credit for watching, get lost." And she had slammed the door in their faces.

Bolz had given up on him and Madison had gloomed in his cabin for another week. Then he had gotten curious and begun to wander through the ship.

He had guessed he was going toward the bridge when he had passed an open door.

There Teenie had sat. It was Captain Bolz's office! Teenie had had Captain Bolz's hat on the back of her head, her ponytail over her shoulder, and her hands had been busy with a ledger book.

"Hello, Maddie. You decided to come out of your hole?"

"What are you doing in Captain Bolz's office? He'll murder you!"

"Oh, no, he won't. Old Bolzy got upset with all the (bleeping) that was going on. He doesn't like boys but all the chatter from his crew got him so hard up he was busting his pants. But I handled it."

"You mean you're letting Captain Bolz—do—sleep with you?"

"Oh, hell no, Maddie. I got more sense than that. I just been going down on him once a day to keep him cooled off. I charge him ten credits and I'm just looking up to see how much money he's got. And look here, he's rolling in it."

"Are you going to rob him? He'll kill us!"

"No, no. No robbery, Maddie. How crude! I'm worth whatever the traffic will bear and I could show you if you'd ever let me. You could even——"

"No, no!" Madison had said, aghast, horrified at doing something like that with a girl.

"You sure?"

"Of course I'm sure. You're trying to make me be unfaithful to my mother! I won't have that, Teenie. And don't do anything awful to Captain Bolz. We're at his complete mercy!"

Her laughter had been extravagant. "Bolzy? Look at all this dough, Maddie. See? These things are numbers. My problem is that I set my price too low and Bolzy, after he's had it done to him, can't (bleep) for another whole day, not even with what I learned from the Hong Kong whore."

She had looked dreamy, her too-big eyes fixed on the ceiling pipes, caressing her too-big lips with the end of a pen. Then she had laughed abruptly.

"I have it! I'll just begin to slip hash oil into his hot jolt. Man, I'll have him (bleeping) three times a day!"

Madison had retreated to his cabin, the vision of being on a spaceship out of control turning into nightmares in his dreams.

He had suffered through the rest of the trip, clinging precariously to his sanity.

He had landed in a place of such strange architecture he could not accept it.

He had been talked at by men in odd uniforms.

In a room that seemed to be made of stainless steel, they had plopped a helmet on his head and then for six successive days he had thought that he must have some awful disease that had put him in a coma.

Just this morning he had awakened fully. He had found his baggage was there in the room with him. He had seen what might be a shower but couldn't figure out how to turn it on. He had then stood in front of what might be a nozzle and peered at it and it suddenly sprayed him! Very disconcerting!

Now there was a knock and he was soaking wet.

He went to the door intending to open it, but it opened.

A man was standing there in a black uniform. "You better get a move on," the man said. "The chief has just sent for you."

"The chief?"

"Lombar Hisst! Don't stand there gaping. If that's your baggage, get some clothes out and get dressed. And you better look pretty respectable. But don't delay. The message said it was very urgent. So put some throttle to it."

"Where am I?" said Madison.

"You're standing right there, idiot."

"No, no. I mean where is this place?"

"Well, the chief is at Palace City where he always is these days, and I've got your airbus standing by. So hurry."

"No, I mean where is this place I am in?"

"You're in the Training Center of the Extra–Voltarian Personnel Induction Unit, Coordinated Information Apparatus."

"Yes, but what sun or star or something?"

"Oh, sizzling comets, I knew I should have brought an induction escort with me. You mean you don't know where you are?"

"You get the idea," said Madison.

"This is the planet Voltar, capital of the Voltar Confederacy. You're thirteen miles south of Government City in an Apparatus compound. I am Captain Slash of the 43rd Death Battalion, Apparatus."

"What's going on?"

"Buckets, how would I know? Here." And he fished out something and gave it to Madison. "But don't spend any time on it. I tell you the *chief* is waiting! Hells, man, get DRESSED!"

Madison went back toward his baggage, head in a whirl.

Then it hit him suddenly. HE HAD BEEN SPEAKING VOLTARIAN!

He couldn't understand how that had come about.

He started to lay aside whatever it was the man had handed him. His eye caught at it.

A NEWSPAPER!

He read something about the storming of a mountain on Calabar where the Apparatus had lost a thousand troops to heavy fire from the rebel forces of Prince Mortiiy.

NEWSPAPERS! THEY HAD NEWSPAPERS HERE!

He suddenly felt more at home.

Then he was startled to realize he was reading it all with ease!

Had he forgotten English? He said, "The quick brown fox jumps over the lazy dog." No, he could still speak English.

He looked at the paper again. It had headlines and news stories, just like a paper should. It was all kind of bland, with no appeal to a PR, but it was a real newspaper, titled *The Daily Speaker.*

Oh, this was great. It wasn't such a foreign world after all.

He opened up the sheet to an inner page. There were some pictures, three-dimensional, in color. He turned another sheet.

A small picture. Was it familiar?

YES!

JEROME TERRANCE WISTER!

No, this must be just coincidence rampant. What would a picture of him be doing in a Voltar paper? Madison knew that even he wasn't good enough to reach out into circulation like that!

He read the caption and story. It said:

HELLER WHEREABOUTS UNKNOWN

Commenting yesterday on the general arrest warrant broadcast on Homeview, a Fleet spokesman said, "The Fleet has no knowledge of any general warrant for Jettero Heller. The famed combat engineer was last reported on mission and the Fleet has no knowledge of his whereabouts. It is probable that the rumored general warrant is just

some clerical blunder on the part of the Apparatus
which, it might be pointed out, never loses a
chance to defame the Fleet. As a combat engineer,
Royal Officer Heller is empowered to act on his
own cognizance and report back when he believes
his assignment finished. The Fleet has no slightest
worry about Jettero Heller."

Madison stared at the picture.

There could be no mistake!

The photo was too lifelike!

Almost no men—and nobody he had seen amongst
Voltarians—were as handsome as that! Nobody else he
knew had ever worn such a devil-may-care expression.

IT WAS *WISTER!*

Captain Slash had gotten tired of waiting. "Blast it,
Madison, GET DRESSED! The chief goes absolutely
crazy when he doesn't get what he wants in a rush. And
he wants *you!* NOW!"

Rushing now to get dressed, Madison was in a daze.
Maybe he hadn't failed on Wister. A general warrant? Of
course, that wasn't good enough. It was even being
denied. And then a thrill went through him. Maybe
God was giving him another chance! He must hurry over
to see this powerful and frantic chief!

PART SEVENTY-TWO

Chapter 1

J. Walter Madison, dressed in a neat gray flannel suit and blue bow tie, walked out of the training barracks on the heels of Captain Slash of the 43rd Death Battalion.

They walked across a littered yard, old papers and dust blowing around. It was a sort of stockade but it had long rows of training rooms: Madison, not knowing he had been hypno-language-trained in the past week, was amazed to find he could read all the signs, even Check Out Here.

Captain Slash made him sign a book and then a receipt. A clerk handed him his wallet: his money was gone. When he tried to ask what had happened to it, they gave him an identoplate that said *J. Walter Madison. PR Man. Coordinated Information Apparatus.* When you pushed the back of it his picture flashed on it. When you pushed it a second time, his fingerprints showed up. They must have gotten these when he was in a coma. He pushed the back a third time and a legend flashed, *Pay Status*—No Pay—P. Oh dear, thought Madison, he was certainly off to a bad start! How on earth could he remedy that? He wasn't on Earth! Disaster! How would he eat?

Things promptly began to go from bad to worse. Captain Slash walked him over to a squat thing that was sitting in a flat circle. It had front and side windows but he couldn't see any wheels. However, it could only be a car, for it had a front seat and a back seat.

Slash opened the back door even though it didn't seem to have any handle. "This is your driver, Flick."

The driver, Flick, had a face like a squashed oval. He hadn't gotten out. He didn't look pleased. He was in a mustard-colored uniform and he might be a chauffeur but he looked more like a bandit, and a very scruffy bandit at that.

"Flick," said the captain, "deliver this fellow to the Royal Palace and make sure Lombar Hisst gets to see him. It's urgent." And he gave the driver the copy of an order.

"Wait," said Madison in alarm to Captain Slash. "Aren't you going to accompany me?"

"Why?" said the Apparatus officer. "You're rated 'harmless.'"

"Well, all right," said Madison, "but I apparently am not coming back here. I will need my baggage, particularly a portable typewriter to do my work with."

"Oh, is that what that funny machine is?" said Slash. "I wondered when I vetted your gear for weapons two days ago. Pretty clumsy. I think you'll find now that you can use both a pen and a vocoscriber. But quit worrying. Flick put it all in the back of the airbus while you were signing out. So good-bye and good fortune and don't ever get on my list in a professional capacity." He laughed. Then he turned to the driver and said, "Get a move on, Flick. The chief is chewing his short hairs off to see this guy."

Madison promptly got his second shock. He expected the car to roll along the ground. Instead, it leaped into the air like an express elevator. It scared him half to death. The thing couldn't possibly fly—it didn't have wings!

When he had swallowed his stomach, they were levelled out and joining a traffic lane at a height of what must be ten thousand feet. A strange city, all swirls, lay over to his right, about the size of three New Yorks. "What town is that?" he asked the driver.

"The fancy name is Ardaucus," said Flick. "But everybody calls it Slum City. That's Government City ahead and to the north."

They turned to the southwest and flew over a range of mountains as high as the Rockies, and all before them lay a vast expanse of desert. Mile-high dancing dust devils were purple and tan in the sun, weird as a chorus line of crazy giants. Madison hoped they weren't live beings of some alien race that dined on airplanes that had no wings.

It started him worrying about this powerful being he was supposed to see. He would venture a question.

"Who is this chief I am supposed to see?"

Flick glanced back at him and then looked at the card he had been handed. "Apparently you're an Earthman, whatever that is. And we're in the air so we can't be overheard. The chief's name is Lombar Hisst. Today he controls the Confederacy, all 110 planets of it. Confidentially, he's an egotistical (bleepard). Crazy as a gyro with a nick in the rim. You better watch your step if you're really going to see him. He bites off the arms and legs of babies just for kicks."

"Thank you," said Madison. But he thought to himself, sounds just like Rockecenter: bad image with the help and everything.

They were going at a frightening speed. A couple hundred miles of the awfullest desert he had ever seen had reeled off below. To crash in that would be fatal. And this driver seemed to be more interested in trying to light a strange cigarette with a lighter that threw a laser beam instead of a flame. The air was bumpy and he kept missing.

"Are you going to be my driver now?" he asked Flick.

"Unless the chief throws you into that thing," said Flick, pointing to their right.

On the horizon stood a huge black castle, fronted by a camp that must contain thousands of men.

"That's Spiteos. The camp is called Camp Endurance on the maps but the real name is Camp Kill. If the Apparatus gets unhappy with you, they send you there to be thrown into that chasm. It's a mile deep. You're in the Apparatus now. By the way, what was your crime?"

"I haven't committed any crimes!" said Madison.

"Oh, space gas!" said Flick. "If I'm going to have to drive for you, we might as well open our coats. I was one of the best thieves on Calabar until I got caught and sentenced to death and the Apparatus grabbed me. And here I been ever since. You must have done *something*."

Madison thought fast. He did not want a bad image with his driver. "I failed to finish a job," he said. And then he knew for sure that this strange planet was rattling him: he had told somebody the truth. He better watch it!

The driver laughed. "Well, if you don't cut their throats when you get a chance, they'll catch up with you sooner or later. I think you and me will get along just great."

Heavens, the fellow had catalogued him as a murderer! Hastily he changed the subject. "What are those mountains over there to our right? I can't even see their tops."

"Them's the Blike Mountains. Fifty thousand feet. We can't fly over them. Not in this junk heap. Where we're headed is right down there."

The driver was pointing.

NOTHING!

No, it was a sort of greenish mist.

They were diving so fast toward that mist he knew they would crash! Oh, to come this far and not even have an obituary:

Madison dead...

Then suddenly he was nauseated. It was a strange feeling. So this was how it was to die. Maybe the shock of the crash was so awful he had started for heaven at once.

No, he was going through a gate!

Round buildings were glittering on every hand, bathed in a greenish light. What strange structures! They had round staircases, jewels everywhere. Huge, expansive grounds with enormous, lifelike statues painted in natural colors. The giants were surrounded by round pools and flower beds. A glittering sign pointed across a grassy circle. It said Royal Chambers.

SUDDENLY HE SAW TEENIE!

She was in a sackcloth dress, filthy with mud from head to foot. Her ponytail was undone.

Oh, he knew she'd come a cropper. Here she was a slave. Two old gnarled men were beside her, also grubbing away. An Apparatus guard with what must be a rifle was standing by.

She had an implement in her hand. Madison's car was skidding along five feet off the ground and it went close by her. She was just standing up, placing her muddy palm against her obviously aching back. SHE SAW HIM!

Then he was by her. Oh, she must have done something awful, to assign her to filthy manual labor. The knight-errant rose in him. "Never mind, Teenie," he whispered, "I'll rescue you if I can."

They stopped in front of a huge, jewelled building with twin curving stairs you could have marched a regiment down.

Two tough-looking officers in black rushed up.

"Delivering J. Walter Madison," said Flick.

"In the name of seven Devils," said one, "where have you been? The old (bleep) is tearing his toenails out waiting for you! Get the Hells up those stairs! Guard, guard! Shove this guy through to the chief, triple pace!"

Hefty hands seized Madison on either arm and propelled him up the stairs and into a corridor at a dead run.

The fatal moment had arrived. J. Walter Madison was about to meet Lombar Hisst.

I have dwelt upon it at length, for it was a moment which would mean much to Voltar's history and Jettero Heller. And, dear reader, I assure you, not for the good of either!

Chapter 2

On every hand the pomp of millennia rose: the golden ropes curved in intricate patterns along jewelled friezes depicting parades and battles down the ages; the glowering eyes of long-dead monarchs frowned at Madison as he went along the curving hall. The consciousness reached him that he was dealing with power ensconced in the awesome traditions of history far longer than man, on Earth, had even known how to use an axe of stone.

He was rushed at length into a huge circular room, jewelled and glittering. It was the antechamber of the Emperor's sleeping quarters.

On the other side of it, a huge desk, carved from a single block of onyx, seemed to be barring a door. All around the desk, machines and equipment had been set up to make an impromptu office.

At the desk sat a huge man, rather swarthy, an odd sheen on his skin. He was dressed in a scarlet uniform, corded round with gold. His eyes had a crazy light.

LOMBAR HISST!

The guards had dumped Madison in the center of the room. Not one to be overly impressed by the trappings of the mighty, Madison straightened up his clothes, picked a bit of imaginary lint from his lapel and sauntered forward.

Without preliminary, Hisst said, "Is Rockecenter all right?"

Madison weighed up the situation. There was concern and worry, not hostility, in Hisst's voice. "Well," said Madison, "he was the last time I talked to him."

"You were close to him, then?" said Hisst.

Any unease Madison felt, he did not show. He was asking himself how good Voltar intelligence was: Did they know the true situation? That Rockecenter would have Madison's head for failing and running away? He saw what appeared to be a TV screen flickering away: How fast were communications between this place and Earth? He decided he would take a chance. He would name-drop. "Oh, yes," he said, careful to sound bored. "I handled delicate things for him: telling the prime minister of England or the president of the United States

what to think, things like that. My account was several
million dollars a year."

"What a salary!" said Hisst. "You must have been
very valuable to him."

"Well, he often said there were a lot of things only
I could handle. I was his top *PR man*."

Hisst frowned. This is what the investigators had
run into and hadn't solved. "What is this thing you
call *PR?*"

"Well," said Madison, "I noticed, talking around,
you don't have a very good image."

Hisst looked angry. "Nothing wrong with my image!
I'm six foot three inches tall. I weigh 271 pounds——"

"No, no," said Madison. "The way people think of
you. The *image* of you other people carry in their minds."

"Huh!" snorted Hisst. "Is it important how I am
thought of by the riffraff?"

"Well, yes, it is," said Madison. "I have heard that
you are the virtual ruler of Voltar."

"Well, of course I am! I can see that what these
(bleeped) Lords think of me could matter. But what does
the riffraff have to do with it?"

"Well, you see, *PR* means 'public relations,' though
the letters don't add up to that in Voltarian. The Lords
and the riffraff are different publics. But if you don't
have the right image, they could rise up and kill you."

Hisst frowned. He was thinking that could very well
happen anyway. They were all against him.

Madison saw the frown. "You know, Mr. Hisst, I
was very close to Rockecenter. I call him 'Rockie' and he
calls me 'Mad.' Many a time, late at night, he used to slip
his shoes off and put his feet on his desk and, over a companionable *Scotch and soda*, he'd confide in me. He
trusted me when he really wanted something. I was, so

to speak, his most intimate confidence man. I think it's time we opened our coats. Is there something you desire more than anything else in the world?"

Lombar's eyes got a bit crazy. The sheen on his face was more pronounced. He leaned forward and spoke in a whisper. "It isn't that I want it so much. It's that I have an order about it. In spite of my being a commoner and the fact that all the Lords hate me, I am destined to become Emperor."

Madison was instantly alert. Ah, he could deal with this. He had heard of it before about Rockecenter. "A call from . . . ?" He left it hanging in the air.

Lombar whispered, "The angels."

Mad knew he had it made. "Did you know they called Rockecenter to rule Earth?"

"NO!"

"Fact," said Madison. "Heard them myself. That's why I became his *PR man*."

Hisst instantly frowned. "What's that got to do with it?"

"Well," said Madison, "when somebody doesn't have a good *PR man*, the riffraff rises up and kills him. BUT if he DOES have a GOOD *PR man*, the Lords, the public, the riffraff rise as one man and proclaim him Emperor by acclamation."

Lombar blinked. This was a brand-new idea. Usually, he didn't bother to listen to people or even answer them. But this Earthman sitting here had been close to Rockecenter. Rockecenter, a commoner, had risen to become the ruler of Earth, and this alone had given Lombar hope that it could be done. Now he was alert to the possibility that some secret technology, heretofore unknown to him, had been employed. He mused on it. It came to him that what this man was saying might get around not having a dead Cling to display. Emperor by proclamation of the public! How novel! But then his suspicious nature began to tell him that it might be too good to be true. He started to sag.

Madison, noting it: "Do you have any other little problems?"

Lombar stiffened. He was instantly wary. He was not going to tell anyone that there was no emperor in that room behind him and no regalia either. Instead, he clutched at another worry. He said, "This (bleeped) Soltan Gris!"

That startled Madison. "Soltan Gris? Is HE here?"

"You know him?"

Madison had detected the fury. "Oh, I should say so. On Earth he went by the names of Smith, Inkswitch and Sultan Bey. Got in the road all over the place. Knew NOTHING of PR. Wrecked things. An idiot!"

"He's down at the Royal Prison and I can't get to him and can't execute him the way he deserves."

"Well," said Madison, "that's a PR problem, too. There are ways. Any other problem?"

"Heller! That (bleeped) Royal officer!"

Madison felt like somebody was giving him candy on a silver platter. The whole room went brighter. But he said calmly, "On Earth he went by the name of Wister."

Lombar, who had never bothered to listen to anyone before, seized upon the information like a starved hound! THAT was the missing piece of the puzzle of why his strategy had failed. "Aha!" he cried. "Gris didn't carry out my idea with the birth certificate! It went wrong because that (bleeped) Gris didn't follow my plans for Heller!"

Madison's hopes soared to seventh heaven. Oh, what

a chance was opening up in front of him! He could finish the job he had been hired to do! He could go home to plaudits and glory! But he made himself look very calm. "Well, Wister-Heller is a PR problem, too. If you really want these things handled, just give me the account and let me get to work. Just give me an office and a budget——"

Lombar cut in. "Not so fast, Madison. Things are pretty delicate around here. I don't know a thing about *PR*."

Madison's hopes fell. But he pointed to the Home-view screen. "Is that a *TV?* May I turn on the sound?"

Lombar shrugged. Madison found a button and upped the volume. The picture was a battle scene on Calabar. Apparatus troops were firing at an enormous snowcapped mountain. The announcer was simply saying that Prince Mortiiy's troops were being blasted out of caves. Mad turned the sound off.

"Now, a good PR," he said, "would have that announcer stating that those Apparatus troops were fighting at your orders to make the Empire safe. And it would have a shot of you leading them to victory even though you weren't even there."

Lombar frowned.

Madison pulled out the newssheet he had been given. He showed Lombar the front page. "If you had a good PR, your name would be all over this, building up the image that YOU were the one to rule. Pound, pound, day after day, week after week, you'd eventually get the message through that YOU and ONLY you should be Emperor."

"They wouldn't print it," said Lombar.

"You would ORDER them to print it," said Madison.

"Hmm," said Lombar.

"With a good PR," Madison said, "not just the riff-raff but every Lord in the land would be bowing down to you."

"Lords bowing to ME? Those stiff-necked (bleeps)? I'm just a commoner! They'd rather die!"

"But if the Lords DID bow down to you," said Madison, "and day after day such things appeared on Homeview, the people would have to assume that you WERE their master and you'd be Emperor by acclaim!"

Lombar shook his head. "Madison, those Lords would never bow."

Madison continued to appear calm. He wasn't. He was playing for very high stakes. He would get another chance at Wister. If he succeeded, Bury would have to admit he had done his job. If he worked Hisst properly, he could be sent home. He would be on top again! He said, "Mr. Hisst (and forgive me if I am already thinking of you as His Majesty), if I get pictures of Lords bowing to you on *TV*—I mean Homeview—will you retain me as a *PR man* with an unlimited budget and a free hand?"

Lombar barked a laugh. "That's a big contract."

Madison said, "But it won't take much to start: just a few thousand credits." Suddenly he remembered Teenie. "And the help of my assistant, Teenie Whopper."

"WHO," said Lombar, "is Teenie Whopper?"

"An Earth girl that came with me."

Lombar suddenly remembered there had been another passenger. "Well, Madison, you can have your Earth girl. But as to money, no. It would be just a waste of cash."

Madison had a sinking feeling. He would have no resources for bribery, no way to hire actors, no way to order Homeview to screen what he gave them. It looked pretty forlorn! But he had to be bold. "But if I succeed in this first bit, will you okay the big contract?"

Lombar could never recall having done so much listening before. No wonder he always avoided it: it was so tiring. He said, "It's impossible to get Lords to bow to me. So I can safely agree to your offer. If you can get such pictures on Homeview, all right. But I'm busy now. Good-bye. Guards! Show this Earthman out."

As it stood, right at that moment, dear reader, Madison's apparent failure with Lombar left Jettero Heller fairly safe; the empty chamber back of Lombar would sooner or later get exposed and the histories of Voltar and Earth might have righted themselves.

Madison's chances of getting much further now looked thoroughly *zilch*. But only at that moment, dear reader, only at that moment. Huge and diabolical forces, already at work on two empires, were about to get a hefty push!

Chapter 3

J. Walter Madison walked down the long curving steps. Inwardly, he felt downhearted: without connections or knowing channels, without money and without even a press card, things seemed pretty hopeless.

He raised a friendly hand to the two black-uniformed guard officers and they merely looked through him and away.

He climbed into his airbus but he didn't have any place to go: he didn't even have a home.

Flick, his driver, said, "Things didn't go so well, eh? At least thank several Gods you are alive."

Was his gloom that obvious? thought Madison. But he did feel down. The chance to get back on the job at Wister-Heller had almost been within his grasp, but his fingers had been too slippery. Curse trying to work with madmen!

"Who runs Homeview?" he said.

"The manager of Homeview," said Flick. "It's on all their program cards. Here's one: I keep it so I know when Hightee Heller is going to sing."

"Heller? Is she any relation to the Royal officer Jettero Heller?"

"She's his sister. Most beautiful woman in the Confederacy, and can she sing! Billions and billions of fans."

Well, that wouldn't do much for him now. He looked at the program. Aha! Homeview was under the Interior Division and that was under Lord Snor. He must be right here in Palace City!

Maybe he could pull something off! He excitedly told Flick to go wherever Lord Snor lived.

They drove through innumerable parks and around innumerable round buildings: there must be thousands of them in these few square miles, all different colors, all basking in this greenish light. But the place seemed unpopulated: patrols of Apparatus guards in mustard uniforms were the only ones upon the walks; Apparatus tanks were the only vehicles.

"Where's all the people?" said Madison.

"Oh, there used to be a lot of them, especially at this time of day: it's near quitting time. Ladies would be strolling with retinues, Palace Guards on every step, concerts going in these parks. But that's all changed. After His Majesty was taken ill he issued an order replacing the Palace Guards with the Apparatus: a lot of families moved to their town or country estates because the

Apparatus would stop and search them. There's plenty of domestics in these buildings but they don't show their faces. There must be only a few hundred thousand people left here now. Used to be two million."

"You seem very well informed," said Madison.

"Ha, ha," said Flick without laughing. "A lifetime as a breaking-and-entering thief sort of trains you to keep your eyes open. Untenanted houses are a prime target. But a murderer like you wouldn't know. You probably got all the dark places in these parks already spotted, though. Here's your address."

They were stopped before a huge round building that evidently combined offices and living quarters. It was bright yellow and had gardens jutting out from its walls.

Madison went up a staircase. An Apparatus guard stopped him, called for an officer. One in mustard yellow came out, looked at Madison's identoplate. "What the blasts is a *PR man?*"

"A special envoy," said Madison promptly. "I want to see Lord Snor."

"Well, you could be a special envoy from the thirteenth Hell," said the officer, "and it still wouldn't do you any good. You might even get into his quarters and you still wouldn't make it. He used to have a wife but she's gone home to her family. He's got a son but he's in page school."

"What's all this family got to do with it?" said Madison.

"Oh, that's the way things used to run around here. If you couldn't see the top man, you saw some member of his family and slid your message in on that channel. But, frankly, I don't think even they could make it now. Lord Snor just stays in his quarters. He hasn't been seen for weeks. Wait a minute." He stepped inside and looked into a door marked CHAMBERLAIN. He talked a moment and then came back. "I thought maybe you could make an appointment for next week or month or something, but the chamberlain says the only ones that see him are the resident doctors who take in the little packages."

"The little . . . ?"

"The white stuff. Don't play dumb. You know as well as I do what's happening with these Lords. Your best chance of getting anything done in the Interior Division is to go into Government City. The clerks all run it from there anyway."

The "white stuff": that meant dope. "Well, thank you. You have been of great help."

"I wouldn't give you the time of day if you weren't from the Apparatus." And the officer walked off.

Gloom settled in on Madison. The day he began to transact business through clerks had not arrived. And the top men? In sudden revelation, this deserted city was explained. Any minute he expected to see an I. G. Barben truck. Lombar Hisst had this place on dope! Did this explain the chief's interest in Rockecenter? Did Rockecenter have a connection to that Earth base in Turkey? No, he doubted Rockecenter even knew about these people. But they knew about Rockecenter.

Madison seldom cursed. He felt a bit like cursing now. You could only deal with top men for the things he had in mind, and with insight he knew that from the Emperor on down, here at Palace City, he would be running into hopheads. Suddenly he understood a bit more about Lombar Hisst: the (bleeped) fool must be on amphetamines himself! A speeder! The signs of persecution were there, delusion was obvious. It wasn't to the point of feeling bugs under the skin or aging or losing one's teeth, but it would get there. And he probably had been crazy to begin with.

A chill hit Madison. He had better get his job done on Heller somehow, some way, and get out of this place before Hisst reached raving paranoia and started to kill everyone in sight!

How long did he have? A few months?

He groaned. He didn't even have any place to start!

"Where now?" said Flick. "It's quitting time. Do I drive to Government City and find a rooming house?"

"I don't have any money."

"Hells of a boss you are," said Flick. "I'm tired of sleeping in an airbus and I bet you have nightmares: killers always do."

"Sleep in a car?" said Madison. This was getting worse and worse. He could see himself becoming an unshaven wreck: not the slightest chance of being believed.

"Well, I ain't going to break into any of these palaces," said Flick. "That would be a fast route to Camp Kill, with all these guards around. Tell you what, we'll fly to Slum City and rob a store. You can shoot the watchman."

Madison wished Flick wouldn't keep building on that image, yet he could see respect for him was dwindling. "I don't have a gun."

"Blowholes! The assignments I get! My last boss lost all his pay in gambling and finally got stabbed in a dice game. Now I'm going to starve to death."

"Don't you have any pay? Any quarters?"

"In the Apparatus? A driver's boss is supposed to provide all that. And I get a murderer who isn't even packing a gun, that's dead broke and has no pay status. Can't you do *anything?*"

It jarred Madison. Yes, there was something he could do. He could be a knight-errant. He could rescue Teenie; that had been allowed. He would do it even though the thought of sleeping three in an aircar presented new problems.

He mentally donned his plumed helmet. "Drive back to that park in front of the Royal Palace. I've got to rescue a girl."

Chapter 4

They drove back a mile and slid along the curving path where he had first seen her. The light seemed bad: apparently in this place they followed day and night, and this must be dusk.

The garden space around the painted statue was all dug up but no workmen were about. Flick stopped.

Suddenly, from under the sculptured purple cloak of some long-dead monarch, an Apparatus guard moved out, rifle levelled. It was the same guard he had seen before. Madison hastily presented his identoplate through the window. The guard saw "Apparatus" and relaxed.

"There was a girl here earlier," said Madison.

"Oh, yeah," said the guard. "They're gone now. You haven't got a puffstick, have you?"

"Give him one," Madison told Flick.

With a very dirty look, Flick complied. He gave the guard an even dirtier look when he had to light it for him.

"They went over that way," said the guard. "Between those two orange-colored buildings."

Flick headed in that direction. "This is getting worse and worse," he said.

Madison privately agreed with him. If he found her, she would probably be covered with mud and this car, not overly clean already, would really ruin all his clothes then. Anyway, she would be terribly happy to see him and know that, as his assistant, she would be free.

They burst into an area of pools. There was a circular series of waterfalls, each one lower than the next, the water spilling off the lips in shimmering sheets, the underlighting turning them into a cacophony of colors.

They would have passed them by but Madison saw a sudden movement on a rim. It was pretty far away.

TEENIE!

She was running along a lip. She dived through scarlet lights into the next pool. She swam across it. She dived through yellow lights in the next pool and swam toward the next fall.

A sign plainly said:

NO SWIMMING

Oh, Gods, she was going to get into trouble before he even had a chance to rescue her!

Frantically, he directed the airbus to a point where she would come out if she dived into the ground-level pool.

She did! Her body glistened as she shot through a sheet of yellow light. She came swimming boldly across.

Madison got out of the car. He waited at the pool edge.

Teenie came to the rim and with an agile leap, sprang up on it, gleaming in the red lights. She was very lean: her stomach and her thighs were flat. Water cascaded from her shoulders and made sparkling rivulets down her legs. She swept her light brown hair out of her big eyes and looked at him.

"Teenie!" he cried. "I've got great news. I've got a chance to get us back to Earth. And you're my assistant now! You're not a slave anymore!"

She shrugged. She turned and walked over to a bench where she had evidently left her purse. She got out a comb and began to whip the water out of her hair with it.

Madison couldn't understand it. She didn't seem glad to see him at all! He walked closer. "Don't you understand? I've freed you! And when I saw the horrible way they treat slaves, you ought to be very happy!"

She gathered her wet hair into a ponytail and put a rubber band around it. Then she went over to the pool waterfall and fished up the piece of sackcloth she had been wearing. She wrung it out and, without putting it on, tossed it over her shoulder. She picked up her purse and began to walk off.

She seemed cross.

Madison tried to find a reason for it. Why was she angry with him? He hadn't been the one who had gotten her into this mess. That had been Gris.

He followed her, Flick driving the airbus at a slow pace behind him. The little procession went down a curving promenade, between two other buildings. They were approaching a gold structure that was ornate but seemed very aged. Vines had crept up its several stories and were tangled in its balconies. The wide, curving staircase was so huge that it made the thin Teenie look like a toy in a giant world.

Madison followed up. Flick stopped at the bottom.

She went through a pair of gold doors you could have flown a Boeing jetliner through.

Madison entered after her.

They were in a mammoth hall, all festooned with golden cords woven into patterns through which three-dimensional painted angels flew against a white sky. The floor was in patterns of clouds. Hundreds of jewelled chairs lined the walls: it must be some sort of a salon.

There was a mound of silken-fabricked pillows in the middle of the floor. Teenie sat down on them and they were promptly spotted with water.

Madison walked up to her, his footsteps sounding hollowly in the vast place. "Teenie," he pleaded. "I know a lot of these palaces are deserted now that families have moved out. But you're just riding for an awful fall. First you're swimming in a no-swimming pool and now you're coming in here just because it's an empty building and you're even ruining those pillows. Please come along and let me get you out of here. Guards may drop by at any time to turn off the lights or something."

She picked up what must have been a priceless silken cover from a low table within her reach and began to swab herself with it, using it for a towel. She was ruining it! Oh, how could he stop her from sure disaster?

"Don't be cross with me," he begged. "I am your friend!"

She gave a short, barking laugh. "You're a fine one to talk. Some friend! On that freighter, you didn't help me a bit. You didn't even volunteer to keep books for me! You could have put up signs, 'The One and Only Too-Too!' You're even a lousy PR."

"Oh, come off of it," said Madison. "I couldn't get involved with a filthy business like that! You were making that poor boy into a prostitute, ruining his life! You even had him smoking pot. You have no conscience! No moral sense of any kind!"

"You're a fine one to talk, sleeping with your mother!"

"That's just the way I was raised!"

"Well, this is just the way *I* was raised!" snapped Teenie. "Have you got any money?"

"Well, no."

"And I bet you came around here just to borrow some."

Madison received a shock. He had sort of wondered if they had let her keep hers.

"I landed with a thousand credits," said Teenie. "I got it stashed. I'll let you have ten credits and that's the limit. You can then proceed to get lost."

Ten credits? He didn't know what things cost but it wasn't enough to sell his pride for. "I wouldn't touch money made out of the body of that poor boy!"

"That 'poor boy,' as you call him, happens to be a catamite that that (bleep) Gris set onto Lord Endow. Lord Endow is the head of the Exterior Division and the top man over the Apparatus, when he can stop drooling long enough. So I taught that 'poor boy,' as you call him, a few little tricks he could do and when he got back here he pleased Lord Endow no end. The goofy old (bleepard) went absolutely delirious over Too-Too."

"Wait a minute," said Madison, in Voltarian, "you just shifted languages. When you started talking about Endow, you shifted to Voltarian."

"Of course I did. And it's *court* Voltarian. What you just said, you said in *executive* Voltarian."

"But how . . ."

"Well, Lord Endow would do anything Too-Too asked, even jump over one of this assortment of moons they got on this planet. And I right away got sent to page school. They hypnotrained me to talk, read and write court Voltarian in five days. But meantime, Too-Too told all the other catamites about the wonderful trip he had had, and boy, were they envious! (Bleeped) by a whole crew for six weeks! He was the hero of the hour! So he's got me teaching the other catamites and we're including all the pages."

"Wait a minute," said Madison. "You must be lying, Teenie. I saw you doing slave work with my own eyes!"

"Well, jumping *Jesus Christ*, Maddie, you really *are* dumb. Is that why you were chattering about me being a slave? Listen, *buster*, I've only got a limited supply of marijuana seed and those dumb gardeners would have wasted it. Sure they got a growth catalyst that matures it in a week, but the old (bleeps) are 160, would you believe it? And they potter and totter when they ought to be drilling and tilling. We're tearing up all the flower beds in sight and planting the whole place properly with Mary Jane."

"Oh, God," said Madison. "More trouble. They'll kill us. You're my assistant now. Please, get out of this palace before they shoot us."

"*(Bleep)*, Maddie! Nobody's going to shoot us. Too-Too told Lord Endow I was a *movie* queen on Earth. So the drooling old (bleepard) gave me this palace. Two hundred and thirty rooms! Some queen abandoned it about a hundred or a thousand years ago, poisoned or old age or something. But all her things are still here: Queen Hora, it says on the silver trays. I'm getting cold."

She snapped her fingers in a peculiar way and two

old men in ornate silver livery, who must have been hovering in one of the several hallways, rushed in. They threw a gauzy silken robe on her that left her twice as naked as before. They snapped up the table cover she had used for a towel and vanished back into the hall.

Teenie snapped her fingers again, in a different way, and two old women trotted out. They were dressed in silver gowns. One bore a crystal jug of sparklewater on a crystal tray with crystal glasses. The other expertly balanced a silver tray which must have had ten pounds of colored sweetbuns on it, topped, each one, with a design which said *Queen Teenie.*

Madison suddenly got the picture.

Teenie had INFLUENCE!

Hope boomed in him like a struck drum. He could almost hear the trumpets blare. Influence could be USED!

The two old women had made their offerings to Teenie, bent to one knee. She had a goblet of sparklewater now in one hand and was cramming an oversized sweetbun into her oversized mouth with the other.

The two old women cast their eyes sideways in a question to Teenie, waiting then for a signal to offer something to Madison.

Teenie shook her head. "Forget him," she said. "He's no friend of mine."

The two old women backed away, bowed and left.

It was more than hunger which made Madison stare after them. He knew just where he stood now. Nowhere.

His hopes of finishing Heller fell crumbling about him.

Chapter 5

A small obituary ran through Madison's head:

Earthman Found Dead

An emaciated body was discovered last night in Slum City. The identoplate had the name J. Walter Madison. No known relatives or friends on Voltar.

Teenie sat there stuffing herself with sweetbuns and guzzling down nutritious sparklewater. Maybe, thought Madison, when the beast in her is fed, she will be more kind.

He waited until her face looked relaxed and then he said, "Teenie, common humanity says that you should help me."

She shrugged. "Why should I? Did you help me on the yacht? No. You didn't even attempt to persuade that (bleeped) Gris to stay aboard! You ran right off with him!"

Ah, so that was what was biting her. No reason to stir it up further: he would try another tack, earnest and sincere. Even frank! "Teenie, I've got to succeed as a PR here. Otherwise I'll never be accepted back on Earth. Did you ever hear of Wister?"

"The Whiz Kid? Yeah, I read something. And that (bleeping) (bleep) (bleep) Gris was snarling about him one day."

"Well, Teenie, the Whiz Kid was really Jettero Heller, a Royal officer of Voltar. And I'm in trouble. I never completed my job on him."

"That's your (bleep), baby. Not mine."

Madison was beginning to feel desperate. That obituary was drifting to the last page, below the classifieds. "Teenie, I've got to make motions of putting Hisst on the throne."

"So what's that to me? He doesn't and won't give a (bleep) what's happening in Palace City. He never even talks to the Lords here and they sure won't talk to him, no matter what he calls himself. He's just a *rat* from Slum City: he'd still have to rule through the Grand Council. He's got them all drugged up, but even so he can only push them so far. They privately laugh at him behind his back. Even if he gets put on the throne he won't last any time at all. I know what I'm talking about, because I been through page school now and I know all the pages and they know everything! So all I've got to do is keep in good with the catamites, raise lots of Mary Jane and sit here in my queen's palace having fun. I've got it made."

Madison's obituary even lost its subtitle. Desperation boiled over. He got down on his knees. "Please, Teenie. Oh, please, help me!"

She laughed at him. She snapped her fingers in yet a different way and two young boys, about twelve, ran out of a hall, stopped before her and bowed.

"You've got to excuse me, Madison," said Teenie. "I have a class starting shortly."

All sorts of arguments were racing through Madison's head. He was hastily examining her own assessment of her situation to see if he could punch any holes in it. Having worked for Rockecenter, he knew that madmen could not be dismissed so lightly. But all he could come up with was that she had INFLUENCE and he needed it desperately.

Then suddenly he registered what she was doing. He was horrified for more reasons than one. Good Heavens, she was going to disgrace herself and not even be able to help him if she would. She had gone insane!

She had signalled to the two boys before her and they were grinning in a knowing way and taking off their clothes!

"No, no!" cried Madison. "Not here! This is a public audience hall!"

Teenie smiled. She said, "I know. And the audience will be here soon. Bye-bye, Madison. If you ever get back to Earth, say hello to Broadway."

Madison knelt there, suffering. He ignored the dismissal. Somehow, some way, he would make her listen to his plea, but right now she seemed to be well on the way to destroying her public image. The huge entrance doors weren't even closed!

The first little boy was looking down, grinning.

Teenie reached her hand out.

Madison stared. He was horrified. "Teenie! What are you doing? Don't make that boy into a queer! Take that out of your mouth!"

Teenie leaned back and looked in disdain at Madison. "They're not being made into queers, idiot. They'll be top-grade catamites when I'm done. It's still early and

I'm just playing around waiting for the audience. You should see what happens *then!*"

He could see liveried people watching for her bidding in the halls. She was really going to destroy herself before she could be of any possible use to him! He said hastily in English, "Teenie, don't perform sexual acts in public! The thing you did there is not socially acceptable! Not even in front of the help! What will the servants think?"

She looked at him, annoyed. In English, she said, "What will they think? Listen, mister, they're so glad to have a live body in the place, they'll put up with anything. They don't get paid in this palace unless they're serving royalty. And you ought to hear the tales they tell about Queen Hora. In the time of their grandfathers she had a new lover every night! And in just the short time I've been here they're saying the good old days are back. What do they think, indeed!" She was angry now and shouting, still in English. "Go ahead and raise your voice to me and you'll see what these servants think of me! They'll slaughter you!"

Madison was suddenly chilled. A hand settled on his right shoulder. He glanced sideways in fear. A man in silver livery was standing there, scowling at him with ferocity!

A hand settled on his left shoulder. He whipped his head in that direction. A second glowering man in silver was there. And both these brutes were carrying strange, sharp axes!

"Your Majesty," said the first one to Teenie, "this man has provoked you in your own palace. Would you care to conduct his trial and execution now or would you prefer to wait until after this evening's ceremonies?"

Teenie considered it. Then she reached for her Earth purse and looked at her Mickey Mouse watch. "Shattering comets!" she said in Voltarian. "I'm running late!" She glanced toward the men. "I can't be bothered with him now. Sergeants, shove him in a chair over there and tie him up." She grabbed her purse and yelled in the general direction of other servants, "Get this hall ready fast!" and raced off up a stairway of gold.

The sergeants pushed Madison backwards across the room and plunked him down in a metal chair. They clamped some shackles on him and bound him there solidly. One of them gave the chains a final yank, unnecessarily hard. "You must be crazy mad, you fool, to insult our queen. She's the most wonderful thing that's happened here in centuries and you just made yourself a lot of enemies. So sit quietly! Not another word out of you. Hammer," he said to the other guard, "you better stay here so you can prevent some other staff from sneaking up and cutting this (bleep's) throat." He turned back to Madison. "Insulting Queen Teenie!" And he spat straight in Madison's face!

Madison cringed. He had not thought he could get any lower. And as the spittle dripped down his cheek, he recomposed his obituary. He added a line:

Body taken to the local garbage dump.

Chapter 6

The hall resounded with the sounds of hurrying staff who dashed about setting up the place. They roped off two large areas, one with red ropes, the other with blue. Before them they left an open expanse. About five hundred square feet of it was suddenly underlit so that it glowed and shimmered. The whole ceiling turned into a blue haze, much like a summer sky.

Two liveried footmen raced out, pushing a big vertical board on wheels. Two more, with the sound of thunder, pushed into view a massive golden throne all covered with sparkling jewels. The seat was twelve feet above the floor, reached by scarlet steps. They placed it in front of the open expanse, across from the ropes.

There was a rumble. On the wall, over to the right of the throne, ten feet above the floor, a whole section moved outward to form a balcony that was a stage. Eight musicians with strange instruments were already in place, adjusting their equipment: they were dressed in shimmering yellow clothing that sparked other colors each time they moved.

A dozen silver-liveried men with axes on tall handles marched in smartly and took positions at the ends of the roped areas and on either side of the throne.

As quickly as they had appeared, the hurrying staff vanished, leaving only the silent musicians and guards. The stillness, after all that noise, was almost like a blow.

There were then some murmurings and footsteps coming from the main entrance stairs.

Madison tried to fish in his pocket, hopeful that he had a kleenex so he could wipe his face, wet with spittle that was too much like tears.

"Sit still!" snarled Hammer and blocked his motion with the axe. Madison froze: little chains of sparks were racing up and down that blade, giving off the odor of ozone. He recoiled: It wasn't just a ceremonial axe as he had thought—it was an electric weapon. Gods knew what it would do! Would the sparks jump? He hoped it wouldn't touch his chains: it could electrocute him! He let the spittle drip. Maybe they were tears now, for he certainly felt like crying. In all of his career as a PR, he had never felt quite so dejected—except maybe that time he had accidentally wrecked the country of Patagonia, or perhaps that afternoon he had icily been dismissed by the president of an international airline Rockecenter had told him to PR, or possibly the dreadful day the presidential candidate Bury had given him as a client suddenly announced he had gone insane. Unaccountable failures dogged his life. He certainly hoped that somehow he would not fail again on Heller: it was his only hope. Or did he have any hope left, sitting here in this overwhelming hall waiting on the whim of a juvenile delinquent from New York? Would that little pathological liar and infant con artist really try him and sentence him to death? He decided she would. Maybe if he threatened to expose her and tell these Voltarians that "*movie queen*" was just an expression, not royalty.... Oh, no! They would kill him if he even so much as looked like he was being critical. She had even taken care of that! He could think of no way to reach her. Actual tears began to mix with the spit.

He became aware that small groups of boys had been coming in the vast front door. They were being greeted by two bowing seneschals in silver and then directed toward the roped areas by polite ushers. The boys were beautifully dressed, some flashier than others. In the main they were handsome or pretty, and a few wore powder and paint. They all had belts with a shining metal plate which hugely, in Voltarian, said *Page*. They appeared to range in age from eight to fifteen, but one couldn't really tell with these long-lived people. There must be two hundred of them here by now, and laggards still sauntered in.

At last a seneschal with a list gave a signal and the giant front doors closed. Another scanned the roped areas: the larger number of boys were behind the red ropes, a smaller, better-dressed number were behind the blue.

An usher gave a signal to one of the seneschals, who pushed a button on his livery.

A spotlight went on, striking at the top of the golden stairs.

Four heralds closed across the bottom of the balustrade. They raised what must be battle horns. A chorded blast struck the hall.

And in the spotlight glare at the stairway top stood Teenie!

She had a golden crown upon her head, ponytail sticking out behind. She wore a scarlet military coat with golden frogs: it gripped her neck with its high collar and fell away to her black-booted heels. In her hand she carried a golden rod that sparked with jewels, a scepter.

Like a benediction from above, a gauzy gold cape,

full of glitter, settled over her shoulders. The two boys Madison had seen earlier were now in golden suits.

Teenie took a forward step to descend the stairs.

The musicians bashed out a cymbal crash! Then they began to play a stately air of celestial majesty. With the two boys in gold carrying her long golden train, in time to the sedate music, Teenie came down the curving golden stairs.

The throng gazed at her in ecstasy.

Followed by the spotlight, she paraded across the hall. With great dignity she mounted the scarlet steps to the throne. Regally, she seated herself, and the two boys gave the train an artistic, curving fold upon the approach. They folded their arms and stood like two small golden statues at her feet. The music ceased.

The seneschal approached the throne and gave a sweeping bow. Kneeling and speaking to the floor, not her, he said, "Your Majesty, I beg to announce the court is assembled. I have further been told to say that there are several virgins here. The courtiers await your pleasure. They beg that you would condescend to caress their ears with the celestial beauty of your voice. They eagerly attend. Long Live Your Majesty. May I withdraw?"

Teenie gave a twitch with the scepter and he backed away. She gazed down upon the lifted faces of the throng across the open space.

The spotlight narrowed to a glittering circle upon her.

She smiled.

A sigh of pleasure rippled like a friendly breeze about the room.

Teenie spoke and her voice was quite commanding and loud: there must be a microphone in the arm of that throne. Her Voltarian accent had changed: she was speaking with the lilt that characterized the speeches of the court.

"Welcome, welcome, my dear, loyal vassals and sweet friends. I spread my love upon you and accept your kisses on my feet. May the blessings of a thousand Heavens rain into your waiting lips." She paused and gave a sly smile. "And into your hips as well." There was a patter of applause. Teenie smiled more broadly. "I thank you from my bottom."

Instant cheers broke out.

Then the boys were throwing her kisses.

Teenie beamed. "I love you, too!" she said.

Wilder cheers racked the hall. The sentries had to twitch the ropes as a warning not to burst across the open space to the throne.

Teenie was laughing. She held up the scepter for quiet.

The two boys in gold saw some signal and rushed up the steps to her. She kissed each one and then they unfastened the chain which held the golden cape and, doing a sort of swirling dance with it, bore it off.

Teenie stood up. "But enough, my darlings, of this ceremony. I fear that I must now go into the stuffy, technical end of life. Are you ready for my lecture?"

Cries of "Oh, yes, Your Majesty!" "Please, please!" rocked the hall. No professor in a school ever got such an invitation to begin.

Madison wondered what in heaven she was going to talk about. Like all good PRs, he was an expert in presentation and stagecraft, and up to now he had been struck with awe at how well the page school had trained her and how she must be working under the guidance of an expert palace staff with all the expertise that they must have. A *technical* lecture after this? Surely Teenie, now on her own, was going to blow it. The foolish girl: good heavens, how she needed his help! And, oh, how desperately he needed her assistance to finish his job with Heller!

Chapter 7

Covered from throat to heels by her scarlet military coat, topped by her glittering crown, Teenie strode to the wheeled vertical board. Madison could not see what was on it. But he was very glad she had good enough sense not to appear naked or exposed before these boys: they were much too young to be subjected to female nakedness, even that as immature as Teenie's.

The hall was hushed. She raised her scepter, using it as a pointer. It must have a microphone in it, for her voice came loudly, with authority, from speakers Madison could not locate.

"Here, my loving students," Teenie said, "we have a graphic illustration of the naked male body." She gestured with the scepter in a sweep. "A front view, a right-side view, a left-side view and a back. Now, I must admit that the artist has made the (bleep) too large for my taste." She turned to them and smiled a too-big smile. There was pleased laughter at her joke. "But somehow getting around that point"—more laughter—"you will see that I myself have marked in certain places with an *X*. Now attend, and no more giggling, for this is serious business and I have left you clearheaded for this part of the program so that the information can slide in and stick. There are 172 of these *X*'s on these four drawings. Can everyone see them?"

Choruses of "Yes."

"They are called the *erotic spots*. Touching them or manipulating them can bring about sexual stimulation, prolong it or cool it off." Jabbing with her scepter she rattled them off, for each one had a name. English? Chinese? She turned to the assemblage, quite out of breath, and smiled. "I know it seems an awful lot, but nevertheless, you must know each one and know just how to use it. You will see these boards again in subsequent evening classes. The palace artist, who is a very splendid fellow really, despite his exaggerated idea of (bleeps)..." She paused to let their laughter pass. "He offered to make copies of this for you, but the information is secret. So these boards will be placed in the basement near the rear portcullis and you can slip in and out to your heart's content and study them. Now mind that you do, for you will be personally examined on each one of them. Got it?"

The two groups nodded vigorously, interest was intense.

"Now," said Teenie, "for tonight's first demonstration. I need a virgin volunteer."

Instantly fifty hands went flailing toward her.

Teenie pointed with the scepter. "I'll take you!"

A boy who appeared to be about fifteen slid eagerly under the red ropes. He was quite pretty, with a clear white skin.

The staff ran out a platform five feet high with steps. The two young boys in the golden suits led the volunteer up it. With expert hands they stripped off his clothes and in a moment had him standing there naked. They withdrew. Teenie mounted the platform.

"Now behold!" She pointed with her scepter to the boards. Then with one finger she touched a spot on the boy near the spine.

INSTANT RESPONSE!

The audience gasped.

Teenie pointed at the boards with her scepter. Then she touched a spot on the lower outside right thigh.

THE RESPONSE DEFLATED!

The audience groaned.

Again Teenie indicated the boards and then, with one finger, touched the lower middle lip of the boy's mouth.

RESPONSE OCCURRED AT ONCE!

She gestured at the charts and then she touched the side of the boy's neck.

THE RESPONSE GREW BIGGER AND STAYED!

Once more she pointed at the chart. Then with one light finger she touched a spot at the lower center of the boy's pubic hair. His eyes rolled up, his chin thrust forward, he gave an ecstatic groan.

HE (BLEEPULATED)!

Gasps echoed in the audience like an echo of the groan. Then there were cries of amazement and suddenly wild applause.

But Teenie wasn't through. She touched a spot at the base of his throat. He straightened up.

ANOTHER RESPONSE!

Gasps of astonishment slid through the hall.

Teenie leaned over and touched his ear with her tongue.

ANOTHER (BLEEPULATION)!

The crowd went mad!

The stern-faced sergeants had to twitch the ropes

quite hard to prevent a forward surge onto the cleared space.

"We could keep this up all night," said Teenie, "and though I'd dearly love to, the program must continue. You," she said to the volunteer, "have been a very good boy. You are very pretty, too." And she gave his (bleep) a pat. It was suddenly erect again. "So thank you for coming up here."

Although dismissed, the boy dropped to his knees and clutched the bottom of her military coat. He kissed it passionately. "O Teenie, Queen Teenie, thank Gods that you are here. I shall be your vassal forever."

She patted his head and smiled. "For that, sweet fellow, my two little grooms will take you into the hall there and in no time at all, you will no longer have to suffer your virginity."

Many behind the ropes had knelt when the boy did. There came a shout of "Long Live Your Majesty!" from 250 lips, more like a prayer than an accolade.

Madison was torn between revulsion at what she had just demonstrated and sheer awe at the power she had over these misguided youths. Oh Lord, he prayed, if I could just somehow channel this INFLUENCE in handling Heller!

Chapter 8

But Teenie never glanced at Madison. She obviously had forgotten him utterly.

The platform and the boards were now being wheeled away.

Teenie said, "Thank you for your patience, lovely court. After the ardors of stuffy technical harangue, I bid you have a moment's relaxation before we go on."

Madison blinked. She certainly taught a very unorthodox class! What more could there possibly be to this after TWO (bleepulations)? He knew she could be taken in hand and educated in good presentation. She had achieved a program peak with "Long Live Your Majesty." There couldn't be anything more. Then he wondered why he should be so anxious to be tried and probably executed. He must think of something!

Teenie had clapped her hands and servants were now passing amongst the boys behind the ropes. They had silver boxes and were handing out a joint to every four boys and lighting them.

Marijuana smoke soon rose sweetly and blue in the hall. The boys had evidently already been instructed in their use for they dragged the smoke in and held it, on and on, while the joints went round. One could see the euphoric surges hit their faces.

Teenie had walked over to the musicians. The bandmaster had come down and was kneeling before her while she conversed quietly with him. Then he kissed the hem of her military cloak and raced back up to the bandstand.

A prolonged chord was struck. The hall was filled with sound. And then Madison could not believe his ears.

ROCK AND ROLL!

Good heavens, how had these musicians ever learned this? It was an old piece of the Beatles! The electric whang of the guitars was there, even if a little strange, but the savage, pounding rhythm surged clear up to the painted angels. Then, as he saw the boys begin to jerk under the pall of marijuana smoke in time to the music, he remembered that Teenie had had an awesome collection of records in her baggage as well as tapes and players. Somebody must have matched current to them and these musicians had practiced to imitate the sound. He expected any minute to see Harrison walk out and begin to sing!

But this was just an interlude. Teenie had retired to her throne. She sat there, buttoned up to her throat, keeping time with her scepter. A servant knelt before her and passed her the pipe of a golden bhong. She took only a small puff of it, seemingly to just be companionable, and then waved the servant away.

The volunteer came back into the vast chamber, beaming and delighted. He whispered to his companions and they shook his hands and kissed him, making him a momentary swirl of attention.

The two boys came back, adjusting their clothes at the door, and then stole a puff apiece from a nearby joint and went once more to take their places near Teenie. One of them made a circle with his finger and thumb at her, an "okay" she must have taught him. She winked and nodded and he grinned and stood once more with folded arms like a statue.

A piece ended. A male singer in a shimmering military shirt came out. He held a microphone in his fist. The music started up with the beat of rock and roll. The audience began to move in rhythm to it. The singer screwed up his face and then he began to move his hips just like Elvis Presley! It so startled Madison to see this that for an instant he had the delusion of being in some Earth nightclub decades ago, and he didn't register for a moment that this was NOT a Presley song! The beat was there but not the meter.

> *Oh, a soldier's life is the life for me,*
> *Tuma-a-diddle, tuma-a-diddle, paw-paw.*
> *In camp and plain, I'm always free*
> *To tuma-diddle, tuma-diddle, paw-paw.*
> *No women ever spoil my view*
> *With tuma-diddle, tuma-diddle, paw-paw.*
> *They're always wanting something new,*
> *Not tuma-diddle, tuma-diddle, paw-paw.*
> *For it is the men that I enjoy*
> *To tuma-diddle, tuma-diddle, paw-paw.*
> *The best there is, I find, is boy!*
> *Oh, tuma-diddle, tuma-diddle, paw-paw.*
> *The enemy I do not mind*
> *If tuma-diddle, tuma-diddle, paw-paw*
> *Can go on in my behind*
> *With tuma-diddle, tuma-diddle, paw-paw,*
> *And if my bunkmates all are kind*
> *With tuma-diddle, tuma-diddle, paw-paw.*
> *Surrounded by ten thousand (bleeps)*
> *That tuma-diddle, tuma-diddle, paw-paw,*
> *All passionate and hard as rocks*
> *To tuma-diddle, tuma-diddle, paw-paw,*
> *Eager to slide in my buttocks*
> *And tuma-diddle, tuma-diddle, paw-paw!*
> *So (bleep), (bleep), (bleep) and (bleep) in me!*
> *Tuma-diddle, tuma-diddle, paw-paw.*
> *And let me (bleep) and (bleep) in thee*
> *With tuma-diddle, tuma-diddle, paw-paw.*
> *Oh, what a love-ul-lee Arm-eee!*
> *With its tuma-diddle, tuma-diddle,*
> **OH! BOY!**

But that was not the end. Teenie had been waving her scepter to the beat and watching the boys sway. She gave a sudden signal. The music went up in volume, battering the hall.

Teenie stood up.

A blue spotlight came on.

She reached up to the collar of her military coat.

She gave a rip.

It fell off!

She still had on her crown. She was wearing a red jacket so short that it barely covered the tops of her shoulders and her breasts, leaving her exposed from throat to crotch. She had on a small, scarlet jockstrap, no bigger than bikini pants, which had a gold metal plate in front. What had appeared to be boots were simply foot platforms, laced with red to her ankles, leaving the tops of her feet bare.

SHE WAS PAINTED FROM THROAT TO HEEL WITH PHALLIC SYMBOLS!

A groan of ecstasy rose even above the music from the crowd.

The singer began to sing the song again.

Between the two kneeling grooms in gold, Teenie began to dance in place. But she was not moving her limbs. All that was moving was her muscles!

Selectedly, in rhythmic time, balanced from right to left, the flesh was jerking and leaping, savage but under perfect control. The spotlight began to change colors in rhythm.

She took a step downward, muscles still dancing. Then step by step she descended, provocative, seductive. And when the muscles leaped the phallic symbols writhed and jerked.

Oh, she had been well taught by the Hong Kong

whore! As she extended her hands and feet, exactly in time to the music beat, the muscles whipped and rippled.

Now she was advancing across the open space, planting her feet so that the heel struck last. The song and music thudded on.

She went all along the ropes, muscles writhing, and her hips began to grind.

The boys watched her with eyes that were glazed with appreciation, awe and passion. Their mouths were open and their breath was coming hard.

Then Teenie turned away from them so they could see her behind and marched with beating steps while her buttocks writhed in time.

The song had rolled off twice again and now neared its end. She began to spin her scepter over her head. She suddenly caught it and shoved it between her legs from behind and threw up her arms.

The cymbals crashed. The lights burst on.

SCREAMS OF ECSTASY AND APPLAUSE CAME FROM THE BOYS!

The two little boys rushed up and put a golden cape on her that covered her, neck to heel. She turned and, holding the shimmering folds to her, made kissing sounds at her audience.

Good God, thought Madison, she certainly peaked that performance! He had not known she could muscle-dance, although he had often heard her speak of her training under the Hong Kong whore.

She certainly held these boys in her palm. Their attitude toward her was expressed in their adoring eyes. If he could only get her to listen to reason. This was a juggernaut of influence to be channelled!

But she certainly must be finished now, and any moment she would come over and say "Off with his

head!" and he never would be able to bring Heller the
fame to which he was entitled.

A tear coursed down Madison's cheek as he thought
how brutal life really was. The plum was almost within
his grasp and yet he sat here starving.

Then he sat up with amazement. This program had
even more to it! But it couldn't have! Not after that
climax!

Chapter 9

At a wave of Teenie's hand, many staff ran out. They
were pushing carts on which teetered mountains of sweetbuns and tanks of sparklewater and canisters, both of
which were seasoned with hash oil. They thrust them
through the ropes and the boys fell on them avidly to
remedy the tight jaw muscles and dry throats Madison
knew the smoked marijuana must have given them.

Another huge board was put in place and when the
tumult had died down and all the boys were contentedly
gulping and chewing, Teenie stood before the new display and raised her scepter for quiet.

"I am glad you liked the dance," she said, "but it
was wholly education—we must always complete our education. I did it just to demonstrate muscle control. For
muscle control is EVERYTHING!"

She had their rapt attention. "Now I want from you
another virgin volunteer."

Several would have dashed forward but she pointed
out a tall brunette boy of perhaps sixteen. The sergeants

let him through the blue ropes. He walked forward: he was very handsome, striding with a lordly, springing gait. His clothing shimmered in all colors of the rainbow.

A herald suddenly appeared behind Teenie's back, whispered something to her and withdrew. "Aha!" cried Teenie as the youth approached. "We have another high nobleman amongst us: the son of Snor, heir to his father, the Lord of the Interior! Advance, milord, if you have come to pledge fealty to your queen."

The boy ran forward and knelt suddenly at her feet. He reached out and grasped the bottom of her golden cloak and pressed it ardently to his lips. "I do acknowledge that I am thy vassal, O Queen Teenie, and do but wait any bidding of your slightest whim."

Madison stiffened with excitement. Lord Snor controlled Homeview and this boy was one of two who had access to him. Oh, God, he moaned, what a prize! But Teenie and her influence seemed light-years beyond his reach. Oh, God, he must think of something to get her to cooperate and give over this notion of executing him. She didn't even know the value of that lordling who now knelt at her feet.

Teenie lightly touched him with her scepter. "Your fealty now I do accept. Rise, my vassal, and embrace your queen."

The boy rose and they engaged in a perfunctory embrace while moans of envy coursed through the room. The boy stood away and looked back at the crowd with a cockiness that said he guessed that would show them.

There was another rumbling roar and servants pushed the platform up on which the first volunteer had stood. It now had a cushioned table on it.

Teenie made another signal and Too-Too ducked

through the ropes and raced away from the crowd to her. He was followed by cheers and calls of "Lucky Too-Too!"

The orchestra began to play again—less volume but a hard and sexy rock beat.

The two golden pages walked Too-Too and the son of Snor up the steps of the pedestal, mounting in the rhythm of the sexy music. They reached the top and turned around.

The music pulsed with a heavy rock beat and pulsing with it came a play of colored lights lacing forward and backward over the crowd.

Teenie settled her crown over her ponytail and walked up to the new display board. She pointed at the picture with her scepter. Single amongst the roving colored lights, a white light glowed upon it. "The artist has drawn a beautiful picture here and I know you will all agree. Attend!" She gave her scepter a jab at it. "This is the sphincter muscle! As you can see on this chart, it is located just inside the anus. It is a ringlike muscle which normally maintains constriction of this body orifice and is capable of relaxing and contracting."

She turned and fixed them with her eye. The music pounded and the lights pulsed. "Now, if this muscle were NOT under your control, it would be disaster, right?"

"Right!" they chorused back.

"IT IS THE MUSCLE OF LIFE AND DEATH!" cried Teenie.

They stared at her with awe.

"When people die," she cried, "it lets go!"

A gasp of horror rose above the beating music.

"Therefore," cried Teenie, "an active sphincter muscle is a sign of life!" She drew herself up sternly and called, "Is yours active?"

The crowd of catamites and catamite initiates responded with an emphatic "YES!"

Teenie shouted, "Then you LIVE!"

Cheers racketed around the hall above the beat of music.

"Now, so much for the technology," said Teenie. "It is in your power to *control* the sphincter muscle. Oh, you say, no, no, not possible. Well, young gentlemen, I must inform you that it is not only possible, you can make it go round and round!"

Cries of "No!" and "That can't be!"

"Ah, yes!" said Teenie. "You can learn to control it, and in your study time in future days in the basement study rooms, I will make available to you a probe. It is a simple matter, no more difficult than finding the control points and discovering how to wiggle your ears. Ah, I see you do not believe it. And so, my courtly gentlemen, I have arranged a demonstration!"

She walked to the platform steps and mounted it to the music beat. The spotlight had followed her and now it fell also upon the two boys who stood there.

She put her hand on the shoulder of Too-Too. "This pretty expert has been trained and is much experienced." Too-Too looked at her adoringly, eyes bright in his painted face. It was obvious that the privilege of being touched by her was almost more than he could bear.

Teenie made a gesture and the two grooms started to strip Too-Too and the son of Snor.

Madison abruptly understood, from his experience on the *Blixo*, what was about to happen. "No!" he shrieked. "No, Teenie, no!"

Instantly the guard was in front of him.

The electric axe was huge in Madison's face.

"Be silent!" snarled the guard.

Madison raised his eyes in prayer. Teenie's voice came to him. "Bend over, dear Too-Too," she said. "Now, grooms, make the lordling here stand upright behind him and do not let him move. Not a muscle!"

The orchestra played devotedly.

The boys behind the rope stared as the colored lights laced across them. They let out a concerted groan of interest.

"Too-Too," came Teenie's voice, "begin!"

Madison could not see around the axe.

Madison shifted slightly. There was a hole in the blade. He could just see the face of the son of Snor. It was wreathed in ecstasy.

"Don't let him move at all!" came Teenie's voice.

The bandleader gave a signal and the volume of the music rose.

The boys behind the ropes were standing with their mouths open in amazement.

The bandleader directed for more volume and the heavy throb was making the curtains jump.

Madison tried to see through the hole in the axe.

A boy in the audience said, "I don't believe it," in a passion-choked voice.

"Those grooms are holding him like a statue!" said his companion, wide-eyed.

Too-Too's horizontal face held a knowing smile.

The crowd was wide-eyed and panting.

Madison, staring, flinched at a scream of ecstasy from the son of Snor.

A moan went through the hall. It had the tension of sexual yearning in it, desire that throbbed as heavy as the music beat.

Teenie leaped down off the platform and sprang up the steps to her throne. The spotlight followed her and she stood, arms raised on high. The music was louder, heavier. She began to sway to the rhythm of it, scepter raised on high, golden crown flashing.

Her golden robe fell from her and she stood there swaying while the phallic symbols writhed upon her.

"Vassals and courtly gentlemen!" she cried. "Hear my Royal command! HAVE AT IT!"

They gave a thankful shout! Behind the ropes they fell upon one another like wolves in heat. The music and marijuana and the tableaux, the pulsing colored lights, had driven them mad with lust that no longer could be restrained.

The air above the roped-off areas was a sudden explosion of castoff jackets and other clothing.

The floor behind the ropes began to sink and with it went the sound of savage music and the lights, the stacks of sweetbuns and sparklewater and the cries of the boys.

A second floor slid over and the crowd was gone.

Chapter 10

Madison knew his time had come.

The servants were rolling the platform away—Too-Too and the lordling had scampered off into the orgy and behind the ropes had begun to hug and kiss. The big board went and then the throne.

The musician balcony was sliding back into invisibility, for the same piece they had been playing had melted undetectably into recordings which still thumped very faintly from the floor below.

The lights in the room went back to normal. The marijuana smoke was sucked away by ventilators. A fresh smell like violets gently replaced it.

Madison cowered in his chair under the watchful eye of Hammer. Little sparks ran up and down the blade of the electric axe. Madison cringed back to keep it from touching his chains.

There seemed to be a gathering of the staff. Men and women in clothes that might be worn by cooks and chambermaids and technicians were drifting in. Even the musicians that had played joined the collecting throng. There seemed to be more than a hundred of them, including the seneschals, heralds and guards. Even the old gardeners came in: one of them had a bouquet of massive flowers.

Madison wondered if they were all there to attend his trial. It made him acutely uncomfortable. Maybe they loved the sight of blood!

Teenie had been talking to some artist-looking fellow and they were now both laughing. Somebody had taken away her golden cape and replaced it with a plain red cloak that hung about her.

She started to walk toward the staircase that led upward. Madison felt a sudden surge of hope. She seemed to have forgotten him entirely: at least with luck he'd live another day. He tried to make himself very small so as not to attract her attention.

The staff had formed two lines now and Madison understood that they were not there to witness his demise. This must be some sort of a nightly informal ritual. Earlier moments might belong to the great Lords, but this was their little gathering, no more than a wishing of good night as they sent her off to bed.

A portly old man, coated in many golden frogs like an officer, probably the major-domo of the place, approached her as she strolled between the two rows of servants. He dropped to his knee and the whole staff instantly knelt. She stopped. He grasped the hem of her robe and pressed it to his lips. Speaking to the floor, he said, "Your Majesty, your staff wishes to thank you for letting them enjoy themselves doing their jobs."

Teenie looked all around at them, beaming and pleased. "Oh, dear trusted people. You are so sweet to be among. I thank you." And she began to name different sections of the staff, thanking each personally. Then she cried, "I love you all!"

They gazed at her with adoring eyes. The major-domo was about to say something else when a squabble broke out. Six women who, from their uniforms, were maids, were hissing and snarling at each other.

An old woman, stern and beautifully uniformed, was at them at once, speaking to them sharply for causing a disturbance. The major-domo went over to them.

It developed that they were having a dispute as to which two of the six should take the night watch and put Teenie to bed. It was quite bitter. It seemed that some of them had been switching watches. The major-domo pointed with authority at two of them whose watch it really was: they would take it! This pair stood promptly taller, their faces very proud. And then they suddenly stuck their tongues out at the other four and raced upstairs to get Teenie's bath ready. The abashed four, who had sought to interlope, looked at Teenie and knelt with both knees on the floor with a trace of fear. She smiled at them and they let out a sigh and then smiled back. It struck Teenie funny and she threw them a kiss and began to laugh. The whole staff began to laugh. Then, "Long Live Your Majesty!" they cried.

Teenie opened her mouth to tell them all good night when the guard captain in flashing silver caught her attention and pointed way over to the wall where Madison cowered.

(Bleep) that guard captain, choked Madison. Teenie had obviously forgotten all about him, for now she frowned and looked toward him as though she had noted some unwanted bug. The staff looked toward him as well and glared: evidently his crime of provoking their darling Queen Teenie had circulated through the whole, vast palace.

The guard captain and Teenie engaged in a whispered conversation. Then, with two guards flanking her, she followed the captain over to where Madison sat.

"They reminded me," said Teenie, in English, "that I have several dress fittings in the morning and gardening in the afternoon. They couldn't find time to fit in a trial, so we'll have it now. Guilty or not guilty?"

"Of what?" wailed Madison.

"In the confines of a palace, unless he is dealing with a person of higher rank," said Teenie, "the nobleman has the power of life and death over offenders to his property or person."

"I didn't offend you!" cried Madison in English. "I was just trying to get your help! You NEED me!"

She turned to the guard captain and, in Voltarian, she said, "He pleads guilty as charged. Enter it in the palace records."

"TEENIE!" cried Madison, "You MUST listen...."

"I don't have to listen to you," she said in English.

"You're guilty as hell and you know it. You never even lifted a finger to stop that (bleep) Gris. You got yourself into this mess because you didn't play ball with me." She shifted to Voltarian, "I therefore pronounce the prisoner guilty and the sentence is to be carried out without fail."

The guard captain nodded.

Madison said, "You haven't said what the sentence is!"

She was speaking in English again. "Well, Maddie, I get all heated up conducting these classes; they sometimes bring me to the brink of (bleep) and I ache. I've always wanted to break that fixation you have on your mother. So you're sentenced to coming up to my bedroom and (bleeping) me until I'm all limp and satisfied."

"OH, NO!" screamed Madison, and cringed back so hard his chains rattled. Then he thought in quick streaks of blue light and inspiration hit him. "Look," he said, "right down under that floor there are 250 boys! I can still hear the music pound! Any one of them would——"

"Maddie," she said sharply in English, "you got your wires crossed. The moment I start (bleeping) one of those pages, the rest would be so jealous of him they'd slaughter him! Besides, I'm making them into perfectly good catamites and it would ruin them."

"You've got men on this staff!" cried Maddie in English.

"They're commoners and they'd be executed if they were found in bed with royalty," said Teenie, continuing in English. "I'm too fond of them to put them at risk. Queen Hora used to use noble guard officers: she had a whole regiment of them. But they are not here. So can the chatter, Maddie. You're for it, me bucko boy."

Madison was shuddering to the depths of his soul. "No," he pleaded. "The answer is no!"

Teenie smiled and it made him flinch. He knew this wasn't all of it.

"All right," she said, glancing at her Mickey Mouse watch, "just sit there and think it over. This guard captain has orders that if you don't come up to my room tonight, then, straight up sharp at 6:00 A.M. you are to be taken to the dungeons and executed with an electric axe. So if you change your mind, your guard here will have orders to bring you up to my room, no matter the hour."

She gave him a little mocking wave and turned away.

The staff insisted that she sit on a little silver seat with handles as she might be too tired after her long evening to walk up the stairs, and they bore her off, up the golden steps and out of sight.

Chapter 11

For a very long time Madison sat, and he sat in the deepest gloom. The metal chair was cold, the chains were colder and the guard's electric axe, with its racing sparks, chilled him even more.

It was dark now in the hall. The rock music from below was only the faintest thumping, more like the mutter of some hungry beast than music.

Half-seen in the dimness, the painted angels on the walls seemed to look at him. He had little doubt that he would be joining the real angels soon and spend the rest of eternity sitting on some cloud holding a useless harp. Madison knew he could never learn to play it.

At length he was able to struggle up out of his shock, enough to think about his terrible conflict: If he did go upstairs he would die; if he didn't go upstairs he would die.

He had been very well brought up: He had to be true to his mother at any cost, even his life. Since he had been a baby it had been dinned into him that boys who did not sleep with their mothers were unnatural and it had been proven to him without doubt, even in his schools, where the word of the psychiatrist Freud was five times holier than God's. Unless one had a firm Oedipus complex, expressing libidinous desires for one's mother, one could never hope to be a genius at his trade. To abandon it would be a negation of his own wits. Without this bright spark, according to all Freudian teachings, he would fall into crass mediocrity, descended to a mere hack or drudge. There was no such thing, according to psychologists, as a genius who was not neurotic. Without that genius—which Madison never doubted—he would die professionally. Like all PR men, belief in himself was the first thing one had to establish and only then could others believe in him.

But his mother had reinforced it by continually reminding him of how indulgent she was. After his father departed she had not burdened him with another whom he could only hate, and how very few mothers would bother to give a son this much attention. His mother was a dear thing, still quite pretty at forty-nine. When he thought of all the sacrifices she had made for him, foregoing all other men, the least he could do was reciprocate and forego all other women. But it went deeper than that: completely aside from any Freudian orders from his child psychologist, made more real with mild electric shocks, he truly loved her. She had warned him repeatedly of the dangers of other women, as had his current psychiatrist, and colliding in life with such heartless creatures as Teenie, he agreed with them utterly. It would not only wreck him mentally to have sex with Teenie, it would break his mother's heart. She would probably commit suicide, a thing she often had to be prevented from doing, and he knew, if that happened, he would promptly do the same.

No, to go up those stairs and get in bed with Teenie would be the end of all he knew. Impossible! That was out. Better to die at dawn. Far better.

His thoughts turned to Heller. Victory had been almost within his grasp when everything had come so unaccountably unstuck. The headlines he had been getting for Heller had been magnificent! He fondly recalled the stories about Toots Switch, Maizie Spread and Dolores Pubiano de Cópula. Absolute masterpieces, guaranteed to stamp the name of Wister indelibly forever upon the public consciousness. Wister would have become known, as those trials progressed, as the greatest outlaw lover in history. And such plans he had had, to embellish and add glitter to the outlaw part of it! Wister robbing the Federal Reserve Bank had been the least of his PR projections. He could have made it all soar to greater and greater heights. He could have had every law-enforcement agency in the world, every one of them from Nazi Interpol right on down to the meanest town cop, absolutely baying on Wister's trail and slavering to catch him. It would have ended with the biggest public execution man had ever known. Wister would have been absolutely IMMORTAL!

Then he brightened up. He could do the same thing here if he had a chance. That the man's real name was Heller made no difference in his plans. He was tireless enough to simply scrub his other work and start anew. They had Domestic Police. They had the Army Division. And even if the Fleet might be lukewarm at first, he could heat them up. If he worked this right, he would have the whole Apparatus behind him.

He began to daydream in the dim and empty hall: headlines about Heller robbing the estates of Lords and giving the proceeds to the poor; Heller robbing spaceships, 18-point type; Heller kidnapping the daughter of some earl or duke and story after story of her pleading with him piteously to be raped—how the public would LOVE it! Headlines of Heller robbing every bank on every planet of the entire Confederacy, each one with a new twist, each one with new blood, each one with new staggering amounts of loot being given to the poor. What a hero he would be! Heller, the most hunted outlaw in 125,000 years! Confederacy history! MAGNIFICENT!

Then he had another idea: He could hyphenate Heller's name. He could call him Heller-Wister and rake in and rake over ALL the earlier stories, spreading them throughout the entire Confederacy. No, his earlier work was NOT lost—it was only being amplified!

Ah, now he was getting somewhere. And he could safely begin to dream the greatest dream of all: Madison walking up to Bury in a sort of offhand way, "Well, Mr. Bury, I finally finished a job for you. Heller-Wister is immortal." And Mr. Bury would take him by the hand, tears of gratitude sparkling in his eyes and in a voice charged with emotion say, "Madison, you are restored to grace. Please, please accept the presidency of F.F.B.O. and please forgive me for ever doubting you for a second. Never again will I chase you in army tanks!"

The glow faded. A chill wind blew in the hall. The reality of the situation was that, right now, if Bury even caught sight of him, even providing he could get home, he would be stood up against a wall and shot. It was death if he did not succeed with Heller-Wister. Death without even the comfort of a blindfold or cigarette: it was a good thing he didn't smoke.

A bit of the rock music from down below beat for a moment more loudly against the floor. The rhythm sounded so much like Earth that it gave him pause. He began to get a sort of hunted feeling: Bury was sort of supernatural—maybe he could even reach him here! When he thought of possible links between Rockecenter and Lombar, he began to shiver. Oh, it was surely death indeed if he did not somehow get to work on Heller-Wister!

The current guard shifted position slightly and the axe emitted a puff of ozone. It brought his mind to Teenie.

Up to now he had been thinking that if he went upstairs and went to bed with her, she would then help him. He realized she had made no guarantees of that whatever. All she had promised was that if he went upstairs and slept with her, he would not be executed at dawn!

It was a problem wherein if he did he would die because of his mother and if he didn't he would die because of Bury. It wouldn't help him at all to go up there.

Obviously, this required some other solution!

He was usually good at getting ideas and had always been proud that, because of the Oedipus complex, he was a genius at it. But tonight his mind seemed bankrupt.

He glanced at his Omega wristwatch. He had been sitting here for two hours! What a long time for him just to sit without getting a single constructive idea! He took a grip on himself. After all, he was a PR man, a true-blue professional.

He would be orderly. He would now skim over everything Teenie had said to him since the moment he found her by the pool. It didn't take long. He tried it again.

Suddenly he stiffened in his chair.

HE HAD IT!

If it didn't work, he would only be dead anyway.

IF IT DID, HE COULD FINISH HIS JOB ON HELLER-WISTER!

Madison looked up at the guard. Calmly, keeping all signs of elation out of his voice so the guard would suppose him to be operating in defeat, he said, "Take me upstairs to your mistress."

OH, GOD, THIS HAD TO WORK!

PART
SEVENTY-THREE

Chapter 1

The guard hissed sharply into a microphone disguised as a silver button.

Instantly a sergeant sped into the huge hall. He looked at Madison's guard, who jerked a thumb toward the stairs, and the sergeant nodded.

With a clank and a rattle they struck off Madison's chains. He stood up and rubbed his wrists and neck.

They thrust him into a washroom and made him strip and bathe. They inspected him. Intimately.

"He doesn't seem to have any lice or bacteria," said the original guard, gazing critically at Madison, "but he's not well equipped. I don't see how he can give her a good time."

"Well, listen you," said the sergeant to Madison, suddenly flicking a knife out of the back of his silver coat, "if you don't act nice and give her a good (bleep), I'll personally use this to cut your (bleeps) off. Is that understood?"

Madison gulped, covered his (bleeps) protectively with his hand and backed up.

They threw a white silk robe on him that still bore a Royal crest and the words *Property of Queen Hora. Do not use this robe for burial. Return it to palace in undamaged condition.*

"Now, what's the proper protocol?" the guard asked

the sergeant. "I don't for the life of me recall whether my grandfather said to deliver the man in shackles or gold ropes."

"Neither one," said the sergeant. "It was a collar and a gold leading chain. Why, there's one of them right over on that shelf." He got it and looked at it. "What do you know? It isn't true the collar had spikes inside it. My grandmother must have made that up. See, look here," he showed the guard. "It's an electric wire. And see here, there's the activating button at the end of the chain. Oh, no! Its power pack is dead. No sparks."

"Hey, lucky!" said the guard, gazing into the power recess in a link. "It's the same type we use in our boot toes. Here, I'll take the one out of my left boot." He did so, and when they tested the collar again, it sparked when the button on the end of the chain was pressed.

They put it on Madison.

"Now," said the sergeant, "if I heard right, the protocol is, you lead him in, bow, and when the queen puts out her hand, you place the chain handle in it, and I think you say, 'Your Majesty, here is one to do your bidding: pray thee, if he does not please thee, I shall be right outside the door with an electric whip.' "

"We haven't got an electric whip," said the guard.

"Well, you can't go changing protocol," said the sergeant. "Don't you go shifting words around. You keep the words just like they are, but if this (bleepard) doesn't do as he is told, use your stinger."

The guard checked the inside of his silver boot to see if his stinger was in place and started to nod, but the sergeant interrupted him. "Like I always tell you, be careful of your weapons. The staff would kill you out of hand if anything happened to displease Her Majesty." He had drawn the stinger out of the other man's boot.

The weapon was a limber rod about fourteen inches long. The sergeant gripped the handle and the tip glowed.

He raised it and gave Madison a slash across the lower thigh.

YIKES! It gave a stinging shock like the bite of a huge insect! Madison yanked the robe aside and stared at his thigh.

"Oh, that was just low power," said the sergeant. "You don't think I'd mark you up just before you went to please Her Majesty, do you? Man's an idiot," he commented to the guard. "Now, when you present him and go back to stand guard in the hallway, you keep your ear to the door and if you hear any protests or arguments or if you DON'T hear some moans and squeals of pleasure, you go right back in and sting the Hells out of him until he DOES do his job! Understand?"

The guard nodded. "Sure is great to have things running normally again."

"Well, yes," said the sergeant. "And you just make sure that Her Majesty doesn't have to wear her thumb out pushing the button on that collar chain. The darling is entitled to all the fun this fellow can give her."

"What do I do when she's through with him?" said the guard.

"Oh, you'll probably have been relieved by that time and I'll be hanging around. But if it happens on your watch and she hasn't told you otherwise, listen to make sure it's all quiet and has been for some time. Then beckon up one of her maids—probably the one on watch at the foot of her bed—and tiptoe in. Now, this is the tricky part: use your ultraviolet lamp and eyeglass so you don't wake Her Majesty, and look very carefully at her face. If she's frowning or sleeping restlessly, take him to the execution hall. If she's sleeping with a slight smile, then get this fellow out very carefully without waking her and send him back to his regiment."

"I haven't got a regiment," said Madison.

They both looked shocked. Then the sergeant said, "That's true. Those clothes hanging there are no uniform I ever saw before. Wait a minute. Maybe this is all wrong. Are you sure you're a nobleman?"

Madison's mind raced. Despite all these horrible arrangements which he only hoped he could escape, he had to get up those stairs and present his inspired idea to Teenie. He drew himself up haughtily. "I," he said, "am one of the *Knights of Columbus!*"

"Is that noble?" said the sergeant. "You see, if a male commoner were to lay hands upon her, protocol requires instant death. So don't go trifling with us."

"A *knight*," said Madison, "in her native language, means a gentleman-soldier. It is one who has been raised by his sovereign to the nobility. I came here as a *knight-errant.*"

The sergeant told the guard. "Well, that may be. Tell you what. When you take him out of her bed, put him in one of the better dungeons and hold him and I'll get this clarified in the morning. If it turns out he isn't really noble after all, we'll have the pleasure of executing him anyway. I sure didn't like the way he was yelling and screaming at her yesterday afternoon. Didn't sound very noble to me! And if he starts yelling and screaming at her again, take him out of there fast! We don't want our dear queen getting upset and leaving us."

The guard gave the chain a yank and Madison, not expecting it, flinched back.

The guard pressed the button in the handle.

It felt to Madison that his neck had been sawed

through! It wasn't an electric shock, it was a tearing sensation. Awful!

"Come along," said the guard. "Her Majesty awaits."

The sole of Madison's foot recoiled from the cold, rough floor stones of the washroom. "You didn't give me any slippers! At least let me put on my shoes!"

"Barefoot is just great," said the guard. And he gave the button another push.

Madison gripped his head so it wouldn't fall off.

He followed.

Everything depended on the next few minutes. He would be a dead man or a hero!

His idea MUST work!

Chapter 2

He wasn't being taken up the golden stairs. He was being led up a circular metal set of steps that spiralled back of the walls. It was very dark and from the deadness of the air Madison suspected it had long been out of use. Suddenly a gate with spikes barred their way: he could see small sparks chasing back and forth, skipping from tip to tip on daggerlike extrusions, ready to impale any unauthorized interloper. No wonder Flick said no-no on robbing these palaces. They were FORTS!

The guard did something over at the side and with the groan of long disuse the portal slid aside.

They seemed to be in a dark box now, another thick door facing them. The guard picked up a dusty microphone and said something, evidently to a remote security

desk—some sort of numbered password. Then the guard
shoved him in front of what must be a closed-circuit
camera.

"Demonstrate that you are not under duress, Jinto,"
said a sepulchral voice.

Jinto, Madison's guard, closed his hand on the chain.
The dreadful tearing feeling ripped at Madison's neck
and an additional yank threw him off balance.

Apparently some security post somewhere was satisfied. Beyond the haze of lingering pain, Madison heard
the slither and snap of several sets of remote-controlled
bolts.

Silently the door slid open and Madison was pushed
forward.

A moaning sort of music caressed his ears.

He was hit with a feminine whiff of fragrance and
he fearfully opened his eyes.

He was standing in a softly lit room of considerable
dimensions. Gently rippling colored lights bathed the
walls in ever-changing pastels, soothing, almost hypnot-
ic. Overhead, at first he thought these must be the open
skies and then he saw that the stars were slowly dancing
in a pattern about a moon which, real as it looked, could
never possibly, in nature, pulse with the same ripples as
the walls: the ceiling was some sort of an illusion that
must change the hour of the day or night on command.

The floor suddenly frightened him. It seemed to be
a thick mist, not a rug, and he was standing ankle-deep
in it. But he was reassured to find it seemed to be holding him up.

The furniture, delicate and curved, bureaus and
chairs and tables, didn't seem to have any legs; they
were just motionlessly floating in place.

The lost feeling he had experienced at his first

glimpse of this place—like nothing he had ever heard of or imagined on Earth—was leaving him. The determination to be successful in his visit gripped him again. Where was Teenie?

Then he again felt all unstabilized. Neither he nor the guard were walking, they seemed to have just been standing. But they were moving! Very slowly and gently this floor, without even so much as a ripple, was carrying them down one wall. What he had thought must be some kind of huge bureau was actually the top of a bed!

Madison stared.

It was a dark area of the room. Moans of pleasure were coming from it.

The moving floor made further progress.

Teenie's hand was visible in a patch of light. It rose up and quivered as she groaned.

The music moaned; the perfume drifted.

The guard gave the chain a slight rattle to attract attention.

The heads of the two maids snapped up with a jerk. They saw who it was and glared at Madison resentfully.

Teenie turned her head slowly and her sex-glazed eyes gradually focused on Madison. Then she closed her too-big mouth and smiled a slow smile.

In a lazy voice, in English she said, "You waited so long, I was finally certain you weren't coming so I let them go ahead—they wring their hands so when they see me all worked up by dancing and unsatisfied." She was coming back to herself now and the musing quality was leaving her voice. The lazy smile turned into a grin. "Well, well, Maddie. You finally decided to let me have a crack at breaking you of this mother fixation." She laughed with delight.

The guard suddenly knelt, bowed his head and courteously placed the handle of the chain in her nearest outflung hand. He said to the misty floor, "Your Majesty, here is one to do your bidding: pray thee, if he does not please thee, I shall be right outside the door with an electric whip."

Teenie glanced along her arm at it, saw the button and gripped it.

The collar almost took Madison's head off. He let out a scream! He clutched at the collar with both hands. Teenie looked at the button and looked up at him. The current was off now and Madison was moving his head about to see if it was still on. Teenie suddenly began to laugh. "Oh, Maddie, I see we're going to have fun! I don't want to hurt you. I want you to have a marvelous time. So you just be a good boy and do whatever you're told and I won't touch the button again."

Madison was not at all reassured. The bizarre room was already rippling and the tearing feeling had jarred his brain so it now seemed to be spinning. Was the moaning still the music or was it him?

Through the daze, he saw that the maids were also laughing now, but there was a note of cruelty in it that was absent from Teenie's: he was only too well aware that with this staff he was not amongst friends. And Teenie was no friend either. She had said so! He was trying to marshal his resolution. The guard, after a glare of caution at him, went to stand in the hall.

Teenie, still laughing, was giving them directions.

One maid got up, wrapping a robe about her. With a silken cloth, she began to straighten Teenie's makeup.

The other maid, a mature and good-looking woman, wiped off her own face with the hem of her scanty covering, got up and began to advance on Madison.

Although he tried to flinch away, she sprayed him with a masculine-smelling powder.

She reached for a pot of grease on a bureau.

Madison looked down at her and flinched.

The maid turned to Teenie and said, "Your Majesty, I think this nobleman must have had a dishrag in his ancestry."

This made Teenie laugh. She was lying on her side now, looking in Madison's direction. "Well, wring him out!" she cried.

Madison snatched his robe about him in panic.

The other maid looked over at him in surprise and then began to guffaw.

Madison now had his hands out, trying to keep the first maid from approaching him.

This sent Teenie into gales of laughter. She finally panted, "Oh, Maddie, you're killing me! Didn't your mother teach you *anything?*" And she went rolling about, screaming with mirth at her own joke.

Madison's eyes were glazed with terror. He was making a blocking motion with his hands.

Two maids' faces were laughing at him as they knelt in front of him.

Madison was backing up.

One maid had the pot of grease.

Madison was staring down at it.

The other was measuring out some hash oil.

"No, no!" shrieked Madison.

Teenie was convulsed with laughter. "Oh, Maddie," she shrieked, "you ARE a clown! This time you're going to be cured of your mother!" She sat up. "After me, you're going to get those two," and she pointed to her maids.

"NO!" screamed Madison.

One of the maids, still laughing, moved forward to grab him.

Madison backed up again. Then he saw something.

The end of the chain was no longer held by Teenie. It fell off the bed and hit the floor.

The maid had grabbed him. Madison was looking around wildly.

Teenie went into new howls of laughter.

Behind Madison was a tall bureau.

The maid was trying to kiss him.

Suddenly Madison lashed out with his fist.

He hit the maid in the jaw.

She went down with a crash.

Like an agile ape, he leaped up on the bureau, using the door handles to climb. He got to the top. He yanked the chain handle up after him to get it out of their reach. He was twelve feet above the floor. If the guard came in, he couldn't even be touched with the stinger.

The sight of him scrambling up and hanging there now had taken them all by surprise. He didn't know whether they would start to laugh again or yell for the guard to shoot him for hitting the maid.

THIS WAS HIS CHANCE!

Into the hiatus, he shouted, "Teenie! Listen to me! There's something you don't know!" Now was the time to launch his beautiful idea. Fate was trembling on the edge of the cliff. Would she listen?

Her attention was on the maid. She knelt at the woman's side to see if there was a bruise on her face. In a second, if she found a contusion or some blood, she would go berserk with fury.

"Teenie!" he screamed down at her. "Soltan Gris is here!"

Her head whipped round. She stared up at him.

"He's here!" shouted Madison in desperation. There *was* a little blood on the side of the woman's mouth and he MUST hold Teenie's attention.

HIS IDEA MUST BE GIVEN A CHANCE!

"He's right here on Voltar!" yelled Madison from the bureau.

Her eyes were on him. The door was also opening and the guard was alert and watching, having heard the raised voice.

"On THIS planet?" said Teenie. "Here?" She was in shock.

"Yes, that's right! Soltan Gris has taken refuge in the Royal prison, a huge castle! Nobody can get to him. He's perfectly safe! They aren't even going to try him!"

"WHAT?" cried Teenie, on her knees but straightening up.

"He's sitting there safe as can be!" cried Madison. "He's laughing at everybody! He's completely beyond reach!"

"THE (BLEEP)!" cried Teenie. Her eyes began to glare.

Madison shouted, "Unless somebody acts, he's going to go scot-free and even get a medal!"

"THE SON OF A (BLEEPCH)!" cried Teenie, leaping to her feet. "You mean after all he's done they're protecting him in safe custody?"

"Exactly!" cried Madison.

Teenie stamped her foot in fury. "Well, God (BLEEP) HIM!"

"And Teenie, if I have your help, I can get him HANGED! You know me and you know what I can accomplish if I'm turned loose! Teenie, if you back me up, then when they stretch his neck I can guarantee that I will personally put your hand on the rope!"

She looked at him: her eyes were furnaces of revenge. "It's a bargain!" she screeched. "Just tell me what you want me to DO!"

He had assured her he would prepare the plans. He had left her pacing up and down the room, pounding a fist in her palm and then shaking it in the air, swearing luridly in gutter English, vowing that if it was the last thing they ever did, they'd have to GET Gris!

The guard had been told to turn him loose and to admit him to the palace any time he called.

Madison, in the lower washroom, got into his clothes. He was trembling with relief.

Earlier, when he had been sitting in the hall, scanning through everything he had heard her say, a line from an Earth playwright had leaped up, and oh, was Madison glad that he remembered his Shakespeare. "Hell hath no fury like a woman kicked in the teeth." It had given him his SPLENDID idea and it had worked.

Tonight he had escaped death *thrice!* Once at the hands of Teenie; again from the threat of being unfaithful to his mother; the third and the far more important one of being wiped out by the deadly Bury.

With Teenie's influence, cleverly working step by step, he could now get on with his job.

Heller, he thought, here I come!

The universe will never again see such magnificent and skillful PR as would now occur!

He had to be clever, he had to be careful, he had to advance step by step. BUT HE WOULD GET THERE!

PR was the one weapon against which there was no defense. Oh, there were pitfalls on the way that would yawn. But, in gleeful confidence, Madison strode into the Voltar night.

Chapter 3

Across another night, twenty-two and more light-years away, Heller was talking on a viewer-phone in his New York office to Prahd on another one in the hospital in Afyon, Turkey. There was no problem in being overheard: the viewer-phone operated on a time-skip at the topmost quiver of energy bands and Earth was far from being up to that technology.

The subject of the conversation also involved time. "You can't rush these things," said Prahd. "I've told you all this before, sir."

"But he DID speak," said Heller. "When I entered the room at the palace, as soon as he was aware someone was there, he opened his eyes and spoke. He even recognized what I was."

"When you got to him," said Prahd, "he must have been on the tag end of an amphetamine dose. It was keeping him conscious. Some time before that, the quantities of speed he was being given must have set him up for a cerebral hemorrhage, because that's what he's got. Speed wrecks the central nervous system and he has had it."

"You mean he won't recover consciousness?" said Heller.

"Look, I'm doing all I can to hold on to this sudden elevation to King's Own Physician. I'm doing all I can to rebuild the nerves and vessels, but you don't seem to understand. It's the central nervous system! It's going to take months."

"So long?" said Heller.

"I'm being optimistic. Did you know it takes a day of therapy for every day of use anyone has been on speed? I don't know how long they had him on it. Could have been years!"

"What you're telling me is that he won't come around soon."

"I think I finally got my point across, sir. Of course, I could bring him around so he'd be alert a bit with some amphetamine, but that would then kill him."

"We don't want THAT!" said Heller. "Completely aside from our duty to protect him, it would be a rotten thing to do just to get our own heads off the block with a signed order. Skip any idea of it. We'll take our chances."

"I didn't mean it as an out," said Prahd.

"Well, don't think of it at all," said Heller. "You and I are quite expendable. He isn't. So you just go on doing what you're doing. Can you switch me over to my lady?"

The face of the Countess Krak appeared on Heller's screen. She threw him a kiss and then said, "Hello, dear. It's just like Prahd said. He's just lying there in fluid, rebuilding. There's absolutely nothing going on."

"I know," said Heller.

"I told them to build up defenses here."

Heller shrugged. "All right. But I don't think anybody will come. Ghoul-face doesn't know we came here. I've been giving this some thought and it's almost funny that he'd issue a general warrant for me: they're questionable on a Royal officer—courts usually just throw them out. It would take a Royal warrant and he just plain can't get one issued. It would have to be signed by the person who's lying there unconscious. Actually, Ghoul-face must be having fits. There was no mention of His Majesty on that broadcast and I don't think Hisst will admit he's gone. If he were to do so, the whole Confederacy would go into chaos. There is no heir: the other Royal princes are dead and Mortiiy is forbidden succession for starting a revolt. The Grand Council would have to have a body before they would proclaim Cling dead. So all Lombar can do is blunder around trying to locate me. He's only got the Apparatus, a small force. The Fleet and Army won't cooperate on the basis of just a general warrant on me. The Fleet would laugh at him. The 'drunk' is on the spot. If he doesn't dare admit I have the Emperor, then I can't think of anything he could say or do to get people incensed against me. He's only got the Apparatus and I'm not afraid of 'drunks.' So I quit worrying."

"Dear, could you be being too calm?" said the Countess.

"That's my profession," said Heller. "Keeping calm."

"I've seen you overdo it."

"What's being overdone right now," said Heller, "is our separation. It's silly you sitting there alongside a fluid tub while I'm having all the fun. I've got an AWFUL lot of things to neaten up and I can't possibly get away from here. So I had Bury contact the air force and they'll be sending a new Boeing Mach 3 Raider for you. They take off and land vertically and can put down in Afyon."

"WHO?" said the Countess Krak.

"A Boeing," said Heller. "All the airlines are messed up trying to get back into operation and their backlogs are awful. You'll be only three hours in flight. I'll have you met at La Guardia."

"I mean BURY!" said the Countess, still in shock.

"Oh, he works for us now. I forgot to mention it. But it's someone else I want you to meet. You'll like her."

"HER?"

"Yes," said Heller. "We need her permission to get engaged."

"WHAT?"

"Look, your clothes are still in the condo, so don't bring much. Now that I have verified there is no sense in your staying there, I'll tell the Boeing to take off. It'll be there about 2:00 P.M., your time. The Silver Spirit will bring you to the condo and you'll be in time to powder your nose and have a lovely lunch."

"Wait a minute, Jettero. You've got me all in a spin."

"They better not spin or we'll court-martial the whole air force. Wear your best smile. Tell you all about it when I see you. Love you. Bye-bye."

"Jettero," wailed the Countess Krak, "do you think your estimate of this situation is safe?"

But he had clicked off and the screen was dead.

Chapter 4

An amazed Countess Krak had been saluted on both sides of the world, had been set down to "all runways cleared" at La Guardia, had not even gone through immigration or customs, and had been rushed, sirens screaming, with an escort of six New York motorcycle police, straight to the condo.

She had managed to slip by the beaming Balmor and, despite the tears and sobbings of an overjoyed lady's maid, was able to change her clothes and get neatened up.

Now as she entered the luncheon salon, she was promptly all messed up again by the hugs and kisses of a smartly uniformed Jettero.

The place was crammed with flowers, the tables groaned with food and strains of triumphal music shook the chandeliers.

Izzy, Bang-Bang and Twoey were clutching at her hands, bowing and beaming in adoring welcome.

There was a one-foot stack of something on the table before her chair, and when she tried to sit down, the stack tipped over and cascaded into her lap and all over the floor. Credit cards! Of every possible company and they all said "Heavenly Joy Krackle," and the Bonbucks Teller one was in a blue orchid corsage. She was trying to put the corsage on when Balmor and two footmen came in with an enormous gold frame.

It wasn't for her.

They put it on an easel. It was some kind of parchment apparently printed by special run. It was a banner headline of the *New York Grimes* and just one story. It said:

> # NO DECLARATION!
> # LEADERSHIP OF
> # PRESIDENT
> # BRINGS U.S. FROM
> # BRINK OF WAR!

The four men went into bellows of laughter!
For the life of her she could see nothing funny in it.

Somewhat petulantly, when she could be heard, the Countess Krak said, "You might at least tell me what you're laughing at!"

"It's for the wall of Jet's study," said Bang-Bang. "We had it specially reprinted and framed."

That told her nothing. She turned to Jettero. "And it was mean of you to leave me hanging in midair about Bury and some woman."

Jettero laughed. "Well, it got you aboard that plane, didn't it? And without a word of argument about how you should stay in Turkey."

That made her laugh. "Oh, Jettero!" she said. "Living with you has its moments! Life is certainly never dull. Now *please* tell me what has been going on."

They were all sitting down eating prawns now and Jettero began to tell her what had happened in New York and Pokantickle but he evidently kept leaving out pieces of it that had to do with how he had accomplished certain things and the others kept stopping him and correcting him and well before he was finished, she was scared half to death at the risks he had taken. She managed to keep herself from going white and finally said, "So Rockecenter is dead."

"No, he's not dead," said Jettero. "He's sitting right there," and he pointed to Twoey. "Between him and Izzy, they own the planet." He turned to him. "So what are you going to do with it, boys?"

"Raise pigs," said Twoey.

"Now there," said Jettero to the Countess Krak, "no problems at all. They've got it all worked out."

"Oh, Jettero, be serious," she said. "I'm sure there's some kind of plan or program."

"Yes, ma'am!" said Jettero. "You've put your lovely finger right on it. There certainly is. At four o'clock this afternoon we're due over at Bayonne. And it's very important that you dress well and look very proper and prim, for if you are acceptable, we can then schedule the engagement party."

"Acceptable to WHOM?" she wailed.

"Well, I can't call her by her title yet because she won't be invested until Saturday. And that's the other thing I've got to take up with her, the coronation party. And we have to decide upon the date of the engagement party, but I should say it should be the following week."

"Jettero, I feel like I am going faintly insane."

"Blame the summer weather, not me," said Jettero.

Balmor came to the door just then and said to Izzy, "Mr. Bury is on the phone, sir. He merely wants to know if Mr. Twoey will be available tomorrow to address the Swillerberger Conference that will now be held at the White House in the afternoon. He says he's sorry to trouble you and he has written the speech. He is just verifying."

"There better be some item on the agenda about pig production," said Twoey.

"Tell Bury he'll be there," said Izzy, "and while he's on the phone tell him to hold up clearing out the Rockecenter offices until I can see to it personally."

The cat had been trying to get her attention and the Countess was very glad of the distraction.

The rest of the luncheon went off in a blur and then, dressed somehow and feeling she looked a fright, she was in the Silver Spirit with Jettero, escorted by two army tanks.

There were things she wanted to say to Jettero, urgent things, but he had the window down and the roar of the huge monsters made it hard to talk. "What are the tanks for?" she said in desperation.

"I haven't had time to separate from service," said Jettero.

"Do they always escort junior officers with tanks?" said the Countess Krak.

"Well, no," said Jettero. "They're probably afraid that I will forget to turn in my sidearms. One signs for them, you know."

"Jettero, for Heavens' sakes, be serious! I'm worried sick about this Voltar situation."

"If you go worrying about everything all the time, all you get done is worrying," said Jettero.

"Some worry is necessary," said the Countess.

"You'll never be a combat engineer," said Jettero.

"I'm not trying to be a combat engineer," she wailed. "I'm trying to become the wife of one."

"Ah, well," said Jettero, "it's a good thing you decided to put your mind on that. Here's your crucial test. We've arrived."

They had pulled up in front of a high-rise which rose grandly beside a park.

Two dark, lean Sicilian men carrying submachine guns were there, looking warily at the tanks. One peered into the Silver Spirit and then relaxed.

"Oh, it's you, kid!" he said. "You better go right up. This place has been in an uproar all day."

The other yelled into a lobby, "Hey! On your toes! It's the kid and his moll!"

They were walking through a mob of men in black suits, and swarthy faces that had appeared from nowhere, apparently specially to get a look at her. She felt she was wearing everything backwards and was missing a slipper, for those eyes were very alert and appraising.

Then a whisper reached her, "Jesus, kid, where did you find HER? Cristo, is she a movie star or something?"

It made her feel a bit better, but at the top of the elevator, a booming voice was heard coming down the hall, "I don't give a (bleep), you (bleepard)! Tell those sons of (bleepches) in Chicago to throw their God (bleeped) drugs in Lake Michigan and begin running rum or I'll put a hundred hit men on their tails. Now get the hell out of here. I think I heard my kid!"

A very old Italian, beautifully dressed, lugging a briefcase, fled out of the room, almost collided with Jettero, looked at him in a cautionary way and said, "Take it easy in there. She's on fire!"

An old Sicilian in a white coat hurried up and gave Jettero a reassuring pat and ushered them into a salon of such elegance the Countess thought for an instant she was back on Voltar.

A middle-aged woman, very blond, was sitting on a sofa in a pose of elegance and decorum. She wore a gold-sequined gown and was idly thumbing through a fashion magazine. Then she looked up and smiled politely and said, in a cultured and modulated voice, "Ah, Jerome. How nice of you to drop in." She extended a hand for him to kiss and he did so.

"Mrs. Corleone," he said with his most courtly Fleet manners, "may I present my fiancée."

The woman languidly unfolded and stood. She was six foot six, over eight inches taller than Krak.

"Ah," she said, extending her hand, "You are the Countess, I presume."

Krak's head spun. What was coming off here? How did this woman know she was really the Countess Krak? No one else on Earth knew that!

The giantess was looking her up and down as though she was some kind of a horse. And then apparently, she couldn't keep the pose up any longer and she suddenly

put her arms around Krak and hugged her and then held
her off and looked at her and then hugged her again and
said, "God (bleep) it, Jerome, this is the most beautiful
lady I've seen in all my life!" She held her off again.
"God (bleep) it, you're more gorgeous than a Roxy girl.
You'd stop the show!" And she hugged her again and
said, "God (bleep) it, yes, Jerome! For Christ's sake,
marry her quick before she gets away!"

After a while, the giantess put her in a chair like
Krak was some kind of porcelain and, gazing at her with
admiration, offered her a silver box with Russian ciga-
rettes—which of course Krak didn't smoke—and called
for cookies and milk for Jerome.

And then she and Jettero began to discuss the details
of the engagement party and decided on Madison Square
Garden and that it would be a week after the coronation.
They had a lot of trouble with the guest list because
Mrs. Corleone had not yet decided what to do with the
mayor's wife: on the one hand she wanted her there and
on the other she didn't, so that part of it was left up in
the air.

They were finally being shown out and Mrs. Corleone turned to Jettero at the door. She said, "No wonder
you would never touch those girls at the Gracious Palms!"

Kissed on both cheeks and getting into the Silver
Spirit again, the Countess Krak's head was in a new
whirl. *What* girls?

To the clank of tanks and the beat of a police heli-
copter that was riding escort overhead, Jettero got her
laughing a bit about his unarmed-combat class at the
UN's "favorite hotel." He was quite witty and charming
about it and she forgave him. But she didn't get a chance
to talk to him at all about Voltar at dinner. Although they
ate in a most exclusive restaurant on East 52nd Street,

The Four Reasons, and although Jettero had said they would have an intimate dinner, he also insisted that the tank officers and crews, two police captains who seemed to have joined the parade and the condo chauffeur also have dinner in the same place; and even if they were at different tables and studiously let Jettero and his lady sit close to each other in candlelight, people kept dropping by who had nice things to say. And from the restaurant manager to the head of Saudi-Yemen Oil, all had to be introduced.

Then they went to a world title prizefight and a whole row had to be cleared out for the tank crews, police officials, bank presidents and a pop star who now seemed to have joined the parade.

The Countess never did figure out who won the fight or why, as she couldn't understand why neither fighter used any proper blows when they were wide open for them and never once even tapped each other with their feet.

The after-fight late supper was about as intimate as rush hour, as they had now acquired the heads of two TV networks and their guests and it drove *Sardine's* half mad trying to serve them all. She hadn't realized that Jettero knew so many people and even though he assured her that he didn't, the restaurant manager himself took over a microphone from the M.C. and convulsed the whole assemblage with a story, which they found hilarious, of Police Inspector Grafferty accidentally getting his face full of spaghetti at the hands of "a certain celebrity" who "shall not be named" as he looked at Jettero.

It was not until they had been in bed for two hours that the Countess Krak found him quiet enough to listen.

"Jettero, I hate to have to bring this up. But please be serious. I'm quite worried about the danger we are in.

You just grazed over it on the viewer-phone. I do not agree with your estimate at all."

He propped his head up on a pillow and she knew she had his attention.

"You don't know Lombar Hisst," she said. "I do. For almost three years I had to work at his orders. He's completely mad. He's entirely capable of blowing this whole planet up simply to get revenge on it if it thwarted him."

Jettero yawned. "I don't think you know what a big job it is to blow up a planet. I even doubt it could be done. It's even a very great engineering feat just to pull off a planet's atmosphere."

"But it could be attacked," she said. "The populations could be mowed down."

"Listen," he said, "you stop fretting your pretty head. In the first place, the planet does have some defenses and they would be an embarrassment to any invader. Even if they were wiped out, which they would be, they still would take a lot of killing. You'd have to land at least a million men to mop the place up. And that would require, in terms of ships, everything the Apparatus has got. In order to conquer Earth, Lombar Hisst would have to pull his ships and troops out of every hangar and barracks in the Confederacy. And they have a lot of other things to do, like suppressing the revolt of Mortiiy on Calabar. Lombar would be spread too thin. And he won't have any other forces available. He can't tell anyone we have the Emperor here and the Fleet and the Army would simply yawn at him if he tried to insist they chase all over the place looking for me. They wouldn't help him invade Earth. They'd think he'd gone crazy."

The Countess rose on her elbow and pushed her hair out of her eyes. "Darling, I know your reputation with the Fleet and even the Army has been excellent and that is as it should be. But I get a horrible feeling about all this. You have forgotten what happened here on Earth: that PR made an awful mess. All that horrible publicity. All those women and all those lies. Remember Madison?"

"Aw, they don't do that sort of thing on Voltar," said Jettero. "That goofy PR technology isn't even known there. And as for Madison, he went in the river."

"Well, call it woman's intuition if you will," she said, "but I've got a bad feeling about all this. Please, won't you worry just a little bit?"

"Lady mine," he said, "a lifetime is composed of a finite number of minutes. What is happening *now* is important. I have seen men who well knew they'd be dead in half an hour enjoy a glass of tup most thoroughly. Others spent the same half hour worrying. They were just as dead but they had missed a glass of tup."

"You're impossible!"

Jettero looked at his watch. He said, "You have just wasted one minute of your life. Don't waste the next one. Give me a kiss."

"Oh, Jettero, I wish you knew Lombar like I do!"

"I assure you, lady mine, that you are just now in much better company. Come here."

And though he smothered her with kisses and though he soon had her mind on other things, he did not, that night or in the weeks to come, succeed in smothering her worries.

Somehow she KNEW it was far more dangerous than he said. But he wouldn't even listen!

Chapter 5

Haggard with the smell of his own brand of danger, three days later Madison was returning to the Royal antechamber, escorting Lombar Hisst.

Keyed up until it felt his whole insides were going to rip asunder, Madison would know now, in just minutes, if he was to stride on to victory or be left expiring in some unpleasant Voltar gutter, a loser cast away. Just a hair's width of miscalculation could expose all and even bring him death.

For three days he had worked and worked hard, with the knowledge that a failure at any given point in a complicated chain could leave him lost and condemned forever upon this distant strand and it would wreck forever his last chance to finish Heller.

The major problem had been to prove to Hisst that he, Madison, was such a magical PR that he could get the Lords to bow to Hisst—a thing which Lombar, a commoner, considered utterly impossible—and to get the action shown through the Confederacy on Homeview.

The sequence of minor problems had been hairraising, each one in itself.

The first incipient nervous breakdown occurred when the son of Snor had been unable to wake his father up long enough to get him to stamp and certify a blanket order giving Madison the run of Homeview. Finally the boy had been persuaded by Teenie to go back and, when no nurses or doctors were about, and out of the sight of the security scanners, get Lord Snor's seal of the Interior Division out of a desk and stamp the order himself.

The next threatened crackup happened when the manager of Homeview at the Joy City Studios had been unable to believe that Lord Snor would issue such an order and had tried to call Palace City to verify it. Unable to connect with Snor, he had gotten back at Madison—he evidently did not like the Apparatus—by giving him a lousy crew. No director, a scrub team of drivers and crewmen and, worst of all, a cameraman whose wife had just left him and who was not yet recovered from a five-day drunk. "A stinking order from the stinking Apparatus to do a stinking event only deserves a stinking crew," he had said, little reckoning that he was putting Madison's life on the line—and he probably would have cheered if he had found out. "We'll put it in the Family Hour, so hold it on time, for we won't reprogram all of Homeview just to insert a stinking clip." Madison had left him wondering what the blazes a *PR man* was and had had to be content with what he got. Hair-raising!

Then a page had had to sneak into a meeting of the Grand Council. It had only been attended by five members and these were all bleary with speedballs. The page had slipped the prewritten resolution under the palsied hand of the Crown who was stamping something else and then he had to get it logged by a clerk who was too deaf to hear things that were being passed. Madison had crouched outside shivering until the page sauntered out, tapping his jacket to signify he now had a legal order to the Master of Palace City to change building names.

It had taken every credit Teenie could scrape up to bribe the Master to order the name wanted and to make the ceremonial arrangements for the right minute of the

day. If this final result, about to be received, did not
work, then Teenie would be after his blood again.

And then there had been the struggle of pages and
sons to get most of the Lords to feel indulgent enough
toward children to agree to attend the affair, followed by
the heroic feat of actually getting them into their robes
and out there.

Throughout the event, Madison had been too tied
up with guiding Lombar to keep an eye on the Homeview crew. It had been HARROWING to have to walk
along with dignified mien and resist all cravings to
watch that (bleeped) cameraman and see if he even had
the thing on, much less pointed at the *exact* required
angle. If Madison had looked, the camera would have gotten him subjective—looking into its lens—like some
gawker. So as of right here and now, walking across the
antechamber, bringing the chief back to his desk, Madison did NOT know what he had in the can.

Lombar lumbered to his desk in front of the bolted
door of the Emperor's bedchamber and sank down in his
chair. There was no telling what his reaction was thus
far: he was completely silent.

Madison went over to the Homeview screen and
with a bit of fiddling got it turned on. He didn't know
how to calculate the transmission time as the signal had
left Palace City through a thirteen-minute future drag,
had been transmitted to the planetary network center at
Joy City and then had to come back and go through time
relays to get back into Palace City time. So he didn't
know how to set the digitals to be sure he was ahead
of the program on the screen's recording strip, which
would give him a replay. His palms were dripping and
his hands shook.

Oh, God, he was about to do a thing which no PR with any brains would ever dream of doing: showing a client a program which the PR himself had not previewed. With a drunk cameraman, heavens knew what was on that strip and if that camera had even wobbled, Madison knew he would be dead.

He abandoned time calculation. He just yanked the strip ahead at random and hoped he was before the start point he wanted.

He got the afternoon "Family Hour." There was a picture of a woman rocking a child and crooning while the commentator went on and on about the joys of motherhood.

Madison stole a glance at Hisst but Hisst was just sitting there, eyes upon the screen. Madison couldn't figure the reaction.

The commentator said that you should never feed a child anything but mother's milk so that "what gets indrawn with sweet nourishment carries with it, on this channel of deliciousness, a soft and vibrant flow of love and family."

Madison wished desperately he knew how to fast-forward the strip. He glanced at Hisst to see how he was taking it: the yellow eyes, aside from their ever-present flicker of insanity, were unreadable.

The picture showed a lot of shots of strange animals rutting in dirt and the announcer condemned all beast milk as imparting only lust and greed, and wound up in style.

Now there came a series of views of ancient buildings. SCHOOLS! Oh, thank heavens, this was finally the start of the program they had just enacted.

A rather nasal commentator voice was running along with a history of schools and began to show those which

had been named after members of the Royal family and
even Emperors.

Madison cast a covert glance at Hisst. He was just
sitting there in his gaudy scarlet Apparatus general's full-
dress uniform, more like a brutish Devil than a man.
One couldn't tell *what* he was thinking.

Then suddenly the part that Madison had been waiting for came on. "... but times change and the parade
of power across the stage of history can ever glitter to
new heights. Yesterday it was determined by Lord Snor,
Lord of the Interior, acting through the Master of Palace
City, to celebrate our dedication to fineness and decency
in tomorrow's noblemen and courtiers and celebrate as
well the glory and dedication of our magnificent and
relentless protector of the realm, Lombar Hisst, Spokesman of the Emperor..." Madison thought the text was
absolutely great, for, after all, he had written it himself;
but he didn't quite like the trumpet fanfare: it sounded
more like razzmatazz. He glanced anxiously at Hisst to
see how he was taking it but Madison could get no reaction at all!

"... by changing the name of the Page Royal School
to the Hisst Royal School."

God, thought Madison, he isn't even blinking. He's
just sitting there! Can't he see I've built in a name association so people will think of him as Royal? Yet, no sign.

There were pictures of the school and past classes,
then a picture of the school as it had been today. (Bleep)!
It looked a bit shabbier! It was a round pillbox of a building enclosing a hidden sports field; big enough, but some
of the blue and red ropes, in stone, had gaps in them and
there was even a broken window!

But the cameraman, even though his camera was

unsteady, had opened up the view and there were the two lines of waiting Lords!

Martial music!

And here came Hisst striding along to go between the twin lines of waiting Lords, each Lord flanked by a son or a page. They were pretty drugged-up Lords but at this distance one missed it.

NOW, right here, this was the tricky part! If the cameraman erred in any way, Madison was dead, dead, dead!

Hisst strode between the two lines.

THE FIRST ONES BOWED!

Then, as Hisst passed, there was bow and bow and bow. The sons and pages were tugging at their sleeves and every Lord was bowing very low.

Madison was watching so closely he was almost losing his eyeballs. One slightest slip of that camera and he would be executed! And the cameraman had been drunk!

Hisst was through the lines. But it wasn't over yet. Hisst would be walking that path again presently at Madison's utmost peril.

On the screen, Hisst stepped into the path of the illusion projector. A technician turned it on. And the electronic illusion of Hisst, two hundred feet tall, like a gigantic red Devil, seemed to pat the top of the school and the speakers boomed out as he blessed it.

Screams of cheers racketed. Totally and only boys, and piping and shrill. Were some of them more like animal calls?

One could not tell what Hisst, there at his desk, thought of any of it. No client reaction! Had Hisst seen something Madison had missed? Oh, pray the Lord, no!

Hisst was walking back now. The martial music

banged and throbbed. Once more he had to pass between the lines of the waiting Lords.

Would they bow?

Would the cameraman slip?

Ah, the first two Lords bowed, then the second two, then the third pair. . . . Madison was watching every inch of that way like a hawk—or more like a chicken that any instant could get its head cut off.

Every pair of Lords bowed!

Hisst climbed into his local ground car on the screen.

The scene shifted to a cathedral and the announcer said, "We will now bring you to Casterly Church for afternoon vespers."

It was over.

Madison, however, knew that his own trial was not. The client may or may not have detected something Madison had not seen. The client reaction was everything!

Lombar roused himself. He pointed at the screen and said, "Play that again!" Was he angry? Was he pleased? Had he suspected?

Madison suffered the agonies of the damned while the strip ran through once more.

Then Lombar uttered a shuddering sigh. He said, "They bowed to me."

Then he sat there for a while.

Then he said, "They bowed to me, Lombar Hisst, a commoner."

Then he shook his head. He said, "If I hadn't been there myself, I would never credit it!"

Then he sort of rotated his head and blinked his eyes and said, "Lords? Bowing to a commoner?" Then, "It's never happened before in the whole 125,000 years of Voltar history!"

Then he was blinking rapidly. "It can only mean one thing. They knew about the angels!"

"Well, I wouldn't count on them bowing all the time," said Madison. "After all, we have to prepare the minds of the people to eventually accept you as Emperor."

"Yes," said Hisst. "Yes. We have to prepare their minds." And he was off into some daydream, spinning in who-knew-what part of the universe.

Madison let him spin for a little while but, after all, this was a client and he had to close.

"So you can now honor your promise to me," said Madison. "An unlimited budget and a totally free hand."

That brought Lombar out of his spin. He fixed Madison with a stare. The yellow lights in his yellow eyes were strange. "You can't have a budget. Only a department or section can have a budget. And it would take a Royal order to create a new one." He checked himself. He must never come so close to saying that there is no emperor or seal back of that door. "His Majesty is far too ill."

"But you promised unlimited funds!" said Madison. "You said if the Lords bowed . . ."

Lombar was shaking his head, annoyed. "Why are you making me listen to you? I don't have to listen to people."

"It's because the people have to listen," said Madison. "To BELIEVE you should be Emperor, they have to listen and I have to see that they listen to the right things and get whipped up about it. It will take PR and it will take time to create the favorable climate. And PR costs MONEY!"

"Money," said Lombar. "I can only authorize pay. That's why nobody gets paid much in the Apparatus. I can't authorize budgets for departments that don't exist!"

"Then," said Madison, "as you are a man of your word and worthy to be Emperor because of that, authorize unlimited pay."

"WHAT?"

"You saw the Lords bow."

Lombar suddenly blinked and began to nod, sort of bowing himself. Madison slid his identoplate across the desk. He saw a basket of forms and found "Change of Pay." He wrote "UNLIMITED" on it and slid it to Lombar.

Lombar looked at it and then filled it out and stamped it with Madison's identoplate and then found his own in his hand and stamped again.

Madison already had the other order written and he slid it under Lombar's identoplate and it came down on it. The order said:

> *J. Walter Madison, in all matters of PR, is to have an absolutely free hand with material, equipment and personnel, and no further authorization required.*
>
> *Lombar Hisst*
> *Chief of the Apparatus and Spokesman for His Majesty, Cling the Lofty.*

Lombar seemed to have forgotten about him. The chief went over to the Homeview and fed the strip back in. He sat down on a stool before it, cushioned his jaw in his cupped hands and began to watch it again.

Madison knew the man was hooked now in more ways than one. It was time to split with his spoils.

He got out into the hall and out of sight and then leaned weakly against a door, for he felt his knees would give way.

It was an awfully good thing Hisst never listened to anybody.

And who would tell him anyway?

In fact, who knew what the swindle was? Everyone else, watching, would have thought Hisst would know.

The cameraman had made it! He had not missed.

Right back of Hisst, in the golden dress of a page, amongst the crowd of boys, had come Teenie!

In the whole walk in and the whole walk out, she had been right back of Hisst, but cut out of the frame.

The Lords had been alerted by their pages.

They had been bowing to Queen Teenie, not to Lombar Hisst!

Madison's knees stopped shaking.

He clutched his goodies to his bosom and sped out of the palace.

Though distant still, victory beckoned loud and clear just over the horizon.

HE HAD HIS CHANCE AT HELLER!

Wild exultation began to pound through him as he finally believed himself that it was true!

HE WAS THE ABSOLUTE CZAR OF PR ON VOLTAR!

PART
SEVENTY-FOUR

Chapter 1

Teenie, standing in the door of her palace, still clothed in the golden page's costume she had worn while walking back of Lombar, received Madison's ebullient good news somewhat grimly. She looked at the authorizations and gave them back.

"All right, all right, Madison. We've got it this far. Now you better start delivering. You can't hang around here and get anything done now. I want Gris's head and I want it bad—rotting preferred. So roll up your sleeves and start sweating!"

The look she gave him was so meaningful and the pop of her bubblegum so explosive that Madison hastily left. She might suspect that this really was a double cross. He wasn't after Gris at all—his real target was Heller-Wister, for only in that way could he come right with Mr. Bury. With Heller-Wister fully handled on Voltar, Madison could only then return to Earth a conquering hero—and not be shot as a deserter.

He hoped Teenie realized that PR was intricate and complex and wasn't done in a minute. The thing to keep your attention on was thoroughness—and GETTING HEADLINES!

Madison knew the image he would have to complete: it was that of a folk hero on the model of Jesse James,

and how well he was researched in such images now—in
the yacht he had travelled all over studying famous out-
laws. Heavens, he fairly ached to put it into effect.

He knew just how to attain results: Coverage, Controversy and Confidence.

What he lacked here on Voltar were Connections,
another *C* which he had always had on Earth.

Well, first things first. He had better get organized.
He didn't even have a secretary, much less a string of
obedient editors and publishers. Money. That was what
he better start with first.

As he climbed into his airbus, he said to Flick,
"How do I get my identoplate changed? Where do I go?"

"You going to get PAID? Oh, you just lie back on
the seat there and relax and I'll have you to the Government City Finance Office twice as fast as this junk heap
will go!"

They took off in a blur. They rushed through the
Palace City gates, outbound, so fast Madison hardly had
time to get nauseated from the time shift to thirteen minutes earlier.

As he drove frantically across the Great Desert,
Flick said, "Oh, but am I tired of eating stale sweetbuns
out of garbage pails like we been doing! You also owe me
a pack of puffsticks. And I know a rooming house where
we can get a room real cheap. Do you feel all right? Are
you comfortable? Should I turn on some music?"

Madison was not paying much attention. He was trying to work out how he would go about setting up in
such unknown terrain. Then he got off into headlines
that kept drifting through his head: 18 point, FLEET
OFFICER GOES RENEGADE but he kept discarding
them. They were sort of pale and lacked punch. He realized this would require a lot of careful planning to really

make it good. He had no support troops, he had no lines and the fact that these people on Voltar were ignorant of real PR was both a blessing and a curse. Every trick of the trade would be brand-new to them, but on the other hand, there were no traditional supports. It was sort of like a man approaching a virgin: the question was, how willing would she be to be raped?

His thinking was interrupted by Flick. The driver had gotten out, opened Madison's door and was now anxiously cautioning him not to trip on the ramp as he alighted. Madison was startled to see how much time had elapsed. They were at the Finance Department.

Following the anxious directions of Flick, Madison went by himself through the scurrying crowds and came shortly to a counter which had a sign:

Identoplate Changes

A bored clerk, in a working coverall to protect his suit, finished downgrading the pay of a disgruntled teacher who had been transferred to a lesser school and turned to Madison. Without interest, he examined the papers. He reached over for his plate-changing machine and then suddenly looked back at the form.

"UNLIMITED PAY?" He went boggle-eyed. He hastily pushed buzzers and Madison found himself surrounded on every hand by Finance Department Security Police.

An officer took the Change of Pay form through a door while the others just stood and stared at Madison. The officer could be seen punching buttons and turning on lights that apparently verified codes hidden in identoplates.

When he came back, he held on to the form and waited. It made Madison very nervous.

Shortly, an old man with a Finance Department executive badge came behind the counter and the officer gave him the form.

"I can't understand it," the officer said. "It's genuine."

"This is impossible!" said the aged executive. "Unlimited pay status? He could buy the planet!"

"Well, it's your business now," said the officer, and at a signal all the Finance Police left. But all along the counters, the word had spread and clerks and others were peering at Madison and whispering.

Another executive came behind the counter and the first one handed him the form and said, "Gods, look at this, Cipho. That guy Hisst gets crazier every day! It's a valid order. But what do we do?"

Cipho said, "What allocations would it come out of? Let me see the other papers."

They examined them minutely. They conferred. Madison got very nervous. He said, "Is there something wrong?"

The first executive looked at him. "We can't determine what budget it comes out of. Your rank is *PR man*, whatever that is, and it's in the Apparatus. Your pay status says No Pay—P, so that means you were to be attached to Palace City. Hisst signed this authorization not only as Chief of the Apparatus but also as Spokesman for His Majesty, so that would make it Royal. We can't determine which letter designation to put after the new pay status. I'm afraid you will have to come back."

Madison's stomach rumbled. He thought of his image with Flick. He thought of Teenie's meaningful look. He thought of his anxiety to get started. "Is there no way it can be done now?"

"Well, it's dangerous," said Cipho. "You might overdraw somebody's budget. You might decide to buy Industrial City or something and then you'd jam all our computers."

"What kind of money is in those budgets?" said Madison desperately.

They went in the other room and came back. Cipho said, "The Apparatus is nearly overdrawn because of the revolt on Calabar. Palace City is nearly empty now, so its allocation is only 50 percent utilized. The Royal expenditures have dropped to almost nothing."

"Money," begged Madison. "How much money is in them?"

"There's a billion Palace City that won't be used and about four billion Royal."

Madison's hopes soared. "Look, just give me a pay status on all three."

"Hmm," said Cipho.

"Look," said Madison, putting on his most earnest and sincere face, "I am a reasonable man. If I guarantee to advise you if I intend to draw more than a billion at any one time and confer with you, will you make it a pay status for all three? That way it would only debit from existing funds."

"You'd have to put it in writing," glowered Cipho.

"It would keep the computers from locking up," said the first executive. "Give him some paper."

They got the signed and stamped undertaking and marked his identoplate Pay Status: Unlimited—APR.

Madison accepted it with a very straight face. Never in his whole career had he ever had a billion-dollar drawing account! Oh, what he could do with that!

They had the look of men who had bested him. And he was very solemn as he walked away.

A BILLION–DOLLAR DRAWING ACCOUNT!

Chapter 2

On the way out, Madison put his new identoplate to use. At the cash-withdrawal counter the pretty girl there looked at the identoplate and stared at him round-eyed. "Unlimited pay status?" she gulped. "How . . . how much cash do you want?"

Madison gave her the first figure that came into his head. "Oh, fifty thousand for now."

She scratched her head. "That will be an awful wad. It will ruin the shape of your suit. Wait right there. I'll see if we have some thousands."

She came back with a neat pack and while she was stamping things, Madison looked at the banknotes. It was the first time he had seen any Voltar money up close. It was gold-colored paper, quite pretty. It sparkled. He petted it. Very nice.

"You wouldn't have some idle time tonight, would you?" asked the girl hopefully.

Madison ran.

He got in the airbus and Flick closed the door for him. "We got some money?" said Flick. And when Madison patted his pocket, Flick leaped behind the controls and they took off.

"I'm STARVING!" said Flick, as he threaded his

way through Government City air lanes. "I'll just drop down to a busy street and we'll get some hot jolt and FRESH sweetbuns off a vendor. You also owe me a pack of puffsticks. I gave one to that guard, remember?"

He dropped down into the parking strip beside the thronged and noisy street. He yelled at a dark-complected old man who was pushing a cart laden with comestibles and other things.

"Two hot jolts, four sweetbuns, one pack of puffsticks," said Flick.

Dutifully the old man handed them in and then held out his hand.

"Pay him," said Flick.

Madison got out a thousand-credit note and handed it over.

"I can't take that," the old man said. "It would clean out the change of the whole street. You only owe me a tenth of a credit. Haven't you got a coin?"

"Wait a minute," said Madison. "Two coffees, four buns, one pack of puffsticks. Ten cents? You must be mistaken."

"Well, things are a little high these days," the old man said. "And after all, I've got to make a living."

"No, no," said Madison. "I'm not haggling with you. I'm just trying to figure out how much a credit is worth. I got it: how much is a good pair of shoes?"

"Oh, call it a credit and a half," the old man said. "They're kind of dear, the good ones I mean."

Madison did a racing calculation. He had been thinking in terms of dollars. As close as he could guess, one credit must be worth at least twenty bucks!

He sank back on the seat in a sudden shock. He didn't have a billion-dollar drawing account.

HE HAD ONE FOR TWENTY BILLION!

A voice penetrated his shock. "Well, pay the man," said Flick. "He's got some blank vouchers there. Just stamp one."

Madison was still in shock. Flick came back to him, stuffed the thousand-credit note into his breast pocket and tapped around his coat and found his identoplate and drew it out. The old man was presenting the paper through the window and Flick, looking at the stamp face, was pushing the button to get it to come up with the right stamp.

Suddenly Flick froze.

He was staring at the plate.

Suddenly Flick cried, "Pay Status *UNLIMITED?*"

He stared at Madison.

The mouth opened in the squashed oval of a face. The mouth closed.

Flick looked back at the identoplate. He worked the button and made the picture of Madison come up. He looked at it. He looked back at Madison. Then Flick shifted the button and stared at the pay status again.

Flick sat back. His eyes were jiggling.

The old man urged the paper at the driver. "Stamp it for my tenth of a credit, please."

Flick got his eyes in focus. He went into sudden motion. He scribbled on the paper and stamped it and said, "THROW THE WHOLE CONTENTS OF YOUR CART IN!"

The old man looked at the paper in shock. Then he hastily began to pitch things through the window. He barely managed to tip up the last tray when Flick took off.

"HOT SAINTS!" cried Flick as he raced into the air. "MY DREAMS HAVE JUST COME TRUE!"

Chapter 3

The airbus was accelerating so rapidly and with such a wild turn that Madison was sent sprawling into the tumbling packs, canisters, chank-pops and jugs of sparklewater. He thought the world had gone vermilion until he found, from the floor of the vehicle, that he was looking at it through a disposable umbrella of that hue which, somehow, had sprung open.

"What the blazes are you doing?" yelped Madison.

"Just hold on," said Flick. "I'll have us there in a minute flat!"

"I didn't give you any orders to go anywhere!" howled Madison from amongst cartons of puffsticks.

"You don't know the place like I do," Flick called back. "Just don't worry. We're not lost. I know exactly where we're going."

The airbus swooped perilously. It wasn't a minute. It was more like ten. And Madison had just begun to get himself sorted out when *WHAM!* they landed.

Flick was out of the airbus like a flash. Madison, prying a sweetbun off his face, heard him chortling. "There she is. Oh, Gods, you beauty! Just what I have always wanted!"

Madison gingerly pried himself out of the car, dabbing at his face. They had evidently landed straight through the open doors of a huge display room. The sign in reverse on the window said Zippety-Zip Manufacturing Outlet, Commercial City.

Flick was standing ecstatically, looking at the ceiling.

A rather good-looking man in a bright green suit came over, somewhat upset about this unorthodox landing but not saying so. "I'm Chalber. Is there something I can do for you gentlemen?"

"That!" said Flick, jabbing with his finger.

Madison had gotten the sweetbun crumbs out of his eyes. They were surrounded by rows and rows of airbuses of every shape and hue. But Flick wasn't pointing at any of them. He was jabbing at the ceiling.

Up there, on a transparent sheet suspended by cables, was a vehicle on display, visible from the air if one looked through the high windows or glass dome. It was utterly huge: it had a flying angel in lifelike colors protruding forward from each of its four corners and it appeared to be solid gold.

"That, that, that!" said Flick. "I've wanted it for years!"

"Oh, I am sorry," said Chalber, "that's the Model 99. There were only six of them ever built and they were used for parades and vehicle shows. It's sort of our symbol of excellence to show what Zippety-Zip can do. It's not for sale."

"Oh, yes, by Gods, it's for sale. Look at that sign on the window. It says, 'We Sell Everything That Flies.'"

"Well, that's just a figure of speech," said Chalber.

"You better start figuring," said Flick. "I WANT THAT AIRBUS!"

"Well, really," said Chalber, "you must realize that when the Model 99s were built, they were never intended for sale. We were merely seeking to prove we could do better than any other manufacturers. One or two of them were presented to noblemen as a gesture of good will. But you gentlemen aren't noblemen."

"You want a fight?" said Flick, putting up his fists.

"Listen, Flick," said Madison. "I don't think we should get into any brawls...."

"Listen yourself!" said Flick. "That 99 has a bar, a toilet, a washbasin with jewelled buttons. It has a color organ and every known type of screen and viewer. The back seats break down into beds that massage you. The upholstery is real lepertige fur. It flies at six hundred miles an hour and can reach any place on the planet nonstop. It is fully automatic. It is completely soundproof and it is pressurized for flights up to three hundred miles altitude. When you land, a piece of the back end pulls out and becomes a ground car and you don't need to walk. The Model 99 has tons of storage cabinets and you can even hide a girl under the seat." He shook his fist at Chalber pugnaciously. "I've had dreams of driving one around, snooting at all the other traffic and I'm NOT going to be stopped!"

"Really," said Chalber. "Be reasonable. The price would be ten times that of a top-grade limousine airbus. I can show you gentlemen some very fine vehicles that——"

"How much?" said Flick.

"That Model 99," said Chalber with a superior sneer, "sits on the books at thirty thousand credits. I am sure..."

Flick still had Madison's identoplate. He stuck it in front of Chalber's face and said, "Will that do?"

Chalber looked at it. Then he went into staring shock. "Pay Status UNLIMITED?"

"Him," said Flick, jabbing a finger at Madison. "Apparatus-Palace City-Royal. Now get that beauty down here! Service it! And don't delay!"

Chalber nodded numbly. Flick threw his hands wide

toward the car and cried, "Baby, come to your Daddy
Flick!"

Chapter 4

After Flick had oohed and ahed over the lowered
Model 99, showing Madison all its beauties, and while
mechanics got dust off of it and fuel rods into it, Flick
raced over to an office communication booth and got
very busy.

Madison, already a car buff, began to warm to the
vehicle. It certainly was FLASHY! Even the angels at
the four corners had a sort of wild grin on their faces as
though they were going to show the world. He thought
for a moment of his poor Excalibur, probably on the
river bottom still in New York, far away, and then dismissed it. This was a car that performed like a jetliner,
with no wings. It wasn't chrome-plated. It was gold-
plated! Every button was a precious stone. The seats
were like sitting on a cloud. He forgot the Excalibur.
This was a PR car to end all PR cars!

Chalber had a lot of papers to stamp and had to show
him how but he was very respectful. Flick came away
from the communication booth long enough to make
sure it was all in order.

"You hold on to this Apparatus junk heap," said
Flick to Chalber. "I'll tell you what to do with it. And
you stand ready to give me two or three mass-passenger
air-coaches if I send for them. I've always wanted some."

He went off leaving a numbed Chalber.

Suddenly Flick rushed out of the communication booth. He was flinging his arms around. He said, "I've got it! Oh, man, my dreams are really coming true. Would you believe it, I've got it!"

Flick was dashing around, checking the Model 99, and Madison couldn't get his attention.

Flick stacked all the contents of the vendor's cart into the hidden cabinets and pushed Madison in like another piece of baggage.

Madison felt a little piqued. After all, it was *he* who now owned the car. Who was boss here anyway?

"Listen, Flick," said Madison mildly as they took off, "I'm glad you got us a nice car but I have other things to think about and do. I am a working PR, you know. I should be about my business getting some connections."

"Feel her!" cried Flick. "Ain't she beautiful? Not a sound from the outside, not even a whirr from the drives. Oh, man, does she handle just like I knew she would."

The car did ride smoothly, actually like a feather. He was startled to look out the window and see the ground rushing by, quite close, at a speed which must be approaching sound. They had left Commercial City but the verdant countryside was such a blur, Madison could not tell if they were farms or parks or what.

"Flick," he said, "I'm sure it's a joy to drive this thing and she is a beauty, I admit. But I see it is now afternoon and I should not be wasting the day."

"Never you mind," said Flick. "Don't you fret. I can tell you're new here. An Earthman, isn't it? I didn't know we had such a planet but I don't know them all. So you just let me handle this so you don't get lost."

They were over buildings now and were slowing

down. The area seemed to consist of a lot of parks and clubs whose signs were even visible in daylight. For a hopeful moment, he thought Flick might be taking him to Homeview, for he could see a gigantic dome ahead with that lettering upon it.

"We're almost there," said Flick. "This is Joy City. That's our destination over there, just beyond that big sign, Dirt Club. Ain't it remarkable?"

"Well, that IS a remarkable advertising sign," said Madison. "A girl in a military hat lying on cannon parabolas. But really, Flick, I think I should go over to Homeview. . . ."

"Not the Dirt Club. That's for Army officers and we ain't Army. No, no. That big bright slab of a building."

Madison tried to see what they were heading for. All he saw was a rectangle of metal that must be eighty stories high and which covered an area of what might be six New York City blocks.

"That's her!" said Flick, hovering to let some traffic clear. "The five top stories of that building was the town-house of General Loop."

"All that?"

"Yeah, he was awful rich. He died a couple years ago and it's too big for anybody to want to live in. The swank residences are all over at Pausch Hills and nobody with that much money wants to live in Joy City: there's nothing but clubs and hotels and amusement parks and the entertainment industry around here. So it's been closed. It must be absolutely crammed with antiques and valuables. Way back before he retired, the owner, General Loop, was in charge of all electronic security for the whole Confederacy. Ever since I heard nobody was living in it now, I've tried and tried to sneak into it, but it's guarded by the fanciest electronic gimmicks anybody ever heard of! An awful challenge: I've laid awake nights trying to figure out how to break in and rob the joint. But back there, I solved it. I'll tell them we're interested in buying it. And they'll show me every security device! Then we'll come back and rob it. Smart, eh?"

Madison blinked. However, before he could protest, Flick received a clearance on a flashing screen on his dash and dived abruptly for the roof. The flat metal expanse was the size of several football fields. He headed for a solitary figure at one end, tiny as a doll in all that vastness. It was waving at them to come in. Flick landed.

An old man in a watchman's uniform was at their door. He was carrying a small box in his hand. "So you're the fellow that wants to buy this place," he said to Flick.

"Yes, sir," said Flick emphatically. "Another dream that's going to come true."

"Why hasn't anybody bought it?" said Madison, not at all happy about what he was getting into. He might be able to use some offices, but this was not even getting a building: it was a planned robbery. He was being steered way off his mark, and the meaningful look of Teenie hovered in memory.

"Oh, they're crazy, of course," the old man said, "but they think the place is haunted."

That was all Madison needed to get along: the robbery of a haunted townhouse. What a headline THAT would make! He tried to think of something that would dampen Flick's enthusiasm.

But the old man was talking, "You can't get into this place without help," he said, climbing in.

"I know," said Flick.

"So I thought I'd better come up in person with the box. They're all waiting for you down below, so if you'll just move this airbus ahead to that small white dot you see there, we'll go in."

Flick, quivering with expectancy, moved the car as stated and the old man pushed at the side of the box.

SWOOP!

Hidden doors whose edges had not been evident activated and they were still sitting in the airbus but it was now sitting in the center of a palatial living room!

Madison glanced up. The door was gone.

Three nicely dressed men were sitting around a desk.

Flick leaped out of the car, looking all around. There were paintings on the walls, vases on stands. He rubbed his hands.

Flick rushed over to the desk. He didn't shake hands. "Let me see the rest of this layout!"

One of the men, gray-headed, said, "We have to be sure this is a serious offer. We came over from the bank just in case somebody really wanted to buy it."

"We got to see the whole place," said Flick.

The three businessmen and the watchman seemed a little cool but then Flick, like a stage magician, flashed Madison's identoplate.

"Pay status UNLIMITED?" gawped the gray-haired man.

Flick gave Madison a broad wink when the bankers weren't looking.

Madison swallowed. This was NOT good PR! The identoplate was now being used as an entrance to case a joint and rob it! He had visions of himself being carted off to jail.

The bankers made haste to show them some of the rest of the townhouse. To see all of it would have taken more than a day. Five floors of this size would have taken far more walking than they had the legs for.

There were apartments beyond count, some quite elegant. Some were like the palatial cabins of ships at sea, some were like those of spacecraft. Some looked like hunting lodges.

There were several bars as big as a tavern, chairs and tables and decor approximating styles of different planets.

There were kitchens that were complex mazes of electronic cooking gear which sent viands upwards which would then appear magically on tables in dining salons without having seemed to travel.

There were rooms which contained such a multitude of screens that one got the impression he could look at any band or transmission on any planet anywhere.

They came to an auditorium that would seat at least two hundred people and whose stage revolved or simply flapped back when another decorated stage rose.

Madison got the distinct impression they were not seeing everything there was to see in these rooms. Something odd about it all, something strange. Spooky. Part of it was that there seemed to be windows but they were all black.

The old watchman didn't seem to be much interested. Flick ran along and the watchman would hit buttons in his box and the doors of rooms would open. Flick would look in, see paintings and hangings of great value and rush on.

"You realize," the watchman said at last, "that if I was not working this box right, we not only could not pass down these halls, for I've opened all the invisible barriers, but traps would open in the floor as well. There's this box for watchmen and such but some of the master suites can't be opened at all until they're voice-tuned to the new owner."

Flick whispered to Madison excitedly. "There's a

half a million credits in loot in this place. It would be the haul of the century." Then he went racing on to glance into more rooms.

"Of course," the gray-haired banker told Madison, "the apartment has regular street entrances and elevators: several of them in fact. But you can only come up to the first floor of these five. The upper ones require special entrance. General Loop was pretty security conscious, I'm afraid."

Finally the three bankers and the bored watchman were so worn out with walking that they simply stopped. "Do you mind," said the gray-haired man, "if we go back to the hangar salon? If you're still interested..."

"Oh, we're interested!" said Flick with a wink at Madison. And he followed them back to where the airbus was.

Flick, arriving there, reached out his hand to the watchman. "Could I see that box?"

The watchman shook his head.

The three bankers sank wearily into chairs, quite worn out from almost two hours of unaccustomed walking. Madison himself felt fagged.

"If you're willing to talk price," said the gray-haired man, "we are open to some serious offers. We know that the place is large, too large. And it could never obtain a hotel license. The entire remainder of the building, all seventy-five lower floors, are separately owned by residential families such as club officials and so on, and they are much smaller. This so-called townhouse is all under one deed that can't be broken down into subdeeds and so it can't be separately rented out or sold in pieces. Now, I am being very frank. The general's heirs want to get rid of it. It would not be honest of us not to tell you. So what do you offer?" Madison was sure Flick would find some excuse. Madison's main problem was how he was going to discourage Flick from a break-in and robbery.

Flick was looking at the box in the watchman's hands. It was obvious the watchman was not going to give it up. Flick sighed deeply. Madison had visions of being part of a break-in that would bring immediate arrest. There was only one way to handle this. As a PR man he knew how to wheel and deal. He would offer a price too low. They would leave and then he would use his authority to argue some sense into Flick. Maybe bribe him.

"Well," said Madison to the gray-haired man, "I'm afraid we can't go higher than twenty thousand credits."

"Sold," said the gray-haired man without even looking at the other two. "The heirs will be very pleased. The papers are already here. I will fill in the amount and you can stamp them."

Madison blinked. Then he suddenly realized the offer was about four hundred thousand dollars!

HE HAD BOUGHT A HAUNTED TOWN-HOUSE!

Chapter 5

"Jumping comets, are you smart!" crooned Flick as they rose up through the roof and flew away. "Now we can rob the place without any watchman even sticking their noses in."

"Flick," said Madison, "we OWN the place."

"Makes no difference," said Flick. "My dream is going to come true! Look, I got the box and a four-foot stack of directions in the bargain. Wow, what an easy break-in this will be! Oh, man, are *all* my dreams coming true!"

"Flick——"

"Oh, leave this up to me. You're smart. I got to admit that now. I was wrong: a murderer can have brains for something else besides nightmares. Wow, what a master stroke! Boy, and I puzzled and puzzled over that for months and months!"

"Flick, it's sunset and I think we ought to call it a day. I got to get up early in the morning and get on my job!"

"Hey, that shows you why you should leave all this up to me. Crime works best by night and you ought to know that."

They had leaped up into the sky and the traffic lanes, strung out like fireflies in the dusk, were falling behind them.

"Flick, we seem to be leaving the towns. Where are you going?"

"Now, don't bother your head. Just because you got one bright idea doesn't prove you know enough to handle everything in sight. Just relax back there."

"Flick, I think..."

"Hand me a sweetbun, would you? They're in that side locker. Have some yourself."

A vast sea was on their left and they were speeding along the coast, a greenish surf drawing ribbons of foam upon the sand in the dimming light. Great scarlet clouds, far to the west, were catching the afterglow of the sun.

Presently, in the fading twilight, the beaches gave way to cliffs and black mountains began to silhouette against the stars. Suddenly Flick pulled his throttle back and pointed.

A huge ebony bulk lay just ahead, sprawling along the top of cliffs that fell a quarter of a mile, sheer, to the sea. Battlements that covered acres were blacker against an ink-dark sky.

"That's the Domestic Confederacy Prison," said Flick. "Two hundred miles from Government City and two miles past Hell Nine. My brother did twenty years here and he told me all about it. It used to be an Army fort that held a million men: huge underground bunkers. But part of it was destroyed by an earthquake that took some of the cliff away so they gave it to the 'bluebottles.' They use it for those sentenced to twenty years or more: place is escape-proof, so they ship in their worst ones from all over the Confederacy. There's about two hundred thousand prisoners there and they never see the light." He slid Madison's identoplate into a slot in the dash.

"You mean we're going in amongst murderers?" said Madison.

"Oh, you kill me, Chief, you really do. Always gagging around. You don't have to pretend with me. I'm your driver, remember?" Flick snickered. "An officer of the Apparatus squealing like a little girl about associating with criminals! And a murderer at that." He thought it was very funny. Then he sobered. "There's their call-in light. Now, you let me do the talking, you hear?"

A glaring light hit them from a battlement and then went off. Four bright blue lights sprang up, bathing a courtyard in an eerie glow.

Flick landed and they got out. Two "bluebottles"

approached and the snout of a gun covered them from a high turret. Flick showed them Madison's identoplate and a torch glared in Madison's face as they compared the picture. Surf sounded with a distant boom and the wind moaned.

"Take us to the warder," said Flick.

They walked across the gritty courtyard, through a rusty door, and shortly were ushered into a stone-walled room where a very old and tough-faced man was just getting his jacket on. "And what's so urgent that you come here at night?" said the warder, scowling.

Flick held up Madison's identoplate.

"*PR man?*" said the warder. "What's that?"

"Parole officer," said Flick. "Apparatus parole officer." And he made a little gesture toward the two "bluebottles" that had followed them in. The warder signalled with his hand that the escort could withdraw.

Flick reached into Madison's coat and drew out two one-thousand-credit notes and slid them into the warder's palm. It was a year's pay.

"Ah, yes," said the warder. "A parole officer. Anybody special?"

"Lead us to your computer consoles," said Flick.

The warder took them down a stone passageway, ushered them into a room where several consoles sat, deserted at night. He waved his hand in invitation and left, shutting the door.

Flick took off his mustard-colored tunic, rolled up his sleeves and sat down before a keyboard and screen.

Madison said, "Flick, you've GOT to tell me what you are up to NOW!"

"Well," said Flick, with a glance to make sure the door was shut, "if you plan a robbery you've got to have a gang."

"You don't need a gang, Flick."

"Now listen," said Flick, "I've dreamed and dreamed of having my own gang. I never had the means to break one out. Now, you're not going to spoil it. You got to be more careful of dreams: they're fragile." He turned to a pad on the desk, a big smile beginning to split the horizontal oval of his face. "Oh, man! Am I ever going to have a great gang. Now I'm going to make a list of absolute essentials, so don't you interrupt."

He began to write and Madison, looking over his shoulder, read:

IDEAL GANG

1 Female for a footman in the car to fool with and feel up when I have long and tiresome waits. '

3 More drivers for getaway and loot coaches and in case I get tired driving.

3 Chefs for cooking in relays 24 hours in case I get hungry at odd times.

1 Scaler to climb up walls and open windows and roof traps in places I think I might get dizzy or my shins barked.

1 Purse snatcher to get keys to houses and opening plates to avoid making noise by breaking locks.

1 Electronics security expert that knows all about security systems and can defeat them.

1 Salesman to fence loot for me so he gets caught and I don't.

1 *Good-looking girl to clean up my room
because I hate making beds. Ha. Ha.*
6 *Whores to sleep with and cook for the rest
of the gang so they leave mine alone.*

He chewed the end of the pen for a bit, then he said, "Nope, that's it. That's just about right. A gang right out of my dreams for sure. Now I'm going to computer out ten candidates for each of these jobs, then I'll get the warder to dig the applicants out of the old bunkers and parade them and I can select the absolute top-best criminals. Perfection!"

He turned to the console and shortly the screen began to show a racing blur of numbers, names, faces and records. Flick was preselecting categories and then entering them by number in on a side, portable computer board. Thousands of names and faces were pouring through.

Madison watched dully, wondering how he was going to stop this.

No master at operating one of these, Flick occasionally hit a wrong key. This got him in a tangle and wrong categories flashed up while he tried to get back.

"Wait!" said Madison, suddenly jarred out of his preoccupation. "What on *Earth* is that category you just passed? Go back to it."

Flick did. "Circus girls? What would anybody want with circus girls? All they ever do is stand around and show off costumes. And there, look at the crimes: life for rolling drunks. That type of criminality is NOT dignified. We're not rolling drunks: we're in the house-robbing business."

"Wait, don't shift categories yet. Some of those carry the educated symbol. Does it say any of them were ever models?"

"What's a 'model'?"

"Pull the printout on those and get them paraded along with the rest."

Flick muttered. He hit another wrong key.

"Hey!" said Madison. "There's an ex-Homeview cameraman doing life for equipment theft!"

Flick was disgusted. "Look, if you're going to put together *another* gang, go over to another console: you're getting in my way."

Madison approached another console and figured out how to operate it. He got to work.

Chapter 6

Madison, two hours later, was feeling more than slightly ill. He was standing in the ghastly blue light of the prison courtyard, one hand on the airbus, trying not to vomit. Naturally fastidious, he feared he'd be smelling that smell for weeks.

The warder, good as his word, had paraded ten candidates at a time in a noisome assembly bunker and Flick and Madison had had the job of interviewing each. Between them, they had examined 480 prisoners. They had selected 48. They had been cursed luridly at the last by the 432 luckless ones who had NOT been chosen.

And here came the fruits of their interviews after being handled on the prison rolls. The small mob was being prodded forward by stingers in the hands of guards. Additional "bluebottles," alert with guns, walked behind.

The night was dark and the courtyard cold with wind in off the sea. The prisoners' rags were blown like tattered banners about their filthy limbs. They stank; their hair was matted; they were thin. The fourteen women and thirty-four men should have been cowed, but they were not.

They came to a stop in the sudden glare of a spotlight on the wall. They had not been outside, some of them, for years. They looked around brazenly. A couple of them barked laughs at the guards, jeering laughs. Flick and Madison had not chosen convicts who looked cowed.

The warder, walking over the black pavement to Madison, heard the laughs and turned around and glared at the group. Then he turned back to Madison and pushed papers at him on a board so they could be stamped.

"I hope you know what you're doing," the warder said. "The people you selected were not the ones *I* would have picked for parole. You passed over many a bird down there that have maybe reformed. Some of these you picked are probably killers we never got the goods on. Those women are a bad lot—capable of anything. I think they fooled you with their looks. But you guys in the Apparatus always have been crazy. We pick 'em up and you turn 'em loose. The government pays us to prevent crime and pays you to commit it. Funny world."

Madison handed the now-stamped papers back.

FIND OUT WHAT HAPPENS NEXT!

A 50% SAVINGS!

*DON'T WAIT —get in
on the whole plot now!*
Order Mission Earth in hardback! $18.95 per
volume. (**Or order all 10 volumes for only $99.95.
A 50% savings!**) *FREE SHIPPING!*

ORDERS SHIPPED WITHIN 24 HRS OF RECEIPT!

PLEASE SEND ME:

___ MISSION EARTH hardback volumes _____
  (specify #s:_____) $18.95 each
___ MISSION EARTH set **(10 vols)** $99.95 _____

CHECK AS APPLICABLE: SHIPPING: *FREE*
❑ Check/Money Order enclosed   TAX*: _____
  (Use an envelope please).
❑ American Express ❑ VISA ❑ MasterCard **TOTAL:** _____

Card #:_____

Exp. Date:_____ Signature:_____

NAME:_____

ADDRESS:_____

CITY:_____ STATE:_____ ZIP:_____

PHONE#:_____

Call Toll-Free 1-800-722-1733   (1-800-843-7389 in CA)

"You got forty-eight killers there," the warder said. "Don't turn your back on them. Good luck."

He walked a few paces toward the prison doors and then changed his mind and faced the tattered, filthy group grinning at him in the wind and spotlight glare. In a loud, harsh voice he said, "Listen, you bird droppings. If any one of you show up here again, I'll put you in the iron box and down in the darkest hole and we won't even bother to bury you when you die. You'll stay free only as long as this Apparatus officer here is still alive. Your papers say you are to be returned here any time he says so. If you run away from him, a warrant goes out for you and back here you come. You belong in Hells, not in free air." He pointed emphatically at Madison. "Obey that man, you (bleepards), or you're dead!"

Madison watched the warder tramp away. The fellow had earned his money: he had turned total control of these convicts to Madison with that speech even though he might suspect that Madison would order them to commit crimes.

Earlier, from the prison, Flick had called Chalber and out of the night here came three air-coaches and an airbus to ferry back the Zippety-Zip drivers. They flashed down out of the night and into the glare of the wall spotlight. They were shiny new vehicles, sparkling and sleek.

A driver popped out of the Zippety-Zip ferry airbus, spotted Madison and came over with papers to be stamped. While he waited, the driver stared at the prisoner group.

Flick had begun to sort them out and move them to stand beside different vehicles. The convict drivers were getting genned in by the ferry people.

"Ouch," the man beside Madison said. "What a Hellish lot! You're actually putting them in clean, new air-coaches!" He looked closer. "What a bunch of killers!" Then he shrugged and took the papers back. "Well, they're your vehicles now. Carry whom you please. Wow!"

Madison went over to the groups as the ferry airbus took off hastily.

Looking into the faces, he began to check his list. It was composed of:

---

1 Director, ex-Homeview, who had been making porno movies on the side.

2 Cameramen who had been caught selling government supplies.

3 Set men whose sets, because they had sold the fasteners, had fallen down and killed actors.

1 Horror-story writer who had frightened an audience of children into convulsions resulting in deaths.

5 Reporters who had been caught accepting bribes to omit names, and other similar crimes.

1 Studio production secretary who had been accepting bribes to ruin the careers of actors.

2 Actors who had been doing long stretches for impersonating officers of various kinds to shake people down.

5 Circus girls, educated and statuesque, who,

> *variously, had been doing time on long sentences yet to be served for rolling drunks, extorting money, setting up people for hits.*
>
> *6 Roustabouts who had been doing lots of time for mayhem and assault, amongst other things.*
>
> *2 Drivers skilled in heavy vehicles who had been doing twenty and thirty years respectively for pillaging their trucks.*
>
> *2 Cooks, experienced in crew logistics, who had been doing time for selling stolen food.*

Madison finished his body check and despite the stench, a pulse of exultation began to course through him.

One thing they had in common. It was chief amongst the several quick tests he had used. If they tried hard, they could lay aside the killer stamp and appear totally honest and sincere. If they concentrated, they could even talk in persuasive voices. Oh, they would require some work and practice, that he understood. But he always expected that. A master at it like himself could drill it in.

A glow of eagerness built up to a fiery excitement within him. What luck!

HE HAD HIS CREW!

The exact people he needed to get on with his job!

He felt he could rise to heights now never before achieved!

Oh, how lucky Heller was, to have him for his PR!

He must not let anything stop him now!

Chapter 7

There was a holdup on departure.

The convicts were all loaded. The felon drivers were at the controls of the air-coaches. No Flick.

Madison looked around the black and gritty courtyard, noting there was a turret gun still trained on them from the wall. He wanted to get out of there before something untoward happened. He didn't want to shout and raise a commotion.

Then he saw a glow was coming from the Model 99. He raced over to it.

Flick was bent over one of the panel screens: three-dimensional colored maps were stopping, shifting, blurring on it. They were all of mountains.

"You're keeping us waiting," said Madison impatiently. "Let's get out of here. What on *Earth* are you doing NOW?"

"I'm looking for a place to take this gang," said Flick. "There's a lot of mountains but it's not like on Calabar. On Voltar, I can't find any caves."

"And what do you want caves for?"

"To train! You got to train a gang. You can't just let them blunder into a job. It all has to go off like clockwork—clip, clip, clip! Now, there's some old ruins on the other side of the Blike Mountains—some town that got knocked out in a revolt ten thousand years ago, it says. And it would do, except only this airbus can cross the Blike Mountains. Those air-coaches can't fly at fifty thousand feet. I got PROBLEMS!"

"Well, Flick, I don't see why we don't go to the town-house in Joy City."

"Oh, no! That would be cheating!"

"Well," said Madison, "you can do what you please, but I'm going to take MY gang there."

"YOUR gang—MY gang! What's this? Are we splitting up? Hells, that could cause a gang war!"

"Oh, we should do anything to avoid that," said Madison. "Look, I've got a compromise. The 76th floor is said to be just ordinary. It's the rest of the upper floors that all the loot is in. I promise faithfully not to let anybody go up to the upper four floors."

Flick frowned. He thought it over. Then he said, "All right. Nobody goes into the upper four floors until we're ready to rob them. So that's settled. We go to the 76th floor of the townhouse."

Madison started to withdraw to signal the air-coaches. "Wait a minute," said Flick. "It will look awful suspicious going into the townhouse in that swank neighborhood with a bunch of prisoners in rags. The cops would be all over us like a blanket. We'll go rob a clothing warehouse first."

"NO!" said Madison.

"Yes!" said Flick. "I compromised on the 76th floor of the townhouse. Now you can compromise on something. I know of the swankiest men and women's clothing outlet you ever heard of. HUGE. Even noblemen's stores get their stock from that place. Besides, I need to put my footwoman in a uniform: she's got awful big breasts and is going to need a big selection to choose a uniform from, or we won't get a fit. So, as long as I've got to get her one, we'll just outfit the whole gang in one go."

Madison looked at him aghast.

"Classy Togs Warehouse is the name. It's in the outskirts of Commercial City, whole area deserted at this time of night. I cased the joint. It's only got one watchman and he's old."

Seeing the determination, Madison felt helpless. "I'm afraid that I'll wait outside."

"Oh, good. You be the whistle man!" And Flick leaped out and raced to the air-coaches, ordering the drivers to follow him, whispering to each they were off to do their first job and get some clothes.

Shortly they soared into the air out of the courtyard and strung out, streaking down the coast. A moon had risen and was bathing the night with a soft green glow. The Domestic Confederacy Prison's bulk disappeared behind. Then even the mountains were gone.

Flick was chortling happily. "Man, we're off on our first job!"

Madison looked down. They were speeding along moon-bathed beach, the surf long ribbons as it purled against the sand.

Madison looked back.

NO COACHES!

"HALT!" he screamed at Flick. "You were going too fast!"

"WHAT?" said Flick. "No air-coaches? I only been doing three hundred. Those coaches can do four hundred easy! They've escaped!"

He flipped the Model 99 around in the air and sent its scanners flashing all around the sky.

NO BLIPS!

No sign of air-coaches on the screen.

"Well, (bleep) them!" raged Flick. "That's gratitude! The lousy (bleepards) have taken off to do their own job!"

"Let's go back the way we came," said Madison. "Maybe they crashed. Can you do a ground search with something?"

Flick punched around and got a metal-detector beam working and registering.

They sped back up the moonlit sand. The tips of the mountains to the north rose once more as they headed back.

Then, A BLIP. TWO BLIPS. THREE BLIPS!

Three air-coaches down there on the sand!

Fearing the worst, they speeded near and did a fast pass.

THE COACHES WERE EMPTY!

"Oh, Gods," said Flick. "They've escaped inland! We'll never find them in that scrub. Where the Hells is the body-heat detection button?"

"You don't need one," said Madison. He was pointing.

The group wasn't inland. It was down in the surf. Were they fighting?

The Model 99 swooped nearer and landed with a thunk in the sand. Madison leaped out.

Convicts were running everywhere!

"WHEE!" they were shouting. "WHEE!"

Madison caught an arm of a naked woman as she raced by. But she was gone, shouting, "Whee!"

He spotted another one who had stopped to catch his breath and quickly went over. It was one of the cooks/logistic personnel.

"What's going on here?" demanded Madison of the naked man.

He was catching his breath. He finally said, "I'm afraid it's all my fault, Chief. Your Lieutenant Flick told us we were going to get new clothes tonight so I said, 'Let's throw all these rags away!' I think they got a little enthusiastic."

A voice was at Madison's elbow. The director, naked as the day he was born, said, "Isn't it great? If my cameraman just had a camera, I could really get it in the can. And show it as the 'Rites to the Goddess of the Sea.' Hells, I'll direct it anyway. YOU THERE! GRAB THAT WOMAN AND PITCH HER OFF THOSE ROCKS!"

Madison raced back to the Model 99. It had every known kind of noisemaker: sirens, klaxons, scream-beams, moans and bomb blasts. He pushed them all. A dreadful assortment of sound racketed across the waves and sand. Naked convicts came streaming out of the water and rushing in from the dunes to see what was up.

Madison found a floodlight knob and pushed it. The immediate scene went a glaring yellow.

He was surrounded now by a mob of naked bodies. He rapidly made a count. The last one was just arriving: he now had forty-eight.

"Blast!" cried Flick, above the thunder of the surf, "How we going to do our job with no clothes?"

"You said the job was to get clothes," somebody yelled.

"That's right!" cried another.

A woman shouted, "You can beat us and we won't put those rags back on!"

Madison saw mutiny in the air. He motioned Flick to be silent. "I think you did just great!" he shouted. "Just be sure you don't leave those rags lying around.

People will think somebody has escaped. So gather them up and we'll be on our way."

The throng disintegrated.

Shortly a pile of rags was gathered in one heap just above the water's edge. Somebody got a laser-lighter from an air-coach and touched off a blaze.

That would have been all right but somebody else promptly found some driftwood and piled it on the flame and then somebody else found some more and they had a bonfire. They thought that was great and, grabbing hands, began to dance around it in two rings going opposite ways.

Then, mysteriously, sweetbuns and sparklewater from the lockers of the Model 99 began to get tossed from hand to hand. They had robbed the airbus!

Then they were all sitting, toasting sweetbuns on long sticks and guzzling sparklewater from jugs. And somebody began to sing a song!

And here's a cheer
To the boys in blue
And here's to the cons
They love to screw.
So let's screw the blueboys
Screw, screw, screw.
And chaw on their carcasses
Chew, chew, chew!
Up their butts
And off with their nuts
And here's to a life of crime!

Flick was seething. "Some gang! Lay into 'em, Chief. Kick some sense into their heads. They've got a job to do tonight!"

"*You* lay into them and kick some sense into their heads," said Madison.

"You're the boss. They've got to learn to respect you."

"*You're* the lieutenant. You've got to teach them respect for me."

"I'm too disgusted," said Flick. "I'm going over and sit in the airbus."

The sweetbuns had vanished. The sparklewater jugs were empty. They had finished the hot jolt and were smoking the puffsticks.

Madison got up. He said, above the surf, "All right. It's getting late. Let's be on our way."

"Just as soon as we wash this sand off!" somebody yelled.

There was a concerted rush into the sea and then they began a water fight.

A statuesque circus girl, body gleaming in the moonlight, rushed out of the water toward Madison. Three more came whooping on her heels. Madison thought they were just chasing the first girl until she was upon him. She grabbed him with a shout. The others jumped on him.

"Come on in!" they were shouting at him.

They had his clothes off so fast he hardly knew when they had been slipped off. Yikes, these girls were expert!

They bore him straight into the sea and pitched him into the teeth of a towering wave. Madison came up blubbering and blowing.

Something pulled him under. He hadn't taken a breath. Then he was on the surface again and being carried into the air.

Buffeted by the waves, four girls bore him back to

dry land. Madison was coughing and sneezing and trying to get his breath.

He was being held horizontally six feet off the ground.

His blurred sight took in faces rushing at him.

They were going to wipe him out!

He stared around anxiously.

In the lights from the bonfire and the car, eyes were glittering. Like wolves?

Suddenly they began to chant, "Hup! Hup! Hup! Hup!" Was this some sort of a convict or guard cry that marched them about?

They were going to the fire. Were they going to throw him in?

They were marching around the fire. Some sort of savage ritual. "Hup! Hup! Hup! Hup!" Like Indians or wild animals!

Then suddenly they all stopped. A male voice—the director's?—began a chant, calling one line and being answered by all the rest.

"Who's the gang?"

"WE'RE THE GANG!"

"Who's the mob?"

"WE'RE THE MOB!"

"Who's the chief?"

"HE'S THE CHIEF!"

And threw Madison in the water!

He came up spluttering.

They paid no further attention to him. They were now trooping off to the air-coaches.

Madison, not knowing how to take all that, but quite certain it was not the kind of respect and image he needed, trudged alone across the sand to where his clothes had been stripped off.

He dried himself with his undershirt and got his clothes back on.

He was glancing around to see if anything had dropped out of his pockets. Nothing lying there. He patted his pockets. He had his identoplate. Then he missed a bulge which should be at his breast. He patted again.

HIS WALLET AND FORTY-EIGHT THOUSAND CREDITS WERE GONE!

He felt himself go white.

He looked at the air-coaches over there in the moonlight. They were all loaded and waiting to go.

He flinched at tackling that mob again.

That settled it. He would have to work on his own image first. He went over to the Model 99.

"Some gang," muttered Flick. "Bunch of lousy beach (bleepards) out for a holiday."

Madison sank back in the seat. He didn't agree at all. That mob was a bunch of criminals. But he wasn't going to tell Flick they had stolen his wallet—no use to harm his image even more.

Chapter 8

When they flew in over the outskirts of Commercial City, it was dark as pitch below. A hill blocked off the moonlight and left the part of the plain they wanted in the deepest shadow.

That was fine by Madison. He couldn't possibly

imagine greater folly than using a Model 99, so recognizable, on a robbery job. Not unskilled in the methods of crime—since these often go hand in hand with truly expert PR—he knew you were supposed to steal some cars and, after the heist, abandon them without fingerprints.

A vast factory complex, spreading over possibly six square miles, squatted in the darkness below, all of it, apparently, devoted to just one company, Classy Togs. In daytime it might well be occupied by hundreds of thousands of workers, and a network of monorails led in from the town and curled and swooped all over the plain and mountainside and then went over to another site, a collection of high-rises, a miniature city in itself.

The Model 99's screens, turned to night frequency, showed it all up plainly, color-corrected to look like day. It was quite startling to then look out and see only blacks and shadow.

Flick was sorting out the buildings. He found the various chimneyed structures where they made cloth and fabric molds and discarded them. He was able to label the many-windowed, low, long buildings, each standing in its park, as design and assembly structures.

"I thought you'd cased this joint," said Madison.

"I did. I saw it on Homeview," said Flick. "It produces, all by itself, .07 percent of all the clothing for the nobility, their staffs and estates."

"That's not very much," said Madison.

"But it's quality we're after and that is the TOP .07 percent. Or maybe it was 7 percent: I always have trouble with my ciphers because they're nothing, you see, and you don't have to bother with them. But I'll convince you: the cloth they make in them factories down there have been used in stage clothes for Hightee Heller. So there's no better recommendation than that!"

Hightee Heller? thought Madison. Ah, yes. He'd heard something: that was Jettero's sister. "That's the Homeview star," he said.

"Star?" sniffed Flick. "You mean *Goddess!* Don't you go running down the girl of my dreams. Hey, there it is! The warehouse! No windows. See it in that snarl of monorails? Here we go!"

They shot down to a truck roadway that ran under the monorails and stopped. They were in a park, close by the warehouse, within a hundred feet of its doors. Three air-coaches came down, *crump, crump, crump,* on the road behind them.

It gave Madison the creeps. Here he was in a glaringly recognizable car, accompanied by three vehicles full of naked cons. He looked around hastily for guards.

The night was very black here, the moon blocked out. Ah, there it was: a watchman's office, marked by a blue light. The office itself was inset into the side of the circular warehouse and close by the main entrance.

His attention was distracted by someone at their windows. It was the scaler, the purse snatcher and the electronics security man, stark naked.

The security man said to Flick, "All the controls will be in that watchman's office. This place will go up like a celebration if we even touch the latch of that front door at this hour. We were talking it over in the coach." But he was pointing at the watchman's windows.

Madison's hair stood up. In silhouette, a watchman could be seen peering out.

"You see?" said the electronics convict. "Our gang ain't complete. We ain't got no slugger to take the watchman out."

"Oh, yes, we have," said Flick. "The chief. He's a first-rate murderer."

Madison groaned. He knew he had set up the wrong image.

"Well, don't hold us up, Chief," said Flick. "Go on over and erase that watchman. Sir."

Madison knew his control of this gang was on the line. But murder?

"When you get in there, Chief," said the electronics man, "you'll find a big board. So as soon as you take the watchman out, remove the activating plate from his belt and push it over a green dot you'll find on the board and all the alarms will nullify."

Madison braced himself. He got out of the airbus. Two of the roustabouts had come up and showed every sign that they were going to go accompany him.

In a firm voice, Madison said, "Don't come with me. I don't want any witnesses to learn how I really work."

"He'll be armed," Flick said.

"You birds stay here," said Madison. And they watched him walk down the road, visible only against the watchman's windowlight.

They saw Madison enter the office and the watchman vanish from the window. A small sound came to them, something falling. Then there was a delay and they grew more and more nervous. "Maybe he's having trouble with the opening plate. Those boards are pretty complex. I better go help."

"You stay here like he said," snarled Flick. "You caused enough trouble for one night."

They became more and more edgy.

Then suddenly someone was running toward them and they tensed.

It was Madison.

He beckoned.

Nervously they followed him.

Madison reached for the entrance door and opened it. At his gesture, forty-eight naked cons slid like whispers into the building.

Flick glanced toward the watchman's office.

"Don't go in there," said Madison. "It would turn your stomach."

Madison firmly closed the door behind them, fumbled along the wall and pushed a panel.

The interior of the warehouse flooded with light.

There were tiers and tiers of shelves of boxes, racks and racks of clothes, men's and women's.

The convicts let out suppressed squeals of delight and began to rush along the racks and tiers. They began to tear down boxes of fancy shoes and grab hats and capes.

At a low word from Madison, Flick called them to come back.

Holding items already grabbed they unwillingly returned.

Madison walked up to a rack of shimmering white dresses, probably expensive beyond belief. He ripped one off the hangings. He was using it to wipe his hands! THEY WERE BRIGHT RED!

Madison tossed the gown, now gory, on the floor.

The convicts stared at him.

Madison went over to a hook and took down a book that was hanging there and looked at it. "Yes, I thought so," he said. "This is the stock book for these rows. It has all the sizes. Now what I want you to do is each one outfit himself for any role he might have to play. Try everything on carefully."

"Oh, no," Flick gasped. "That will take time. On a job like this you grab and run!"

"And wind up with a sloppy-looking gang?" said Madison. "Take your time. We've got hours to dawn."

"There are sometimes roving watchmen, too!" said Flick.

Madison let out a snort. "They're not roving anymore."

The convicts hastened back to the shelves. They began to grab stock books. They began to look at sizes. And soon they were very busy indeed.

The circus girls paraded around, getting opinions on which costumes were the most provocative until Madison told them they had to look like ladies of quality and, on this new thought, had to select all over again.

Flick kept trying different tunics on his footwoman to see which ones best showed off her breasts until Madison forced him to find his own and then match hers to that. He had to correct that again when Flick found some lepertige tights that left everything on her front bare. "But," argued Flick, "I found some for myself and they match the upholstery!" In the end, Madison did manage to get them into shimmering violet uniforms but he had to let them take the tights as well: it was the footwoman, this time, who was protesting. She LOVED them!

The two actors who had been impersonating officers had to be argued down into more junior ranks when they found whole racks for generals and admirals.

The horror-story writer couldn't find anything gruesome enough and Madison had to force him into a wardrobe for scholars and lettered men.

The director went crazy trying to decide whether he could direct best, dressed as an archbishop or a lord, and

Madison had to talk very fast to get him to choose clothes of a working executive.

What was most trying about it, to Madison, was that he really didn't know the styles or what they represented. He was finally saved by the studio production secretary finding vast books of fashion plates which showed what was now in style.

After that, it was plain sailing. He firmly got them to outfit themselves as, each one, people of quality, working people, domestics, executives and actors.

At last he could turn to his own wardrobe. And he had very little trouble with that. He found the racks for top-flight executives like presidents of companies and, in a conservative way, got himself into the height of fashion.

Throughout, he had thought that the warehouse stank a bit and then, smelling some cloth to make sure it didn't make him sneeze—for he had some minor allergies—he realized that the bath in the sea had not been total for these convicts: they still stank of the prison; the odor clung to their matted hair and beards and seemed to ooze out of their skin.

The Apparatus! He had smelled this smell at the training center. He had smelled it in their old car. The Apparatus smell was the smell of convicts! So THAT was why it stank!

He shuddered at the thought of their contaminating these new clothes. He persuaded them, before they left, to dress in their working clothes and not their finery.

"It's coming on to dawn," said Flick nervously. "We better be getting out of here. If we don't, we all could wind up back at the Domestic Prison."

With several trips they got their loot into the coaches and then came back one final time, at Madison's order, to wipe the place clean of fingerprints.

Madison waited at the door. The crew finished on the various floors and came down.

Madison was standing at the entrance. He was humming a little song. The director tried to get by him and peer into the watchman's office. Madison blocked him.

"But it must be a great shot!" the director said. "Dead bodies bleeding all around."

"Your stomach wouldn't stand it," said Madison. "I don't want those new clothes all stunk up with vomit."

"Gods, ain't he a cool one," a convict whispered. "Wipes a whole watch force out and hums a little song."

Another convict tried to peer in and Madison shooed him off. "What'd you use?" the convict said. "You didn't have any weapon."

"My bare hands," said Madison. "I love the feel of the running gore when I rip out throat arteries. So smooth, so slick. And it has a lovely smell. You should taste it!"

The convicts let out a gasp. One retched. They stared at Madison.

He shooed them off to the air-coaches and sauntered after them, humming his little song.

Even Flick looked at him a bit white-eyed as he climbed in.

Madison was still humming as they all took off.

And he had something to hum about.

When he walked into the watchman's office, he had disregarded three levelled guns from three tough watchmen. He had pointed to the viewer-phone on the desk and said, "Connect me to your owner, please. The president of the company." He had held up his identoplate and they had.

When the startled president of Classy Togs was blinking into the viewer-phone from his bed, Madison had told him, "I am an Apparatus officer. I'm outfitting an Apparatus crew who must not be recognized. We are therefore getting clothes out of the warehouse without the help of clerks. Take an inventory in the morning, see what's gone and put the amount on the bill."

"Wait a minute," the president had said. "The Apparatus is poor pay!"

"Oh, this is on my personal account," Madison had said. And he had pushed his identoplate into the viewer-phone slot.

"UNLIMITED pay status," the owner had gasped. "Hot Saints! Go ahead! Take the whole blasted warehouse! WATCHMEN, STAY OUT OF SIGHT! DON'T YOU DARE LAY A FINGER ON THAT MAN!"

In retrospect Madison liked the touch of taking the bottle of red ink off the watchman's desk and sloshing it on his hands.

He ended his song with a laugh. He had certainly repaired his image with this crew.

And yes, he had. The sound of that laugh turned the blood of Flick to ice.

BARE-HANDED! And he liked it. Oh, Flick told himself, by Gods, they'd have to think twice before they crossed the chief. A REAL murderer for sure! A PROFESSIONAL! And he LOVED HIS WORK!

"We're heading for Joy City right now, sir," said Flick.

Madison heard the tremor, the fear and the respect in that voice.

It made everything complete.

He had total charge of this crew!

It didn't hurt at all to use the techniques of PR to improve one's own image.

Now he could REALLY PR Heller-Wister!

PART
SEVENTY-FIVE

Chapter 1

Dawn had not yet arrived, for all Flick's fears. A moon had set and it was very black night in the countryside below. But ahead it was a different matter: the whole sky was aglow. Very shortly, at this speed, they would be entering Joy City.

Madison wiped a hand across his face. "My nose is bothering me," he told Flick.

"Try a chank-pop, sir," was the prompt response. "Them convicts didn't touch them. They're in the bar compartment. Try a yellow one: that's 'summer blossom sighs.'"

Madison got one out: it seemed to be just a small round ball. He twisted and turned it, trying to make it do something. In the dimness of the airbus he didn't see the indented line that you press. He, in some annoyance, tried squeezing the whole ball between his palms with force, the way he was sometimes able to crack walnuts, a small fruit of Earth.

POW!

Instead of just opening, it exploded and hit him in the eye. The scent-fog, misdirected, struck his forehead and the roof of the airbus.

"Summer blossom sighs" might be just great—he could catch an errant whiff of it—but Madison grated to himself that he'd be blasted if he was going to lose one eye and the top of his head every time he tried to remedy the miasma of Apparatus stink!

When he could see again, the airbus seemed to be full of light. He looked down and saw that they were entering the vast and brilliant expanse which was Joy City.

They had not yet passed over the main clubs and lakes and amusement parks but, as they were coming from Commercial City, they were still over the market service areas of the pleasure metropolis. Sitting in the center of an interlace of rails and roads he saw what would be on Earth a shopping mall. There were other malls scattered about to left and right. This one below was vast but only seemed to be two stores: *Restaurant Supplies*, one said; the other one said *Beauty*. "What's that?" he yelled at Flick.

"'Beauty'?" said Flick. "Oh, there ain't no dames down there if you feel horny, Chief. That's where revellers buy things to repair the ravages of all-night revelry."

"Go back, go back," said Madison, "and land. We need food and I think that shop might sell just what I need!"

Flick braked around into a dive, the air-coaches followed after and they all landed—thud, thud, thud, thud—adjacent to the two shops.

Madison jumped out and yelled, "All cooks front and center."

"Yes sir! Yes sir!" came the cries, and five cooks streaked to him from the air-coaches.

Madison led them into the sparse mob of predawn restaurant shoppers who were picking up their supplies for the coming day. The place was vast; on every hand stood small mountains of comestibles.

Madison waved his hand across the acres. "Get anything you want," he told the cooks.

The five looked at him, round-eyed, stunned.

"ANYTHING?" gawped the oldest one. "Why, this is the choicest market on Voltar! WHAT A CHIEF!"

They rushed off like a battle charge.

Madison sped the other way, for even in their new working clothes those convicts smelled like the Apparatus.

He rushed into the Beauty Supply vendors. He sped though the aisle toward a place where stood three idle clerks. "SOAP!" yelled Madison. "And LOTS of it!"

A clerk turned and picked up a small bottle and handed it to him.

"No, no," said Madison. "LOTS of it!"

"Well, just one drop of this will give you a whole bath," said the clerk.

"No, no," said Madison, "I'm trying to get rid of Apparatus stink."

"That," said another clerk, "would be VERY beneficial. In fact, I wish we could sell you a solvent that would get rid of the whole Apparatus."

He had their interest now. "I've got fourteen women and thirty-four men. They haven't shaved, they haven't bathed, they haven't cut or coiffed their hair for years. They STINK!" He looked around. The stacks of goods bore no placards or advertising signs. "I need stuff to cut beards and hair, shave them and polish their teeth, make them look like high-class people and also to cut toenails and make them tan—and no chank-pops!"

"High-class people?" said another clerk. "From Apparatus thugs? Sir, we heartily agree. You DO have a problem. Come on, boys, let's help him out. Start getting what he needs."

"In QUANTITY!" said Madison.

They laughed and began to rush around with carts, grabbing big boxes and cases and grosses of this and dozens of that.

Madison had never heard of most of these things. Nothing seemed to have any labels, just numbers. It began to be borne in upon him that, while he had seen a little bit of advertising in the Confederacy, real marketing was an unknown commodity.

These people had so much technology, such a stable economy, such cheap fuel, that they weren't fixated on having to market some new invention every day, and lives were not lived around logistics as they were on Earth. PR was a creature which had grown out of advertising, and these people, despite their high culture, had never developed it. That meant that they would really have no inkling of PR. It made him feel powerful. He could, he realized suddenly, get away with anything, no matter how old and stale, and never even be suspected.

Madison was trying to think of some of the oldest and hoariest PR tricks that had long since become pure corn on Earth. He realized they would all work, even selling the Brooklyn Bridge, and he began to laugh in delight.

A clerk had paused with a piled-up cart. "I'm glad you're so pleased, sir. I wanted to ask you if you'd also want some paint masks and party things."

"Oh, there'll be a party," said Madison. "In fact, it will be a ball!"

"Right, sir, we'll add it to the order," and the clerk rushed on.

At last they took it all through the lighted night and the clerks crammed it in the airbus until there was hardly any place for Madison to sit.

The five cooks and roustabouts were handling the comestibles. The air-coaches, already crammed to overflowing with clothes, had to have their new loads strapped in crates on top.

Madison stamped mounds of cards handed in to him by clustered clerks, and then, with a flutter of vegetable leaves and papers streaming out behind, the convoy took off.

Chapter 2

The glittering lights and parks of Joy City spread out in a symphony of shapes and sparkles. Signs and decorations, even at this hour, shone like jewels and suns, illuminating more than a hundred square miles dedicated to companionship and gaiety. Here clustered as well, in enormously tall buildings, large domes and shining fields, the amusement industry of the Confederacy, dominated by a silver hemisphere which, with its surrounding skyscrapers and parks, comprised Homeview. Madison, flying near it in a sky-traffic lane, was impressed: NBC, CBS and ABC together would have fit in just one of those buildings. He slavered when he thought of what he could do with those facilities that reached 110 planets. Like a concert pianist who beholds a marvelous instrument, he ached to get his fingers on it. Oh, what tunes then he would play! And he even had the order from Lord Snor in his pocket that would let him do it!

His attention was distracted by Flick's slowing

down. They were approaching the townhouse which had belonged to General Loop.

The building stood like a steel slab, floodlit with a greenish light. The top four floors had no windows but all the rest of the seventy-six levels below did. A strange-looking building of harsh architecture: itself an enormous rectangle, everything else about it was rectangular. Madison had thought he must have had an exaggerated idea of its size, but now, looking at it as they eased down to it, he saw indeed that it was two New York City blocks wide and three long. Huge!

As they dropped lower, he glanced about. He was surprised to see that it was very far from the tallest, biggest building in this sector: Although separated from it by broad parks, many other structures were far higher and, in their much more elegant architecture, covered, most of them, far more ground. This steel rectangular shape was definitely an oddity in the landscape of joyous Joy City: a sort of a grim, hard-nosed slab. What would General Loop want with all that space? And why would his heirs be so anxious to get rid of it they would accept almost any price?

Flick dropped the airbus down opposite to the windowed seventy-sixth floor, holding it about a hundred feet out from the side of the building. He was talking the air-coaches into line beside him to their left. Flick had a box in his hand.

"Find a red dot," Flick was saying, "and hold while pointed at it. You there, Number Two, get into line: you dump that air-coach and I'll have your head!"

Madison looked over Flick's shoulder through the forward shield toward the building, across the empty space. He looked down. Yikes! but the ground seemed awfully far away. He glanced at a digital dial on Flick's panel:

it read that they were 912 feet above the park below! He looked up. The top of the building rose another 200 feet!

An errant gust of wind rocked them. A wisp of cloud passed like a ghostly hand between the airbus and the building side. Yikes! He suddenly realized that he was almost as high as the Empire State Building! He glanced around: several structures in this area were much higher. It reassured him in a dazed way. Well, their townhouse was NOT as high as the Empire State Building; it just covered about six times the ground! More stable, then. He felt better. Then a wisp of cloud passed by their lights that looked even more like a ghostly hand, even curled fingers to clutch at him. He felt worse.

"What's the holdup?" he said to Flick.

"Them dumb drivers can't find their red dots on the building side. This blank space all along here is hangars. I got our blue dot right ahead. See it?"

Madison saw the glowing blue dot. But there was no door!

"I can't go in until those bird droppings we got driving the other coaches find their truck dots. The dumb primates would sit out here all night. And if I let them go into a passenger slot with that load they're carrying on top, they'd crash."

The babble of voices from Flick's speakers was getting more frantic.

"Oh, blast," said Flick. "This red button here must be their dot activator. I forgot to push it." He did so.

Coaches one, two and three promptly answered up. They had their red dots.

"Well, blast it," then said Flick. "Drive on in!"

"At that steel wall?" came the combined babble. The consensus was they'd crash.

"You tell 'em," said Flick and pushed a microphone at Madison.

Wondering if he was sending forty-eight people plunging to their death, Madison said, "This is the chief. Drive!"

Resigned mutters.

Three air-coaches moved ahead at the red dots and steel wall.

Gasps of surprise.

Invisible tractor beams had grabbed them, each of the three. The steel opened. The building swallowed them!

Flick drove straight ahead. Beams grabbed the Model 99. Just as he was sure they would hit solid steel, there wasn't anything in front of them.

There was a gentle thud as they sat down. Lights came out with a flare. They were in the seventy-sixth floor hangars.

Flick was out. He was yelling at the electronics man. "You get these coaches set up with their own beams! I'm no blasted nursemaid, sitting around all night. You fix this airbus, too, so it can go in and out!"

Madison looked around. The place was just a hangar with doors opening to passageways. Twenty or thirty vehicles could line up in here.

"Everybody out!" Flick was yelling. "Find some galleys and get that food stored. Find a hallway near bathing rooms and unload this airbus into it. Then find some living quarters for yourselves and store those clothes."

The gang had gathered around Flick and now started to move off.

"Wait," said Madison. "There's enough soap and beauty supplies here to wash the whole Apparatus. I want every one of you to bathe, bathe, bathe before you go to bed. Got it?"

They started off again. "Wait!" shouted Flick. "One more thing: Don't nobody, and I mean nobody, go into ANY upper floor. You birds stay on this level, the seventy-sixth. If you go up above, it would be cheating! We got to plan how to rob the upper floors, so don't go jumping the gun! Got it?"

They all did, or so they said, and got busy.

Madison wandered off.

He seemed to be walking *through* doors that didn't open or close and he found it a bit disconcerting, but he supposed he could get used to it. Walking down a passageway he found that every hundred or so feet there was a tube which evidently went down to street level: they were just polished, rectangular shafts and he wondered if he would get nerve enough ever to simply step into empty space and hope he didn't fall 912 feet. He had put a bottle of soap in his pocket at the Beauty store: he took it out now and tossed it in a shaft, wondering what would happen.

It went down at an alarming rate. He listened for a far-off crash.

Suddenly the bottle reappeared, coming up to his level. It simply stopped there in midshaft. It must have gone to the bottom, hadn't gotten out onto the street as expected and had been brought back up to the floor again.

Madison reached into the shaft and retrieved the much-travelled bottle. He put it in his pocket, wondering if he would ever have the nerve to use these elevators. He decided he would specialize in airbuses.

He began to look into rooms. They seemed to be the sort of salons and sleeping quarters one might expect the very conservative rich to have in such a culture as this: posh, but a bit on the military side, even stark. It was sort of as if someone had put together a monastery out of the most expensive materials. Nothing warm or homey about it. However, he felt he could make good use of all this: there was lots of it. He found quantities of potential office space. He found an imposing apartment for himself with huge windows which gave a fantastic view of Joy City and the Homeview complex.

Down a hall where the beautifying supplies had been stacked, he could now hear running water and yells.

He became aware, suddenly, there was someone in the room behind him. He turned.

It was one of the circus girls, the one named Trotter. She was tall and statuesque, a brunette, quite handsome. She was wearing a sleeping robe and it was open widely all the way down the front from bare breasts to bare toes and she had on nothing else.

Madison flinched. "Get on some clothes!" he said.

"You ordered us to pick up working clothes!" said Trotter. "These ARE my working clothes. What's wrong?"

"Please leave," said Madison.

"Captain," said Trotter, "I just came to warn you about these other hussies. You have a tendency to be careless and you shouldn't trust them. Do you know that some of them are *criminals?*"

Madison backed up. They were ALL criminals and that included Trotter. And she was an imposing chunk of woman, an awful threat!

"Now me," said Trotter, moving sensuously closer to him, "I'm different. And I'll prove it."

Madison could not back up any further unless the window opened up. Yet she came on. She had already bathed and perfume engulfed him. She was reaching out her hand.

Then he felt something in his palm! It was *not* her fingers!

He looked down hurriedly.

HIS WALLET!

He gawped at her. Then he hastily looked into it.

"You see?" said Trotter. "You can trust me. I didn't want anyone to rob you when we grabbed you on the beach so I just slid your wallet in between my legs. That isn't all you can slide there, hmmm?"

Madison checked the cards; they were all present. He counted forty-eight thousand credits: it was all there!

"Th-thank you," he said.

She was sliding up to him closer and she was too close already. "You just shouldn't leave valuables lying around with a gang like this. The only lying around that should be done is on beds, hmmmm? I spotted right away how cute you were and knew I'd better defend you. So why don't I make up that bed over there for you and why don't we just climb into it. I think a favor like I just did you is worth a little piece, don't you? Hmmm?"

Oh, this was an emergency with Madison. Her bare breasts were touching his jacket as her robe swung even wider. He thought fast.

"Trotter," he said with his best sincere-and-earnest look, "you are so devastatingly beautiful, that I had my eye on you from the very first moment. You are so tall, you are so handsome, you walk with such a wonderful grace, that you cause the heart to stir in even the coldest and most indifferent of men."

Her eyes began to glow. Her bare breasts heaved with a shuddering sigh of delight.

"So therefore," said Madison, praying that his pitch

would work, "I am saving you as the star of the very first porno movie that we make."

"A bare-(bleep) movie?" said Trotter.

"Yes, indeed," said Madison, "with men climbing all over you and with the very best angles. A whole mob of them, fighting amongst themselves to be the first to get you, while you stand proud and stately, pushing them off with your feet until at last, you drop a golden robe, baring yourself totally to the camera and then, disdainfully with scornful finger, point to the one you will take and you do it then on a silken bed while the others grovel weeping on the floor."

"Hot Saints!" said Trotter. "And I'm the star?"

"Yes, indeed!" said Madison.

"Oh, blazing batfish! I can't wait to tell the girls!"

She rushed out, robe flying. Madison quickly figured out how to lock the door.

This life was not without its perils. But he felt a surge of confidence. She had bought the image he had built and swallowed it, hook, line and sinker. PR had triumphed once again. But he felt no surprise. After all, it was his trade and he was a master of it!

The movies he was going to make had nothing to do with Trotter. They would have everything to do with creating a brand-new image for Heller, one that would be stamped forever on men's minds: an outlaw! Hunted and chased by everyone! Famous beyond belief!

He turned back to the window. I wonder, he thought sadly, where Heller-Wister is right now. Already wanted on a general warrant, he was probably alone and shivering in some dark cave, unknown and depriving posterity of his potential notoriety. Well, he thought, with a confident smile, I can remedy that. With this crew I can do anything!

Oh my, won't Mr. Bury be proud! What a triumph for good, plain, old-time Earth PR! What an opportunity to show what he could really do!

Chapter 3

The crew were all bedded down, they had been bathed and fed. Being convicts, they did not care what the time of day was: it was always night in the Domestic Confederacy Prison.

Thus, quiet reigned throughout the nearby halls of floor seventy-six. A weary Flick was just reporting all was well. Madison lay back on his own austere but ample bed.

"They're all asleep, sir," said Flick. "You certainly got them under control, and we've got quite a gang. When I've had some rest myself, I can get busy and begin the plan how we're going to rob the upper floors. Oh, sir, you have no idea," concluded Flick in an emotion-choked voice, "how wonderful it is to have a dream like that come true."

Madison nodded. He had his own dream. He could be tolerant.

Flick gave Madison a single, cross-arm salute and turned to go to his own rest.

A wail was coming from somewhere.

It got louder.

Someone was shouting a single word. And shouting it with panic that held the raw screech of terror!

It wasn't a word Madison knew. It was being repeated over and over.

Pounding feet raced toward them. A single man flashed by Madison's open door, screaming that word loud enough to hurt the ears!

"The scaler!" cried Flick. "Come back here!"

But the man raced screaming straight on, tearing through the berthing apartments of the crew, still screaming!

PANDEMONIUM!

The crew began to yell. They were chasing the scaler, trying to get him to stop, shouting to head him off as he rounded turns.

Flick had vanished. Madison hastily climbed into his pants and raced toward the bedlam.

They had managed to cut the scaler off and herd him back and Madison was just in time to see two roustabouts jump on him.

The crew clustered wide-eyed.

The scaler continued to scream the word. He was writhing around, frothing with terror.

Madison yelled, "What's he saying?"

The horror-story writer, from the other side of the crowd, shouted at Madison through the tumult, "He's from the back country of Flisten, from his eye shape and long fingernails. They're like monkeys, those people."

"What's the word he's using?" shouted Madison.

"I don't speak Guaop," the horror-story writer yelled back, "but I know that word. It means 'ghosts'!"

Madison imitated the syllables. They sounded like "slith-therg." He bent over and yelled it back at the scaler.

The small man repeated the word louder and pointed with a frantic hand toward the ceiling.

"Well, (bleep) him!" raged Flick. "He's gotten into the upper floors!"

"What does he mean, 'ghosts'?" shouted the director. He yelled down at the man on the floor, penetrating the din, "Where'd you see these ghosts?"

The Flisten man simply screamed louder and pointed harder upward.

The director promptly ran off down the hallway toward the first place the scaler had appeared.

The whole crowd went chasing after the director. Madison and Flick were left, trying to get the scaler to calm down and tell them more. He shortly began simply to sob and Madison and Flick looked up to see that the whole crew had run off. They could hear them clamoring down the hall and they sped in that direction.

They were just in time to see a woman on the tail end of the mob vanish up a ramp which led to the seventy-seventh floor.

"Come back!" screamed Flick. "You're cheating!"

He and Madison rushed up the ramp.

There was a clank right in front of their faces. They collided violently with what must be a sheet of bullet-proof glass which had dropped as a barrier before them.

They could not get through.

From where they were hammering on the glass, they could see three corridors branching out. The crew was in there, split up into three mobs, racing along into the distance, looking into rooms and everywhere for ghosts!

Suddenly, the group in the right-hand corridor halted.

CHAOS!

They began to scream and retreat.

BLUEBOTTLES!

With raised stingers, a squad of police was charging straight at them!

"Oh, Gods, they were wise to us!" howled Flick. "Come back here. QUICK!"

The group in the middle hall suddenly blew apart and began to run.

SOLDIERS!

They were kneeling and firing at the criminals with deadly expressions! Flame slashed and roared in the hall.

The group in the left-hand hall heard the commotion. They turned around.

Too late!

ASSASSINS WITH ELECTRIC KNIVES WERE BEHIND THEM!

The group fled onward in total panic!

Madison and Flick looked anxiously back into the right-hand corridor.

IT WAS EMPTY!

They looked into the middle corridor.

NO SIGN OF THAT GROUP!

They looked into the left-hand corridor.

NOBODY THERE!

THE WHOLE CREW HAD VANISHED!

A wispy, filmy shape, a ghost indeed, drifted down toward the glass barricade and LAUGHED!

Oh, it was a horrible sound!

Madison and Flick fled.

Chapter 4

In Flick's room, he and Madison looked at each other. It was all quiet now.

They were scared stiff but that was not what dominated their thoughts.

THEY HAD LOST THEIR CREW!

Flick had managed to get his gasping under control. "Let me think. Where could they have gone? Ah, I have it! That watchman warned me there were traps. They've fallen into floor traps. I think the lights must have gone out or something because we didn't see anyone drop, but that is the only thing that it can be. The crew must be up there someplace in floor traps. We've got to go back up there."

"I haven't got a gun," said Madison.

"You got your bare hands," said Flick. "And they're deadly enough."

Madison knew he would have to think fast. He did. "What about that box the watchman had?" said Madison. "What did you do with it?"

"It's in the airbus."

"And where were all those directions they gave us, that big stack?"

"Yes," said Flick, coming out of it. "It should tell us where the traps are. Maybe the crew is locked in somewhere."

In short order they had the four-foot stack of directions and manuals and began to look through feverishly. They couldn't make too much out of them. But now, armed with the box, they went back up to the top of the ramp.

Flick found the right button. The glass was one of the barriers the watchman had mentioned. It rose.

Flick found another button on the box that said General Disarm. He pushed it and they walked into the first hall of the seventy-seventh floor.

They didn't find anything. The place was terribly quiet except for their own footfalls. Flick flashed a torch about.

No sign of the police.

They walked into the middle hall where that segment of the crew had vanished.

No soldiers. Nothing.

They walked into the left-hand hall and even though it seemed to stretch endlessly before them in the dark, they found no assassins.

Madison mourned. It was not only a haunted townhouse, it was a hungry townhouse. It had eaten up all their crew. No wonder nobody had wanted to buy it!

"Maybe there are some other panels somewhere," said Flick. He led the way down a side corridor.

They seemed to be in a big room but it was terribly dark. Flick played his light through the place. It seemed to be a tavern. There were tables and chairs around on the floor and a natural wood bar, all polished.

Flick walked over to the counter and looked under it. "A panel!" He stabbed an eager finger in.

Abruptly the room was full of light.

It was also full of babbling sound.

AND AT EVERY TABLE SAT ARMY OFFICERS DRINKING TUP!

They were deep in conversations and laughing, very friendly to each other. One group at the far end was singing an army song. They all wore uniforms of long ago that were covered with mold!

A captain at a nearby table turned and seemed to look at them. "Come in, drink up!" he said.

Flick fled as though pursued by demons!

Then Flick found out those were Madison's running footfalls behind him.

Flick stopped and caught his breath. "Comets, but this is an awful place. The ghosts of all his brother officers, long since dead, carousing in that tavern. It makes your blood run like winter ice."

"Maybe the crew got into one of these side rooms," said Madison.

"Oh, I don't like this," said Flick. "There's nothing like this on Calabar. That's an orderly place. When people get killed, they have the decency to stay dead. It's more gravity than here, you know. It holds corpses in their graves better. (Bleeped) Voltar! You mind what I say, Chief. You murder any people on this planet, bury 'em with WEIGHTS!"

Madison went into a room and Flick followed him. The torch, flashing around, showed what seemed to be a bed and a chair and a table. There was a huge, black window with an easy chair over to the side, placed as though inviting one to sit in it and look through the window.

Madison saw a square box just inside the door and went back to it. Flick was examining the bed: it didn't seem to be a bed but just a block of stone.

"Chief," said Flick. "I seen something like this once. It was a sacrificial altar on Mistin. This place makes me nervous."

Madison opened the wall box. There were several buttons. He pushed the biggest one.

A ROAR OF SOUND!

The whole window lighted up!

Through it one could see the red and glaring flames of a Hell!

Devils were stoking a fire!

There was a long, drawn-out scream when two more devils threw a maiden into the scarlet blaze!

Flick had stopped, stunned, staring at the scene.

Madison turned around to look at the room.

THREE RED DEVILS SAT IN THE CHAIRS!

A dismembered man appeared, bleeding gouts of blood on the sacrificial altar! Another devil above him brought down a knife! The victim let out a scream.

The devil in the easy chair turned to Flick and said, "Stay around. You're next!"

Flick tried to rush from the room. He hit Madison in the door and they both went down.

On hands and knees and then on foot they fled down the hall.

Finally they ran out of run and stopped with shuddering breath.

"I don't like this place," said Flick.

Madison bolstered his own nerve. "Look, Flick, we've got to find the crew. Let's try in here."

Flick nervously pushed his torch around this new room. It was obviously a rather posh salon. Various lounges sat in the expanse. The floor was bare and the walls were bare. It looked like somebody had half moved out.

There was a long buffet table and Flick opened a door of it, probably expecting vases or valuables. It was a panel instead.

"Don't touch the big one," cautioned Madison. "I don't know what will happen."

Flick sorted down a rank of buttons and pushed one. The salon lights came on.

Now that they could see it better, it was a very nice room, even though the walls and floor were bare.

There was a big set of glass doors at the end. Flick pushed another switch and it was as if floodlights had turned on in a lovely garden. A fountain was playing out there and birds could be heard to sing.

Emboldened, Flick touched another button.

Suddenly, the room was beautifully decorated!

There was a rug on the floor.

Vases with flowers appeared on small wall tables.

PAINTINGS APPEARED ON THE WALLS!

Hastily, Flick turned the switch off. Vases, flowers, rug and paintings vanished!

"OH, MY GODS!" cried Flick. "The objects of art we meant to rob are JUST ELECTRONIC ILLUSIONS!"

Madison suddenly understood. He had seen Lombar Hisst in his red uniform step in front of a thing the Master of Palace City had had placed before the building, and an apparently solid Lombar Hisst, two hundred feet tall, had appeared over the building blessing it.

General Loop was crazy as a coot on scenery with his officers and devils and all. But he was smart as a whip on theft and security.

THERE WAS NOTHING TO STEAL!

Tears were running down Flick's face. With leaden steps he dragged himself away. With a sad, sad voice he muttered, "There goes my dream," and fumbled off to the seventy-sixth floor, leaving it all to Madison to find the vanished crew.

It was a moment of agony and gloom.

Chapter 5

Madison had worked for hours rescuing the crew. Belts underneath the upper-hall floors had shunted them to a "prison" on the seventy-sixth floor and they had been waiting there in fear of being returned to the Domestic Confederacy Prison when Madison let them out.

An embarrassed electronics security man had explained that he also had been taken in, for he said the devices were not of a type in general circulation outside the security forces. He recovered a spare from an electronic parts storeroom and, after he had figured it out, showed them all it was just a chip about the size of a pen point which, put in the path of a microscopic projector, gave images in the air which could move and emit sound. The spare, fortunately, was not of any ghost but of a small boy taking a pee and the crew morale had been restored, even if the laughs were weak.

The scaler had gotten over his fright after a few convulsions, aware now that people were laughing at him and anxious to make amends.

General Loop, they all agreed, had been purloining government property and devices, and this made him a fellow criminal and so, somehow, made it all right. Whether he had done all this just to exercise a hobby or scare his fellow officers half to death was entirely beyond their interest. Madison had another theory—that manufacturers, knowing Loop was somewhat crazy, had installed the devices in the hope of getting a contract after showing what they could do. Madison had noticed different makers' names on the activating boxes; he didn't think any of this was in use or known to the government at all. He had not found a single Security Forces stamp on anything. If it were government property or even known to the government, it would have long since been taken out. But he didn't disagree with the crew; they needed all the solace they could get.

The crisis was over. The crew had slept. And Madison now had other things to do.

In a seventy-sixth floor briefing room which General Loop had probably used to address his own staff, Madison had assembled his gang here today for purposes of his own.

They looked much better now: the men had shaved and cut their hair, the women were coiffed and made up. They were gaunt but good food would handle that. The prison pallor still showed through but a few days under sunlamps would turn them a more natural color. The stink was gone!

The cooks were lounging in the doors, the rest sat on chairs and benches. And all eyes were on Madison as he stood upon the raised platform at the front of the large room.

"I have gathered you together this afternoon," said Madison, "in order to clarify for you why you are really here. I am certain some of you have probably wondered, and the very essence of a team is a common purpose.

"Now, I know some of you were curious as to what *PR man* really meant. It does *not* mean 'parole officer': I just told them that so I could spring you."

The crew sat up more alertly. It made them feel better to know that they were not in the hands of just another Apparatus officer but with one who now seemed

to be saying that he had other goals and might well be
a master criminal in his own right, only using the Apparatus for some crooked purpose of his own. His popular-
ity rose.

"The actual meaning of *PR*," continued Madison,
"is PUBLIC RELATIONS. That is the activity in which
you will now be engaged."

They nodded but now they looked puzzled. They
had never heard of this. The only relations they had
ever had with the public consisted of victimizing it.

"As this will be your work," said Madison, "I had
better explain in detail."

Madison stood up very straight. His face began to
glow. His own love of his subject took over. In a voice
more suited to a cathedral, he said, "PR is one of the
noblest pursuits of man!"

His audience was jolted. They stared at him wide-
eyed.

Madison was off. His voice contained the caress of
eulogy. "Public Relations is an art that FAR transcends
mere painting and crass poetry."

The audience gawped.

"It is," crooned Madison, "the magic of telling people what to think and bludgeons them to change their
minds."

A roustabout called out, "Now that's more like it.
Do we hit soft to stun or hard to kill?"

Madison smiled a beautiful smile. "You always hit
to kill."

The gang buzzed and nodded. "Got it," came from
many voices. Then someone in an aside to his neighbor
confided loudly, "That's what his Lieutenant Flick said
last night. He's a killer! One of the greatest murderers of
all time!"

Everyone began to applaud, even the cooks at the door. Then they stood and chanted, "The chief! The chief! The chief!" Madison, an expert at timing and stage presence, knew when speeches should end. He bowed.

The tumult had died down as the people were now departing.

Madison became aware of something. No Flick. He called out, "Where *is* Lieutenant Flick?"

The driver footwoman said, "He's in bed. He didn't even touch me. I can't do my job. I think he's down in the mouth. Even suicidal."

Madison, in alarm, immediately passed through the halls to the apartment which had been appropriated by Flick.

The man was lying with his face to the wall. He appeared to be completely caved in. Madison had to shake him by the shoulder to get any response.

"What's the matter?" said Madison.

"Life is over," muttered Flick.

"Why?" said Madison.

Flick moaned, "Don't ever rob a man of his dreams. It's death."

Madison looked down at him. The lethargy was pronounced. He knew he couldn't live with him in this condition. He thought fast.

"Don't you have any other dreams?" he said.

Flick groaned and then at length turned over on his back. "Just one, but it's impossible. I shouldn't even think of it."

"Tell me," said Madison.

"It's a dream I get and then always have to abandon. It's to meet Hightee Heller in person." Then he groaned, "But she has billions of fans. I couldn't even force my way through such a crowd. I haven't even ever been able to afford a ticket to her personal appearances. So forget I even mentioned it. No, life is over for poor Flick." And he turned back to the wall with an awful, shuddering sigh.

Madison went over to the window. The mammoth dome of Homeview was gleaming in the late day sun. Something clicked inside his head.

Lombar was trying to find Heller. Madison also had to know.

The orderly outline of a plan began to form on the glass before his eyes in Old Century 10-point type.

---

1. On some off chance, Hightee Heller might know where Heller-Wister is. If so, she might be tricked into telling Madison.

2. If she doesn't know, then she might have lines she can use—unwittingly, of course—to get somebody to tell her.

3. He would have to have an excuse to see her often so she could spill the information to him when she got it.

Then suddenly, the whole sheet jacked up and a banner, 22 point, all caps, seemed to flow across the glass:

BUILD THE IMAGE BEFORE YOU FIT HELLER TO IT!

"YOWEEE!" shouted Madison. He sprang into the air, he danced around the room. He knew EXACTLY how to go about it now!

"What the Hells is happening?" said Flick, afraid that Madison had gone crazy.

Madison came to the side of the bed. He put on his most sincere and earnest look. "Flick," he said, "if I introduce you to Hightee Heller in person, will you give up trying to pull off robberies?"

Flick stared at him. Then he saw from the sincere and earnest look that Madison wasn't joking. "I'd have to," said Flick. "If I met Hightee Heller in person, I couldn't pull off no more robberies. I'd be a changed man!"

"Good," said Madison. "It's a bargain, then. If I see that you meet her in person, the crimes we do from here on out are only the ones that I order. Agreed?"

Flick nodded numbly, not daring to hope.

"All right," said Madison. "Get up and get dressed. We've got work to do!"

Madison rushed out, ecstatic with his plan.

Oh, he was really on his way now! The smell of eventual victory was in the very air! He could REALLY get on with his job with Heller!

Chapter 6

The first thing Madison did was get from Flick the name of a certain type of crooked jeweler.

Flick and his footwoman got into the Model 99. Madison sprang into the back.

They flashed out of the hangar and sped across the sky, Slum City a vast smudge and sprawl in the distance, growing larger.

"I know this fellow personally," said Flick as he drove. "He's from Calabar like me. But we ain't never been in the same line really. He's rich, I'm poor. I robbed houses. He received the goods from thieves who looted tombs. The world thinks he's respectable and I know what they think of me: I got caught and wound up in the Apparatus. He married a jeweler's daughter and wound up owning a 'legitimate business.'"

Shortly Flick pointed out a square which looked to Madison like an island in the middle of a ghetto sea.

They landed and the Model 99 in all its glitter instantly attracted a swarm of tough-looking, hooting kids. Suddenly Madison was aware that this footwoman had other uses than being felt up. She was out of the car like a tiger. She had somehow gotten hold of a stinger. Her target was the biggest boy and he got the weapon in the teeth with a shower of sparks. He didn't get a chance to recoil more than a foot when the footwoman had him by the arm. In a sort of a whirling motion, she swung him—his feet left the ground—and like a scythe, used him to take out the whole front rank of hooters.

There was the departing rush of hasty feet. Into the dying echo of the screams, the footwoman thrust the stinger in the belt of her violet uniform and stepped to the door. She opened it with a bow. "Watch your step, sir. There's garbage."

If he hadn't seen the killer look when she sprang out of the airbus or heard the wild animal snarl of satisfaction when she used the stinger, he would have been completely taken in by the sweet and demure smile she now exhibited. She appeared to be the mildest and kindest person you would ever want to meet. Ah, he thought with pleasure, he had quite a crew! Totally deceptive!

Madison, immaculately attired, stepped around the garbage—which happened to be the unconscious body of the one she had used as a weapon—and, with Flick, made his way to the jewelry store.

And that is exactly what it seemed to be: a store that sold the cheap gewgaws displayed behind bulletproof, steel-barred windows.

An old man in a black cloth cap that had a light and an examination magnifier on it directed them through the back of the store and shortly they were in an opulent office quite at variance with the rest of the establishment.

A very greasy, overfed man came forward from an ivory table to greet them. His head was a squashed oval like Flick's: maybe the heavy gravity of Calabar did this to them!

"Flick, my cousin, I am so glad to see you are still out of jail. My, look at the violet uniform! Are you in the Palace Guards?"

"Cousin Baub," said Flick, "you got to meet my new chief, Madison. We're still in the Apparatus, but there's a difference."

"Well, Cousin Flick, I did hear the Apparatus had taken over the guarding of Palace City. But is your friend here safe?"

"He's a full-fledged criminal in disguise," said Flick. "I vouch for him."

"Well, all right. Sit down, my friends. But I must warn you that we're very too full stocked up, so if you've stolen something from the palaces, I can't give you much price."

"That's very good news," said Madison, and he took a seat. "You see, Baub, we are buyers, not sellers."

"Ho, ho, Cousin Flick. We HAVE moved up in the world!" said Baub.

"*Mister* Baub," said Madison, "I am sure that when you receive stolen gems, you recut them and remount them so they will not be quickly recognized."

"Yes, that's true. But good stones are of such size that their refraction indexes are known and we have to be very careful."

"*Mister* Baub," said Madison, "I know you are a man of discretion. I want an absolutely stunning stone in an absolutely stunning setting the like of which has never been seen before and WON'T be recognized."

"Aha!" said Baub. "You're talking about the 'Eye of the Goddess'!"

"If it has a name," said Madison, "it must have been known."

"Nope," said Baub. "It can't be known. Because I just this minute invented it."

Madison laughed with delight. Here was somebody he could do business with, almost in his own line.

"A few years ago," said Baub, "over on Calabar, where everything is very big, some thieves got into a very ancient, pre-Voltarian tomb. Up to that time the tomb had been unknown, but the thieves were not. Police were on their trail and caught them and the tomb contents were inventoried and added to the National Treasury. They had rounded up the thieves and had sent them en route to an interrogation center, but the air-coach crashed in an updraft that slammed it into a hundred-thousand-foot mountain range—things are big on Calabar—and that was that. One thief, however, right

at the tomb, got away. The police never knew he existed."
He looked at Flick. "That thief was me."

Baub sat back, nostalgia taking over. "Oh, them
were the days. I had a whole bag of stones. They had
never been recorded nor listed. One by one I spent them
and had myself a marvelous misspent youth." He sighed.
"But that was seventy years ago and youth has fled."

He got up and went into another room which seemed
to have a complex array of vaults and returned carrying
a small bag of silk which he laid on his desk, and resumed
his seat.

"In that haul, there was one stone I never could get
rid of. I never even dared show it. I couldn't say I had
found it in a stream bed because it was already cut. And
I warn you that the moment it appears on the market,
questions will be asked, because it is too remarkable. If
it fits your purposes, here it is."

He opened the bag by laying out its sides and there,
blazing on the silk, was a jewel the size of an egg. Madison moved closer. He could not credit what he saw. He
blinked.

"I don't know how the ancients did it," said Baub.
"And I don't know if it is natural or artificial. But you
are looking at an emerald totally enclosed in a diamond.
The emerald is top color and has only one flaw. The diamond is a perfect blue-white. And I can't sell you this
unless you can absolutely guarantee that where it came
from can be totally explained by you."

"I can guarantee that," said Madison. "How would
you mount it?"

"It's too big to be anything but a crown jewel or a
pendant. Following my suddenly invented name, I'd say
one might put it in an oval setting, the stone held in gold
like open eyelids with strings of little diamond chips to

look like eyelashes above and below, and we hang it on a broad chain of gold net. It's heavy, you know. Feel it."

Madison said, "Can you put it on the front of a net gold cap so it looks like it's in the middle of a forehead?"

"Wow," said Flick. "What a blazer that would be!"

"How long to make it up?" said Madison. "I want it fast."

"Oh, I could put the old man on it. Gold net is easy to weave. Two days."

"All right," said Madison. "Now what's the price?"

"Oh," said Baub, looking shifty, "it's a momento of my lost youth. Say a hundred thousand credits."

Madison translated it to dollars. There never had been a stone worth two million that he knew of. An actor named Richard Burton had given an actress named Liz Taylor one of the fanciest stones on Earth, and though he had only read about it, he thought it had only been about a million and a half. And he wasn't going to use any identoplate for this transaction. Too risky.

Flick, however, saved him. "Oh, Cousin Baub, I thought you were a friend. You know very well you've never been able to get rid of this, and here I bring you a customer and you drive him out of the shop with a club. You don't even have to give me the 10 percent I always get on purchases I make for him. We'll give you five thousand credits and that's the lot."

"I wouldn't dream of it," said Baub.

"Listen, Baub," said Flick. "I'm family. Remember?"

Baub sighed. "Not a credit less than thirty-five thousand! Plus the setting and cap."

"Thirty thousand *with* the setting and cap," said Flick.

"NO!" said Baub.

"Twenty thousand," said Flick.

"NO! NO!" cried Baub. "You just offered thirty thousand!"

"Bought," said Flick. "Give him the money, Chief."

Shortly afterwards, walking back to the airbus, still ably defended by the footwoman, Madison said, "I didn't know you got 10 percent of everything I spent!"

Flick said, "Runs me ragged going back to collect it. And I just saved you seventy thousand credits, so you see I'm worth it. But on this present deal, I'm not taking any commission. I won't do anything crooked on anything connected to Hightee Heller. She's sacred! 'Eye of the Goddess'—that suits her perfectly! Now I'm actually beginning to believe that I WILL get to meet her personally!"

Madison grinned as he got in. "The Eye of the Goddess" wasn't all he had planned for Hightee Heller.

Chapter 7

Two days later, Madison was on his way to see Hightee Heller. Flick had barbered and bathed himself almost down to the bone. He had polished the Model 99 until, another criminal had said, the angels on its four corners screamed. He had sternly left the footwoman home. One would have thought he was engaged in the greatest adventure of his life: he kept bubbling.

Madison hoped that he himself looked all right. He missed being in a neat Earth lounge suit, his fighting uniform. He had chosen a steel-gray business tunic and

pants, devoid of any ornament, but the very shimmer of
it said it cost a fortune. The sleeves, being a pointed
cuff, had worried him: they might brush things off
tables unexpectedly. Accordingly, he had practiced for
half an hour reaching for things. He had fluffed his hair,
had put just a touch of glitter in it and then brushed it
until it shone. He had practiced his most engaging and
ingenuous smile before a mirror for over an hour.

But that was not all the preparation he had done. He
had had the horror-story writer sweating for a whole day
and a night. One of the reporters had been expelled from
the Royal Academy of Art and could write a little poetry.

Madison's own musical background should have been
extensive but was not. His mother had planned, when he
was eight, that he should have a career as a concert pianist. He had been labored over by numerous teachers until
he was twelve, at which time the last one, like his prede-
cessors all had, found Madison playing ragtime when he
should have been memorizing a concerto of an austere
classic nature. The man had whipped him soundly. His
mother wouldn't stand for that, the man had been fired
out of hand and Madison had finished his musical career
with a sore bottom. He only hoped he could remember
enough not to make some awful, gauche slip. He would
be talking to a very accomplished musician. Details, in
such an extensive caper as this, were everything.

He had gotten his appointment very smoothly. A
house clerk had answered her viewer-phone at her home
in Pausch Hills. Madison had told him that he had a message from Hightee's brother, Jettero Heller.

The clerk had relayed the fact and a background
voice—Hightee's—had said, "Does he know where Jettero is? I'd surely love to find out."

Madison knew at once that Hightee did not know.

He went at once, smoothly, into the second phase of his plan to locate Heller-Wister for Lombar, after which he would get into his image-building.

"Tell your mistress I can't give her the message over the phone: her brother ordered me to give it personally. I am an Apparatus officer on detached duty to Homeview. My name is J. Walter Madison."

He promptly got his appointment for one o'clock, and here he was, flying in through a warm sun to land on the rooftop estate of Hightee Heller.

He was impressed! The estate looked like it comprised several acres that rested high in the air, crowning an elegant building. One could see for miles and miles from such an aerie; the view was not even blocked by neighboring buildings and looked down on other lovely estates. A place for the angels, even unto a wisp of wandering cloud! At least that was what Flick was crooning as he put the Model 99 down on the roof target. He was very disappointed to see a house clerk in black awaiting them instead of Hightee.

"The lady is expecting you," the clerk said. "She is in the summerhouse. I will escort you."

Madison sternly told Flick to stay by the car and followed the black-suited man down a curving path. The first thing that struck Madison was that the trees were full of songbirds trilling their hearts out in melodies and harmonies.

"However do you keep the birds in?" he asked the clerk.

At that moment two birds of gorgeous plumage swept down and inspected the briefcase Madison was carrying and then fluttered accusingly in front of his face.

"It's not a matter of keeping them IN," said the clerk. "It's a matter of never being able to drive them

away. They sometimes hear the music from the oratory
and they come for miles around to sing with Hightee.
And they always fly with her when she takes her walks."

What struck Madison was the total absence of
guards. This clerk didn't even have a telltale bulge in his
close-fitting black coat. They hadn't even asked for an
identoplate on landing, or now. He could be anybody,
even an assassin. Nobody had even asked to look in his
briefcase. Very, very lax. And it might be very useful.

He had to make sure. "Don't you have guards and
security and things?" he asked. "It makes me nervous
for her."

The clerk snorted. "Lady Hightee has fifteen billion
fans who would tear anyone to pieces if she was hurt.
And who would touch the sister of the hero of the Fleet,
Jettero Heller? Only a madman would so much as frown
at Lady Hightee, and it is very plain you are not one of
those."

So there was no security, Madison filed away.

They came to the summerhouse, a grill of golden lat-
tices through which the summer sun splashed in gentle
patterns.

She had been working at a table with a sheet of music, probably memorizing a lyric. She came forward to
the door, hand outstretched in welcome.

Madison flinched. He had never in his life seen such
a beautiful woman. She was wearing a casual artist's
smock of shimmering green. Her hair was the color of
Heller's but it was fluffed into a glowing halo. Her eyes
were an electric blue that made you feel very warm. The
presence of her was an aura that seemed to make the day
go brighter.

Madison came out of his shock, took the hand, bent
over it to kiss it but the touch of her on his palm almost

paralyzed him. Oh, yes, indeed, this was Hightee Heller. Even the three dimensions of Homeview screens couldn't begin to do her justice. For an instant he thought he was going to kneel despite himself.

Still bent over the golden fingernails, he summoned up his most engaging and ingenuous smile. He was very glad he had practiced it. The presence of this woman had almost knocked him flat and gawping. In fact, for the barest, fleeting instant, out of pure admiration for her, he had qualms at going forward with his plans. But he recovered quickly.

She was graciously waving him to a seat as she resumed her own swinging chair. As soon as she had sat down, Madison perched himself on the edge of the indicated armchair. He wished those patches of sunlight didn't make her glow. It made it difficult to proceed.

But Madison held on to his smile. "Forgive me for seeming so much at home, but Jettero has spoken of you to me so often, I feel that I know you."

She smiled. "Oh, Jettero and I have always been close. He is such a wonderful person."

"One of the finest fellows that ever lived," said Madison.

"Probably the finest and most honorable man alive," said Hightee.

"A prince among princes," said Madison. "I bless the day when he honored me with his friendship."

"You know him well, then?" said Hightee.

"Oh, intimately," said Madison. "It often makes me feel humble when he tells me how much he trusts me. How heartening it is, when all else is black, to know that one has such a dear friend as Jettero. I don't know what I would do without him."

"I have always felt," said Hightee, "how fortunate I was to have a brother like that."

"And such a future!" said Madison.

"There isn't a young officer in the Fleet that doesn't try to emulate him," said Hightee.

"Oh, he will rise to the top," said Madison. "Inevitable success."

"His superiors swear by him," said Hightee.

"I am sure he will achieve universal renown," said Madison. "In fact, he deserves everything that can be done for him."

"Indeed he does," said Hightee. "Ever since I was a little girl, I've felt more confident in life knowing he was there. I've always felt I was one of the luckiest girls alive to be his sister."

"And I have felt I was one of the luckiest fellows alive to be his friend," said Madison.

"You really have a message from him?" said Hightee, eagerly.

"It's more interesting than just that," said Madison. "In fact, he made me swear on my honor that I would not fail to see you personally and give you this present from him."

He opened up his briefcase and removed a large jewelry box and said, "From your brother with his love." And he handed it to her with a bow.

She opened it. The sunlight hit it and it hit back, breaking the light into a thousand colored pieces. Sitting in its new setting, nestled into the gold net cap, the jewel quite took her breath away. She had never seen anything like it: an emerald inside a perfect diamond.

She put it on and the jewel in the center of her forehead drove the sunlight frantic in the summerhouse. She took up a small mirror and looked. Then she took it off and gazed at it. When the pulse in her lovely throat slowed down, she gazed at Madison. "Where could he have possibly acquired it? It must have cost ten years' pay!"

"Oh, he didn't buy it," said Madison. "It is quite a story. It's called the 'Eye of the Goddess'. Jettero is so brave and so commanding that it was presented to him by the Aga Khan when Jettero saved the life of his son."

"Oh!" said Hightee. "Tell me!"

"Well, Jettero made so little of it that he did not give me many details. He never brags."

"How like him," said Hightee.

"But it was headlines in all the newssheets. The son of the Aga Khan was on a *tiger* hunt—that is a very dangerous beast—and Jettero happened to be flying by and pulled the Aga Khan's son right out of the jaws of the tiger, barehanded."

"Oh! How dangerous!"

"Well, Jettero is nothing if not the most courageous fellow alive. But you know, he is so modest, I'll wager when you see him he won't even mention the exploit. Probably just laugh and say it never happened."

"That's my brother. Go on."

"He's so unwilling to take well-earned praise," continued Madison. "And when the Aga Khan presented him in gratitude with this family heirloom, do you know that Jettero actually blushed? I know. I was right there and saw him myself. He slid it into his pocket and he whispered to me, 'The only reason I'm not giving this back is because I think Hightee would like it.' "

"Oh, how sweet."

"But that's Jettero," said Madison. "He also said, when he made me promise to give it to you directly when I arrived on Voltar, 'Tell her I won it shooting dice and say it's a bauble she needn't even thank me for.' But I could never bring myself to lie to you. So I have told you the truth. Don't mention it to him that I did. He'd half kill me!"

"But good Heavens, I have to thank him."

"Oh, I thought of that. Wear it on your next Home-view appearance and, without saying how he got it, since that would embarrass him and reveal I had told you the truth, casually mention that the jewel is a gift from your brother Jettero and dedicate your next song to him and all his brother officers of the Fleet. And then sing some song about far places and loved ones at home and then say you don't know where your brother is and long to hear from him to thank him for the gift. And his brother officers, hearing it, wanting to help you thank him, would tell you where he is now. I'm sure the resulting fan mail would come in in a flood. Any of your fans, let alone his brother officers, would be eager to relieve your anxiety about where your brother is."

"Oh, it's a lovely idea. But you just saw him. Don't you know where he is?"

"Alas," said Madison, shaking his head sadly, "the two of us had a little farewell party for each other. We were going different ways. And it was only after his ship took off that I suddenly realized he had not told me where he was going. But it's not important that I know. It is only important that any anxiety you have be relieved. So I have written this little card for you that you can use for your lines and you can locate him and send your thanks to him that way."

She read the card and the lines. "Why, this is sort of sweet."

"And you could let me know as well," said Madison.

"I worry about him. He is too brave. And also, of course, I miss him."

"Well, I certainly do thank you," said Hightee, rising, "for bringing his gift."

Madison rose, too, but he said, "Oh, that isn't all that I have brought."

PART
SEVENTY-SIX

Chapter 1

Hightee Heller looked at Madison with a bit of wonder. "You mean, after that beautiful gift you brought me from Jettero, you have something *else?* My, you *are* a man of surprises. But come, let us stroll a bit: I've been sitting all morning."

J. Walter Madison hastily grabbed his briefcase and followed her out of the summerhouse. They were instantly accompanied by songbirds.

The acres of the rooftop estate were artfully landscaped with curving paths and pools and waterfalls and trees so that every few yards, on any path one took, one was looking at a new presentation.

Sauntering along, hands thrust into her artist's smock pockets, Hightee looked sideways at him. "Now what is this something else?"

"Your new musical!" said Madison. "I've brought it!"

"That's unusual," said Hightee. "Normally I originate them and my own staff develops them."

Madison hadn't known that: on Earth artists didn't write them; they just sang and acted in them. But he plunged ahead. "Well, the order to do it comes from Lord Snor himself. He's a great admirer of yours, as they all are. When he heard one of the songs from it, he said, 'THAT'S HIGHTEE!'"

"He did? That's funny. He's as deaf as a rock."

"To everything but a bone-phone," said Madison hastily. "They put bones into the probe, I mean prones into the bobe. . . ."

Hightee laughed. Then she said, "I'm sorry I got you all flustered. Maybe Lord Snor did wake up and listen to what goes on on Homeview. Stranger things have happened."

Madison was floundering in his briefcase. The impact of Hightee Heller was a bit much for him. But he was a veteran and he got himself under control. "Look, I better play you one of the songs from it. Where can I find a *piano?*"

"A what?"

"A keyboard. I'm not any pro but I tinkle away."

Hightee was walking away from him. He quickly followed. Then he noticed that some of the vine-covered walls they had been passing were actually the sides of structures. She opened something that looked like a garden gate and Madison, coming up behind her, found himself looking into what must be a musical-equipment repair shop.

A middle-aged man was standing over a bench which was littered with electronic components and shells of what might be instruments. He looked up, saw Hightee, smiled and laid down a tool.

"Jarp," said Hightee, "have you ever heard of an instrument called a *piano?*"

"No," said Jarp. "What's it look like?"

"Teeth," said Madison. "It has lots of keys like ivory teeth."

Jarp turned to Hightee. "He's talking about some primitive mouth instrument."

"No, no," said Madison. "It's quite sophisticated.

You play it by hitting the keys with both hands in chords. You mean you don't have a keyboard? Oh, dear!"

"What scale is it?" said Jarp.

"Eight-note major, thirteen-note chromatic."

"Do you know the notes?"

When Madison nodded, Jarp dug around and found the remains of a chorder-beat that operated on finger proximity. Madison, after a couple of sour tries, managed to get it to hum the right numbers of vibrations. Jarp turned on a recorder and Madison, moving his finger closer and closer and holding it each time he had the right note, ran the chromatic scale.

"All those notes on one instrument?" said Hightee.

"Yes," said Madison. "Eighty-eight total."

"I know," said Jarp. "He's talking about a chorder-bar." He turned to Madison. "When you put a finger down on a long bar, it sounds a note. When you put it down softly you get low volume; when you put it down hard you get high volume. But you were saying something about a keyboard or keys. What's it look like?"

Madison found some paper, but he was making such a bad job of it, Jarp took it away from him and with a long sheet of paper, using Madison's hand span for an octave, shortly had a piano keyboard drawn. Jarp looked at it and scratched his head. "Never saw anything like it. It must work mechanically: you strike a key, you say, and it takes a hammer and hits a string. How clumsy! I guess it must be a blood brother to one of those stick harps they once had in the back country of Mistin. Used to jump around naked beating them before they did their spring mating."

"Well, see what you can do," said Hightee, "and bring it to the practice room when you finish." Madison followed her out. They were shortly on a path that wound round a waterfall, the birds flying escort. "Now what's the story of this musical?" said Hightee. "The book. I hope it isn't about spring mating."

Madison laughed easily and donned his most engaging smile. "No, hardly. It's really a great vehicle that will show your lovely voice off as never before. You see, there's this mythical planet named Terra. The whole story is a fantasy, you see."

"Oh, I like fantasy. *Prince Caucalsia* made a great hit. But go on."

Madison wished he could just give her the treatment. But it was in his briefcase and she was using the time to get some exercise in. He and the horror-writer had sweat their brains out on it but he hadn't thought he would have to give it verbally. He hoped he had it straight.

"Well," said Madison, "this fantasy planet Terra is ruled by a huge monster in a red suit with horns and a tail."

"You're describing a Manco Devil."

"Good," said Madison, who had never heard of one. "I'm glad you've got that straight. So this Manco Devil rules all the people. And they haven't got any money and they are starving. Now, in the opening scene we show the people all huddled and starving and praying and the Devil comes in and kicks them around."

"How awful!"

"But wait," said Madison. "The Devil has a huge court of Devils and one of these has lost his Devil child and an old nurse has put a HUMAN child in its place to fool the Devil and the Devil raises this human child, thinking it is his own.

"So the sight we saw in the first scene—the main Devil kicking the people around—is witnessed by this human child, who is now a young man, and he decides it's bad."

"Good for him," said Hightee.

"But the Devils in the court all think this son is one of them. They think he's a reliable officer of good repute. But really, he's planning to help the people. So, whenever he can get away, he puts on a mask and starts robbing *trains*."

"*Trains?*" said Hightee. "What's a *train?*"

Madison said, "This is a fantasy."

"Oh."

"Now, the Devils all ship their valuables and money on these *trains*."

"Ah, a *train* is a space-liner between planets," said Hightee.

"Well, kind of," said Madison. "And the hero robs them."

"You mean the fellow goes CRIMINAL?"

"Well, he HAS to," said Madison.

"Oh, I don't think that would go down well. People despise criminals."

Madison said, "Well, this isn't really criminal. It's in a good cause. He robs the trains and he gives the money away to the poor and they DON'T STARVE!"

"Listen," said Hightee. "It's the people who raise the food. If they didn't raise the food, they couldn't buy anything with the money the hero gives them."

"Oh, the Devils grab the food and the people have to bribe them to get it back. So suddenly the Devils find out WHO the bandit is. A Devil's own son! So they declare him an OUTLAW! And there's a lot of fighting and the Outlaw escapes."

"Hurray!" said Hightee.

"But the Devils finally catch him," said Madison,

"and hang him. Hang him up high and very dead. The people all cry——"

"Wait a minute," said Hightee. "I don't see any part in this for me. There's no girl."

"Well, I was coming to that. You're the hero's sister."

"Then I must be a Devil, as he was a stolen child."

"No, no. The Devil stole a brother and SISTER! I forgot to mention it. And in the musical, the sister warns and saves the hero time and again. And SHE'S the one who sings all the songs. The Outlaw just runs around shooting people, and the sister, in the songs, describes what he is doing. And all the people begin singing her songs."

"So there're a lot of choruses."

"Exactly!" said Madison. "Now the last scene when they hang him is the great one. All the people are there watching him choke out his life on the scaffold——"

"How grisly!"

"And the sister comes in and sings a great song, a kind of a dirge. And then the Devils realize that *she* was the one who tipped him off all the time and they hang her on the spot!"

"No!"

"Yes. Right alongside her brother on a second scaffold. And then two graves open up and huge skeletal hands come out of them and grab the bodies off the scaffolds. And then the people all rise up and sing the song she had been singing and remember the Outlaw forever!"

Hightee Heller was staring at him, wide-eyed.

Madison held his breath. Would she fall for it?

A speaker underneath a flowering tree opened up and interrupted them. "Hightee, the instrument is ready."

Chapter 2

Madison, as he followed her into the music practice room, knew he had better be awfully lucky or awfully good or both.

The place was a domed room with no flat surfaces to reflect sound. It was decorated with huge enlargements of Voltarian single notes in pastel blue that hung in various places as baffles to further break up the sound. The interior of the dome was a pastel yellow. Jarp was hanging something from wires in the middle of the room. It was the drawn piano keyboard but the keys were vertical and it was raised five feet above the floor.

"No," said Madison. "You sit down to it."

"No musician ever sits down," said Jarp. "It must be awfully lazy music."

"Give him what he wants," said Hightee. "I can't see for the life of me how you play such a thing. Keys?"

At Madison's direction, Jarp had a band helper get a stool and then they supported the keyboard horizontal and firmed it in place.

Madison, on his part, couldn't possibly see how it would work. The keys, white and black, were simply drawn on paper. They had no action up or down at all.

He summoned up his nerve. It was all or nothing. He struck one of the painted, motionless keys with one finger and he got a sort of a howl.

"Oh, no," he said. "A *piano* doesn't sound like that. It vibrates more like a *harp*."

"Let's see if we've got the notes right, first," said Jarp.

Madison limbered up his fingers, wishing he had at least tried to entertain people since he was twelve. He ran the whole scale from bottom to the top. Yes, the notes were all on pitch. But no piano ever HOWLED!

"The tones are wrong," said Madison. "A *piano* note is bright and bubbling."

"My word," said Jarp. "Well, here's the adjustment tool and that's the panel over on the right end. The first slot is 'attack,' the second is 'decay.' The next one is 'overtones' and the bottom one is 'percussion.' See what you can do."

Striking one picture of a key with one finger, Madison fiddled with the controls. He began to perspire. He got rid of the howls and got some sharp striking notes but it still didn't sound like a piano. Far too dead now.

"What's this second box under the top one?" said Madison.

"Well, that thing I pasted the picture on is a chorderbar. I moved the contact points under it so they match the pictures that you drew, only I can't figure why anybody would want pictures to play an instrument. You simply press the right spots hard or soft. And you don't want that second box. That's drums, cymbals and bells."

"Ah!" said Madison and promptly went to work with his tool on the second box. He found another slot Jarp hadn't mentioned: it was "resonance."

Striking one note repeatedly, he thought he finally had it right.

He wiped off his hands, flexed his fingers, and without daring to hope, experimentally struck a chord. It felt so weird not to have anything move.

Everything, he felt, depended upon this now.

He took a deep breath and began to play "Beale Street Blues."

He got very interested. This thing was putting out sound like the most jangly honky-tonk piano he had ever heard.

He was making an AWFUL lot of flubs and sour chords.

Too much depended on this. He was rattled. He stopped playing and wiped off his hands again. He shook his fingers in the air. What piece had he been enamored with and had played a lot? Then he remembered. It was Scott Joplin's music they had used in the movie *The Sting*. It seemed very appropriate.

He started playing. This instrument really did have a wide dynamic range; the soft was soft and the loud was LOUD! He started to give it the heavy downbeat of ragtime.

He glanced sideways at his audience of two. He could tell nothing from their faces.

He thought he had the instrument now. He reached over to his briefcase and whipped out a sheet. "Now this," he said, "is one of the lyrics of the musical." Nothing had been easier than to come up with music, for he could pirate the entire library of Earth ragtime and blues and simply get words written to it. He had lifted the tune "The Trickster Rag" from a Broadway musical comedy, *The Con Man*. The ex-Royal Academy reporter had put new words to it.

"If you would like," said Madison, "I will play the melody through and then you can sing it. It's called 'The Outlaw.'"

Hightee took it, looked at it. Madison went through the tune and then Hightee began to sing:

We hunt him here,
We hunt him there,
For he is hiding everywhere:
    The Outlaw!
In your favorite boudoir,
If you hear a randy snore,
Don't look further anymore:
    The Outlaw!
If you step into a bank
And see the muzzle of a tank,
Don't ask who you have to thank:
    The Outlaw!
If there is a town to steal,
If the jewels are very real,
If the beauty has appeal:
    The Outlaw!
He'll take anything you've got,
Your money, girls, the whole lot,
And leave you tied up in a knot:
    The Outlaw!
He will use the smartest lure
To take riches from a boor
And give it to the very poor:
    The Outlaw!
So for this man, strike up the band,
And give to him a helping hand,
For he will give us the whole land:
    THE OUTLAW!

Her brilliant voice died away.

"Of course," said Madison, "when you sing it in the play, you will be wearing black shorts and boots and a wide-rimmed black hat and you will have a gun on each hip and then draw and hold up the audience at the end of the song. And then the Outlaw himself rushes amongst them, robs them and runs off to give it to the poor. Terrific theater!"

A man who must be her bandleader had drifted in.

"That's an amazing downbeat," said Hightee. "What do you think of it, Tink?"

"Primitive," said Tink. "It probably came from the backwoods of some planet like Flisten and then got refined a bit. Drums. You know, comes from beating sticks on logs. And the downbeat is probably some kind of a charge motion at a wild animal. Hunter enactment dances. You know, chug chug CHUG, chug chug CHUG."

"You are absolutely right," said Madison. "Except it comes from the blacks of Africa and it got to New Orleans and caught on all over the place. It's called jazz."

"You sure got that chorder-bar sounding crazy," said Tink. "Why didn't you tune it up for him, Jarp?"

"*He* tuned it," said Jarp defensively.

"It's tuned to represent a *honky-tonk piano*," said Madison.

"Why do you need the pictures drawn on it?" said Tink.

"Listen," said Hightee, glancing at her locket watch, "I've got to run. I have a show to do this afternoon. I'll walk you to your car, Madison. Somebody tell my maid to bring me a jacket and tell my driver to run out an airbus."

Madison walked with her out of the music practice room. He had no clue as to whether he had won or lost. An awful lot depended on getting this image built so he could fit Heller to it.

Hightee seemed to be a bit thoughtful. They came

to the landing target. She stopped suddenly, "A MODEL 99! Good Heavens! I didn't think they ever would sell one!"

Madison had forgotten all about Flick. Suddenly he decided he could at least use this meeting to prevent further robberies. He said, "My driver will be delighted to show it to you."

Flick, scarlet-faced, trying to go down on his knees but too frozen to even make them bend, just stood there.

Madison said, "Flick is trying to ask you if you'd honor him by letting him drive you to the studio."

"That would be an adventure. I've heard these ride like a cloud." Her maid was hurrying up with her things and she turned to her. "Send Tink and the others in my car. I'm going to take a ride in this Model 99."

Flick managed to get himself unglued enough to open the door for her. When she and Madison were in, Flick, beet-red and gasping, slid under the controls.

They flew to Joy City and Flick managed it without ever taking his eyes off the mirrors which showed him Hightee in the rear seat.

They landed on a target marked *Hightee* which jutted out of the huge dome. Attendants rushed forward. One yelled back over his shoulder, "Hey! Here's Hightee in a Model 99!"

Flick had a sudden, obscured fight with the attendants and opened the door himself. Although he seemed to be having great trouble breathing, he stood there, straight as a rod, waiting to help her out and bow.

But Hightee did not get out. She turned to Madison. "You know, Madison, you're a nice fellow. But any friend of Jettero's would be. I'm absolutely bowled over by that—what's its name? Piano beat? You get the writer to do the rest of the book and I'll do the show."

When she had disappeared inside the dome, Flick said, "You're an absolute wonder, Chief. I actually drove her in the car! I'm a totally changed and reformed man!"

Madison didn't even hear him. As they took off, he was grinning from ear to ear.

He had a stage image being manufactured by the most popular star on Voltar, the guy's own sister! And he would soon, with other media, fit Heller to it.

He would soon put an end to this mediocre hero worship Heller now experienced and push Heller's name to the heights of true immortality.

And he began to hug himself. He had a bonus! When the musical had been aired and when she had found Heller for him, he would have another headline. It would run:

HELLER BURNS TEMPLE
KILLS THOUSANDS
OF PRIESTS

ROBS SACRED IDOL
OF PRICELESS EYE
TO GIVE PRESENT
TO HIS SISTER

Sure-fire! She would even have shown the evidence on Homeview. He could use the story on an off day when he didn't have more exciting news to print about Heller.

He was REALLY making progress now!

Chapter 3

They were nearly home when Flick turned around. "Chief, I just thought of something. When you were busy with Hightee Heller, you got a viewer-phone call from Queen Teenie."

Madison was jolted out of his euphoria. All his influence rested on Teenie Whopper, who was busily misrepresenting herself as royalty and holding her position through making page boys into catamites. It was, however, to Madison, the equivalent of a Royal command.

"Go up and hover!" he commanded nervously. "If she gave you a connection, call it back at once!" He was very jittery: apparently, due to time lag, it was difficult to call from Palace City. Was Teenie in town?

A piece of upholstery unfolded and a viewer-phone was staring him in the face.

Teenie's face appeared. She looked provoked. "I've been waiting out here in the desert beside this God (bleeped) message center for an hour! It's going to ruin my complexion!"

"Oh, I'm sorry!" said Madison.

"Why didn't you call back?" she snarled.

"Oh, I've been meaning to call you. But I got tied up."

"Tied up with Hightee Heller! You owe me a progress report on Gris!"

"Well, actually," said Madison, "I've been working up to that."

"Listen, Madison. This 'all promise and no delivery' is just the way PRs work. I know! You get busy, you lunkhead. I'll come back to this message center at sunset and if you don't have something to report on Gris by then, I'll have your cotton-picking head!" She hung up violently.

Women! Oh, his mother had taught him well. They were *trouble!*

He thought fast. He glanced at his Omega watch and saw that he only had about two hours left of the day. He thought faster. Suddenly, he said, "Fly me to Government City, Royal Courts and Prison!"

"What the blazes? Chief, are you all right? Did Hightee run you out of your head?"

"It's another woman. An almost-woman."

"Look, Chief, we were just lucky getting in and out of the Domestic Confederacy Prison. You get near a Royal Prison and that's that!"

"Fly!" said Madison.

They flashed above the traffic lanes and lanced along toward Government City.

Madison soon saw the forbidding structure. It was perched upon a craggy hill, a fortress disdainful and aloof from the mundane matters of the worlds.

Flick didn't land in any courtyard: that was forbidden to anyone except the Emperor. Instead he landed on the sloping road outside its gates. He wouldn't move any nearer than a steep one hundred yards.

"Good-bye, Chief," said Flick. "It was great while it lasted."

"Shut up," said Madison. He got out and toiled up the pavement. It was heavy going for him, due to the increased gravity.

Above him loomed the towering pillars of the outer

gate. As it was still daylight, guards were standing there, stiff as statues, on the other side of the heavy grill.

"I want to see somebody," said Madison to the nearest guard.

The man just kept on standing there. Madison was not as much as a fly.

Madison got out his identoplate and showed it. The guard didn't even look at it.

An officer was coming up, electric saber clanking. "What's this unseemly disturbance out here?"

"It's no disturbance," said Madison. "I've got to see somebody in here."

"Well, that's informative," said the officer. "All it lacks is his name, your business and what plot you are involved in to subvert the machinery of state. Be off."

"Look," pleaded Madison, "this is a matter of life and death."

"There's plenty of both in here," said the officer. "They're doing life, most of them, and we have assorted brands of death. Now get out of here!"

"Please, please," said Madison. "It's my life I'm talking about."

"Talk away," said the officer. "In living memory, no one has had the nerve to walk up this road to this gate and ask to get in...."

The statue guard said, without moving his mouth, "Correction, sir. Gris did."

"Gris!" said Madison. "That's it. I am his dearest friend. I must see him!"

The officer bent his head way forward and looked at Madison through the bars. He suddenly walked off and Madison fidgeted nervously. He could see the officer talking into a courtyard call box.

The officer came back and gave a signal to open the

gates wide enough for Madison to slip through. Then he gave another signal. The gates clanged shut and two guards ceased to be statues and abruptly took Madison by the arms, one on each side, and marched him forward saying, "Hup! Hup! Hup!" the same way Madison had heard his criminals chant. Was he under arrest?

They followed the officer into the main entrance and through the vast echoey halls. The officer opened a door and they were in a courtroom. They walked Madison straight across it and stopped him in front of a door.

The officer frisked him, appropriated his identoplate and went through the door. He came back and held it open.

The two guards catapulted Madison into a room. It was a stone-walled chamber but it had a rich rug on the floor. A huge block of stone, like a desk, had another rich hanging thrown over it. An old man, dressed in black, was in a chair behind the desk staring out the window.

The man swivelled the chair around. He picked up Madison's identoplate and looked at it. He fixed Madison with a wintry eye.

"So you're a friend of Soltan Gris. Well, well. I am Lord Turn. You can speak freely here."

Madison took it that they must be alone but he heard a clank behind him. The officer was standing against the far wall, keeping an eye on him.

"I just wanted to make sure he was all right," said Madison, lamely. "I want to see him."

"Do you have a Royal order?"

"No," said Madison.

"Then how could you possibly expect to be able to see a prisoner here?"

"I am very close to Lombar Hisst, Spokesman to His Majesty."

"Hmm," said Lord Turn. "Tell me . . . Madison? Do you know anything of the crimes of Gris?"

"Well, sir, I did not come here to testify. He may——"

"No, no. This is not a court you're standing in. You couldn't testify anyway unless a court was in session. Let me put this another way. Do you know Royal Officer Jettero Heller?"

"Well, yes, Your Honor——"

"Your Lordship," corrected the officer fifty feet away.

". . . Your Lordship," said Madison. "I do know Jettero Heller."

"Do you know where he is?"

"Well, no, Your Hon—Your Lordship."

"Blast!" said Lord Turn.

"I know there's a general warrant out for him," said Madison, "and I would be happy to——"

"General warrant, piffle," said Lord Turn. "I am holding his prisoner here. And I am quite sure that Jettero has a very good reason to put this Soltan Gris in Royal custody. But I DO wish the lad had given me a note or something to say what Gris has DONE!"

The conversation had gone all sixes and sevens for Madison. He realized he could not now say that Gris was a criminal to end all criminals, as he had already said he was his friend, thinking they would let him have visitors. Maybe they could get him for contempt or lying to a judge. The cold chill of this stately place was gnawing into him.

"I'm looking everywhere for Heller myself!" he said in a desperate effort to appear helpful.

"And you haven't found him?"

"No, Your Lordship, but I have lines out."

Lord Turn looked at him and then barked a short,

dry laugh. He punched a couple of buttons on his desk and a court clerk appeared first, being just next door.

Lord Turn said, "This is a man named Madison. I see what this is all about now. It's just another crude attempt by Lombar Hisst to bypass all normal procedures. For some reason, Hisst does not want to produce a Royal warrant or even a Royal pass. He's sent another man in here to see Gris." He turned to the guard officer. "Did you find any poison on this Madison here?"

"No, Your Lordship."

"Oh, heavens," said Madison, "I wasn't sent here by Hisst!"

"You just said you were," said Turn.

"I just wanted to make sure my friend Gris was all right!" wailed Madison.

A warder had come in in response to Turn's second buzz. He rattled his opening plates.

"Is the prisoner Gris all right?" said Lord Turn to him.

"Chipper as a songbird, Your Lordship. Just sitting there all day and half the night dictating his confession. He's on his third roll of vocoscriber paper. Singing like a songbird, too, Your Lordship."

"Well, maybe someday we'll know what this is all about," said Turn. "That's all, Warder. Now, Clerk, look at this identoplate. Stamp it on something. And leave an order at the gate that this Madison is to be let in if he ever finds where that dear boy Jettero has gotten to."

Mistaking this for kindness, Madison said, "Could I see Gris for just a moment?"

"And," said Lord Turn to his clerk, "issue another order for Gris not to be permitted to stand near windows. I think Hisst is trying to assassinate him." He turned to Madison. "Now, as for you, if I find out that

you have found out where Jettero Heller is and have
NOT told me, I will have you picked up on a judge's
order and thrown into a detention cell until you tell me
why you withheld the information." He turned to the
guard officer. "Throw him out!"

Chapter 4

Madison picked himself up off the pavement, wishing the guards had not taken the order so literally.

Flick kept out of sight until he was sure the gate was
closed and then he ran out and, accompanying the limp-
ing Madison, tried to brush him off.

"I told you not to go near that place," said Flick.

Madison didn't like this decline of image. "I
shouldn't have gone for the guard's saber. I should
have aimed for his windpipe."

"Comets! Well, at least they threw you out instead of
in. Even His Majesty is careful how he orders that lot
around."

As Madison climbed into the airbus he noticed the
sun was almost set. He had Flick go up a few thousand
feet. He thought hard for a few moments and then suddenly a plan came to him.

He straightened up his clothes, put on a reassuring
face and called Teenie.

She answered instantly. "That's better!" she said.
"I'm sure," and there was a threatening edge in her
voice, "that you have good news. Did you see the
(bleepard)?"

"Oh, yes," said Madison. "And Teenie—I mean, Your Majesty—you would be absolutely boiled over. I spoke of you and he gave the most insulting laugh I have ever heard."

"WHAT?"

"And he leaned back, idly eating grapes—he's getting fat as a pig—and he said, 'Madison, when you see her, give her my best: up her (bleep)!'"

"Oh, the (bleepard)."

"Yes, I thought so, too. They've got him writing his memoirs and he showed me some of them, what he thought were funny passages about you. He absolutely rolled on the floor with laughter over his own jokes! Oh, I could have killed him, but the warders were right there and they'd taken away my knife. Such a crass exhibition of unfeeling callousness, I have never before witnessed in my life."

She had gone white as a sheet.

"He's bragging," continued Madison, "of how he led you on just for the pleasure of casting you aside."

She was grinding her teeth. She suddenly snapped, "That settles it!"

Madison went into sudden alarm. He had overshot his mark. He had not intended for her to do anything. His plan was very simple: he would simply begin to try Gris in the press and push it to such a public pitch that the Emperor would have no choice but to issue a Royal order for a trial. Then, under that guise, he would get Gris to start testifying all sorts of accusations against Heller and he could make these into headlines that would shake the universe.

It was a very good plan. Just plain straight PR, Earth style, done all the time. But it required preparation and work and time. It didn't need any sudden interventions.

Teenie had not gone on speaking. Madison said,
"What settles what?"

"They're not even going to try him, are they?"

"Well, they will if I work on it hard enough."

"Yah? Well, Madison, you be out here at dawn tomorrow. I see back of you on this viewer-phone, you've
got a new car. Fuel it up. We're going to take a trip."

Before he could say a word, she had hung up. It left
him in quite a quandary.

That was the trouble with amateurs. They got ideas.
And ideas from an amateur PR were mostly useless and
ideas from Teenie might be very deadly.

He very well recalled the chaos Gris caused. Everything had been running along well until Gris tried to
muscle in on the PR business. Amateurs just didn't
understand the smooth nuances of it.

Madison scanned over his plan again. It was quite
standard and flawless. Create a public storm around
Gris, using the media, and then get the trial itself to
create a public storm around Heller. And even if His
Majesty, for some reason, illness or otherwise, didn't
stamp an order for the trial, public pressure would make
it vital that Lord Turn change his mind. It would work.

What in Heaven's name was Teenie planning? It
could well wreck everything! He had only intended to
keep her interested! Not throw her into a stampede of
senseless activity!

Oh, he mustn't let this gorgeous victory elude him
just when it was beckoning.

He thought of the sad plight of Heller, shivering
unknown in some lonely hideout, waiting for Madison
to rescue him for posterity. What a waste of material!

Knowing how to handle Gris and Heller in PR
terms was easy. Handling an almost-woman like Teenie

might be quite something else! What a potential obstruction!

"Eighteen point," he said, "quote Madison on Edge of Cliff."

"What?" said Flick.

"Go home," said Madison. "We need rest. Tomorrow is going to be an awful day."

At that very second, but more than twenty-two light-years away, the object of Madison's concern, Jettero Heller, was not shivering in any dark cave. He was riding down Fifth Avenue, New York City, Earth, deafened by the roar of the ticker-tape parade that was celebrating the investiture of new top officials for New York, but which was being led by Babe after her assumption of the title *Capa di Tutti Capi* and whom people were now starting to call "Queen Babe." Heller, resplendent in U.S. Army full dress, on the seat beside her, was smiling into the newsreel and TV cameras, totally oblivious of the storm that threatened his whole future on Voltar and his good name and the future existence of Earth as well. The Countess Krak, on the other side, wasn't smiling. She had a premonition that was giving her nightmares.

Chapter 5

Madison, as ordered—what else could he do?—was before the entrance of Teenie's palace at the crack of dawn. His fingernails were not in very good shape: he had been chewing them all night.

A guard captain came out, saw Madison and promptly went back in. When he came out a second time, he was buckling an electric saber around his silver tunic and he was followed by two sergeants with electric battle-axes. They took positions beside the airbus door, waiting for Queen Teenie to emerge.

Madison was in no mental state for any kind of a wait. The morning had already started badly enough. Flick, at the townhouse, when he got into the car, was seen to have an eye that was rapidly turning black. His footwoman had gotten in, disdainfully aloof, and then during flight had elaborately ignored Flick.

From various veiled remarks, Madison had gathered that Flick had been incautiously raving about Hightee Heller and both his bedroom girl and his footwoman had cleaned up on him.

Women! thought Madison. They were always trouble.

And here came more trouble: Teenie, in a suit that was a shimmering jet black, came out the door, drawing on a pair of long, red gloves. She was wearing her crown pulled forward on her forehead and her ponytail was swishing out behind like the tail of an angry cat.

She didn't comment on the car. She simply got in and took the best seat.

The guard captain got in and then both sergeants.

"Where in hell do you think you're going?" Teenie said to the guard captain.

"We're not going to trust you with that man," the guard captain said, pointing at Madison.

"You got good sense," said Teenie. "He's a PR and they don't deliver, never."

At that moment the major-domo, very portly, came

running down the stairs, clutching rolls of scrolls and trying at the same time to get into his ceremonial robe. He sprang into the airbus.

It did not leave much room for Madison and he had to sit on a ledge across from Teenie.

"Where are we going?" said Madison.

The major-domo ignored him and, leaning forward, passed a slip of paper to Flick. The driver looked at it, glanced back to see if the doors were closed and then took off.

Thinking that they were going into Government City or some such place, Madison was very alarmed when, having emerged from the gate and gone through the nausea that always resulted from the violent time shift, Flick headed the airbus west of south.

As they built altitude, the desert wind devils dwindling in size, Madison tried to lean forward and see the map on Flick's screen. It looked blank!

The alarm on Madison's face must have been very pronounced. Teenie scowled at him and said, "Take it easy, buster. You've got a long ride. Three hours at the very least."

Madison reached for a music panel and turned it on, hoping that it would soothe the savage womanly breast. Then maybe she would tell him what this was all about.

Teenie reached over right after him and turned it off. "I don't want anything spoiling my concentration. I got a whole military campaign to plan."

"Military?" he gagged.

"Of course! You have gone palsy-walsy with Gris and I just gave up on you. Stronger measures are indicated, buster. And don't try to pry out of me the battle plan. For all I know, you're just acting as a spy for Hisst. Militarying and spying go hand in hand."

She had been talking to him in English and Madison continued in the same language. "I'm no spy, Teenie. I'm on your side."

"That remains to be seen," said Teenie. They rode for a while and then Teenie seemed to have completed her plans, for she popped a piece of bubble gum in her mouth as though to celebrate and a small smile began to play around her oversized and now busy lips.

"I should know where we're going," said Madison. "After all, I've got a right to know where I may have to walk back from."

"You wouldn't ever walk back from the place we're bound," said Teenie. "Not unless you brought a pair of Jesus shoes. It's an island, two thousand miles southwest, surrounded by the sea."

"Are you running away or something?" said Madison.

"Boy, did you ever get up into a fog. Too early for you, I guess. I *own* the place!"

"You own an *island?*"

"Sure, mac. It's the place Queen Hora died."

"Was she exiled?" said Madison.

"Oh, hell no, Madison. She just got tired of smuggling her officers into Palace City and, as she was getting old, she simply moved to her island. It's part of the Treaty of Flisten."

"Teenie, you're losing me."

"Well, you ought to be like me and do your homework. I been sweating it out with the major-domo here and I got it all straight. I bet you thought I was a fake queen."

"Oh, no," lied Madison. "The thought never crossed my mind!"

"Oh, yes, you did. I can tell. So let me put you

straight, buster. I'm the real article. No fakery about it, completely different from your profession. You see, Queen Hora was what they call a Hostage Queen. You got to know a lot about treaties and things. And I'm getting to be pretty expert now.

"About thirty thousand years ago, Voltar conquered the planet Flisten. The only reason the planet surrendered finally was Voltar promising that the Royal Family of Flisten would be preserved. This was all right with Voltar because it gave them an axe to hold over Flisten's head and the Royal Family was moved to Palace City as hostages. It's a pretty common Voltar maneuver: there's four or five such hostage families in Palace City.

"Anyway, the Flisten Royal line finally dwindled out because Queen Hora, in spite of all her time in bed, never had any children. And when she died on Relax Island——"

"So that's the name of the place we're going to," said Madison.

"Don't interrupt," said Teenie. "I'm trying to complete your education. So when Queen Hora died on Relax Island about fifty years ago, it put the Exterior Division on the spot. You see, the maintenance of the Flisten Royal Palace—my palace—and the Flisten island—my island—was paid for out of Flisten taxes. The treaty was executed by the Exterior Division even though the planet is now under the Interior Division. The Flisten Royal Family stayed under the Exterior Division——"

"You're getting me all mixed up."

"You don't need any help. Get the wax out of your ears and listen. So when Queen Hora died, it put the Exterior Division on the spot, like I been trying to tell you if you'd just stop fidgeting. Old Endow and the other officials count on the Flisten taxes for graft. And they been trying to justify to the Flisten taxpayers how come they still paid the Royal tax. And when I showed up, Endow put me in the slot. The old treaty is still valid, the Exterior Division still get their rake-off and everybody is happy as clams. Of course, I can't never go there, because that's part of the treaty, but I'm the real Queen of Flisten, sure enough. It's even awfully legal: about ten years ago His Majesty, Cling the Lofty, issued an order to Endow to head off a Flisten tax revolt by appointing a Hostage Queen of Flisten. But old Endow couldn't find anyone that wasn't from the Confederacy and who could be trusted to keep their mouths shut about the graft. So when Too-Too showed up and Endow was ecstatic over him, the old (bleepard) suddenly remembered the order and with one stroke of the pen, between strokes on Too-Too, he executed the blank patent Cling had signed. So there. I'm no fake. I'm a real queen!"

"Well, I'm very happy to hear it," said Madison. "But when I get finished with my work here, you can go back to Earth."

"Hah!" said Teenie. "I don't think you've heard a single thing I said about hostage queens. If Voltar takes it into its head to invade Earth, the Apparatus will knock off any royalty around there or anybody calling themselves queens or kings and Endow will appoint me the Hostage Queen of Earth. I won't ever be able to go back there but Endow will get his whack at the taxes——"

"Teenie, this is madness!"

"There you go," said Teenie, suddenly speaking in a Park Avenue accent, "I try to educate you in Palace City politics and you insult me. And you're just a commoner, not Royalty like me." She blew and exploded a bubble for emphatic emphasis.

They had reached the coast and were now departing,

at six hundred miles an hour, across what seemed a green and endless sea. No wonder the map Flick was using looked so blank. It was mainly water.

Madison nudged the footwoman in the front seat—he couldn't reach the driver. "Tell him," he whispered, "to turn on something that describes Relax Island."

"I'm not talking to him," the footwoman whispered back. "He says he's reformed and if he doesn't re-reform, I'm going to black his other eye."

"You've already done him damage enough," whispered Madison.

"No, that was his bedroom girl. I haven't begun on him yet."

Madison had the distinct sensation he was living in a madhouse. Teenie with her jabber about becoming Queen of Earth had thoroughly upset him. And now here was another woman acting up. Oh, but his mother had been right!

He had the sensation that his best-laid plans were going up in smoke. He thought sadly about poor Heller-Wister as they flew across what seemed an endless sea, going further and further, as he thought, from any sensible PR approach. What the blazes did Teenie mean by "military"?

Chapter 6

Flick, nervously navigating and driving at ten thousand feet, looked all around: there was no land now anywhere in sight, only heaving green sea.

He pushed a button on his panel and in a screen alongside of the map, Madison read:

> RELAX ISLAND, formerly known to the ancients as Teon, stronghold of the since departed sea people. Royal preserve of early Voltarian monarchs but fell into disuse fifty thousand years ago. Deeded to the Royal Family of Flisten after the Treaty of Flisten. Located in the semitropical grid 18/103, Western Ocean, 883 miles from the central continent mainland. Area 305 square miles. Surrounded by vertical black cliffs 2000 to 5000 feet in height, no beaches or harbors. Highest altitude, 9056 feet, Mount Teon located at north end, which, though snow-capped in colder months, blocks inclement storms. Island formed by geological upthrust of volcanic peak but volcano long since extinct. Mean annual temperature 76 degrees. First view, clouds usually clutching Mount Teon or reflective sky discolor. Warning to fishing craft and all aerial traffic, do not attempt to land.

Madison was chilled. What a bleak and awful place *that* must be! Black cliffs, no harbors, warning not to land. What on Earth was Teenie thinking of, coming out here?

Flick leaned toward him and whispered, "I think I'm lost. You're supposed to just punch in the grids but I think this Model 99 is lost, too! I forgot to read my ground distance meter when we left the mainland. That ocean down there is full of toothers, some of them fifty feet long and if they don't get you, the airborne flying batfish will. Visibility is getting bad. Can you get permission to turn back?"

Madison turned. Others had not heard Flick but the fact that he had moved caused the guard officer to glare. Teenie was deeply lost in her own thoughts, scowling.

Madison said to Flick, "For heaven's sake, find the place. I'm not tackling any more women today!"

"Me neither," said Flick. And he began to peer to the left and right.

There was a mist across the sun which made visibility poor. "Haven't you got a radar?" said Madison.

"You mean beams? Oh, yeah, beams," and Flick hastily began to twiddle knobs. The screens stayed blank. "I ain't no ocean pilot," said Flick. "When I crash 'em I like to have somebody find the remains. Look at that distance meter. We've already come twenty-one hundred miles."

"Wait a minute," said Madison. "You're only scanning ahead. What if we already passed it?"

Flick hastily twiddled more controls and shot the beams behind them.

THERE WAS THE MOUNTAIN!

They'd passed right over the top of it with only a hundred feet to spare! It had been hidden by morning clouds.

Madison let out a gasp of relief. They had overshot by twenty miles! Flick slued the airbus around, reducing speed, dropping altitude.

Instantly, the moment they changed course, their speakers boomed, "Warning, warning Model 99-3. This is Satellite Monitor Control, Planetary Defense. We have a Slaughter Warhead ready to launch. Do NOT attempt to land on Relax Island."

Perspiration started up on Flick's low forehead as he hastily veered off. He grabbed a microphone. "I been ordered to land here!" And he hastily grabbed Madison's identoplate and pushed it in the slot.

"We're sorry, that won't do," said Planetary Defense. "There's been no landing on Relax Island for fifty years, but you're not the first one to try. Clear off at once!"

A hand was plucking Madison's sleeve and he turned to find the major-domo pushing something at him. It was an identoplate. He passed it to Flick who withdrew Madison's and put the new one in the slot. His hand was shaking so, he could hardly get it in.

"Is this a trick or something?" boomed Planetary Defense. "We'll have to clear this with Government City. Stand by."

Madison and Flick looked at each other in dismay.

There was a pause, then, "Would Your Majesty accept our apologies? We are merely being diligent in executing Exterior Division orders that no one may land on Relax Island without the express approval of Your Majesty. We bow."

The major-domo grabbed the mike. "Her Majesty graciously thanks your diligence and watchful eye and verifies that the order is still in force. She releases you to your duties."

"We kiss the hem of her robe. Out."

Flick said, "Phewww! A Slaughter Warhead! You were right, Chief, in saying this would be an awful day." He passed Teenie's identoplate back over his shoulder to the major-domo.

Madison had been electrified by the exchange. Teenie wasn't lying, for once. Even Planetary Defense and Government City had her registered as a queen.

And seconds later, he got another shock. They had

dropped below the cloud layer and there, dappled in patches of sunlight, lay the island.

It was BIG! He hadn't realized that it took so much ground to make up 305 square miles. From four thousand feet, you couldn't even take it all in.

There were gentle hills and forests. There were waterfalls and rivers. There were squares of fields walled by stone on which crops were growing. There were herds of animals in meadows. And there were little villages with white walls nestling here and there in the brilliant verdure of folded hills. Dropping even lower, he saw that the masses of color were flowering trees and flower gardens.

He tried to compare it to any island he knew of on Earth for beauty. Tahiti? No. It was ten times that.

WHAT A PARADISE!

"Where do I land?" squeaked Flick.

"In front of the palace," pointed the major-domo.

Madison saw it. It was partially up the slope of Mount Teon and so masked by flowering trees that the size of it was obscured until they were almost landed. Then it burst upon him that he was looking at a building that must be a thousand feet long, curving elegantly upon the mountain breast. It was only three stories high but it must reach back into the mountain.

There was a landing target, the usual blue circle nearly gone. Weeds were pushing through the stone steps which led down to it.

Then Madison took a closer look. All along the curving palace front, what he had taken to be green scallops of decoration was moss, hanging on faded metal ropes which bore only a fleck or two of gilt. Dead limbs from forgotten storms littered the curving steps and terraces.

They got out and stared at the palace.

"Jesus!" said Teenie.

A door opened, one that was inset into the massive entrance grills.

An old man with a stick in his hand, gray beard flying, raced toward them.

"Be off! Be off!" he screamed. Then he drew himself up in his tattered rags and shouted, "You're trespassing! This is the domain of the Planet Flisten. Fly away fast or I'll call the guard!"

The major-domo waddled up to him. "Governor Spurt, I will wager you do not even *have* a guard! Down on your knees, you oaf!"

"Down on my knees in Hells for you!"

The major-domo turned, "That is an insult you cannot forgive, Your Majesty. This place is a disgrace: the walks are clogged with weeds, the fountains aren't even running. Compare it to the beautiful condition you found your palace in Palace City in, hold an immediate trial and let us fertilize the grass with his blood. That is my recommendation. I await your command."

The old man had been gawping. Now he began to shake. "Did you say 'Your Majesty'?"

"Her Royal Majesty Teenie the First!" said the major-domo and unsnapped the Exterior Division scroll before the bugging eyes of Governor Spurt.

"Oh, my Gods!" wailed the old man. "We have a QUEEN!"

Faces popped out of palace windows.

The old man rushed forward and fell prostrate at Teenie's feet. Talking, blubbering really, with his face pushed into the pavement, he said, "Oh, forgive me, forgive me. Mercy! We did not know you existed. We did not know you were coming. We have had no warning. Fifty years ago when dear Queen Hora died, Exterior

Division people came and locked up all the chests. We have had no money for paint or material of any kind. No one has come from the mainland. None of us can go. We raise our own food and fish in the sea. We have not forgotten protocol, we drill it every week! Please, please, Your Majesty, don't execute me on the day your coming has made the happiest day of my life!" Then he stopped for a moment and said, "No. You can go ahead and execute me if it will give you the slightest moment of pleasure."

Governor Spurt reached out and put her foot on his neck and he clung to it, caressing it.

"I don't want your life," said Teenie. "I want you to show me the deepest, rottenest dungeon that you've got."

"Oh, good, you'll put me in it. It is more than I deserve."

Teenie looked up. The earlier shout of the old man had been overheard. At least two hundred people, young and old, had come scurrying out of the palace, half-naked and in rags, and were now prostrating themselves on the terrace, steps and landing target. They were all sobbing.

Teenie turned to the major-domo. She removed her foot from the back of Governor Spurt's neck. "Will you tell this idiot to get up and lead the way to that dungeon?"

Madison had a chill. Was that why she had brought him here? To put *him* in it?

"Your Majesty," said the major-domo, "if you are choosing to be merciful despite this man's offense, could I recommend that you at least let me tell these people to clear some of the debris off the steps and brush the halls so that it will not soil your feet to enter?"

Teenie gave a slight motion with her hand. Governor Spurt instantly kissed her foot and scuttled backwards.

He leaped to his feet and bawled at the crowd, "GET BUSY! CLEAN THIS PLACE UP FOR YOUR QUEEN!"

One would have thought, from the ferocity and volume of his voice, that he would have blown them all over backwards but this was not the case. They rose with awe upon their faces and like a wave across them, the look changed to adoration. They started throwing kisses and then took up the bellow of a big fellow at the back: "LONG LIVE THE QUEEN!"

Governor Spurt finally got them going back inside.

Restlessly, Teenie paced about. She had something on her mind and she was not paying too much attention to her surroundings. But, inwardly driven to be in motion, she walked up a path, all weed grown but festooned with heavy-scented flowers, and came to a spot where she could overlook the valleys below.

Madison, somewhat anxious, trailed after her. He looked at the breathtaking view. "How lovely," he said, hoping it would soothe her. "It's a garden spot like I have never seen before. Even the softness of the breeze kisses one. And how restful! Even the song of the birds is a lullaby."

"Shut up," said Teenie. Then she looked around. "It's a pretty place, all right. Too (bleeped) pretty, if you ask me! I thought, like it said in the book, it was all black cliffs and rocks."

One of the sergeants came up with a message from the major-domo. "It's cleared enough for you to enter now, Your Majesty. But please watch your step, some of the paving is loose."

Teenie gave her red glove cuffs a twitch and promptly strode down the path. She stamped up the steps and across the terrace. They had the gigantic front doors open now and the ragged staff was lined up on each side, all kneeling, trying to catch her eye.

Governor Spurt was waiting with a burning torch. But Teenie paused beside her major-domo. "If you can get any sense into these people, have somebody assemble my regiment out in front."

The major-domo bowed and turned back and Teenie followed Governor Spurt.

Men who had suddenly remembered they were sergeants and guards were opening doors ahead of her. A man who was probably the seneschal, for all his rags, was jangling opening plates as he hurried on ahead.

"What are you doing with that wooden torch?" Teenie's Palace City guard officer demanded of Governor Spurt. "Where are the lights?"

"Oh, sir," said Spurt, "we ran out of fuel bars way back when I was a boy. Even this wooden torch is a luxury. So many of the people here were nobles and courtiers and high-level technicians that they had quite forgotten folk arts. It took us three years after dear Queen Hora died to work out how to weave the hair of the woolly animals into rope. We never have reevolved the skill of making cloth. We do very well to just weave baskets to carry fish and food, and we could only do that because some of them, as little girls, used to make flower garlands and flower caps. It is a terrible shock, when you are a high-level technology, to suddenly have to flounder with the primitive. The steppingstones upward to a high technology all disappear and one tries in vain to go back down them: everyone has forgotten how."

"I didn't ask for a lecture," said the guard captain. "I asked you where the lights were. I see we are entering tunnels back into the mountain and I'm not letting Her Majesty go any further until there's light."

Spurt hastily said, "Oh, I'm sure the electronics and electrical devices all work. There just isn't any fuel...."

The guard officer pushed him aside and strode ahead. Looking along the walls, he finally found a panel. He scraped off the mold and dust, found the catch, opened it and then, taking a spare electric saber battery from his belt, pushed it into a slot.

Nothing happened.

Disgustedly, he recovered his battery and with an acid glare at the governor said to Teenie, "Your Majesty, this place is getting impossible. I think these tunnels go way into the mountains and deep down. I must ask you not to proceed."

"I got to have a dungeon," said Teenie. "The deeper and darker and more awful, the better. Lead on!"

Following the sputtering, sparking torch, their shadows eerie on the walls, the group proceeded.

At length, having descended very deep into black rock, they came to a series of openings. There was a guard room. Then there were chambers lined with cells, their doors all corroded and hanging awry. Finally there was a large chamber which seemed to contain a forge and the remains of whips. Teenie patted a slab of stone which lay, filth-encrusted, at its center.

Madison realized it was a torture chamber and when he saw the look on her face by torchlight he felt his hair rise.

She found there were two cells just beyond it, little more than dark holes. She took the torch and peered into them, one after the other. She found some old shackles.

"These," said Spurt, "are left over from the ancient Teon sea people. I've only been down here once, when a courtier sixty years ago lost a pet snug. These dungeons scared me half to death. Could I ask Your Majesty to withdraw from such an awful place?"

Teenie was testing the remains of a door on one of the holes. "This has got to be repaired," she said.

"Oh, yes, Your Majesty," said Spurt. "We'll clean it all up."

"No," said Teenie. "Leave it as filthy and awful as possible. I only want it fixed so no one can ever get out. And repair those torture implements, too."

Madison could stand it no longer. "Teenie, what ARE you up to?" he said in English.

"This," she said, "is all for Gris."

"Gris?"

"Yes! The moment I heard torture dungeons existed over here, I had to come at once. They're torture dungeons, all right. A real horror picture. They'll do just fine. I am going to put Gris right there in that hole and then every day for the rest of his life I am going to torture him and hear him scream and blubber and beg. I'll carve on him for years and years!"

"Wait a minute, Teenie. You haven't got Gris. He's in the Royal Courts and Prison!"

Teenie, in the torchlight, fixed him with an awful smile. "That's my military campaign. Queen Hora kept her regiment here. I'm going to smuggle them out and in the dark of night I'm going to storm the Royal Prison and get Gris!"

"Teenie, you can't ask that of anyone. It would be death to try!"

"The men of the regiment were all Flisten nobles, sworn to give their lives at the whim of their queen. In each generation, only the strongest of their descendants were permitted to join the regiment. You are going to get me the arms and transport! And I am going to get Gris!"

"Teenie," said Madison in shock. "Teenie, listen to me. I can get Gris brought to trial. It will take a long time and lots of work. I can hammer away in the media, try him in the press and absolutely force them to try him. And," he added in desperation, for his whole plan for Heller depended upon it, "I can guarantee the trial will go on and on! He'd suffer mentally no end!"

"That isn't the suffering I want to see," said Teenie. "I want him right here under my sharpest knife. For years."

Real desperation seized Madison. He could see them both being killed. "Teenie, what if somehow I arranged it to get him sentenced at the trial and into your custody?"

"I'd have to wait too long," said Teenie. She turned to the governor and began to give minute orders about the cell and the torture chamber and the implements. It took her quite a while.

A radio crackled on the guard captain's belt. It was the major-domo. "Please inform Her Majesty that her regiment is assembling. They've had to get word to the villages and farms. But they should all be ready for review by the time you have come out."

Madison had not realized how deep they had come into the mountain until he tried to walk back up. The foul and ancient air didn't help him catch his breath as he toiled on up the ramps. It took them nearly half an hour to get back into the halls.

A sergeant knelt and would have used a handkerchief to brush off Teenie's boots but women from the palace pushed him aside, and though their cloths were animal skins, they got the stains and mold off Teenie's black suit, boots and red gloves.

Then Teenie walked through the hallways and salons toward the big entrance door.

She strode across the terrace. She reached the top of the outside steps.

She stopped dead.

About five hundred men were standing there in an orderly parade. Their faces were handsome, their physiques magnificent. Obviously the product of noble lines, every one, the titled sons of officers of long ago, mothered by titled ladies of Queen Hora's court. They were young and they were splendid, despite their rags.

An old man, evidently their colonel, stood straight as a ramrod before them. At the sight of Teenie, he and the whole regiment knelt.

"Your Majesty," the colonel bawled, "we have not forgotten protocol. We lie ready to do our duty. We are only too anxious to do Your Majesty's bedding."

From five hundred throats, a song arose:

> *Oh, welcome to us,*
> *Oh, welcome to us.*
> *We greet you, dear Queenie,*
> *And promise sex plus!*

And then, at a signal from the colonel, they all rose up.

But what had stopped Teenie was the flowers in their hair, whole crowns of them. They had no weapons in their hands nor any sign of any.

They began to form rings by squad and then began to dance, plucking flowers from their garlands and tossing them into the air as they circled with skipping, mincing steps like girls.

Teenie sank down on the top step.

She lowered her head and began to cry.

The regiment stopped in consternation. The major-domo waved his hand at them and they scattered like chaff and vanished.

Teenie's sobs grew very marked.

Madison knelt beside her.

"They aren't soldiers," sobbed Teenie. "They were bred for bed. Oh, Maddie, what am I going to do?"

Madison did not tell her he could recruit five hundred criminals that would take on a Death Battalion in a day! Oh, no. It didn't suit his plans. He was very clever, that Madison. He didn't even push her.

"Maddie," she said brokenly, after she had sobbed for a while, "do you think you actually could get Gris sentenced to my custody?"

"Well, as I am very fond of you, Teenie, as a favor to you, I am absolutely certain that I can."

"Then I'll help you follow your plan to try him in the press," said Teenie, feeling a little better, "and when he is sentenced get custody of him."

A ragged maid was trying to dry Teenie's tears with a scrap of animal fur.

Teenie looked at Madison suddenly. Her eyes went very hard. "But there's one thing you got to know, Madison. If you fail to get me custody of Gris, you'll be right there in that cell yourself!"

Madison had no slightest idea of how he could possibly accomplish such a thing. He had just been talking.

He backed up, nodding in little jerks. "I won't fail you, Teenie."

Gods, was he in for it now!

PART SEVENTY-SEVEN

Chapter 1

The second Madison entered the townhouse in Joy City he got to work. He felt that he was marching to the solemn beat of drums and that noble victory beckoned from a nearer point.

How could he fail? He was the most accomplished PR since Julius Caesar, of this he had no doubt. Caesar, an Earth king of long ago, had come, he had seen and he had conquered all of Gaul. Madison would do the same to Voltar. Lack of confidence was not one of Madison's faults. Historians, dear reader, may wish it might have been, for when all this cover-up is exposed, it is very plain that J. Walter Madison was bent upon a course which would alter the history of not only Voltar but of Earth. Some poet once said that the pen is mightier than the sword: in this case one was testing if PR was mightier than the combined good sense of all the leaders of two empires. And as we follow the actions of Madison and others, we shall certainly see if it was. So read on, dear reader, read on. You'll be flabbergasted!

Teenie, he had left at Palace City. Reencouraged, she was making plans to ready up the island for the receipt of Gris, but reconciled that his incarceration there would take some time. Madison had even gone so far as to discuss with her how she could shake loose Endow from some of the maintenance money for the island to buy an air-coach and some fuel bars and new torture implements. She had decided to teach Too-Too, Endow's dearest catamite, a new way to kiss and was sure that would do it. So Teenie was no barrier, at least for a time, though he shuddered at what might happen if he failed to get her custody of Gris.

He now had his roustabouts clear out a seventy-sixth floor large salon and set it up with tables. He sent out a crew logistics man to get vocoscribers, paper, pens and copies of every newspaper published, not only on Voltar, but on all 110 planets.

Then he called together four of his criminal reporters and stood before them, tall and commanding in the glittering light of dawn.

"You are now," Madison said, "creative artists. Lay aside the habits of drudgery and facts. Unleash your imaginations. You are now, from this moment, public relations men. At once, without delay, begin to write news stories of the crimes of one Soltan Gris, an Apparatus officer languishing in the Royal prison."

"Could we know something about him?" the most senior criminal reporter said.

"He is a blackguard," said Madison. "That's all you have to know. We are going to try him and find him guilty in the press, and by that, force them to bring him to a public trial. That done, we have other game in sight."

"Wait a minute," said the leading reporter. "I don't think anybody has ever done this on Voltar. People might not think it's fair."

"It's up to you to manufacture crimes so monstrous that the public will be ravening after his blood. Do that and all thought of civil rights are swept aside. That's *PR* at its best."

Another criminal reporter said, "You used a funny term there, 'public trial.' I never heard of one. On Voltar, trials are private and they simply announce the crime and sentence."

"Aha!" said Madison. "Star Chamber proceedings. Well, we can attack that in due course. Right now get very busy and dream up the crimes of Gris and we'll get them into print."

The four went into a huddle and then one said to Madison, "We know lots of crimes because we knew lots of criminals in prison. But could you give us some guidance in this?"

"Guidance?" said Madison haughtily. "You mean you want me to do your jobs? No, no, my friends. Let your imaginations take over, let the paper roll. After all, you are now *PRs*!"

They nodded and got to work.

Madison now called the roustabouts and had them set up a seventy-sixth floor music salon. He was delighted to find that Hightee's staff had sent over the reworked chorder-bar with a note that they had duplicated it—making another but without the "pictures." Madison sat down to it and began to record *ragtime*, and the ex-Academy of Arts reporter and the horror-story writer listened in amazement and got to work on the musical. Madison left them arguing about whether the choruses should be danced by skeletons or ghouls and went on to his next project.

Corralling the director and the rest of the available staff, he turned over to them what apparently had been General Loop's drill hall, one of the largest rooms he could find on the seventy-sixth floor.

Madison told the director, "You take over here. Get rid of their prison pallor, show them how to wear clothes.

You are really running a sort of actors' school just now. And above all, get them trained so they can hold a sincere and earnest smile without strain. We've got to get rid of the killer look."

"That will be tough," said the director. "They're killers!"

"Well, nobody is asking you to change that," said Madison. "The final product is sometimes killing. But it is done in a different way: it's called *PR*."

"Got it," said the director and promptly went to work.

Madison then went back to see how the reporters were coming along. They looked up from their work. They were all smiles.

"We've got it," said the leading criminal reporter. "We've worked out some great copy. 'Soltan Gris, the Apparatus officer, has been detected rushing all over the farm country of this planet poisoning the wells. He's been killing grazing animals that way like flies.'"

Madison looked at the copy. These fellows were on the right track but they were kind of green. He had expected that. "That's fine, boys. But add this for a bit of zing: The mangled body of the informant who told you was found immediately afterwards, drowning in her own blood."

"Hey," said a reporter, bright-eyed with admiration, "that's genius!"

"No, that's just *PR*," said Madison. "You'll get the hang of it quickly enough. Now, the four of you revise it, make duplicates of your release, and get it to the city editors."

"Right!" the four reporters chorused, obeyed him and rushed out, on their way.

Madison smiled. Oh, things were going well. Just

like old times. And when he got Gris on the stand, he could coach his lawyers on how to get him off: simply accuse Heller. Copy, copy, copy, miles of headlines!

J. Walter Madison was in his element!

Chapter 2

Madison was feeling very much indeed in his element as he ate supper that evening. He was waiting for tidings from the reporters he had sent out and he was very confident that the news would be good.

He had even arranged a little internal PR caper to get peace back and he was having dinner with Flick: Flick had the best and most chefs.

So Madison was in a combination dining room and kitchen of the seventy-sixth floor and Flick was at the other end of the table. Flick was looking pretty bad: both his eyes were blackened now, for, as his footwoman had promised, one more raving mention of Hightee Heller would collide with her fist and Flick had incautiously raved anew about Hightee Heller.

Flick's "bed-maker" was a willowy brunette with very deceptive beauty. She had been doing thirty years for passing herself off as married and then blackmailing men she picked up with threats of mayhem from a nonexistent champion wrestler husband. Her name was Twa. She was draped over the counter of the sparklewater dispenser.

"I can't believe what you told me," she said incredulously.

Flick's footwoman, whose name was Cun, was lounging, still in uniform, against the door on the other side
of the table. "Well, I seen it," she answered the other girl.

Flick, distracted from his elsewhere thoughts, glanced
up from his plate. "You two don't belong in here. Can't
you let me and the chief eat our supper in peace?"

Madison grinned and covered it with a sip from his
canister. Flick was in a fair way of getting himself killed
by these two, and Madison had set up another scenario.

"You may have seen it," said Twa, ignoring Flick,
"but how do I know you really have the eye to judge?"

"Listen," Cun bristled. "Before they threw me in
the jug for outright spite, I was a bodyguard for the rich-
est whorehouse madam on all Mistin. I'm telling you,
there was five hundred guys, half-naked, handsome as
Gods, standing there in front of that palace just begging
to (bleep). And they were the heaviest hung birds I ever
seen. And I tell you I've seen plenty. I never was no
whore, you understand. But I had to pass on lots of men.
So I *am* an expert!"

Flick was very uncomfortable, staring at his plate
through swollen, discolored eyes.

"Yeah," said Twa to Cun, "but you're just pushing
it on the basis of mass observation. Wasn't there a particular one?"

"Oh, there was that," said Cun. "He was young and
he was handsome: he had silky black hair and the softest
eyes. And when they scampered off, he almost knocked
me down. It wasn't no accident. He whispered, plain as
day, 'You see that flower tree over there? It's nice and
soft behind it and I have something pretty hard that
needs handling. I haven't had any in ages, and boy, do
you look good!'"

"NO!" said Twa. "REALLY?"

"Oh, that's a fact," said Cun. "And there was a big blond one, what a MAN! They're all aristocrats, you know. And as he rushed by, he said, 'Hey, cutie, do you know where I can find a willowy brunette?' "

"Oh, boy," said Twa. She turned to Madison. "Chief, can me and Cun run an errand for you to that island?"

"SHUT UP!" screamed Flick.

"We can leave Flick home," said Cun. "I can find the place."

"YOU'RE STAYING HERE!" howled Flick.

"Why should you care?" said Twa. "You're not interested in us. All you can talk about is Hightee Heller."

"SHE'S TOO NOBLE FOR YOU TO EVEN SPEAK HER NAME!" roared Flick.

"Noble, that's the key," said Twa. "Five hundred noblemen just slavering to get a girl's back to the grass. Get the old Apparatus bus ready, Cun. I'll go get my coat. I think I saw the chief nod."

Flick was past Cun in a flash. He slammed the door violently and stood before it, glaring at them as he barred their way.

"All right, all right, all right!" shouted Flick. "The minute I finish my dinner, I'll see both of you in the bedroom. Strip and get ready. I've re-reformed."

"And no more mention of Hightee Heller?" said Cun.

Flick looked beaten in more ways than one. "I promise," he said.

Madison beamed, benign as a god. He had carefully coached the women. He had restored everything internally. It was an odd employment of his craft, using it for peace, but by the simple expedient of advising the girls to PR the regiment, he had changed the mind and behavior of Flick. It just proved to Madison how much he himself was a master of his trade. Microcosm or macrocosm, it didn't matter; for bad or for good, it didn't matter. What mattered was that one could command, without fail, the destinies of men. The Supreme Being must feel this way from time to time as he directed the courses of the universe. The only reason Madison hadn't done it the other way around and gotten Flick killed was that he didn't need him for a headline.

Chapter 3

Shortly after midnight, it was very difficult for Madison to descend from his cloudy heights to assimilate bad news.

The four reporters stood about his bed like lost wool animals, looking like they had been chewed upon by fangers who had taken great satisfaction in it.

Copy dangling limply from his hand, the lead reporter said, "They won't take it."

"*What?* A good sensational story like that?"

"They never heard of 'handouts' before. We tried every editor we could get past the door to. They wanted sources and every one said they'd send out their own reporters, but why bother?"

"Didn't you try bribes?"

"That's what we were doing time for. We didn't think you'd like it if they put us right back in, what with the iron box and all."

Madison waved them out of there with advice to have a drink and go to bed.

He was certain he knew what the trouble was: they

FREE

Send in this card and you'll receive a free MISSION
EARTH POSTER while supplies last. No order required
for this Special Offer! Mail your card today!

☐ Please send me a FREE Mission Earth Poster
☐ Please send me information about other books by
L. Ron Hubbard.

ORDERS SHIPPED WITHIN 24 HRS OF RECEIPT!
PLEASE SEND ME THE FOLLOWING:

___ Battlefield Earth paperback	$4.95	_____
___ Final Blackout hardcover	$16.95	_____
___ MISSION EARTH Vol 1 paperback **SPECIAL**	**$2.95**	_____
___ MISSION EARTH Vol 2 paperback	$4.95	_____
___ MISSION EARTH Vol 3 paperback	$4.95	_____
___ MISSION EARTH Vol 4 paperback	$4.95	_____
___ MISSION EARTH Vol 5 paperback	$4.95	_____
___ MISSION EARTH Vol 6 paperback	$4.95	_____
___ MISSION EARTH Vol 7 paperback	$4.95	_____
___ MISSION EARTH Vol 8 paperback	$4.95	_____
___ MISSION EARTH Vol 9 paperback	$4.95	_____
___ MISSION EARTH hardback volumes (specify #s:_____)	$18.95	_____
___ MISSION EARTH HB set (10 vols.)	$99.95	_____
___ MISSION EARTH Sound Editions (vols 1-8 now available: #s:_____)	$14.95	_____
___ Writers of The Future Volume I	$3.95	_____
___ Writers of The Future Volume II	$3.95	_____
___ Writers of The Future Volume III	$4.50	_____
___ Writers of The Future Volume IV	$4.95	_____
___ Writers of The Future Volume V	$4.95	_____

CHECK AS APPLICABLE: SHIPPING: *FREE*

☐ Check/Money Order enclosed   TAX*: _____
(Use an envelope please).

☐ American Express ☐ VISA ☐ MasterCard   TOTAL: _____

Card #: _____

Exp. Date: _____ Signature: _____

NAME: _____

ADDRESS: _____

CITY: _____ STATE: ____ ZIP: _____

PHONE#: _____

Call Us Now at 1-800-722-1733 (1-800-843-7389 in CA)

Copyright © 1990 Bridge Publications, Inc. All rights reserved. 0801901596
* California residents add 6.75% sales tax.

were simply inexperienced and deficient in salesmanship. He wrote an order to the director to practice them in sincere and earnest expressions and went back to bed.

It was obvious he would have to break the first ice himself.

Accordingly, brisk and early in the morning, he dressed himself in his most conservative and expensive suit, practiced expressions a little in the mirror, picked up fresh copies of the well-poisoning story and went to the hangar.

A very exhausted Flick told his smug footwoman to take the controls, for he could hardly see and in addition, now, had trouble in even getting his hand up to point the way. PR had really worked!

Madison had decided there was no reason to start at the bottom. As the top of his profession himself, he had better start at the top.

By a slight misrepresentation to underlings, startled by the blanket order from Lord Snor to Homeview, Madison gained audience to the publisher, no less, of the *Daily Speaker*, the most widely circulated newssheet on Voltar.

In the lofty office which overlooked Commercial City with disdain, Noble Arthrite Stuffy kept Madison standing. "I understand you have some message from my cousin, Lord Snor."

"Actually," said Madison, "I came because I have a sensational news story. Headline stuff. Here it is."

Noble Stuffy read it and tossed it back, "It's written in news format. Is it supposed to be a story?"

"Yes, indeed," said Madison. "Print it and you'll increase your circulation."

"We already circulate more than we can easily handle. Why would anyone want to increase their circulation?"

"To get better rates from the advertisers."

Noble Stuffy frowned. "Advertisers? We don't print advertising. I think you have us mixed up with notice-board cards. Where did you say you were from? Let me see your identoplate."

Madison handed it over, expecting to be able to answer questions about *PR man* and bowl this publisher over. Instead, Stuffy snarled, "The Apparatus? You're from the Apparatus? Well, let me tell you, whatever your name is here, this isn't the first time the Apparatus has tried to get something changed or a story pulled. I suppose you have a Death Battalion waiting at the door or some such other poppycock. You have just become unpopular."

Madison didn't like the tone. He was used to editors and publishers bruising their heads against the floor before the PR of the government. "I could get a Royal order that you'd have to publish anything I say!"

"Hah," said Stuffy. "You just get your Royal order and I will get you a revolution as quick as blink. Seventy thousand years ago a monarch tried to force papers to report the soirees of his commoner mistress and they even erased his name from history. Royal order! Oh, this will be rich when I mention it at luncheon at my club to other publishers."

"I could start another paper and give you such competition, I could wipe you out!" grated Madison.

"Hah, hah!" said Stuffy. "There hasn't been a new newssheet started in fifteen thousand years. Try it and the other papers will buy up all the available paper and leave you nothing to print on but gutter stones. Now you better leave before I ask somebody to throw you out."

Madison departed. He went to other papers. He got the same treatment. He also found something else that was discouraging: These papers were all chains that republished, with local sections, on every planet of the Confederacy, and where it had looked like there were tens of thousands of newspapers on the 110 planets, in reality there were only about seventy-five.

Not letting himself look or feel downcast, for after all he was a veteran PR, he told himself he at least had a blanket order for Homeview.

It was getting on toward evening by that time but he phoned them from the airbus.

"Homeview?" he said to the bright face of the receptionist. "Please connect me to your news section."

"News section? We don't have a news section, sir."

"You give out news!" said the incredulous Madison.

"Oh, yes, sir. I'll connect you to the announcers' rest lounge."

The sleek face of an announcer came on: he was sipping hot jolt. Madison said, "Who is your ace news commentator?"

"Our *what?*" said the announcer.

"Don't you have a news staff?"

"What would we want with that?" said the announcer. "Whoever is on at those periods, we just read items from each page of some leading newspaper. We use a different paper every day and give them credit. Oh, I see what you must mean: you mean the camera coverage of lordly and notable people. Do you want me to connect you to our social director?"

"No!" snarled Madison and hung up.

He sat while Flick hovered above the lanes. Confound it, Madison told himself, I can't run a PR campaign on billboards! And come to think of it, the only signs I have seen just told what store it was.

"Take me home!" he snapped at Flick.

Once there, he soaked his feet. It was the first door-pounding he had done in a decade. It was making him cross.

Then, fortified by supper and easy in bare feet and a robe, he went into the reporters' workroom and began to go through the stacks of newssheets that had been purchased. He had an idea that what he was up against was that curse of the PR profession, journalistic truth. Long, long ago, on Earth, they used to talk about it to graduates in journalism. But these days, they even awarded Pulitzer Prizes for the most false story of the year. The Voltarians, with all this nonsense about sources and accuracy, were definitely on the wrong road: even the corniest weekly in Podunk could give them lessons.

He was reading lead stories now.

NEW MONUMENT
DEDICATED

And another:

LADY PROMPTON
ORPHANAGE
SPEECH IN FULL

Those were *headlines?* How ghastly!
Pages two to seven were usually social news.

> # WIFE OF LORD ELD GIVES
> # PINK SPARKLEWATER
> # PARTY

And

> # DAME ALT GIVES
> # GARDEN SOCIAL
> # AT ALT ESTATE

And

> # EDITOR'S WIFE
> # ANNOUNCES
> # WEEKLY AT HOME

Madison exploded. HOW DULL! These people had never grasped the idea that news is *entertainment!*

There was a little hope: several papers, on inside pages, bottom, carried news on the revolt in Calabar, and on the back page of one paper, five lines said that a couple of lovers had been found suicided in a river. Lacking anything else, those stories had the blood to make them headlines!

WHAT A BACKWARD CIVILIZATION!

He had better reform them fast!

Although his determination was strong, he knew he needed more than that. He needed some point of entrance to penetrate this media wall.

He went to bed and stared at the ceiling. No ideas. Eventually, he slept.

Factually, dear reader, not just Heller's fate but that of both Voltar and Earth were hovering in the balance in that dark chamber.

Chapter 4

At dawn, the searching fingers of the sun pried gently at his eyelids.

He lay in the semi-world, half-awake, half-asleep. A thought was drifting through his semiconsciousness.

One of the proper purposes of newspapers, ran the thought, was to cause trouble and worry people. Thus, it followed, a primary intention of all Earth media is to make people go mad.

He stirred. Something was tugging at his mind for recognition. He suddenly realized that he had never seen any psychiatrist on Voltar or any sign of one. Not even a psychologist.

Aha! The Confederacy, through its deficient media, was not only not causing insanity, it was not even curing it! Suddenly an idea hit him.

He struggled out of bed. He got on a robe. He went into Flick's room.

Flick, black eyes now yellowing, was lying spent between the naked bodies of Cun and Twa, both of whom were snoring peacefully through gently smiling lips.

"Flick," said Madison, "what do they do with the insane on Voltar?"

"They sic two women on them and kill them," said Flick, trying to free his arms and sit up.

"No, seriously," said Madison. "It's important that I know."

Flick crawled weakly down to the foot of the bed and sat, too spent to progress further. He said, "The insane? Let's see. Well, when they say somebody is insane, it's not very hard to figure out they're right. They get staring eyes and rush about or flop. They don't know anybody and, when they talk, they say crazy things. So they send them to a big prison far up north and that's that."

"What happens if they get well?"

"Get well? That's a funny term. You mean if they go sane again? Well, if that happens, they watch them for a while and then they let them out."

"You mean they don't shock them or operate on their brains?"

"For pity's sakes, why? How come somebody should punish them? They don't work on them or touch them at all. I had a cousin once was sent to the Insane Detention Camp on Calabar: he went crazy as a gyro with half a wheel gone. They kept him for half a year, didn't do a thing but feed him, and then they let him back out. He was all sane again. I'm sure glad they didn't damage him: my aunt would have raised a thousand Devils if they had."

"Have you ever heard of a mental doctor?"

"Nope. Don't think I ever saw a doctor that went crazy."

"I mean a *psychiatrist?*" said Madison.

"Look, Chief, I been sitting here awfully patient and every muscle aches, but couldn't we lay off foreign words at least until I have had some breakfast and wake up?"

All this talk had stirred the girls. Twa said, "You don't need any breakfast yet," and reached for him.

Madison left. He felt blocked again.

He went back to his room and paced.

The idea he had had was not really his. It was a historic milestone of the PR trade. It had come to him when he realized the primary purpose of Earth media was to make people go mad. And this had jarred into view one of the PR triumphs of the century.

The American Psychiatric Affiliates, many decades ago, had had a terrible problem with the media. At that time, nobody in his right mind would print anything serious about psychiatrists; the breed was regarded as just a bunch of vicious fakes and quacks, destructive at the very least with their electric shocks and murders.

But PR had saved the day. In league with the World Federation of Mental Stealth—an organization composed of ex-Nazis who had murdered the millions of Jews as well as all the "insane" in Germany, and who were running from the Allied forces—the American Psychiatric Affiliates had pulled the most cunning coup of the age.

They had done such a marvelous job on the media that now, today, a psychiatrist could commit murder several times a day, including Sunday, and could do anything, even exhibit himself in front of children, and the media and every page and frame of it would praise him to the skies and say how scientific and necessary it all was.

Yes, their PR procedure had indeed worked and continued to work. Resoundingly, psychiatry and psychology were now considered totally above all law and even the highest in the land licked their scruffy, bloodstained boots.

Madison, with his command of PR history, knew exactly what they had done, how they had gone about it and continued to go about it down to the finest, minute detail.

But there was one small flaw in his plan: he didn't have a psychiatrist.

Chapter 5

Madison, grim determination in his eye, got dressed and had some breakfast and then got on the viewer-phone. He was trying to locate Lombar: he was not at Palace City, he was not at his office in town. He seemed to have vanished.

From what he knew now of Apparatus offices, he hazarded that Lombar must have a chief clerk. By using his blanket order from Hisst that gave him a free hand in all matters of PR, he finally got through several shunts and wound up looking at an old man of very bitter visage.

"I need information," said Madison.

"Well, I'm not giving any over a viewer-phone, no matter what authority you've got. Tell your driver to land you at Camp Endurance." He clicked off.

Flick, up and around now, went into a deeper gloom. "I knew it would happen sooner or later: you been ordered to Camp Kill. They'll simply take us out of the car and throw us in the chasm. That's what they do with criminals the Apparatus can no longer use." And he would have gone off to bid the staff farewell if Madison hadn't grabbed his arm and shoved him toward the hangar.

Far above the traffic lanes, at six hundred miles an hour, they went over the mountains, crossed the Great Desert with its dust dancers and, after a harsh challenge, were permitted to land at the camp.

Troops were marching here and there and for some time the three of them simply sat in the landing area, unapproached.

"They're getting the execution squad ready," Flick told Cun. "They will probably rape you first. Then over we go. I've just got time to re-re-reform so I can go to my death thinking about Hightee Heller."

Cun hit him.

A smart young officer, followed by a squad, came out to the car. He looked somehow different than others who were around. His squad came to a military halt, very precise. The officer leaned in the window. "I'm Captain Snelz." By chance of changing duty rosters, it was the very same man who had been the fast friend of Heller and the Countess Krak. "Is your name Madison?"

Flick cowered back and Madison had to reach over and get his identoplate, just used in the slot. Snelz looked at it. He clicked the buttons on the back.

"Hello, hello," said Snelz. "Unlimited pay status? Well, it just so happens the canteen is on the way and you won't mind setting up some drinks for me and the squad before we proceed. I'm your escort."

Madison got out. The hot desert wind hit him. He stared at the huge black bulk of the castle and then he felt himself being pushed along. "Wait a minute," he said. "I am supposed to see Lombar Hisst's chief clerk, not attend a military review. What is this place?"

Snelz said, "You must be new in the Apparatus not to know this is Spiteos. Where are you from?"

"Earth," said Madison.

"Earth?" said Snelz. "You mean Blito-P3?"

"That's what they call it here," said Madison. "The right name is Earth."

"Hmm," said Snelz.

They got to the canteen and Snelz ordered tup all around. When he had washed the desert dust out of his throat, he said, "By any chance did you run into an officer named Jettero Heller on Earth?"

"Oh, yes," said Madison. "One of my dearest friends."

"Hmm," said Snelz. "How is he?"

"Oh, splendid, splendid," said Madison.

"You didn't come back here with him, did you?" said Snelz.

"No, I'm afraid I didn't have that pleasure," said Madison.

"Then you know his lady," said Snelz.

"Oh, yes," said Madison. "Lovely person."

"What does she look like?" said Snelz. "Just to make sure we're talking about the same person."

"Oh, lovely, lovely," said Madison. "Very lovely."

"But, confidentially," said Snelz, "didn't you think she was a little short for him? I mean, a girl only five feet two when Heller is six feet six."

"Oh, I thought her slightness was one of her most charming features," said Madison.

"Well, drink up," said Snelz, "and I'll run you on through to the chief clerk." Other than that, Snelz didn't seem to have much more to say, which was not strange, now that he knew Madison was a fake.

Madison paid for the drinks and they got onto a zip-bus and were shortly speeding through the tunnels. They got out and made their way to an elevator. They sped to the high tower where Lombar had his main clerical office, and Snelz pushed Madison in and composed himself and his squad in the passageway to wait.

The criminal old chief clerk frowned at Madison. "I know you have a blanket order. You probably think, by seeing me, you can get to see the chief. . . ."

"No," said Madison. "Actually, I want to see *you*. I know very well that chief clerks really run things."

"Well, you're the first one to ever mention that! What can I do for you?"

"Two things. As the Apparatus is actually an intelligence activity, I can only suppose that you have lots of information on people. So the first one is, I want to know if you have data on publishers and editors."

"Blackmail, you mean. It's a fact that we have informers in their houses and in their offices, but it's a dry run. We've tried for years to get something really good on them but all we hear about is just domestic spats. Tiresome trash. You won't find any twists."

"Nevertheless," said Madison, "I want everything on every publisher and editor and everyone around them."

The old chief clerk shrugged, called another clerk and led Madison to the central data console.

With the clerk operating it, they shortly had torrents of printouts coming from the machine.

After a while the chief clerk came over. "You remind me of Gris. He sneaked in here one day and ran this machine totally out of paper."

"It's important," said Madison.

"It's trash," said the chief clerk. He picked up a corner of the roll and in a snide voice read, " 'Lady Mithin this morning accused her husband of being an unreasonable boor when he complained the jolt was not hot.' I can see you now trying to blackmail Noble Mithin, publisher of the *Voltar Vigilant*, with that!"

Madison suddenly found himself looking at reports from informers, doormen and such, who had noted his calls on publishers the day before. Yes, the Apparatus ran quite a network. Well, he could run quite a network himself: he would have to see that proper false reports were fed into their system.

The paper eventually amounted to a formidable bale: the rolls had had to be replaced twice.

"I hope that's all," the old chief clerk said.

"Well, no, it isn't," said Madison. "Anywhere on Voltar or in the Confederacy, is there a real *psychiatrist?*"

The old chief clerk shook his head.

"A *psychologist?*" said Madison.

The old chief clerk shook his head again.

"A *psychoanalyst?*" said Madison. "You know. Somebody who handles mental illness?"

"Mental *illness?*" said the chief clerk. "That's a funny term. *Mental* things don't have any germs or virus connected . . . Wait. I just remembered something. What was that first word you used again?"

"Psychiatrist."

"Aha, yes! That crazy Doctor Crobe, when he came back from Blito-P3, was yapping about treating 'mental illness.' He was refusing to go back into his laboratory because he was now that funny word you just used. He's right down on the first sub-level here."

"Crobe? Can I have him?"

"Oh, and welcome," said the chief clerk. And he promptly wrote out the order of custody.

Chapter 6

Doctor Crobe was lying on a filthy operating table, obviously in a bit of a haze.

The rest of Snelz's squad had stayed outside, guarding the cart of printouts, but two of them and Snelz preceded Madison into the rooms.

Snelz punched at Crobe with a stinger a couple of times and the man writhed around, blinking.

The smell of the place hit Madison like a club. Old dried blood and decayed tatters of flesh stained the floor and furniture. He stared at the dirty doctor.

Suddenly, Madison recognized him. Too long a nose, too long in limb, weirdly misshapen. This was the same man Smith had sent to his office and that he had sent to Bellevue Mental Hospital in New York! His luck was in!

"Get up," said Snelz. "You're being handed over to this man."

"I will not go," said Crobe. "I am busy."

Madison, looking at Crobe's eyes, had a strong suspicion.

A twisted sort of assistant was timidly peeking in. Madison said to him, "What's the doctor so busy on?"

The assistant shook his head. "There are no more freaks being made: the chief is interested in other things. He must be talking about his bottles and pans. He has been working for a week on them and just yesterday, he flopped down on that table and this is the first time he's moved."

"Show me," said Madison, with a sudden flare of hope.

The assistant led him deeper into the maze of rooms and stopped, pointing at a laboratory bench.

Madison smiled a smile of exultation. It was more than he had ever hoped for. There was a pile of moldy seeds. There was a pan to collect the fungus. There were the tubes and vials. Doctor Crobe had been making lysergic acid and from it, lysergic acid diethylamide, LSD!

Yes, there was a gallon jar full of crystals and next to it, three gallon jars full of liquid!

He had suspected it the moment he had taken a close look at Crobe's eyes. Many a psychiatrist and psychologist augmented his income by making LSD in his kitchen and spreading it around. And Crobe had been so industrious he had enough there to knock out a billion people: it only took one one-hundred-thousandth of a microgram to produce a full-blown trip.

"Pack up all this stuff," Madison ordered the assistant. He went back to Crobe and looked at him. The man had evidently finished his task and had celebrated by sampling his wares!

"Don't worry," said Madison to Crobe. "We're taking your *cookout* along and all your *LSD*."

"You know it?" said Crobe, suddenly interested.

"Oh, yes," said Madison. "*LSD* is wonderful stuff. Don't know what I would do without it." Which was a complete lie: he had never touched it in his whole life and wasn't ever going to, nor any of his crew either. Talk about poisoning wells! That was nothing compared to what Crobe could do. With that much LSD poured into waterworks, he could disable the whole planet.

The assistant came out of the back, wheeling the LSD and paraphernalia on a cart.

"What the Hells is this?" said Snelz. "Are you carting away the whole castle?"

Madison flashed his blanket order in front of Snelz. Then he had the assistant push the cart out the door and into the hall.

Crobe rose right up and followed the cart.

Snelz stared. He had thought it would take two soldiers to force Crobe to leave. He made an experiment. He pushed the cart along himself. Crobe ambled right on after it. "Magnets," said Snelz. "It must be magnets."

Back once more in the landing area, Madison shuddered at the idea of letting the filthy Crobe ride in the Model 99: he could hardly bear to be near him, such was the stench. Using his order, he commandeered an air-coach and loaded Crobe in.

"I better send a couple soldiers," said Snelz, "just to make sure he gets to where you want him—and of course to make sure we get the transport back."

Madison shrugged. They loaded the printouts, the LSD, the cooking paraphernalia and Crobe into the shabby air-coach.

Snelz told off a corporal and a soldier and they got in.

"Well, I certainly do thank you," Madison said to Snelz.

"Say nothing of it," said Snelz. "Any friend of Heller's is a friend of mine."

Madison, as they took off, wondered if he had detected sarcasm in that voice. Well, it was of no importance. Riding across the desert, the air-coach close beside, Madison was experiencing his own kind of glow.

He not only had his data, he also had a real Bellevue-trained psychiatrist. And there was a terrific bonus: he had gallons of LSD!

He couldn't possibly lose!

He could follow the American Psychiatric Affiliates caper right here on Voltar. He didn't even have to dream anything up! It had all been done and proven utterly before. Earth ran on it, right this minute. Pure perfection!

The stepping stones were leading him right up to Heller! Oh, it would be no swift thing. But it was sure and it was certain that he would succeed.

A feeling of power surged through him.

Chapter 7

The ensuing days were a blur of activity for Madison. One part of his project overlapped with others and he was everywhere at once.

His very first action was to turn all six roustabouts loose on Crobe and bathe him and soak him and bathe him again and again until he smelled less bad. It was a terrible job.

Madison then got him tailored and provided with a wardrobe of respectable professional clothes, after which the director, with many curses and much sweat, began to get him into shape.

The four reporters that Madison had put on were clipping social notices and making a huge social calendar that covered a major wall.

He checked the wardrobe of the five circus girls, augmented it and turned them over to the director.

He delighted Chalber at Zippety-Zip by purchasing some air limousines.

He went and saw Teenie and, into her wide-eyed stare, gave her certain instructions and she, assured that it would wind up eventually with a captured Gris, fell to with a will.

Madison discovered the Apparatus Provocation Section and pried them loose from many false but seemingly valid identoplates.

He got the electronics man busy on the upper floors.

He even managed to get in, to keep him happy, another clip on Homeview of Lombar. With his own crew this time, using the occasion of a national holiday, Confederation Day of Delight, he had Lombar dedicating a new cemetery for the dead of the Calabar Revolt. It fitted the day, Madison explained to the dumbfounded manager of Homeview, because of the close-ups of delighted smiles of Lombar viewing the as yet unused grave markers in a truck. Lombar, however, thought it was great when Madison explained to him that he was building Lombar an image of "Don't trifle with Hisst, the most ruthless and relentless man in the Confederacy."

At the end of ten days, Madison, everything else going well, wanting to see Teenie, had to fly from Joy City to Relax Island. Flick had left Cun pointedly behind. They had a pass stamped by Teenie.

This time, being more experienced, they took no chances of flying over the top of the mountain and, coming in low, almost collided with the side of a five-thousand-foot cliff, coal black, that gave Madison quite a shock. But, rising up over it, they were rewarded by the stupendous scenery of the valleys and hills.

They landed in front of a much-changed palace. Evidently Too-Too's new kiss had worked like magic on Lord Endow. The whole vast front was stripped of moss and glowing in new gilt, the paths were trimmed and neat, the shrubbery pruned, not a single errant twig obstructed the terrace, and even the paving stones, firmly gripped in new cement, had ceased to teeter. Staff, and possibly some construction companies, had worked miracles.

Two stiffly standing guards, shimmering in silver uniforms, stood on either side of the door. A properly robed seneschal came out and bowed Madison in.

"Her Majesty is in the third music salon," he said. "Follow me, please."

Expecting to see Teenie being played to with soft airs suggested by the climate and beauty of the place, Madison was a little startled to find her stripped to the waist, wearing a pair of blue pants with red side-stripes and nothing else. She held a stinger in her hand.

"Madison," she said without preamble, "you just got no idea how dumb these (bleepards) are!"

Madison had no idea who she was talking about. They were the only ones in the room. There were mirrors on all the walls which cross-multiplied their images, and although there seemed to be several hundred Madisons and Teenies, that did not make them any less the only occupants of this large and ornate salon.

"Watch this," said Teenie. She barked out, "Hike!"

A woman, dressed in noble clothes, entered by a far door. With leisurely and cultured steps, idly gazing about her, she wandered toward a pedestal which must be a performer's platform. Madison recognized one of Teenie's Palace City maids.

"Let him go!" cried Teenie.

Instantly, from another door, a man in officer's uniform raced into the room. He spotted the woman. He made a beeline for her.

He tore the robe off her. He knocked her down. He hauled her over to the performer's platform. Keeping one foot on her so she couldn't escape, he half tore off his own clothes. He leaped on her and was just about to spread her legs when Teenie moved forward with a yell.

"No, no, NO!" cried Teenie and stabbed him in the butt with her stinger.

That didn't stop him. Not for a second. Teenie grabbed hold of the hair of his head and sought to pull him upward.

Two sergeants had rushed in and they backed up Teenie. They got the man out of and off the maid and held him there.

"Madison, that's the third God (bleeped) time he got it wrong! In a row!"

"Teenie, maybe he doesn't understand what he's supposed to do."

"Oh, he understands all right," she snarled, jabbing him in the belly with the stinger. "He is supposed to walk up to her and bow, then kneel and kiss her hand and request her company for a stroll in the park, AFTER which he is supposed to make an improper proposal. But they know (bleeped) well that after the proposal they just get sent back to barracks, so they use these lessons as a chance to get by me and tear off a piece before I can stop them."

"Well, Teenie," said Madison, looking at the wilted officer, "I wouldn't dare to advise you, but has it occurred to you that if you let him actually take a girl to a bedroom and do it, IF he did all the rest right, they might revert to protocol? It's called 'reward' in animal psychology. I know, I studied it in college."

"You got it all wrong," said Teenie. "That's the trouble with them. They're acting like a bunch of beasts! Five hundred God (bleeped) noblemen, my (bleep). They're just five hundred God (bleeped) animals!"

"I think even their fathers and grandfathers were led to the queen with an electric collar on them," said Madison. "I think maybe their protocol requires them to act that way."

Teenie became thoughtful. She sent for Governor Spurt. He came racing, all dressed up, now that the chests had been unlocked. He came to a halt with a clank of office badges and bowed low.

Teenie dragged him over to the side and had a low-voiced conversation with him.

She came back shortly. "By God, Madison, you're right. It wasn't animal psychology that was missing—who'd miss it—it was the standing Royal orders! Queen Hora wanted to be hit and stripped and raped!"

Governor Spurt soon returned accompanied by a clerk in black and three footmen carrying a table and other things. They set them down.

Teenie, with their help, drew up a document which altered former Royal orders. The clerk, with a flourish, handed her the Royal Seal of Flisten—a two-pound carved emerald—and she stamped and signed it.

"It won't do any good to do any more training until the heralds yell it all over the island to make it legal." She got up, a maid dropped a cloak over her shoulders and Madison followed her out onto the terrace.

Teenie sat down on a balustrade and stared out across the valley. A footman handed up a silver tray which held a piece of bubble gum, bowed and withdrew.

She chewed for a while and, when she could blow a bubble, did so. "This queening business is pretty tricky, Madison. You can get away with anything so long as you do it with the proper legal actions. But I'm learning."

"This certainly is a lovely place," said Madison. "Birds singing and the air is like perfume. They're really making progress fixing it up."

"Oh, the contractors are getting the panels and machinery working. I've got two air-coach trucks making daily runs now. I'm having trouble with the villages: they keep organizing dancing festivals of welcome. But the main holdup is in Commercial City: they never heard of some of these torture instruments and they're having to be handmade. How's it going with publicity?"

"You mean PR. I think I'll be in business in another two or three weeks."

Teenie sighed. "I guess I'll just have to resign myself to it. How long do you think it will be until I get my hands on Gris?"

"Two or three months," said Madison.

She looked at him crossly. "You sure are slow! Well, you didn't come down here sightseeing. What do you want now?"

"I just wanted your permission to send in a camera crew and get some blank passes. I want a little travelogue."

She shrugged. Then she said, "While you're at it, tell your cameraman to be sure and take some pictures of that dungeon. I want something to remind you with in case you get ideas of not coming through. Call it animal psychology." And she popped her bubble gum emphatically in his face.

Chapter 8

One week later, Madison called his staff together.

"I think we're all organized," he said. "I just want to tell you that if anybody flubs, he will be subjected to one or both of two penalties. He or she will be forced to take a dose of LSD and if the offense is *very* bad, the offender will be forced to have a psychiatric treatment. Is that understood?"

They squirmed. It must be pretty bad if the chief, a known murderer, looked that grim about it. They shivered, they went pale under their newly acquired tans. They said they understood.

"All right," said Madison. "It's all systems go!"

The five circus girls rushed off, got dressed as noble ladies.

Five air limousines took off, headed for five different social functions.

Five false identoplates that said, incontestably, that they were noble ladies from distant Confederacy planets got them entrance to estates and ballrooms.

The PR war was on.

They had their orders. They had been drilled and drilled. They were to circulate amongst the guests and at any opportunity, talk about the marvelous new doctor from a planet of very advanced culture named Earth that had developed a marvelous thing called *psychiatry*. And would you believe it? The root of all mental disturbance was sex? Amazing! But he was curing people in droves. It was the latest thing, quite the rage.

For days and days, on and on, for dozens and then hundreds of soirees and balls and at homes, the whispering campaign pounded on.

The two officer-impersonators, dressed now in solemn scientific garb, attended on the heels of the circus girls, thoughtfully and conservatively confirmed the rumor and also brought Madison his feedback.

Madison, with a dungeon waiting, watched the campaign nervously.

Very few people, even on Earth, realized that psychiatry and psychology were just the creations of PR and had no other substance.

Freud's theory that everything was sex had remained scoffed at and neglected until he had married into a New York advertising firm and then the advertising men began to push it, and until this day sex was the dominant basis of all Earth advertising. The PR on psychoanalysis was so good that it overrode the fact that a third of the patients committed suicide in the first three months of treatment. And there were no cures of record.

Madison was following the general PR pattern psychiatry had pursued so successfully. He even had LSD available, a milestone of psychiatric success which had permitted it to capture no less than the head of the largest news magazine in America, make him an addict and convert him to the psychiatric cause. Loose, of *Slime* magazine, had thus become a primary crusader for psychiatry and LSD and a relentless hatchet man for any other technology that arose that psychiatry thought might constitute a threat.

Madison did a little praying when, at the end of ten

days, it was announced that the famous psychiatrist would give a lecture to a very select few.

An auditorium on the eightieth floor had been made ready. Limousine after limousine arrived on the roof. Seat after seat was taken. Madison began to breathe more easily as he watched through a peephole.

Doctor Crobe, an electric collar hidden beneath his professional tunic neckband in case he departed from his coached speech, came to the platform and began to speak of the work of Sigmund Freud in the field of sex. It was a good speech. It should be: it was taken straight out of Freud, for Madison had found, much to his delight, that the old Soltan Gris office contained complete translated transcripts.

Crobe droned on. He had a small speaker in his ear that could prompt him if he forgot any part of the speech. He filled the air with *ids* and *egos* and *censors*. And then he got down to the nitty-gritty of it: if wives were dissatisfied sexually with their husbands, inhibitions could build up. The censor was only a thin veil at best, and with the least prompting, the terrible insanities which lurked below could burst out and bring terror. Everyone was inhibited. It all depended on whether one was sexually satisfied.

Applause greeted the lecture. It was not surprising. Most of the people attending were the wives of publishers and editors.

Then Doctor Crobe, as he was supposed to do, said that as a special favor, he would grant interviews that very afternoon to a favored few.

He got five.

They were taken to a room equipped as a hospital. The two actors, now garbed as medical technicians, took their pulse and weighed them and did other banal things. But they also looked into their mouths with a tongue depressor. And unbeknownst to the women, that tongue depressor had on it a small dose of LSD.

Madison held his breath. Lady Arthrite Stuffy was one. She was the wife of the publisher of the largest newssheet in the land, the *Daily Speaker*, the one where he had first been rebuffed so cruelly.

Out of sight, but with everything on monitors, Madison watched the five being escorted to their interview rooms.

Lady Arthrite Stuffy, much younger than her husband, was led into the first room that Madison and Flick had earlier entered and turned on the black window.

The sacrificial altar had been covered with a velvet cloth. The room looked quite ordinary. The young woman, at the direction of the courteous medical technician and assisted now by one of the criminal whores garbed as a nurse, lay down on the block.

The other women were led into different rooms of the same nature.

Doctor Crobe entered the room of Lady Arthrite Stuffy. His collar was on remote control. He knew better than to depart from the arranged speech.

"Now just compose yourself," said Doctor Crobe. "Just lie there and go over all the rows you may have had with your husband. By doing so, we will penetrate the veil of the subconscious. If we can get back past the *censor*, we will then know what you are inhibiting. And we can clear away any latent *neurosis* or insanity. I will be back shortly."

The nurse remained, smiling a reassuring smile.

He went to each of the four remaining rooms and did the same.

Madison looked at his watch. The LSD would really bite in about an hour.

Doctor Crobe kept circulating, telling each one to think deeper about any husband troubles.

The hour was up.

Lady Arthrite Stuffy said to the nurse, "All this thinking is making me a little nauseated. My heart seems to speed up when I dwell upon the terrible arguments we have had."

It was the signal. Madison watched his monitor closely to be sure the subjective stage had been reached. He pointed at the electronics man beside him and gave a signal. The button was pressed.

In every LSD trip, two things were important: the first was the "set" or state of mind of the person; the second was the "setting," where the person was at the time of the trip.

The lecture and the directions to think of quarrels with the husband were the "set" and now came the "setting."

Devils appeared in every chair!

The window lit up and Demons threw a maiden into the roaring fire. Another body seemed to be lying where Lady Arthrite was and a Devil plunged downward with a knife.

LADY ARTHRITE SCREAMED!

In the next room, the woman there, on proper timing, was suddenly leaped upon by howling beasts which rushed in from a window that disclosed a jungle. Savage toothers attacked the third woman as she sank to the bottom of an engulfing sea. Timed precisely with the LSD, the fourth woman was being murdered by bats with daggers in their claws while a cavern howled. In the fifth room, the spaceship cabin was beset by space pirates from some ghastly planet who tore a superimposed body limb from limb.

The screams of the other women were no less loud than Lady Arthrite Stuffy's.

All five writhed and bucked, each one carefully attended by a "nurse" who was making sure she stayed there.

Gradually the illusions were faded down and the women were let go into their trips. Started like that, they must have been bizarre indeed, but they lay back, not protesting, spinning with time and space all tangled and with no sense at all to contradict the unrealities of it.

Some hours later, when the drug was wearing off, Crobe came back.

"I see," he said, "that we penetrated the *censor*. We now have in view the inhibitions. The case, I have to tell you, is very grave. There is no cure except to have sex with a handsome young man." It was the standard psychiatric remedy.

"Oh," shuddered Lady Arthrite, "it would ruin my reputation."

Crobe had even been taught to smile, with a little help from the collar. "Not as much as going suddenly insane due to domestic opposition. That would be fatal. But there is no risk at all. We have a private sanitarium where you could go and you would only have to say you had decided to take a rest."

"A hospital?" said Lady Stuffy.

"Hardly that," said Crobe. He opened up a folder and handed her some photographs of Relax Island. They were just stills but they were of some of the views. They had been dipped in perfume and in each one a different handsome officer was talking with a lady.

The jangled senses of Lady Stuffy were soothed and

caressed by the views. She was also still in the end grip of LSD where the victim is in a highly suggestible state.

"How lovely," she panted. "And it will cure these awful subconscious inhibitions?"

"Absolutely," said the well-drilled Crobe. "The matter is extremely urgent. It is plain you need the best possible professional help. We will keep it absolutely secret that you are potentially insane. Here is your ticket on the air-coach in the morning. Be on it."

When Crobe had done the same to all five, Madison did a rapid calculation. At five a day, it would take fifteen days to hook all the wives of the publishers of the seventy-five biggest news chains. Actually, he was organized to handle ten a day. He decided he would put the pressure on and speed it up.

He grinned.

He could almost smell, now, the Heller-Wister headlines!

PART
SEVENTY-EIGHT

Chapter 1

It was the last week in August in New York. The weather had been warm, even hot, but a cool, sunset breeze was blowing across the landscaped terrace of the condo, rustling the leaves of shrubs.

The Countess Krak was sitting in a garden chair, petting Mister Calico and watching Jettero Heller at the umbrella'd table as he brought his combat-engineer log up to date.

"Jettero," said the Countess Krak, "do you know the date?"

"I was just going to ask you," he said, looking up, pen held thoughtfully against his nose. "Was it Tuesday or Wednesday when they finally let me out of the army?"

"I'm not talking about that, dear," said the Countess Krak. "It lacks just three days to the date you said it would take war vessels to arrive here on Earth if they started the same night you brought the Emperor out of Palace City."

"It was Wednesday," said Jettero and busily made an entry.

"The ships might not have started the same night," said the Countess, "but they could have left within the next twenty-four hours."

"Was it at the new mayor's reception that Bury gave

me the news about the last refinery being decontaminated? Or was it at the engagement party?"

The Countess Krak sighed. What a trial that engagement party had been! Madison Square Garden, three bands and a symphony orchestra, five chorus lines from Broadway shows. And Babe Corleone, despite Jettero's instructions, had stepped up to the microphone and said, "Ladies and Gentlemen, it is my pleasure to announce the main engagement: My son, Jerome Terrance Corleone is going to up and marry no less a personage than the Countess Krak. How about that?"

And afterwards, when bands were playing and thousands were dancing, Mamie Boomp, who had come up from Atlantic City, said to her, "She really got the intelligence services screwed up about your sailor. Almost every delegate at the UN knew him at the Gracious Palms as a mysterious prince and then they found out he was really Rockecenter's son, which was fine, but when she made that announcement a while ago it threw them in a spin. They approached the Crown Prince of Saudi-Yemen, thinking I might be able to shed some light on it, and I set them straight. It's obvious that Rockecenter was secretly married to Babe Corleone. That made them happy. I like to keep these genealogical matters straight."

That wasn't the only genealogical matter that had been gotten straight. Jettero had had Professor Stringer revise Babe's family tree and put Prince Caucalsia at the head of it. She had been bowled over and would have accepted it even without the thick album of evidences he had put together for her, tracing the descendants of the Manco refugees through Atlantis, to the Caucasus and finally to Aosta in the Alps where Babe came from. And it was true that she had the same blood type, a bit different from the usual lines of Earth, that Krak, from

Manco, had. Jettero had given Babe the tiara with the Manco arms that he had had made at Tiffany's and Babe had worn it in public ever since. It was one of the reasons the press referred to her constantly as "Queen Babe."

But it was the TV crews and cameras that worried the Countess Krak. With all the exposure they were getting, if Lombar Hisst had a single agent operating on Earth, he would have no trouble whatever in finding Jettero. And all during the weeks that followed Krak's arrival in New York this last time, she had had more than an uneasy feeling that they were going to get hit and hit hard.

"Well," said Jettero. "I think that brings it up to date. Babe will address the UN next week and get nuclear bombs outlawed. Congress in its fall session will decriminalize drugs and take the profit out of the scene. The fuel situation is handled and will gradually phase over. The atmosphere is cleaning up and the poles are stable. It's been a lot of work to clean up this planet, but I think it's nicely on its way."

"I don't like it," said the Countess Krak.

"What? It's a very nice planet. A little goofy with its fake psychiatry and psychology, but now that Rockecenter interests aren't organizing and financing them to keep the people down, even that may someday come straight."

"I didn't mean I didn't like the planet," said the Countess Krak. "I don't like the situation. We're sitting ducks."

"Well, I must say," said Heller, "that you're a very pretty duck. Don't you think so, Mister Calico?"

The Countess Krak was just drawing her breath to tell him she wished she had his iron nerve when Balmor, the butler, came to the terrace. "Sir," he said, "that special phone in your study keeps buzzing and buzzing. I know you told me not to answer it but I think, sir, it needs attention."

Chapter 2

It was Faht Bey on the viewer-phone. He looked very agitated. He was calling from the Turkish base.

"Sir," he said, "I think you better come over here at once."

"What's the matter?" said Heller. "Has Prahd's patient taken a turn for the worse?"

"No, Prahd says there is no change. It's something else. I've got some news from home and I think you better come over here and do the interrogation yourself."

Heller looked at the sweating face. The Emperor wasn't dead. It was too soon by three or four days for even a scout vessel to get here from Voltar. Obviously Faht Bey didn't want to discuss it on the viewer-phone because other members of the base there could be monitoring.

"All right," he said. "Expect me."

He went back to the terrace. "Dear," he said to the Countess Krak, "I'm going to take a Mach 3 to Turkey."

"I knew it!" said the Countess Krak. "Something has happened."

"Nothing has happened. It's just that Faht Bey wants me there for a talk."

"I'll get packed. I'm coming with you."

"That's my pleasure," said Heller.

Shortly after dawn in Afyon, Turkey, Heller, the Countess Krak and Mister Calico debarked from the Air Force plane and got into the waiting Daimler-Benz.

Having left the Countess and the cat at the villa, Heller was shortly afterward sitting across the desk from Faht Bey in his office.

"Thank Gods you got here," said Faht Bey. "I think we're in for trouble." And he passed to Heller a demand despatch from the Apparatus General Staff.

"It's the *Blixo*," said Faht Bey. "She came in last night."

"But the ship must have left a couple days before I made my call on Voltar," said Heller. "Nothing had happened there at the time the *Blixo* departed. And she wouldn't have picked up anything in passage. She's just a freighter."

"Well, Gris had couriers that travelled on the *Blixo*. Two catamites that alternated. This one is Odur: we've got him in detention and he's scared to death. He had that despatch for Gris: at the time, nobody on Voltar suspected that Gris was no longer here. You better read it."

Heller sighed. A demand order for information was not much to be alarmed about. He read it:

APPARATUS GENERAL STAFF

To: Soltan Gris
Secondary Executive Section 451

  You are hereby and herewith directed to furnish any and all current information on the defenses of the planet Blito-P3, local name, Earth.

> *You will diligently compile, at once, without delay, numbers of troops and populations to be slaughtered.*
>
> *You will give us your estimate of potential pockets of resistance that might form and have to be obliterated.*
>
> *Your viewpoint for the information required shall be the assumption that only Apparatus forces will be used in the all-out assault, so accuracy is mandatory without any allowance made for reserves or reenforcements from Voltar of Apparatus troops.*
>
> *Authority for this demand is contained in Chief of Apparatus Order 345-nb-456-Blito-P3 attached.*
>
> Captain Maulding
> Secretary to the
> General Staff
>
> OFFICIAL

Heller leafed over to the next sheet:

> *EXTERIOR DIVISION*
> *CHIEF OF APPARATUS*
>
> To: General Staff, Apparatus
> 345-nb-456-Blito-P3
>
>   *It has been determined that forces are internally at work on reference planet inimical to our interests.*

If at any time the supply of opium, heroin or amphetamines ceases to arrive from reference planet, you are to withdraw all Apparatus forces from the Calabar revolt and proceed forthwith to reference planet Blito-P3 and launch a full-scale Class One assault, destroying its defenses and populations but taking care to preserve only the inhabitants of Afyon, Turkey, and that opium-producing area and the I. G. Barben factory complexes in New Jersey, United States.

Ignore the Invasion Schedule.

Plan without cooperation of the Army or Fleet.

This is your highest priority. Get it in the planning stage at once.

LOMBAR HISST
Chief of Apparatus

OFFICIAL

"Well," said Heller, "you have been holding incoming freighters, but as of this moment, since not enough time has elapsed for him to know they will not return, he isn't aware of any curtailment of shipment. This planning——"

"You better talk to the man we're holding in the next room, sir." Faht Bey pushed a buzzer.

Captain Bolz was brought in by two guards. His hairy chest was heaving with indignation.

"Bolz," said Faht Bey, "this is Royal Officer Jettero Heller, a combat engineer of the Fleet operating on his own cognizance and therefore officially. You had better tell him what you told us."

"I got plenty to say!" roared Bolz. "As a blasted Royal officer, I know you can have me exterminated, but I'm going to have my say anyway! I come in here, innocent as a virgin, doing my duty as an Apparatus freighter captain, two days ahead of schedule after a competent passage and what do I find? A whole base wearing Fleet insignia! An order putting my ship under detention! I think you've all gone crazy!"

"Quite likely," said Heller. "And I am sorry for any inconvenience. Now, what was this information you had?"

Bolz lost a lot of his glare. He looked down at his big feet and shifted them uncomfortably. "Well, these fellows here know well enough that I was carrying contraband Scotch whisky and they probably already told you. A captain that never gets paid has to have a little profit——"

"The information," said Heller firmly.

"Well, I didn't have room for a cargo of I. G. Barben amphetamines once I had the whisky aboard, so I left them in the storeroom here."

"And when you arrived on Voltar somebody noticed it?" said Heller.

"The amphetamines were on the manifest," said Bolz, "but they weren't aboard. I happen to know that Hisst always checks the drug shipments against the manifests, because every time I try to pinch a little cargo, he has appeared personally to scream."

"Then there has already been a cessation of shipment," said Heller, looking back at the Apparatus General Staff order. "Now, where is this catamite?"

Faht Bey led the way down the tunnels and they came at length to the detention cell.

There sat Oh Dear, his pretty, made-up face streaked with tears. He recognized, from Voltar press photos of yesteryear, Jettero Heller. "Oh," he sobbed. "A Royal officer. I have one request before you kill me: take the magic mail card back so they don't kill my mother."

"You're not going to be killed," said Heller with a trace of disgust. "All I want from you is any other information you might have had for Gris."

"Where is Gris?"

"Apparently dead," said Heller.

"Not really?" said Oh Dear. "Oh, what utterly marvelous news. Oh, I just can't wait to tell Too-Too! We'll have a celebration party! I'll buy ribbons——"

"The information," said Heller.

"That the General Staff despatch was very urgent," said Oh Dear, "and that I was to keep Gris up day and night to compile it and that I was to return with it."

Faht Bey said to Heller, "That means at least three months until they hit. Six weeks going back, six weeks for the Apparatus invasion fleet to arrive here. Add the time it takes them to assemble and board."

Heller said to Oh Dear, "Is that everything you had?"

"There was a message that Gris was assured he'd be the next Chief of the Apparatus only if there was no halt in drugs."

"A promotion?" said Heller. "But Hisst is the Chief of Apparatus."

"Well, you see, the plan is that Hisst will be moving up to Emperor. Any time now. And that's all I had, I swear it."

He was too shaking-scared not to be believed.

As Heller left he saw the Countess Krak at the end of the corridor. She was coming out of the cell that still held Utanc—Colonel Gaylov.

"Dear," said Heller, "your woman's intuition seems to have been right. The Apparatus has a plan on foot to use its own forces to smash this planet. Hisst is crazy insane."

"Then we've got to get off it right away," said the Countess. "We and you-know-who must not be here when they crack it up."

"And waste all the work I've been doing for a year?" said Heller. "This is a nice planet."

"Opinions differ," said the Countess Krak. "Psychology, psychiatry, perversions beyond belief and a population that doesn't even raise its voice when some nut like Rockecenter is ruining it. It's not worth saving, Jettero. We'd better get a move on."

"We've got time," said Faht Bey. "It will take more than three months for them to make the voyages and hit the place."

Heller shook his head. "How long ago did you stop the first freighter?"

"Oh, that's been about four weeks now," said Faht Bey.

"Then they will know for sure, within a couple weeks, that it didn't come back. But it was Bolz that triggered it. You haven't got three months. You may not even have five days."

"What are we going to do?" said Faht Bey. "When they find out we stopped the drugs, they'll slaughter us to a man and go right on with their invasion. We won't have anything left to stand on even if they miss us."

"Steady, steady," said Heller. "I admit this is quite a

problem. We've got to make sure Prahd's patient is secure, we've got to move this base and we've got to safeguard this planet."

"What?" said the Countess Krak. "Try to stand off the whole Apparatus fighting force? Please, Jettero, please. Don't try to save this planet!"

"I'll come up with something," said Heller. "And make no mistake. Whatever else happens, I am going to make every effort to save this planet."

"Oh," said the Countess Krak in a voice of despair, looking at the set expression on Heller's face.

None of them knew that none of their estimates were correct. Just four days short of arriving, an Apparatus Death Battalion was approaching with orders to find any hostile influence at the base and destroy it. That happened to include, at that instant, every Voltarian on Earth excepting only the *Blixo*, its crew, Captain Bolz and Oh Dear. This was no major invasion, not yet, but it could be the preliminary of mass slaughter. Lombar would go crazy for revenge against the planet for getting in the way of his ambitions.

The wings of death hovered over Earth.

Chapter 3

In the coolness of the patio at the villa, Jettero Heller paced up and down. His mood of grimness did not match the tinkle of the fountain.

For weeks the Countess Krak had been after him to

give some serious thought to their plight but had made
no penetration in his easygoing attitude. She was learning something about trying to live with a personality like
his: with peril a constant companion, a combat engineer
took joy in life when he could and tended to shrug off
dangers he considered minor. But once he conceived that
something should be done about a situation, his dedication to getting it handled was a little awe-inspiring.

She had thought he would simply shrug and leave
the planet to its fate. His carefree attitude did not carry
over into his suddenly confronted tasks.

She sat on the fountain's edge, hopeful that at any
moment he would simply turn and say, "You're right. It
is too much for us. We'll just put the Emperor in the tug
and go someplace nobody ever heard of."

He turned all right. But he didn't say that. He said,
"What do we know of Prince Mortiiy?"

She chilled. Calabar was writhing in the toils of raw,
red war. What he inferred was even worse! But she said,
managing a calm voice, "Nothing good, I'm afraid."

"Good, bad, what does it matter?" said Heller. "I
need information."

He was asking her because she had lately been enter-
taining him with bits of Royal history she had read in the
books Gris had left in her cell during her captivity. Suddenly she grasped an opportunity to discourage him
from some mad course that could end in their destruction. He wouldn't believe her unless he saw it himself in
print. "Wait right there," she said. "I'll get the books."

She returned in minutes with the latest supplement
of the *Compendium* she could find. It was only a year old.
She fluttered pages. There it was and she showed him,
reading aloud:

*MORTIIY, ex–Royal Prince. Proclaimed rebel.
Denied succession by Royal Proclamation.
Banished from Royal family.*

Mortiiy, the youngest of three Royal sons of
Cling the Lofty and the late Empress Fohl, was
considered so distant from succession in his youth
that he was permitted to follow his chosen career
as an officer of the Fleet. Graduated from the
Royal Academy rather than Protocol School at
Palace City.

Served with the Fleet with no very notable
distinction: three times excused courts-martial;
striking and, in one instance, killing an officer
superior in rank; not tried due to Royal lineage.
Much given to brawling.

At the age of seventy, some ten years ago,
Mortiiy's oldest brother, heir to the throne, was
killed in an air-limousine accident. As this left
only one heir at Palace City, the Grand Council
ordered Mortiiy to return from the Fleet and
assume his princely duties, which he did.

For a time, Mortiiy behaved himself and
supported his brother Glit, who had become the
heir and of whom Mortiiy appeared very fond.

However, during a banquet Mortiiy, possibly stimulated with strong drink, took his father, Cling, to task on the outrageous accusation
that Cling, not liking the eldest brother, had con-
nived to have him murdered under the apparency
of the air-limousine accident. Mortiiy advanced
the weird theory that a technician had tampered

with the machine. His father, Cling, despite this grave provocation, did yet speak to him further and demanded that if this was true, the technician be produced. Alas for Mortiiy, he had killed the offender in a rage of grief over his brother's death.

Mortiiy was placed under house arrest for a considerable period, becoming very gloomy and surly, refusing to apologize.

When, five years ago, the heir to the throne, Glit, was found dead in his chambers after a short illness, two Lords approached the palace of Mortiiy to inform him that he was now the heir to the throne.

Instead of receiving the news graciously, Mortiiy flew into a rage, grievously injured both of them, raced to his father's palace, shot down the guards and gained audience.

Mortiiy accused Cling before the entire court of being a murderer of his own children, renounced any succession to "a throne drenched in family blood," fired a shot which narrowly missed Cling and then, killing several, seized an air-tank outside and made his escape.

Proclaimed now by Cling an outcast from the Royal family and with no right to succession to the throne, Mortiiy turned up at the Royal estates on Calabar. He subverted the guards and raised the standard of revolt. He was proclaimed a rebel by Cling.

His Majesty has been overheard to say that he would bestow vast estates upon the man who

> *brings in the head of Mortiiy, so deep has the insult rankled.*
>
> *Due to Cling's advanced age and the length of his reign, efforts have been made to find and choose an heir apparent. But those clearly eligible in direct line have passed away. Succession must be chosen by a conclave of Lords and the Grand Council.*

"So you see, Jettero," said the Countess when she finished reading, "if you are thinking of taking His Majesty to Calabar and joining the rebel forces you'd seal his fate. Mortiiy would simply kill him."

"Mortiiy is not a madman," said Heller.

"He'll do until one comes along," said the Countess. "He is no longer in line for the succession. The whole fighting force of the Apparatus, as we heard when we were on Voltar, is engaged in a full-scale attack to wipe him out."

Heller did not answer her. Instead he went to see Captain Bolz, who was sitting in his ship under heavy guard.

Bolz looked up the instant Heller appeared. "No sense talking to me," he said. "I'm not going to join the (bleeped) Fleet and neither will my crew. We're sensible people. We belong in the Apparatus and we are going to stay there!"

"I am sure," said Heller, "that, with your smuggling, you find it far too profitable. But I'm not asking you to join. All I'm asking you to do is take back a cargo to Voltar."

"WHAT?" said Bolz. "So all this talk about no more drugs was just wind."

"It will take several days to get your cargo here from New York, so if you will promise to sit quietly and give no trouble, you can go home with it and you won't be in any trouble at all."

"That's fair," said Bolz.

Heller went immediately to Faht Bey's office. He put in a long-distance call to the president of I. G. Barben and you could almost see the sweat spurting back out of the phone when the man realized who he was talking to.

"Now hear me carefully," said Heller. "I want a ton of tablets made. They will be composed of 50 percent antihistamine and 50 percent methadone. They will be shaped and packaged and marked as amphetamines and you will get them to the airport in Afyon, Turkey, by jet within four days."

"A ton?"

"Correct," said Heller. "See to it."

The antihistamine, he knew from his studies, would give a semblance of reaction like amphetamines; the methadone would counteract heroin. If Lombar ran out of drugs, let the Lords withdraw more easily with that. He doubted anyone would detect the difference. It bought time.

He wrote a despatch to Bolz telling him to be on the lookout for it, load it up when it came and go home. And he wrote the despatch with an ink that would fade to nothing in a couple of days.

He found Faht Bey. "How many freighters do you have that will operate?"

"We got the old ones running. Two more have been stopped here. Five freighters."

"Good. That's enough. Disassemble the base and load it and all personnel. Break your neck and be ready to go as soon as possible."

"It will take days," said Faht Bey.

"I hope not," said Heller. "If we do this right and we are quick, we can save this planet."

Chapter 4

There seemed, suddenly, to be a thousand details to what had looked like a simple undertaking. Family connections who had been unaware of extraterrestrial husbands and domestic connections who had never known who their employers really were had to be cared for somehow, at least decently set up in life. Faht Bey remarked that the Apparatus would simply have killed them and then hastily said he was just commenting, when he saw Heller's look.

The New York office had to be shut down and its personnel hauled back.

Heller found out from Prahd that there was now a lot of trained Earth staff, including doctors, and that made up Heller's mind. He phoned Mudur Zengin at the Piastre National Bank.

"Make up papers," Heller said, "transferring amounts which have been scheduled for 'company maintenance, Afyon' over to 'hospital and disease-eradication use.' Make them up so they stay in effect pending any cancellation from me."

"That's an awful lot of money for health," said Zengin.

"We're earmarking a good chunk of it for drug rehabilitation," said Heller.

"That's a big job," said Zengin.

"Right. Maybe we can undo some of the damage that's been done. Would it be asking too much to fly the papers down here?"

"Not at all," said Zengin. "I'll come myself."

Krak got hold of Heller. "That Russian spy colonel is still sitting there in his cell. You were holding him in case they needed more when they tried Gris. Remember?"

"Well, he hasn't got a country anymore," said Heller. "He can't be very dangerous. Put a hypnohelmet on him and suppress his memory of the base and let him go."

"It's not that simple," said the Countess. "There's the two little boys he corrupted. They're caving in, nobody can do a thing with them. I had an idea. France has been exporting an awful lot of drugs."

"What's that got to do with Colonel Gaylov?" said Heller. "He was also exporting heroin. From here. To keep the international KGB network running."

"Well, those that commit crimes like that," said the Countess Krak, "will often turn completely around and campaign against such deeds. What I want to do is send Colonel Gaylov to France with the two little boys."

"You must be awfully mad at France. They'd corrupt the whole nation!"

"No, I don't think so," said the Countess. "You see, I've been talking to the colonel and he's absolutely spinning with the glory of it."

"Of what?"

"To show up in France and use the old KGB network to convince everybody he's the reincarnation of Joan of Arc. I didn't even touch the helmet. He's sure he can be the greatest Joan of Arc that ever lived!"

Heller gave her a sizable draft on the Grabbe-Manhattan Bank in Paris, to be paid out to Gaylov, month by month for years.

When she put him and the two boys on the plane the following morning, there was a holy gleam in ex-Utanc's eye. Standing there in a silver travelling gown, he/she said, "You are an angel and I bless the day I met you. I can in truth say that I was visited by the Lord of Hosts on high. France is about to become the holiest and most drugless place on Earth." And they were gone.

Handling Babe was not quite as happy an occasion for Heller.

He got her on the phone and said, "Mrs. Corleone, I'm terribly sorry to have to cancel out on the wedding you had planned for the cathedral next month."

Babe, startled, said, "She's left you?"

"Oh, no," said Heller. "It's just that things got pretty urgent."

"Oh, I get it. You're going to pull a fast justice of the peace before those nine months and the stork catches up with you. Well, all right, son, Mama understands. Just don't forget to name the baby Giuseppe after 'Holy Joe' if it's a boy, or Alma Maria after me if it's a girl. And get that beautiful countess into bed and resting as soon as you're hitched and you leave her alone until she delivers. You hear me now, Jerome, and don't interrupt. You're not doing me out of a grandchild, do you hear?"

"Yes, Mrs. Corleone."

"And can this 'Mrs. Corleone' stuff. You can't soft-soap your own mother. Get that girl to the justice of the peace quick, you hear me?"

"Yes, ma'am."

"All right, then. And come back when the coast is clear and she can be seen in public again. You're a dear boy, Jerome, but you sure as hell take a lot of guidance. Keep your nose clean, kid." There was an audible sniff. "I got to run off now, something's in my eyes. Bye-bye, son."

Heller's own eyes, as he hung up, were wet. He doubted that he would ever see her again.

Chapter 5

Regulations required that an installation on a foreign planet could not be abandoned without being destroyed. There were many reasons for this: included amongst them was the misuse of such a base for piracy and smuggling.

Jettero Heller, as a competent combat engineer, did a competent job of setting it up. He used metal-disintegrator mines. These, inserted near connection boxes and along conduits, would cause an atomic shift of heavier metals to silica: with a surge of enormous heat from the converted atoms, every piece of metal that comprised the hangar area would become sand. This meant that the tension-beam boxes would go and the twist and stresses in the rocks that had been restrained through a thousand earthquakes would no longer be braked. The result would be a furious flash of fire and then a wall collapse. It would simply appear that an earthquake had caused the mountain to collapse into an unsuspected fissure.

He attached the fuses to a central firing box and this he triggered to a remote control.

"Bolz," he said to the captain of the *Blixo*, "I am going to have to trust you. You will not join the Fleet. Your cargo will not arrive until the day after we are gone. When you have loaded and exited spaceward, your last act must be to push this button." And he gave him the very small box.

"What will happen?" said Bolz.

"Well, don't experiment," said Heller. "The *Blixo* had better be up there a couple miles when you do it. Every piece of metal in this hangar will disintegrate. A human body contains a lot of iron and anybody standing around will also become sand. So don't leave anybody in here."

Bolz looked at the remote. "It doesn't have a safety catch."

"Why should it?" said Heller. "You'll find it pretty hard to push. It won't go off by accident. But my order to you is *don't delay in leaving here.* And when you do, push it."

Bolz smiled quietly to himself: not only would it not go off by accident, it would not go off at all. Contrabanding was too lucrative, he was becoming rich; he could buy an old space tub, retire from the Apparatus and smuggle to his heart's content. "All right," he said, "I'll be glad to do you this favor in return for my liberty and life. You have my word on it, Officer Heller." And he put the remote in his pocket.

They were almost ready now. The freighters were loaded with every piece of repair equipment and supplies they could salvage. They had even dismantled the line-jumper and stowed it in a hold. The thousand details were coming to an end. It was the evening of the third day.

Heller called Izzy, Bang-Bang and Twoey and told

them guardedly that he had to take a trip and rang off quickly so that they would not suspect this "little trip" was forever.

According to arrangements with Prahd, an ambulance brought Cling the Lofty in the fluid container with all connections active. The Emperor was still unconscious. The tub was masked by an opaque cover and no one could see who was in it.

The tug was in the deepest recess of the overcrowded hangar.

Heller got hold of Bolz and Oh Dear. Without seeming to do so, he positioned them so they could see the fluid container with an unidentified being in it being loaded aboard the tug.

"Odur," said Heller to the catamite, "you are a courier. I have something for you that must arrive in no other hands than those of Lombar Hisst." He produced a triple-sealed packet.

Oh Dear stared at it, unwilling to touch it. He was stunned at this irregularity. Something from Royal Officer Heller to Hisst who was his bitterest enemy?

"Take it," said Heller. "Do not tamper with the seals or he will suspect you have opened it. And if he suspects that, he may very well kill you when he reads it."

"Oh, no!" shivered Oh Dear. "I don't want to take it if it's that dangerous!"

"Well," said Heller, "I'm very afraid that you would find it very dangerous not to take it. If Hisst found out you had it and didn't deliver it, then he certainly would kill you."

Oh Dear let out a small scream. But he took hold of the packet, holding it like it was burning his fingers.

Heller pointed up to where Prahd was carefully getting the fluid tub into the tug airlock. "Also, you and

Bolz should both notice the fact that a sick person is being put aboard the *Prince Caucalsia* with a doctor in attendance."

The significance of it did not register with either one. But they dutifully noted it.

The Countess Krak came out of the tunnel from the villa, pushing mounds of luggage and boxes on a cart. The hangar crew who had been handling the fluid container with Prahd assisted her in loading them.

Heller, going over to give her a hand up the ladder, suddenly stopped. "What's that yowling?"

"I don't hear anything," said the Countess Krak.

"Lady, what are you up to?" said Heller.

"It's just the cat."

"We've only got one cat. It can't be making that much noise."

"Jettero, you are cruel. You expected poor Mister Calico to go all the way off to Voltar and leave Earth forever without a lady friend."

Heller looked at the boxes now being swung into the airlock. "A lady friend? But that sounds like more than two cats."

"Lady friends, then. It just accidentally happened that Mudur Zengin brought down half a dozen female calico cats yesterday. There's also a couple of males. You wouldn't want them getting inbred, would you? But if you don't like the yowling, maybe I can teach them to sing. Good. I knew you would agree." And she went on up the ladder.

Heller shook his head over the cargo he was carrying. An Emperor, a cellologist and nine cats.

He walked across the jammed spaceship hangar: made for five freighters, it now held six and the tug. A knot of officers that carefully excluded Bolz was waiting for him. They were the captains of the five ships and Faht Bey.

Heller motioned for them to bring their heads in close. "Your rendezvous point is coordinates 678-N/567B/978R. Write it down. 678-N/567B/978R." He watched while they did so. "It is a seven-week voyage. I will be five days on the way so I will land and make arrangements and then come out to the rendezvous point in space and guide you in."

"Sir," said one of the captains, "these coordinates are on the edge of the star Glar. I have to inform you that there is war in that area."

"I know," said Heller. "That is where we are going. The Confederacy is under the control of Lombar Hisst: the safest place we can go is to take sanctuary under Prince Mortiiy on Calabar."

A shock went through them.

"We will be welcome, I think," said Heller, "because we carry repair tools, technicians and men. Mortiiy has managed to hold out for five years. The Apparatus is the only force pressing the attack there. Calabar is an awfully big planet."

"Sir," said another captain, "there must be some other reason."

"Well, yes there is," said Heller. "I have reason to believe that if Lombar Hisst knows I have gone there, he will commit all his forces to the attack of Calabar."

"Is there some benefit in this?" said Faht Bey.

"Yes," said Heller. "He will not then attack Earth. You have a right to know that the reason we are going there is to save this planet."

They looked at him doubtfully. Then one said, "Maybe you figure he will whittle down all his forces throwing them against Calabar."

"That he will," said Heller. "Unless something happens to sour my relations with the Fleet and Army, neither one will cooperate in what they will consider to be an insanity—full-scale war just to get hold of me. But I don't want to seem to have such a grandiose idea of my own importance. I happen to have something Hisst wants very badly. He'll come for us, all right, and unless by some fluke he gets Fleet and Army help, he'll shatter himself against the hundred-thousand-foot peaks of Calabar."

"Well, we've all wanted to get out of the Apparatus and be free men again," said another captain, "and we're willing to work for the chance. But how will Hisst know that you have gone to Calabar?"

"That's why we didn't seize the *Blixo*," said Heller. "I just gave the courier on it a letter to Lombar Hisst. I told him what I have. And I told him we would be waiting for him on Calabar. He'll go crazy and throw in everything he's got. And, without help from the other services, that will be the end of Lombar Hisst."

They grinned suddenly. They rushed off to their ships.

One by one Heller watched them as the spaceships shot up into the night.

Heller waved a hand to the captain of the *Blixo*, "Be sure you have a good passage to Voltar!" he shouted. He went into the tug's airlock, closed it and sent the *Prince Caucalsia* spaceward ho!

Chapter 6

Captain Bolz smiled and scratched his hairy chest
The hangar and base, empty now of everything excep'
the *Blixo*, had ceased to exist as an extension of Appa
ratus authority. He had his own plans.

In his cabin he got dressed in Western clothes. He
put a wad of Turkish lira in his wallet. A frightened Oh
Dear stared at him.

"We're supposed to wait for our cargo and go," said
Oh Dear. "I'm certain Officer Heller is right. If I don't
deliver this and Hisst finds I have not, I'll be dead."

"To Hells with Officer Heller," said Bolz. "They
left that Daimler-Benz in the yard of the villa. Even that
old driver with the funny laugh is still hanging around.
I'm going out there, stop him from stealing the car and
go on up to Istanbul and see my friend the widow."

Bolz stopped to give his mate orders to pick up the
cargo when it arrived by air and load it and then, with
a jaunty air despite his bulk, went out and found Ters
who, for a consideration, was shortly rolling him in luxury through the night to Istanbul.

Throughout the entirety of the next day, a frightened
Oh Dear waited. He hardly concerned himself with the
arrival of the cargo when it was brought in by the mate
and crew from the airport in the afternoon. Oh Dear conceived that Bolz might be deserting and this would leave
him captainless and unable to get back to Voltar. He

didn't speak a single Earth language: he saw himself stranded.

Dusk came, the light vanishing above the electronic illusion. No Bolz. If he had been there, they could leave in an hour.

The upper hole in the mountain went black. The hours dragged. Oh Dear began to be afraid of the hangar. It was so empty that his footfalls as he paced scared him with their echoes. He began to get the idea that the place was peopled now with ghosts.

Midnight came and went. One o'clock took forever to arrive. The digitals of his watch seemed to be motionless and refusing to move onward toward two. Then it became two and then two-thirty.

A loud sound somewhere made Oh Dear scream.

It was Bolz.

He had brought a truckload of counterfeit Scotch. He got his crew out and they got it aboard.

Bolz was himself pretty drunk and considerably smeared with lipstick.

It was three o'clock in the morning when the captain finally began to mount the ladder to the airlock as the last one aboard.

There was an abrupt roar overhead.

Wonderingly, thinking a freighter might have come back, Bolz got down off the ladder and stared up at the hole through the mountaintop.

He froze.

The black tail of a warship was sliding in!

Plain upon it was the symbol that looked like a fanged snake. And some letters!

THE 243RD DEATH BATTALION!

The hulk, too big for this hangar, came down with bristling guns. It hit the floor with a thud.

A hundred black-uniformed men poured out of the six locks, blastrifles ready!

Bolz, too shocked to move, was instantly seized.

A squad raced into the *Blixo*.

Shortly the whole crew of the freighter and Oh Dear were being prodded down the ladder to the hangar floor.

Bolz couldn't register what was happening. He had no way of knowing this was the battalion that had been sent by Lombar to "search out any traitors that were confederates of Heller's or took his orders and exterminate them." For the *Blixo* had left a couple days before the order had been issued by the crashed Lombar Hisst.

A man in a black uniform with scarlet gloves, taller than Bolz, loomed over him. "I am Colonel Flay of the 243rd Death Battalion. Who are you and where is everyone here?"

"I am . . . I am . . . Captain Bolz of the *Blixo*, this ship. I have an urgent cargo of drugs for Voltar."

An officer yelled from the *Blixo*'s airlock, "Colonel, this ship is carrying contraband drink!"

The colonel glared at Bolz. "A smuggler!"

"I'm captain of an Apparatus freighter!"

"In those clothes? Answer me. Why weren't we challenged? Where is the personnel of this base?"

"They've gone!" quavered Bolz.

"Gone where?"

"We don't know!" screamed Oh Dear, who was being held by a Death Battalion soldier. "I am a courier to Lord Endow!"

"Ha!" said Colonel Flay. "Travelling with a smuggler? Bend that pretty fellow over a rifle and make him talk."

"No! Look at my identoplate——"

Two soldiers grabbed either end of a rifle. Another

grabbed Oh Dear's head, a fourth grabbed his feet. The first two held the rifle horizontally in the middle of his back. The second two pulled. Oh Dear's spine began to crack. He screamed.

"Tell me where the others have gone!" roared Flay.

"We don't know!" shrieked Oh Dear. "Look at my I.D.!"

An officer fished in Oh Dear's pockets. He looked at the identoplate he found. "This just says he's a clerk in Section 451. That's this planet. He's no courier."

"Make him talk!" said Flay.

They pulled on Oh Dear harder.

"You better talk! You know where they have gone well enough. Don't lie again. TALK!"

Oh Dear went into a high-pitched keening as his spine stretched and cracked. He was able to get out, "I have a despatch. I have a despatch. I have a despatch! I must get it through!"

"To Hells with your despatches," said Flay.

Oh Dear had fainted.

Flay gave a signal and soldiers grabbed Bolz. One of them pulled his head back with a handful of hair and another hit him in the body with a fist. Bolz grunted with the force of it.

"Where have they gone?" demanded Flay.

"They did not tell us!" cried Bolz.

The colonel snapped his fingers and an officer put a light in his hand. Flay walked up to Bolz and shined the light in his eye. "Are you lying to us?"

Bolz writhed, trying to get away from the light. The only thing which was registering with him was that this colonel might discover that he intended to keep this base for his own use.

"His pupillary reaction," said Flay, "shows that he is lying! Hit him!"

The blow echoed through the hangar.

"Once more," said Flay, "I am going to ask you politely and then we will really get to work on you. Where has this base crew gone?"

"I DON'T KNOW!" screamed Bolz.

"Hit him!" said the colonel.

It was the last order he ever issued in this life.

The blow hit the button remote in Bolz's pocket.

There was a searing flash throughout the hangar!

The Death Battalion, the warship, the *Blixo*, the crew, Captain Bolz and Oh Dear glowed, suddenly outlined in incandescence. They shifted color upward from red to yellow to violet. They went black. They turned to silica, momentarily holding shape, then they became molten glass.

No one in the base was left alive.

The wall boxes that held the beams in place turned into sand which, under the ferocity of heat, turned to liquid dribble.

And then with a shuddering roar, the walls of the hangar twisted and began to cave in.

The slide of rock went on for quite a while.

Fantastic heat fused the inside of the mountain.

Then there was nothing left of the Earth base.

And buried there, because of the delay and self-interest of Bolz, lying under the pile of shuddering glass which had been Oh Dear and under the countless tons of boiling silica above it, was the ash of the despatch which had been designed to stave off an invasion of Earth.

It would never be delivered.

PART
SEVENTY-NINE

Chapter 1

Oh, Madison had little doubt now that he would be able to finish his job with Heller. In the foreseeable future he would have not just the Apparatus but the entire Army and Fleet on Heller's trail.

Oh, what headlines that would make!

He was standing at an upper-story window of the Royal mansion on Relax Island, waiting for Teenie, who was unaccountably delayed. He had landed in the rear of the palace so as to stay out of sight. He was down here to tell Teenie some good news and give her some evidence.

Through the window came one of the softest and most perfume-laden breezes he had ever felt. The magnificent view of the valley below soothed his nerves. And one particular ten-acre square of the farmland down there would soothe other nerves as well: it was smoothly rippling with a flourishing crop of marijuana—Panama Red, if he recalled aright when Teenie, working a crew from her five-thousand island population, had told him what she was doing.

But no labors jarred today the tranquil scene of the terrace. A masked woman, middle-aged, an editor's wife, was strolling along the balustrade, loosely gowned and indolent. From time to time she turned her eyes away from the view and cast glances expectantly along the front of the palace.

Ah, here came what she was looking for. A gallant young officer in a brilliant silver uniform approached her at a slow pace. He stopped, he spread his hands admiringly, he bowed. She stopped and steadied herself against the balustrade. The young officer approached closer. He said something in a low voice and the woman laughed coquettishly. He took her arm and they began to stroll together.

Madison admired how well Teenie had taught her regiment. He knew that their lessons did not include just deportment.

And here behind them smoothly appeared a musician with a chorder-beat. But the tune he was playing and the tones had been taken from Teenie's record collection: it sounded exactly like a romantic gypsy violin.

The officer and the lady sauntered down the wide palace steps. Followed by the violin music, they strolled along a path. They entered one of the many secluded nooks. Each one, Madison knew, had a softly padded bench. He could just see the end of one through the flowering trees.

A begging babble reached his ears.

Presently, as he expected, he saw the woman's gown being laid gently on the bench end.

The musician was now behind a tree, his back to the nook, but the violin music played on.

In the limbs above, a branch of blossoms began to weave.

The musician's face was watchful, intent. He was playing faster now.

Blossoms exploded and the petals showered down.

The music now was mild and slow.

An attendant in silver livery who bore a silver tray sped across the terrace. He entered the nook.

Shortly the gray-blue smoke of marijuana rose.

The violin music played on.

Madison looked down at the terrace. Another publisher's wife had come out. She was masked, but Madison knew her husband published the *Daily Conservative.*

Another officer came out of the palace. He stopped, he bowed, he approached. He whispered something in her ear and she handed him a flower.

They sauntered down another path.

Another musician followed them.

The pair entered another nook.

From the palace now came a third officer. He strolled to the first nook. Madison faintly heard his voice, "I say, old man, may I cut in?"

Above the second nook a branch of blossoms was going in a circle.

The second musician, back to it, played faster and faster.

The branch of blossoms erupted in a blast of petals.

The second musician smiled and began to play dreamily.

The attendant with the silver tray approached the second nook at speed.

Out from the palace came a third publisher's wife.

The violin music played on. And Madison knew it would play on for the rest of the day. And other violins would play for the twenty other wives who would be sporting in these gardens this afternoon—after sporting in their bedrooms the entire night before!

Aside from marijuana, any LSD trips they had now were totally full of handsome young officers!

Madison stole a peek at the clipping book he was carrying. The first batches of women were long since

returned home. Just to test his muscle he was getting psychiatry good coverage. Page after page contained news
stories about the marvelous cures it was effecting, how
magnificent Crobe was, how misguided any other form
of treatment was and how all rival ideas should be
crushed out. Life had become impossible for publishers
and editors unless they ran columns and columns about
this marvelous new science imported from Blito-P3!

Oh, there was no doubt of it that psychiatry had
all the answers. They had won press domination on Earth
the very same way: get the wives of the publishers and
editors on the couch and being liberally (bleeped)
and you got all the column inches you could ever want!
And woe betide any competitor in the field: he would be
slaughtered!

A voice behind him jarred into his mood. "What
the hell have you become? Some God (bleeped) voyeur?"

Chapter 2

It was Teenie and she looked very cross. Her air
limousine must have landed in the back near his, for he
hadn't heard it. She was drawing off a pair of black
gloves and two maids were hastily attending her. This
was her upper dressing antechamber.

"Oh, Teenie," said Madison, "you have done so
well. Organizing this place and training the officers as
you have was a superhuman feat. And look: here are the
first fruits of victory!"

He shoved the clipping book under her nose. She

shook off a maid who was trying to comb out her hair and reorder the ponytail and took the book.

She looked at it. "I don't see anything here about Gris."

"No, no. This just shows the dawning of press control. Right now they're just bragging about psychiatry. Isn't it marvelous? Some of this is front page! It's never been done before in the history of Voltar! Influencing their press."

"Listen, buster, I'm helping you for just one reason. You'll forget that to your sorrow! I want that Gris spread-eagled on the block down there and hours and hours every day filled with his screams. I've thought of things way beyond anything dreamed up by Pinch. And all the way here from Palace City today, I've been thinking up new ones! Oh, I'm MAD!"

"Teenie," said Madison anxiously, well aware it could be himself, not Gris, on the block down there, "what has happened?"

"The (bleepard) has ruined Too-Too's life, that's what."

"Too-Too? How?"

"That (bleepard) Gris just reached out and smashed him!"

"WHAT? Has Gris escaped?"

"No such luck, for maybe then I could trail him down and capture him. He's still in that stinking Royal prison hiding out from us. And (bleep) all *you*'ve done to get him out and into that dungeon. I'll let Too-Too tell you—if he can talk."

She turned and gave a signal and a guard rushed off. Teenie took an agitated tour of the ornate dressing ante-chamber. She looked like an angry and frustrated menace to Madison.

There was a clatter at the door and two white-coated men brought in a stretcher. One of Teenie's maids from Palace City was beside it: she was sponging at the forehead of its burden.

Too-Too lay with ashen face, seemingly a corpse. The men laid the stretcher down upon a sofa and the maid swabbed anxiously at the unconscious visage.

Teenie brushed the maid aside. She bent down and stroked Too-Too's pretty face. The makeup was already smeared. Too-Too did not respond.

Teenie turned to Madison. "I brought him with me in the hopes the quiet here would help. And I also wanted you to hear what a (bleepard) that Gris is. I'm going to have to use mouth-to-mouth resuscitation." She snapped her fingers and a footman raced in with a silver tray. Teenie took a joint out of a silver box and lit it. She then knelt by Too-Too. She took a puff from it and then laid her lips on Too-Too's and blew.

Too-Too began to cough on the smoke. Teenie took another puff and, steadying him, pried his lips apart with her tongue and blew.

Too-Too went into a spasm. He had sat up. He saw Teenie and put his arm around her and began to cry.

Teenie held him off and made him puff the joint. This time he inhaled deeply and then the smoke blubbered out amongst his coughs and sobs.

Teenie made him do it again. He became calmer.

"Oh, Teenie, dear Teenie," Too-Too said, "my life has come to an end. Hold me close, dear Teenie, so that I can perish in your arms."

"Hush, dear Too-Too, you'll live many a day to be (bleeped) by many men yet. We're going to get that (bleepard) Gris. I'll even show you the dungeon where he'll be tortured. Now tell this man here what you told me so he'll get off his (bleep) and begin working like he meant it!"

"It's too painful," said Too-Too. And Teenie had to get him to puff the joint again.

Too-Too, in a broken voice, began to talk. Gris had forced him and Oh Dear into being couriers and informers by a mechanism known as magic mail. Every three months, by mailing a card through a certain slot, an order continued to be held. But for some reason the *Blixo*'s schedule had been advanced and although Too-Too had mailed the last card he had been given on Earth punctually, as he thought, it had been late.

The order which had been held had already gone. The commander of the Knife Section on Mistin had received it. Due to internal Confederacy delays between planets, Too-Too had only now been informed.

HIS MOTHER HAD BEEN MURDERED!

Screaming it out, he went back into a collapse and Teenie had to work hard to revive him. After more mouth-to-mouth marijuana resuscitation, she said, "Now, Too-Too, start from the beginning and begin to spill all the crimes you know that Gris has committed."

Madison listened. This catamite knew quite a bit. It was all headline stuff. Actually, Madison had not been too interested in Gris, regarding him just as a way to get to Heller. But as he listened he began to get fascinated. This was juicy copy!

Finally he said, "You say he gave you orders to kill old Bawtch and two others in your office. Won't that implicate you?"

"Oh, no!" cried Too-Too. "I couldn't murder anybody. I simply told Lombar Hisst. We just transferred Bawtch to another section. That was when Hisst began to set Gris up."

"For what?" said Madison.

But Too-Too had spent what little energy he had and was collapsed again in Teenie's arms.

"Now you've heard it," Teenie said, her eyes smoldering as she looked at Madison over Too-Too's head. "Don't let any grass grow under your feet. GET THAT GRIS!"

Madison grinned. With material like this, how could he miss? It would open the door to Heller with a crash.

Chapter 3

Four hours later Madison, in a hurtling Model 99, was hot on the trail. He had been very intrigued by the information that Gris had been "set up." He also knew from recent past experience that the media here had a nasty idea that one should have documents and proof for stories. While this was far from insurmountable—one could always forge and find false witnesses—it might save him time if he could get his hands on the real thing and, thanks to Too-Too, he was certain that, somewhere, a lot of evidence existed.

He had been cautioned by Lombar's chief clerk not to barge in all the time on Lombar Hisst, so the logical target in this case was the old chief clerk himself. The man would be, he thought, at Spiteos or the palace.

Madison, having crossed the green seas and now with the mainland under him, was still trying on the communications system to locate his quarry.

Suddenly into his calling, a harsh voice broke in: "Divert! Divert! This is Apparatus Traffic Surveillance. J. Walter Madison, divert from your course at once and proceed to the Office of the Chief of Apparatus, Government City, without delay."

"Oh, boy," said Flick, overhearing it, "you're in trouble."

"Why is he in trouble?" said Cun who had bullied herself back into her job, Relax Island or no Relax Island.

"It means they been looking for him," said Flick to Cun. "It means they were calling earlier and it means you was out of the airbus instead of standing by its phone. I bet you got yourself (bleeped)!"

"I did not!" said Cun savagely. "I was just peeking."

"I'll bet you were," said Flick. "How come the front of your uniform is wet?"

"I was getting a drink of water. It was you that was getting all hot. And over a scullery maid, too!"

"Peace!" said Madison. "Head for Government City. Do you know where his in-town office is?"

"You can't miss it," said Flick. "Upper end of the town, on the cliff above the River Wiel. You can always tell it from the dead bodies in the streets around it."

"I hope you're joking," said Madison.

"Well, yes, actually I am," said Flick. "He has a chute so he can dump them into the River Wiel."

They sped across the green countryside and soon were over the masses of tall buildings which housed the bulk of the government. The vast area at the upper end skirted tall cliffs which fell into the River Wiel. This section was the oldest and most decayed part of Government City, and the Apparatus, while not the oldest, was certainly the most decayed part of the government and had fallen heir to it.

There was a square, occupied by a central building which was surrounded by broken pavement and monuments to forgotten glory. All of this would seem to indicate that the Apparatus was also old but this was not true: the service was really quite young as things in Voltar go. It was only that the other parts of the government would no longer live in this place where the fountains no longer ran and the statues were missing heads and legs.

As the Model 99 swept in to land, there was immediate trouble to find a parking place. Wide as the surrounding pavements were, they were covered with randomly parked tanks and vehicles.

Flick squeezed in between a personnel carrier and a flight command car, each of which bore a general's guidon. Cun opened the door while ogling some of the drivers.

"There's something going on here," said Flick. "These are the vehicles of the Apparatus General Staff! You watch it, Chief. They're the most vicious (bleepards) in the Confederacy!"

Madison got out. He felt a little conspicuous in his gray business suit. He made his way through clusters of officers and men in mustard uniforms, black uniforms, green uniforms, every one of them badged with the Apparatus symbol which, if you looked at it from a certain angle, did resemble a bottle.

An overly dressed young woman with a snug on a leash was sauntering in front of the main door. Another one, considerably underdressed and with a hard face, was impatiently twirling a cane. The latter accosted Madison, "How much longer is this silly meeting to go on?" she said.

"I have no idea, madam," said Madison.

"Well, if you're going in there, you just tell General

But that his mistress has been waiting for five (bleeping) hours. I'm fed up!"

Madison went up the broken steps. Two sentries in mustard barred his way. An officer bawled at him, "Madison? Where the blast have you been? Get the Hells in there and fast!"

Madison found himself being propelled across a cluttered lobby and then down a flight of stairs. The officer thrust him into a crowded room.

The place looked more like a cave than an office. It also stank.

Generals in red uniforms were sitting in chairs around the rough rock walls. In the recorded strips of this meeting they look just like Manco Devils.

Lombar Hisst was sitting behind a desk, also uniformed in red. He was turned sideways, watching a staff officer with a remote control in his hand who was electronically chasing an orange arrow around on a projected map.

"This is *Omaha*," the staff officer said. "According to earlier intelligence advices, it is a sort of military nerve center. Estimates are that it will take a million men, after it is occupied, to hold the position and fan out eastward."

"A million men!" commented a general. "That means no supplementary reserve."

"Well, if we are denied the right to simply bomb *New York* . . ."

"That has to be denied," said Hisst. "It would obliterate the installations that must be seized in operational condition in *New Jersey*. That requires a solely infantry approach, moving through cities on a slaughter basis. Are you afraid of casualties?" he asked the first general with a sneer.

"No," said the first general. "I was simply hoping that some way the Army could be coerced into participation. We only have about four million troops. When distribution to other continents is examined..."

"We could simply concentrate on the *United States*," said another general.

"No, no, no," said a general with artillery badges. "There are more than twelve nations that are nuclear armed, according to reports. Failure to make this an infantry action on all continents could result in some hysterical nuclear involvement. If the objectives of the chief are to be attained, we have to prevent their use of hydrogen bombs from one country to another across oceans. I think you would find the objective areas totally contaminated and unusable."

An aide bent over Lombar, "Your Excellency, the Earthman has finally arrived."

All eyes swivelled to Madison. (To do him justice, he might not have understood completely that what was under discussion was an invasion of Earth, for the meeting transcripts do not, of course, give internal thoughts of those speaking. Madison's own logs shed no light on this.)

The general of artillery was the one who spoke. "What is the range and thermal penetration potential of an MX3 missile?"

Madison said, "I'm sorry. I don't have it at my fingertips. But I don't think it's much to be worried about. The full project was, if I recall, challenged by the General Accounting Office because of cost overruns and was suspended. I remember reading about it."

"Ha!" said the artillery general. "Good man. So that's a system we don't have to worry about. Now what about the satellite killers? Those could be used against spaceships."

"Well, only the *Russians* developed those. They received a lot of TV coverage. So I should think that if you avoided the sky-space over *Russia*, they would be no problem."

"Aha!" said the artillery general. "Show us this *Russia*."

Madison walked up to the front of the cave and with a "With your permission" took the remote from the staff officer. He mastered it and the projector began to throw up Earth maps. He found Russia and showed them. (Madison would not have known, since it had happened after his departure, that there was no Russia now.)

Hisst moved restively. He glared at the generals. "All right, you can go and wrangle someplace else now. But get a general operational plan on this desk by tomorrow!"

They rose and their aides got their papers together and they left. Lombar, after a bit, became aware that Madison was still there.

"You've been dismissed!" said Hisst.

"I wanted to see you about Gris," said Madison.

"Gris, Gris, Gris! Well, (BLEEP) Gris! He's the one who is the cause of all this trouble!"

"Could I ask what all this trouble is?" said Madison.

"Amphetamines! Intelligence!" shouted Hisst. "If the sun didn't rise tomorrow and I investigated, I can promise you it would lead to Gris! The *Blixo*, on its last arrival, should have brought amphetamines. It didn't. Now there has not been one freighter since! He never kept his intelligence reports up and now we're going blind."

"I can get him!" said Madison.

That got through to Hisst. But he shook his head.

"I've sent three assassins into the Royal prison. Gris is still alive! It's impossible."

"You don't want him dead," said Madison. "You want him talking."

"He let Heller get away from him," said Lombar in his usual disconnected way. "I'm going to kill him!"

"I can get Heller, too," said Madison.

"Heller has turned all Earth against me," said Hisst. "I am certain that right this minute Heller is racing through the streets of that planet screaming at the people to attack me! He's a scourge! The Army and the Fleet won't make the slightest effort to smash him!"

"Please," said Madison. "Let's open up our coats. Is there some reason you don't want Gris to talk?"

The unpredictable Lombar suddenly broke out laughing. Madison did note later that, with Lombar, he very often felt like he was dealing with someone who was quite insane.

"Did you set Gris up some way?" pursued Madison.

Lombar was still laughing. Finally he said, "If I were ever accused of anything, nothing could be proved. Every order that ever went to Blito-P3, every shipment that ever came from there, bears only the name of Soltan Gris. He stamped his life away!"

"Then you wouldn't mind if Gris came to trial?"

"What's a trial got to do with it?"

Madison said, "A trial that was public, that was reported in the media. Blow by blow."

"That's a funny idea."

"You can even try him first in the media and then he's certain to be found guilty in the court. That's the proper way to do these things."

"How strange."

"You'd emerge the hero," said Madison. "It would help build your image."

"Oh, trials have nothing to do with this," said Hisst, suddenly looking angry. "My problem is how to get the Army and Fleet cooperating."

"Is that very vital?" said Madison.

"He asks me if that's vital," Lombar asked an invisible spectator who wasn't there. "I'd have to withdraw the whole Apparatus from Calabar to invade Earth. At least the Army and Fleet could take over there!"

"You need the cooperation of the Army and Fleet," said Madison. "I CAN GET THEM FOR YOU!"

Lombar stopped. Finally he said, "How?"

"Let me have all the files and witnesses on Gris. I will get him into the press and on trial. Then I will get him to accuse Heller. It can be done so that the whole Army and Fleet will go chasing after Heller like mad dogs!"

"Really?"

Madison took the clipping book he had been carrying. He flopped it open on the desk before Lombar. "These stories are just trial balloons. I wrote every one. They'll print anything I issue. All I have to do is use the media, and the Army and the Fleet will be in your hands!"

Lombar was staring at the book, leafing through it. "They are publishing what you say?"

"I control the media of the Confederacy. It's just a tool. I can use it to whip up a storm that will give you all the support you will ever need for anything you want to do. I can mold public opinion like it was clay! And that is the key to all your projects."

"Miraculous!" said Lombar, still staring at the

book. "Crobe? A hero?" Yet here were touched-up pictures of Crobe, front page! Laudatory! Paper after paper!

"There, you see? And that's just an exercise to try my muscle. A nothing."

"Madison, if you can make them think that that demented old criminal is a hero, then it should be no difficulty at all to make a deserving, preselected man like me..."

"An emperor," Madison finished for him.

Hisst's yellow eyes grew round and then began to glow. He stood up, towering over Madison a foot. He took one of Madison's hands in his and stroked it. Then he turned and bawled toward the door, "CHIEF CLERK! GIVE THIS MAN MADISON EVERYTHING HE WANTS! EVERYTHING, YOU UNDERSTAND, OR I WILL HAVE YOUR HEAD!"

Chapter 4

Outside the sun had almost set. The square was nearly deserted and the Model 99 looked lonely in the rubble.

Madison handed Cun an enormous stack of printouts, gave Flick an address card and got in.

"You had us worried," said Flick as he got the Model 99 moving. "Cun was talking to the driver of that general's tank beside us: he said that was the whole Apparatus General Staff in there planning a full-scale invasion. When he said 'Blito-P3' we flipped! Ain't that the planet you're from?"

Madison was lost in thought and did not reply.

"Now, I'm from Calabar," said Flick. "All that war over there worries me. They slaughter whole towns, butcher the kids, rape the women, burn the lot. I should think your hair was standing on end thinking of the Apparatus invading your planet."

"Oh, war is just war," said Madison in a bored voice. "I'm a PR man. Most wars are started by PRs. So what's there to be excited about?"

"Listen to that, Cun," said Flick. "What a cool one! But I guess that kind of attitude goes along with being a murderer. And speaking of murder, get your stinger out, Cun. This neighborhood we're moving into is a perfect 'X marks the spot.'"

They pulled up before a place that was more fallen down than standing: the reek of garbage assailed their noses. Madison walked up some steps at the risk of a broken ankle and banged on a door.

A man with two tufts of gray hair standing out on either side of his head poked his nose out. "Go away. I've just this minute gotten home. I'm entitled to a little peace."

"Is your name Bawtch?" said Madison.

Bawtch tried to close the door but Madison's foot was in it. "I've come to you for information about a man named Gris."

"GRIS! Get out of here!"

"He's in the Royal prison," said Madison, "laughing at you all. I'm trying to get him brought to trial."

"*Come in!*" said Bawtch.

For a revelatory half an hour, Madison, in Bawtch's best chair, listened entranced. "So then," he finally said, "I could count on you as a character witness."

"I'd walk across the Great Desert just for a chance to testify," said Bawtch.

"And if I asked you to give a lecture on him, you'd talk?" said Madison.

"Indeed I would," said Bawtch. "Now, thinking this over, I can give you a couple names. They're just down the street." He wrote an address and handed it across.

At the door, Bawtch shook him emotionally by the hand. "Count on me, Madison."

They rolled around the corner and down a hill. They halted before a very decayed boarding house—For Gentlemen Officers, it said on a twisted sign.

A harsh-faced woman came to the door. Madison had learned his lesson: "I'm here to get you to help me hang Gris. I presume your name is Meeley. You were once his landlady."

"To help you hang..." She whirled suddenly and yelled in the direction of the kitchen. "SKE! COME OUT HERE! WE'RE IN LUCK! SOMEBODY WANTS TO HANG GRIS!"

Madison found himself in a parlor, drinking hot jolt. He listened while Ske, Gris's old driver, poured out his tale of woe, interrupted with curses and tales of woe of her own by Meeley. He gathered that Gris had given them both counterfeit bills and had they tried to pass them they would have been executed. But, knowing Gris, instead they had gone straight to the Finance Police with complaints of their own. Their bitterness against Gris had bound them close together.

Oh, yes, they'd testify at any trial. Gladly, gladly, gladly! At a lecture? Well, they were not really very presentable but they'd be only too glad to say anything Madison wanted.

Smiling like a toother that was all set to snap up his prey, Madison returned to the townhouse in Joy City. He ignored dinner. There was no time for that. He called his whole staff together.

He stood upon the platform in the briefing room. He stood very tall.

"Loyal and hard working staff," he said, "this is a milestone. At times PR finds itself on a pinnacle. We are about to influence the courses of empires. We are about to direct the very destiny of the stars. Now listen closely."

Chapter 5

Two days later, a very select audience of ninety women sat in the lecture hall on the eightieth floor of the townhouse, conscious that they were being especially favored by an invitation to this highly educational lecture by the famous Doctor Crobe.

They were also conscious, but this was never mentioned, that if they didn't cooperate, they would never again get another chance to "get cured" at Relax Island. Also—although this, too, was never even hinted at—if they weren't agreeable, somebody might forget to renew their free supply of pot.

What was discussed amongst themselves and to others quite freely was that, as members of high society, they had a positive duty to use their positions—and their husbands—to do good. It didn't have a spoken name but they were all members of a very exclusive club made up entirely of those fortunate enough to have been "enlightened" at Relax Island.

Madison had had a little trouble with Crobe. He had sneaked an extra dose of LSD into himself outside his rationing and two roustabouts had had to stand him up in alternate hot and cold showers to bring him around.

He stood now on the lecture platform, aware that he would get a small jolt through his hidden electric collar if he goofed up, and steadied himself against the desk.

"Ladies," he said, repeating what the ear speaker told him to, "you are aware that as the chosen inner circle of the enlightened few, your . . . your social . . . social position has responsibilities. The society we live in is . . . is unfortunately a cesspool of unrestrained insanity and monstrous abuses. Lurking, hidden, out of sight . . . out of sight from common and unenlightened view, the brains of men . . . seethe with lusts and ferocity unimagined. It frightens me to see the dangers to which this society is exposed and how ill it . . . it . . . it handles them. It requires stern measures louder it requires STERN MEASURES!" He took a deep breath and steadied himself with his fingers against the desk top.

"Lean forward. There is a case so monstrous, would you know it, that I do not even describe it to you lean back and stop. You are, after all, gently nurtured ladies and I must not speak of it lest I offend your ears don't go on."

"No, no," cried Lady Arthrite Stuffy in the front row, well aware of her position as the leader of this select group. "Go on, go on! Do not be afraid to offend our ears."

"Oh, yes, go on!" came others' calls.

"Look as though you need coaxing," said Crobe.

"We don't need coaxing!" cried a woman. "Tell us!"

"Go ahead. Well, this case, ladies, is so shout it vile that you will cringe. It is a singular and notable case. It is so notable that it falls totally outside the Freudian band of psychosexual pathology!"

"No!" came several cries.

"The case," said Crobe, "is not anal. It is not oral. It is not genital! It is not even latent! Shout a monster."

The women looked appalled.

Crobe sat down suddenly in a chair. "A woman has come forward to describe this case as an eyewitness. Introduce her."

Meeley came forward timidly to the platform. Then took confidence from the expectant female faces. "What he says," said Meeley, "is true. I was his landlady. He never had women in his room. He closed the door when he went to the bathroom. He never spoke properly to anyone. When he wasn't sneaking in and out, he was lurking in the dirt and filth of his room. There is no describing his obscene and awful thoughts. He also plotted day and night to get me executed just because I used to smile at him and wish him good day. When he skipped out we could find no one to occupy his room. It had such an awful reputation that it is empty yet!" She broke down sobbing and an usher led her off.

Then came Ske. "I was," he said, "his long-suffering driver. The deprivations I experienced during that unhappy period of my life have left a brand upon me so deep that my very soul is seared. He used to sit in the airbus trying to hide the grinding of his teeth. And for my faithful service he tried to get me executed. I cannot describe the obscenities that surrounded him!" He broke down as coached and fled the platform.

Old Bawtch came forward. "I was his chief clerk and it ruined my life. The murders and crimes of this man, strung end to end, would reach half across the universe.

The insane things he did culminated in orders to take my life."

He left the platform. Crobe, somewhat revived, stood up. "Now, ladies, you can plainly see that insanity rages. The diagnosis of this case is so monstrous that in all the annals of psychiatry there has never been one like it. I have simply look calm and professorial brought up the case to show you how the claws of insanity have dug into the very depths of our culture look like that's the end."

"Wait!" cried Lady Arthrite. "Who is this case and where is he?"

"Look toward the door. Is the man who informed me of this case still here?"

"Yes," said an usher promptly.

An actor dressed as a warder of the Royal prison came in reluctantly. He was wearing a mask. "Doctor Crobe," he said, "I told you about this case for the good of the society. If it got out that I had informed you of what the government is doing, it could cause me to lose my job."

"Tell them tell them they will all regard your identity as inviolate."

The actor turned. "The man is being held in the Royal prison to avoid his being brought to trial. He sits in his cell, protected. What is feared is that if he ever was put before a judge, the things he would divulge would shake the government to its very foundations. Even if they tried him, it would be done in secret. What we warders fear is that he will be released upon the society through a back door and strew the streets with the gruesomely mangled bodies of the poor and innocent. While I know naught of your *psychiatry*, from just viewing him in his cell, I would say that, in a long career of handling malefactors, he is easily the worst I have ever seen. He defies all descriptions! Yet THEY are hiding and defending him."

"What is his name?" said Lady Arthrite Stuffy in an enraged voice.

"His name," said the actor, "is Soltan Gris!"

Chapter 6

Like a maestro conducting a vast orchestra, J. Walter Madison went to work on Soltan Gris.

The highest social circles of Voltar were buzzing about the scandal and, quite in addition to demands from their wives, publishers and editors could not turn anywhere without colliding with the outrage.

The first headlines read:

> ## MYSTERIOUS PRISONER
> ## HIDDEN BY AUTHORITIES

And this was quickly followed up with:

> ## WHO IS THE
> ## GOVERNMENT REFUSING
> ## TO BRING TO TRIAL?

And then:

> # IDENTITY REVEALED!
> # PRISONER IS
> # APPARATUS OFFICER
> # SOLTAN GRIS!

Quickly then, edition after edition and day after day, the documented catalogue of the crimes of Apparatus Officer Soltan Gris began to appear, each one juicier than the last.

They began with:

> # APPARATUS OFFICER
> # GRIS ILLEGALLY
> # EXPORTED METALS

Immediately after that:

> # APPARATUS OFFICER
> # GRIS ORDERED MURDER
> # OF OWN OFFICE HEAD
> # AND CLERKS

And then:

> # APPARATUS OFFICER
> # ORDERS MURDER OF
> # MOTHER OF
> # DEFENSELESS BOY

And a picture of the sobbing Twolah and faked photos of his mother's body and funeral began to send ripples of rage through the population.

It was at this time that Lord Turn received a viewerphone call from no less a social leader than Lady Arthrite Stuffy.

"Lord Turn," said Lady Arthrite, "I do not think you realize that public opinion is growing. WHEN are you going to bring that prisoner to trial?"

"Lady Arthrite," said Lord Turn, "would you please keep your nose out of the affairs of the Royal prison?" And hung up.

This, as it was recorded, gave the *Daily Speaker* an exclusive:

> # JUDGE TELLS PUBLIC
> # "HANDS OFF GRIS!"

This, of course, made all the other papers livid: they had been scooped. They began to bombard Lord Turn with tricky calls of their own. This made Lord Turn furious. He was so angry that he refused to explain anything to anyone. The headlines grew worse and worse.

Now, unfortunately for Soltan Gris, when he had been blackmailing the Provocation Section of the Apparatus, the head of that section had been radio-recording back to his own office down by the River Wiel during the whole time that he had been shadowing Gris to get the goods on him. And a recording of every single one of these crimes Gris had pulled at that time existed, with pictures and sound, in the Provocation Section. Gris, unaware of this, thought he had handled it with the final murder of that chief. And now Madison began to feed these crimes one at a time to the press.

HYPNOTIST MURDERED
BY APPARATUS
OFFICER GRIS

And then:

SUPPLY COLONEL
MURDERED BY
APPARATUS OFFICER
GRIS

And then:

ELECTRONICS WIZARD
SPURK FOULLY SLAIN
BY APPARATUS OFFICER
GRIS

———

BURNS THIRD OF
ELECTRONICS INDUSTRIAL
QUARTER TO HIDE
VICIOUS CRIME

And the final one of the series was complete with photographs of a body falling ten thousand feet.

> ## BROTHER APPARATUS OFFICER SLAIN IN DASTARDLY EFFORT TO HIDE DAMNABLE CRIMES

The footage was even shown on Homeview, which was beginning to take an interest.

The question was starting to buzz through the streets: If the government had an officer who had been committing all these crimes, just why was it refusing to bring the villain to trial?

But Madison was saving a *pièce de résistance.*

When Bawtch had been overheard chortling "he had Gris now" and about a forgery, he had NOT been talking about the Royal signature forgeries at all. At that time, he didn't even know about them.

Gris, in his carelessness, had left the old cloak of Prahd's beside his office desk. He had intended it to be found beside the River Wiel. And in that cloak he had wrapped a very bad forgery, a suicide note. Unfortunately, he had written it on a piece of paper which had been under a document when he stamped it for Bawtch. And dimly under the writing on the Prahd suicide note could be seen the identoplate outline of Soltan Gris!

The recorded strips of the dead Provocation Section officer had shown Soltan Gris calling on Prahd Bittlestiffender.

All evidence for a murder charge was there. So Madison, through one of his reporters, called the attention of the Domestic Police to the crime.

The Domestic Police traced it down, accompanied by a horde of reporters, and found that young Dr. Prahd Bittlestiffender was nowhere to be found. They then issued a warrant for the arrest of Soltan Gris.

Young Dr. Prahd, the most promising cellologist to graduate for some time, was extolled by his professors as a real loss to his profession. The act of cutting him down in his early youth could be looked upon as a crime against the whole population, who so desperately needed his services. The act of a madman!

HEADLINES!

Then the Domestic Police asked Lord Turn for the custody of Gris so they could try him and execute him. It was, of course, refused.

HEADLINES!

The questions began to race through the population. Why was the government protecting this raving lunatic of an Apparatus officer? Why would they not let him be brought to trial?

Written by his ex-Royal Academy of Arts reporter, Madison began to circulate the words and music of a ballad. It was printed on a single sheet and seemed to be the creation of an unknown. Shortly it was being reprinted in the press and sung on every hand. It went:

In the name of the government he murdered and killed.
Many an innocent victim he has chilled.
He is an Apparatus officer!
Why does the government love this cur?
He grows fat on his victim's blood,
Then with glee stamps them in the mud.

Coddled and protected for his crime,
They extoll his virtues as sublime.
We are demanding his life should cease.
WE WANT THE BLOOD OF SOLTAN GRIS!

Mobs took to marching in the streets singing it at the tops of their voices.

Actually, some time since, J. Walter Madison had fully expected Lord Turn to simply give in and say, "All right. I'll try him." And in the case of the Domestic Police, "Here he is. Try the Hells out of him."

If he could only get Gris on the stand accusing Heller, Madison knew he would have it made.

But he had reached an impasse. The fury boiling in the streets was not moving Lord Turn up there in his high castle.

Other measures were needed.

Chapter 7

Madison was busy far into the night, laying out his plans. There were several things he had to do. Amongst the first of them was to keep Lombar Hisst hopeful.

Accordingly, one morning, Madison caught Hisst at his desk before the closed door of the Emperor's bedroom. Hisst was going over the details of the invasion plan of Earth.

"How soon," he greeted Madison, "do you suppose we can have the cooperation of the Army and the Fleet? If they can supplant our Apparatus forces now active in the Calabar revolt, we can get on with invading Blito-P3 and bring it to heel."

"I'm working on that project day and night," said Madison. "In fact, that's what I'm here to see you about: that and the far more important question of making you Emperor. You see, all these things tie together neatly."

"How?" said Hisst.

"It's simply a matter of image," said Madison. "With enough image, you can do anything. Now what I need to know is what exact image do you favor? How do you want the public to think of you?"

Lombar sat back. His yellow eyes grew dreamy. "Totally formidable," he said finally.

"That's what I thought," said Madison. "A man of iron will. One who will brook no nonsense. The public yearns for strong and merciless control. The figure of a vengeful God."

"Exactly," said Lombar Hisst. "I have finally discovered why I listen to you. You are extremely perceptive and are not afraid to speak the truth to your superior."

"I only do my duty," said Madison. "Now, I know that you are very busy. But it just so happens that there are some riots going on at this minute in Slum City. It is a marvelous opportunity to create image. The mob is being contained by two battalions of the Apparatus. I have a camera crew standing by. If your good judgment tells you that you should utilize this priceless opportunity to create image, we can go there in your private tank and you'll be on Homeview in a trice."

"A mob," said Lombar, "that needs quelling? Where's my cap and stinger?"

An hour and a half later, Lombar stomped up the steps of the prepared stand before the faces of an assembled five thousand people. The Slum City square was cordoned off. For once Madison had not had to put out any money for extras or actors in such a demonstration. Due to the Gris publicity, the two Apparatus Death Battalions were having more trouble keeping additional spectators out than containing the ones that were in: they had tank roadblocks on every side street that entered the area.

Madison had handed Lombar his speech. It was a good speech: the horror-story writer, under Madison's close direction, had been up all night writing it.

In his red general's uniform, Lombar loomed above the crowd. The speakers boomed as he began to read his speech.

"Citizens of Voltar! You are misguided. Law and order must triumph every time above mob rule. Our domestic tranquillity must not be shattered by questions and challenge of your government. I stand here, strong and powerful, formidable and determined to crush all opposition to the sovereign state. In me you see the image of stern power! I will not ever retreat from my stern duty to bring all malefactors to trial."

A wave of satisfaction swept through the vast throng. Madison's camera crew, supplemented by three more camera crews from Homeview on the manager's own initiative, were carrying this speech to all Voltar and, on delay, to every other planet.

"I will have you know," roared Lombar, in fine form, "that the characters of Apparatus officers should not be impugned by the crimes of Soltan Gris. Apparatus officers are men of sterling virtue and unblemished honor. I am proud to number myself amongst them and to be their chief.

"The rivers of blood spilled by Gris, the graveyards jammed with corpses, are all the work of Gris and Gris alone. This foul fiend must not damage the brilliant innocence of other Apparatus officers or mine!

"My very soul cries out to do him justice. With these two hands I could separate his spine, vertebra by vertebra, and take the utmost pleasure in it. I would love to deliver him even into the hands of this mob and let him be dismembered!"

Wild cheering began at the back and swept forward in a roar.

When the hysteria died, Hisst swept on. "Alas, His Majesty lies ill, too ill to be disturbed, and in this time of public crisis, I do not wish for anything but tranquillity. I am therefore carrying forward His Majesty's deepest wish and I am assuming the temporary powers of Dictator of Voltar."

There was a shock of stillness. The crowd stared. They had never heard of such a post or position.

But the speech gave no time for discussion. Lombar had never heard of the position either. He had not read the speech beforehand. But suddenly, although he could not imagine what it might embrace, he accepted the post with a surge of unbridled elation. It was the stepping-stone he had been seeking.

Filled with divine fervor, he read on, "I pledge on my honor to bring peace to Voltar, tranquillity to its people, and I will stamp out ruthlessly any dissidence or question that will damage the state. I am backed by the sterling and honest officers of the Apparatus and I will gather in the support of every other branch of service, or else!

"Now, as to the matter of Gris, due to the obstructionism of the Royal prison, other means will have to be used. The danger is that this foul fiend will be released upon the population to work his will again. Fortunately, there is a new tool that can be used. It is called *psycho-therapy*. It is that which will be employed. And I shall use my new powers to see that it is properly applied. So I promise you that the matter of Gris will be successfully concluded to the satisfaction of everyone."

The crowd was confused. Then they began to get the idea that *psychotherapy* must be some kind of torture. They began to cheer.

Lombar came to the last paragraph of his speech. He waited for a lull and then he boomed it out, "O population of the Confederacy! I promise you that I and all the other officers of the Apparatus, honest, unimpeachable and dedicated, will bring peace and order to the state no matter WHAT we have to do. I thank you!"

Delight raged. Lombar came down off the platform feet taller than he had climbed up it.

The two Death Battalions stood there dumbfounded. Their officers had to scream at them to block back the surging crowds so Lombar could get into his tank. The din of cheering for Lombar was deafening. He stood in the turret and waved. His tank took off.

"My Gods, Madison," he said, "your genius is almost as great as mine. But this post of dictator, won't it have to pass the Grand Council?"

Madison handed him the G.C. order, all stamped and signed. Only two members had been present but the pages were good pages. They had done what Teenie told them to.

"A man named Napoleon," said Madison, "moved from dictator to emperor with ease."

"GODS!" said Lombar, quivering. And for minutes he just stared into space.

It was not until they were flying across the Great Desert that Lombar spoke again. "You know, this opens the door to total cooperation by the Army and the Fleet. We will be able to handle both Calabar and Earth with ease. You seem to have solved everything. But I do have one question. What is this thing called *psychotherapy?* Some new long-distance method of execution?"

"You leave that to me," said Madison.

Lombar nodded and forgot about it.

PART EIGHTY

Chapter 1

Madison was handling the "psychotherapy."

He was in the observation slot back of the wall behind the eightieth-floor townhouse auditorium. He was grinning. This had to work, and when it did he would have his trial. And with the Gris trial, he would have Heller.

The editorials in the papers had been a very mixed lot on the subject of Lombar's speech, none of them less stunned than Madison's own staff. On his return his reporters and crew had said, "We made a dictator, bango, just like that! But what's a 'dictator,' Chief?" Some of the papers were of the opinion that a "dictator" was one who spoke into a dictating machine. Others, since the word had been translated directly over into literal Voltarian, said that it was a more forceful kind of spokesman and was a natural outgrowth from that earlier title. But the majority seemed to gather that Lombar had assumed much more embracive powers and, if the Grand Council order had not been showing up on their consoles, they would have had to assume that Lombar had authored some kind of a coup; they were not at all sure what. But none of the papers missed the point that the Apparatus was suddenly the senior force of the state.

The Apparatus didn't miss it. Their officers, with few exceptions jailbirds, joked to one another about their "unimpeachable reputations" and their "honor." They began to put on airs. Apparatus officers had never dared go into the better hotels and restaurants and clubs, and suddenly it pleased their fancy to show up and bully waiters and managers around. Apparatus troops began at once a game of holding arms and walking up streets shoving everyone else off the walks. Underpaid and unpaid, they began to find ways of being paid.

But Madison ignored all that. He was on to bigger game: Heller. His ways of arriving there were entirely PR. Deadly!

This "psychotherapy" action had begun with his discovery of a postcard in the Gris dossier. It said:

SOLTAN GRIS!

   YOO-HOO, WHEREVER YOU ARE.
   The baby came on schedule and he's beautiful.
   It's a he.
   Now, I don't want to have to go to your superior officer and make a fuss. It would be much nicer just to climb in bed with you. So when are you going to turn up and do the right thing and marry me?

                                        Pratia

PS: Any commanding officer: You can come out and see me about this any time you like. I hope you're handsome. I am very pretty again now that my belly is flat and we can talk it all over. What do you like for

---

> *breakfast? I can be found at Minx Estates,*
> *Pausch Hills.*
>
> *PPS: It has the softest beds and the loveliest*
> *swimming pool and a summerhouse with a*
> *bed in it. Smack. Smack.*

Now, Madison had known better than to put his handsome face in that trap. So he had sent the director and one of the circus girls dressed as people of fashion and an actor as Gris's "commanding officer."

Now, here in the auditorium, a hundred ladies of the "club" were gathered in breathtaking suspense, and Madison's grin widened as he peered through the slot from which he could view them. Although many were middle-aged, they looked in full bloom. They had recaptured some of their lost youth and life, viewed through a marijuana haze and sex, and seemed remarkably attractive.

Crobe took the stand. This time they'd kept the LSD away from him, and expecting more if he delivered, he was on his good behavior. The little speaker was in his ear and all he had to do was repeat the script being read over it.

"Ladies of quality, ladies of fashion, ladies of sparkling eyes and resurged youth," Crobe began—and it was pretty good even though he was saying it in a very flat voice—"I know how concerned you have been about the state's reluctance to try the insane lunatic Gris. As you doubtless read or saw on Homeview, Lombar Hisst, Dictator of Voltar, promised that *psychotherapy* would be attempted in the Gris case.

"Now the grave danger, ladies, is that Gris will be released upon the public totally insane, that he will continue to slaughter and burn and rampage throughout a helpless population.

"Hisst, poorly advised, directly ordered me to attempt a solution through *psychotherapy.* It was reasoned that if the foul fiend could be made sane, it would then be safe to turn him loose.

"I demurred. I tried to point out that this criminal lunatic Gris was entirely off the Freudian scale. Most of you heard the lecture where I took that up took that up took go on go on.

"I said to Hisst, 'The chances of success are so remote they are not worth . . . calculating.' He ordered me to do it anyway. Then I told him that anyone chosen to do this thing might very well be facing certain death. But he said, 'What is one woman more or less? Find a volunteer and make her do it!' "

"The brute!" ran the whisper around the room.

"Now, as you know you know you know quit repeating, according to Freud, sex is the basis of everything. If the true sexual basis of a criminal could be awakened, he would reform and become sane. That is proven scientific fact like all *psychiatry.*

"So what will be attempted is to bring light into the life of Gris in the hope that it will reform him, bring him back to sanity and remove him as a threat from our society."

The women nodded.

"But," cried Crobe, "as I told Hisst, the experiment, while noble, has two drawbacks: one, the chances of this working on somebody totally off the classification scale are almost nonexistent; and two, it is almost certain death for the volunteer. Shout yet we have actually found a volunteer."

Crobe stood there, since no words were coming into his earphone now. An usher led forward the volunteer.

It was the Widow Tayl!

She was dressed in purest white. She looked virginal. Her head was bent forward, her smoothly straight hair fell across her face. She clasped her hands in front of her. She had been directed to perfection, to look like a maiden being brought before the altar in a primitive sacrifice. She stood before them, eyes cast down.

"This woman," said Crobe, "in a spirit of purest patriotism, is willing to risk her life in this undertaking. I regard with awe her devotion and fearlessness in servicing... serving the state and people. I give you Pratia Tayl wait for applause."

The assembled women stared. They felt a surge of awe. Then some began to cry.

"I am therefore," said Crobe, "appointing a committee under the chairwomanship of Lady Arthrite Stuffy to call upon Lord Turn and insist that he permit the marriage and nuptial night of Gris and this woman in the Royal prison."

The audience gasped.

Madison grinned.

Chapter 2

A very disturbed Lord Turn faced the committee of ladies in his chambers the next morning. Nothing like this had ever happened to him before. But he had never been pounded by press in all his life and he was getting cowed. Even his own family was not speaking to him lately, and this mass of determined women he saw before him were, many of them, on remarkably good terms with his family.

"But Lady Arthrite," he sputtered, "nothing like this has ever happened before. A marriage to take place in my prison? It's unheard of."

Lady Arthrite fixed him with a gimlet eye. "Lord Turn, we have consulted legal experts. Our family attorneys tell us that there is no regulation *against* it! You are NOT covered by the law this time. Any objection by you would be purely personal!"

Lord Turn digested that. He was a letter-of-the-law man and he knew she spoke the truth. It had suddenly become too personal. Then he grasped at an out. "Marriage is a thing to which the man must agree. I doubt very much that Soltan Gris would want to get married!"

"He must be asked and we must hear if this is the case."

Lord Turn raised his eyes to the ceiling. There were no regulations up there to be read. He looked back at Lady Arthrite. "Very well. We will go ask Gris."

Now, the Apparatus is an intelligence service and it has ways and means of getting information. And, this time through a warder's wife, Madison had learned that Soltan Gris had finished writing his confession.

Actually, Gris, these days, had put on some weight through lack of exercise, and food eaten regularly. Just now he was sitting in the tower cell wondering what to do with his time.

He had delivered the massive confession. For a couple of days thereafter he had worried a bit, thinking he would now be executed. Then he began to realize that

judges take a long time to read things and maybe he had
a few more breaths of life left to breathe.

The orders that he stay away from the window did
not have to be repeated to him: he knew in his bones that
Lombar Hisst would move the planet to get at him. He
had heard some crowd shouting something or other outside the prison on some occasions but he had not dared
go to the window to look and he could not understand
what they were saying: they were too distant. No information had come to him. He knew nothing whatever
about the press campaign against him.

He was somewhat puzzled therefore to hear many
footsteps coming up the tower stairs and a buzz of voices.
Female voices? How strange!

There was a jangle of opening plates and then the
groan of his iron door.

A guard came in and pointed a weapon at him.

The room was suddenly full of women!

Gris's wits promptly went into a spin.

He recognized none of them.

Their gaze upon him was hostile in the extreme.

Panic gripped him and there was no place to run.

A hooded figure, very slight of build, advanced
toward him. It came very close.

He felt a note being pushed into his hand.

Almost hysterical, he glanced down at the note. It
said:

> *If you don't say yes I will tell them about*
> *the baby and they will tear you limb from limb.*

The figure before him then lifted a hand and took
hold of the top of her hood and pulled it off.

Gris went into petrified shock.

IT WAS PRATIA TAYL!

"For the good of the state," she said, carefully coached, "I have volunteered to marry you." And, out of sight of the others she jabbed a finger at the note.

Gris, very close to fainting, could not speak.

Lord Turn, at the back of the group, snarled, "Well, answer her! Speak up so we can get about our business!"

"Say yes," hissed the Widow Tayl.

Gris took a look at her slitted, determined eyes. He looked at the hostile faces of the other women.

It suddenly occurred to him that he could buy a little more life. He could postpone his execution simply by setting a forward date, a month away, for this marriage.

"YES!" he shouted.

Lord Turn was amazed.

Hope suddenly lit the faces of the women.

"Good," said the Widow Tayl, "we will be married right here this afternoon. Be ready."

Gris tried to open his mouth to speak.

The cell was empty and the door clanged shut.

Chapter 3

Madison, of course, had the headlines set and ready to go. By noon, papers were all over the streets with variants of the headline:

> SACRIFICIAL BRIDE
> TO REFORM GRIS

Of course, there were statements by Crobe to the effect that it was a nearly impossible feat. He could not possibly guarantee any success due to the fact that Gris "had come to him too late"—the usual psychiatric hedge they used on Earth.

But what attracted public attention, as Madison knew it would, was the probable fate of a beautiful woman. Thousands upon thousands of people began to gather on the lower slopes of the Royal prison. Many were weeping, none had any hope, all thought it was a cruel thing to do and all thought that the nobility of Pratia Tayl was beyond any possible estimation.

Madison didn't even need his own camera crew. Homeview had covered the deputation going in and coming out and it was down there now in the afternoon sunlight, putting on the air live this vast throng of gathering people, getting close-ups of faces, getting opinions. He had hardly had to tell the manager of Homeview what to do at all.

For Madison had another mission of his own. With Apparatus-provided credentials and in the uniform of a General Services officer, he was going to act as the "bridegroom's friend," a necessary personnel of the ceremony.

The guards searched him for weapons and poison and promised him that they would be watching through the slot with a gun on him if he so much as made a gesture at Gris. And they let him in.

Gris was lying on his bunk in a state of collapse. He had failed utterly to buy his month. The thought of being married to the Widow Tayl was only offset by the fact that he would not live very long anyway.

The bunk was actually an inset ledge in the stone.

When a pad was on it, as now, it had only about four feet of clearance to its overhead.

He saw what he took to be a General Services officer being let in. That didn't necessarily mean Apparatus. He had expected they would send someone to help him get ready, and sure enough the fellow had some boxes under his arm. He was also reassured when he saw a gun barrel trained through the cell view-slot. So he lay there watching.

Then suddenly the features under the cap began to register.

In horrible shock he shot upright!

He hit his head!

It didn't knock him out. It sent his wits spinning. He thought he was at 42 Mess Street, New York City. No, he must be on the yacht *Golden Sunset*.

Madison? It was MADISON!

"Oh, no," said Gris. "No, no, no!"

Madison found a stool and sat down beside the bunk. "Well, Smith," he said in English, "I mean Gris. I certainly hate to see an associate of Mr. Bury's in trouble. Don't be concerned. I am here to help you out."

Gris went into terror. "Oh, please, dear Gods, Madison. Don't act as my PR!"

"Of course not," said Madison. "I am your friend. I will do everything I can to see you come out of this in great shape."

"Oh, no, no, please. Please Madison, don't help me."

"Oh, nonsense, Gris. That is what friends are for. Now listen to me carefully. You are going to get out of this with flying colors."

"You mean . . . you mean I have a chance of getting off?"

"Oh, more than a chance, Smith. There are people

working day and night to keep you from being executed. It's the very last thing your friends want!"

"I have friends?"

"Why, of course you have! You have no idea how much has been done for you already. We're going to get you brought to trial."

"WHAT?"

"Absolutely. Not only that, it will be a fair trial. You don't think the Widow Tayl is desirous of becoming a double widow, do you? Why, no. She's got money by the ton and she will hire the very best attorneys. I can assure you that you have a very long and very interesting life ahead of you."

"Madison, for the love of your mother, don't torture me this way. I haven't got a chance. You're just up to something horrible. I know it!"

"Oh, Smith, I'm shocked. You are not my client. I'm still working on Heller."

"You are?"

"Of course. You and I are just the old team, Smith and Madison. Same as always. But I probably haven't got all day to talk to you, so you better remember what I'm telling you. When you get up on that stand, I want you to accuse Heller as the sole reason for all your woes."

"But that's true," said Gris. "He is!"

"Excellent! I knew you would agree. So when they put you on trial . . ."

"They won't try me. They'll just execute me. And if I ever walk out of this prison, Lombar Hisst will have me cut down ten feet from the gate."

"Don't give it a second thought. I am Lombar's right-hand man—or he is mine, I forget which. So if we get you to trial, you do what you're told. Understand?"

"All you want me to do is accuse Heller?"

"Right."

"Any and all crimes I can think of?"

"Right!"

Gris started to come out of it. He began to see some light. "They'll realize he's the one behind all this."

"Right."

"I'll do it."

"Good. Now we've got to get you ready for your wedding."

Madison had to keep his smile from spreading into a triumphant grin. Gris didn't even suspect how absolutely diabolical the *real* plan was!

Chapter 4

Late that afternoon, the marriage took place in the prison.

Lord Turn would not permit camera crews inside and they had to be content with what they could shoot from outside the courtyard gates.

The late afternoon sun made the grim old castle a dark silhouette and fell upon the countless thousands of people who covered the flanks of the hill. Priests were passing amongst them, exhorting them to pray, and the crowd sat or knelt, young and old, covered with a blanket of buzzing sound.

When the marriage priest and the friend of the bride and friend of the groom appeared at the gate, exiting, the priest made a sign that the marriage had been performed. A combined sigh of hope from thousands of throats swept down the hill like a wind.

All eyes were fixed on the highest tower now, for they knew that the sacrificial bride and the hated Gris were there, alone. Nobody from the crowd left: they knew that at midnight the wife would depart the prison. They prayed for her. Would the therapy work? Would she ever be seen again alive?

The sun went down. The moon Niko rose: it bathed the ancient fortress with an eerie light; it made the uplifted faces a greenish haze on the hill.

The crowd did not miss the fact that an ambulance stood outside the gates, a medical team ready. As the Homeview announcer said, when the cameras panned it, it was there to grasp the possible hope that the bride, no matter how abused, could be treated and kept alive.

But what went on outside the prison and what went on inside were two different things.

During the ceremony, Gris had been numb as stone. Pratia Tayl, on the other hand, with sparkling eye, had been chattering like a loose cogwheel. And when the two friends and priest had left, she was not even disconcerted by the fact that a guard remained at the blastgun slot, ready to intervene.

Pratia had brought a basket containing a wedding feast which had survived the minute inspections and tests given it. With movements not unlike a golden songbird, she hopped about, spreading the comestibles upon a glittering cloth. She was popping bits and pieces at Gris's mouth—and missing much of the time—even before they sat down formally. They were missing because Gris was too numb to open his lips.

"Oh, you just wait," prattled Pratia, "we'll have such fun. You won't have to work anymore, for you'll be out of the Apparatus. And all you'll have to do is simply lie on a bed and I'll throw food at you like this. Your heaviest exertions will consist of simply sleeping and (bleeping). Isn't it marvelous? Have another berry."

Gris was in the total grip of unreality. He had been peacefully in this tower for months, his only companions a vocoscriber and his materials. Occasionally, the inmate in the next cell would scratch on the wall; now and then a bird would sit on the window ledge and chirp and fly away. All this commotion sounded to him like a din. There seemed to be, as well, some sort of a swelling moan outside he could not account for, for he was still under orders not to go near a window.

Sex was far from attractive to him these days. Since Prahd had changed his anatomy, women had given him nothing but solid trouble. Also this marriage had not bought him any time. He really didn't believe he'd have a trial. He had confessed his life away; the best he could hope for was the most painless execution Lord Turn could give him. During the ceremony, the more he had looked at Madison, the less he believed what Madison had said. The record of J. Warbler Madman was a proven thing to Gris. After his momentary hope, Gris had backslid.

"Oh, have some of this pink sparklewater. It is the very best: extremely nutritious," said Pratia. "It will get your strength up." And she laughed a little bell-like laugh. "You're really going to need it." Then she shook a finger at him. "Don't be so unresponsive! You simply must stop worrying. Three of the very best attorneys in all Voltar will defend you. Trust me!"

"I don't think any of you understand," said Gris. "I am Heller's prisoner. For some reason His Majesty has not issued orders to finish me off. But he will. He will.

Even if you could help me, I just confessed to every crime in the book. I don't believe you and I don't believe, Gods forbid, Madison."

"Oh, don't be so gloomy. Look there! It's already dark outside! Now have you had enough food and drink to feel really fortified? You have. Good. Now you just turn your back and I'll fix up the bed there and WHEEE!"

He sat facing the blank wall and heard her working busily in the stone alcove. She had brought a roll of bedding and he had no idea at all what she was up to.

Finally, she tapped him on the shoulder. Woodenly, he turned around. She wore a gown that was so transparent it made her nakedness an exclamation point.

The alcove had been draped with white gauze and a blue blanket of shimmercloth lay upon it.

She was plucking at his clothes, unfastening things. Like some sort of statue, he stood there and let himself be stripped. The only motion he made was to step out of his boots and pants.

"Oooooooooh!" cried Pratia, standing back and staring. "LOOK what we have here! Oooooh! Why, Soltan, what has happened? WHAT an imPROVEMENT! Oh, Soltan, that is positively DIVINE! I never DREAMED there could be one like THAT!"

Gris looked at her with resignation.

She was staring round-eyed. "No WONDER you never answered my postal cards. Women must have been haunting you in MOBS!"

Gris looked like he had been whipped.

She frowned. "But I see you are not responding." Then she smiled in inspiration. "Oh, I know what will get you excited. A picture of our son. It will make you want to have another one just like him!"

She rummaged in her purse. "I had this taken just yesterday. Here it is. Isn't he BEAUTIFUL?"

Gris looked at it. It was a baby, two or three months old. It was smiling and wide-eyed.

Abruptly Gris took hold of it and approached the light. Yes!

Straw-colored hair! Green eyes!

He glared at her. "This is Prahd's baby!"

"Oh, no, it's yours. There's lots of hair like that in my family and green eyes, too. Just because you have brown hair and eyes doesn't mean a thing. He's your son, all right. The registry papers show it. And now he's all legal, not even a bastard since this afternoon. Aren't you proud?"

It was just like Nurse Bildirjin's baby. "This is Prahd's," he said.

She laughed delightedly. "Why, you're jealous! Oh, this is wonderful! So you do love me a little bit after all. Well, come right over to this bed and you'll get all the love you want!"

She dragged him over to the inset bunk and through the gauze.

The guard was watchful as he stared into the cell across the sights of his blastgun.

The white curtains that hid the bed were moving.

Pratia's robe was thrown out of them and hit the floor. Her voice was reproving. "Come ON, Soltan. This is no time to be shy."

The guard was very watchful as Pratia's voice said, "Now, now, Soltan. Don't be naughty. You've been living in all this stone. Use it as an example."

A bird lit on the cell window ledge and listened. Pratia's voice was a little strained. "Well, I suppose it is the lot of women to do all the work."

The guard frowned.

"Oooooooh!" cried Pratia as the startled bird stared. "What QUANTITY!" The bird flew hastily away.

The guard's face glowered. Pratia said, "Now, Soltan, be a good boy. Aaaah, that's better. Now let me concentrate."

The white gauze curtains were twitching.

Pratia's face was staring up at the close-to ceiling of the inset bed.

Gris was staring down at her wonderingly.

Pratia's face was very rapt, looking upward.

Puzzled, Gris was looking down at her. He decided she must be staring at something above his head.

Gris turned sideways to look upward and find what she was gazing at so raptly. Had she put something up there?

It was a three-dimensional picture. Big as life! Full color!

HELLER!

Gris suddenly began to scream.

He leaped out of the alcove. The curtains caught at him and he felt he was being seized.

His screams rose to total volume!

He was wrestling on the floor with the curtains!

Guards pounded in! Now he knew they were after him.

His screams battered the walls and sliced down the passageways. They tore out the window and into the night.

Outside, a moan rose from thousands of throats.

The camera crews went tense.

The ambulance started its motors.

Alarm gongs racketed in the courtyard!

A tense throng, in agony, watched the ponderous doors swing open.

A stretcher crew raced in.

In the darkness of the courtyard, the men in white were loading something. One of them was an actor: he expertly tossed a blood bag under the sheet, observed by no one.

And then into the glaring gate lights, before the eyes of cameras, attended by the men in white, the stretcher came to view.

Thousands groaned!

People shrieked in horror.

On it lay the sacrificial bride, sheet showing only part of her face.

AND DOWN FROM THE STRETCHER RAN A TORRENT OF BLOOD!

PANDEMONIUM!

The crowd tried to charge.

Guards with flashing guns fired over their heads!

A platoon struggled to get the prison gates closed.

The stretcher was slid into the ambulance. It took off with a roar!

Madison looked back through the rear windows of the ambulance.

WHAT A RIOT!

AND ALL ON HOMEVIEW FOR THE WHOLE OF THE CONFEDERACY!

He sat down by the stretcher. He took Pratia Tayl Gris's hand and patted it. He was grinning from ear to ear.

"Oh, you did wonderfully," he said. "I am very proud of you."

"Well, I certainly hope all this works," said the most dedicated nymphomaniac on Voltar. "I just can't wait to get my hands on him again. Did you know he is now ENORMOUS?"

"Oh, I think the rest of it will come off smoothly," said Madison.

"This PR is great stuff!" said Pratia. "Where's it been?"

Chapter 5

The rest of Madison's caper was not long in following.

On the very next afternoon, an incredulous Lord Turn, already sorrier than sorry that he had said yes to the marriage, looked at the Royal prison seneschal. "WHO?" said Lord Turn.

"They're asking for permission to land in the courtyard," said the seneschal. "It's an air limousine and the identoplate of the occupant says 'Queen Teenie.' They are saying that as the occupant is Royal, they have a right to land."

"That must be the Hostage Queen of Flisten," said Lord Turn. "But a hostage monarch doesn't have access to this place!"

"That's what I told them. But they said royalty was royalty and that they have urgent business with Your Lordship that will NOT wait."

"Well, it's a moot question," said Lord Turn. "Are those Homeview people still hanging around outside?"

"No, Your Lordship."

"Well, nobody will notice. It can't be anything very

important. Probably wants some retainer locked up and
I'll have to tell her no, but I better do it in person or
they'll feel insulted. Tell them they can land."

He got into a new robe and straightened up his desk.

Very shortly, two heralds stepped in and halted. In
unison, they said, "Her Majesty Queen Teenie! All rise!"

A silver palanquin, covered, borne by two husky footmen in silver, was carried into the chamber.

"Kneel!" said the heralds.

Lord Turn, suffering, stepped to the side of his desk
and knelt.

The footmen set the palanquin down.

A blue-gloved hand swept the front curtain of the
palanquin aside. A young voice said, "Rise. You may sit
at your desk."

Lord Turn was irritated. Hostage monarchs had no
business here. But he rose and seated himself at his desk.
Then he looked into the curtained chair. She was sitting
there, crown on head, scepter in hand, robed in gold.
Her eyes and mouth were very big but she was actually
quite beautiful. Then he realized she was little more
than a child and he could not repress a fatherly smile.
What possible trouble could a teen-age hostage monarch
cause? None that he could imagine.

"Well, what can I do for Your Majesty?" he said,
wondering if it would be protocol to offer her some candy.

"It is not what you can do for us," said Teenie. "It
is what we might be able to do for you."

"Really?"

"Yes, really," said Teenie. "We are quite used to
judges and courts and so on and we know how much
trouble they can get into."

"About what?" said Turn, a trifle amused.

"Gris," said Teenie.

"GRIS?" cried Lord Turn. "OH, NO! NOT MORE GRIS!" He dropped his gray head into his hands, clutching his forehead.

"Yes, Gris," said Teenie. "He is the vilest, most underhanded, unprincipled villain alive! Before I became the Hostage Queen of Flisten, I was a movie queen on the planet *Earth*."

"*Earth?* What country?"

"*Moviola*. But it doesn't matter. This Gris, a terrible villain, was hauled before my court there and sentenced to life imprisonment. He escaped. He is actually my prisoner. It would save you a great deal of embarrassment if you simply turned him over to me so he could finish his sentence."

"Oh, I couldn't do that. It's the wrong venue. I think I know what planet you mean now. Blito-P3—it's been in the news. It's not conquered yet. There are no treaties. And even if we were talking about Flisten, it would be the same. There is no possible way under Heavens that I could turn Gris over to you."

"No matter what?"

"Not even faintly possible."

"It could save you a lot of embarrassment if you changed your mind."

Lord Turn sighed. "I'm sorry, but it's impossible."

"Oh, well," said Teenie, "It was a nice try. So I guess I'll have to spill it to you."

"My dear . . . I mean Your Majesty, I would give half my head to get rid of Gris. But unfortunately I cannot. However," and he smiled, "I can't possibly see how he could cause any more trouble."

"It's plain you don't know Gris," said Teenie. "He lies, he cheats, he steals. But this time he's really done

it. He has committed a crime right here in your own
prison."

Lord Turn shook his head. "That's impossible."

"You don't know Gris," said Teenie. "This time he
has *really* done it. And that's why I thought I could help.
When I saw his picture on Homeview, I said, 'NO! It
can't be! But there he is! That's Gris! He's done it
AGAIN!' "

"My dear ... WHAT has he done again?"

"The very same crime I sentenced him to life imprisonment for. BIGAMY!"

Lord Turn's eyes went round with shock. Bigamy
was a capital crime on Voltar. "No, no, there must be
some mistake. You must have the wrong man." He was
pleading with himself, please, not more trouble with
Gris.

Teenie said, "If he confronted me, you would know
in a second that it is true."

"Oh, I hope there is some mistake," said Lord Turn.
Then hastily, "Look, Your Majesty, we can settle this
immediately. If you will consent to moving your palanquin into the courtroom, I will have Gris brought down."

Teenie nodded and they carried her chair out into
the main courtroom. They set it down in the empty hall
before the witness seat and enclosure. Teenie shut her curtains.

There was quite a wait. But at last, a very manacled
Gris was brought, closely escorted by six armed guards.

Gris had not known why they were fetching him.
The curtained chair meant nothing to him. But when he
saw that he was not being taken to an execution chamber,
and it was probably just a matter of some questions, some
of his morale returned. He sat down in the railed witness

box, trying to make a good impression on Lord Turn who was now taking a seat on his judge's dais.

"Gris," said Turn, "have you ever been sentenced to life imprisonment?"

"All my crimes are in my confession, Your Lordship."

"Well, that may or may not be," said Lord Turn. "I've not read it. So please just answer truthfully, were you ever tried and sentenced in a country called *Moviola?*"

Gris had had a very hard night. But he knew that the last thing he must look was guilty about anything. After all, his crimes had all been done because of Heller and he had explained that in his confession. He forced an easy laugh. "That's ridiculous," he said.

"There is someone here who says otherwise," said Lord Turn and waved a hand at the closed palanquin.

Gris managed a confident smile. "There isn't anyone on Voltar who could allege such a falsity." And he looked easily at the curtains.

Suddenly, a blue-gloved hand shot the covering aside.

TEENIE!

Gris went white.

He leaped back!

He hit the rail of the witness box and went right through it!

With a rip of splintering timber he reached the limit of his shackles!

His velocity was so great he parted chain links!

He hit the wall!

He madly tried to get through it!

With a shrieking, frantic moan, he realized he could not escape.

He fainted.

Lord Turn looked at the crumpled heap of severed

chains, fallen plaster and Gris amongst it, lying there unconscious, now, upon the floor. Lord Turn, in the saddest voice said, "Oh, no."

Lord Turn took a long breath and looked at Teenie. "Well, Your Majesty," he said, "I guess that settles it. I have no choice now but to bring Gris to trial for committing a crime in my own prison."

"I said it would be embarrassing," said Teenie. "Pratia Tayl was the fourth time he got married. He's not guilty of just bigamy: it's QUADRIGAMY!"

Madison, two hours later, was dancing with joy. His plan had worked perfectly. He had brought Gris to trial. He would make sure the trial was public. WHAT HEADLINES THAT WOULD MAKE! And Gris would accuse Heller. Madison had it made! He could see it now! The greatest manhunt in the whole universe! The Fleet, the Army, everybody! All after Heller! Headlines, headlines, HEADLINES! What ecstasy!

Oh, it was great to be a pure genius at PR!

Chapter 6

On a lonely mountaintop of Calabar and in the screaming wind, Jettero Heller stood, stung by the horizontally hurtling snow, half-blinded by the night, surrounded by thirty blastguns ready and eager to blow him apart.

It had taken him many days and several different applications of command location geometry to find the headquarters of Prince Mortiiy.

The voyage from Blito-P3 had only taken five days. It had been quite uneventful. The trouble had come when he had had to penetrate the Apparatus planetary net all tangled up with the beams and defenses of the rebels.

Using one identification or another, he had managed to slip through and the *Prince Caucalsia* lay up there now, twenty miles above them, invisible to all intents and purposes but, with her vital passengers, a total loss if anything happened to him.

He had come down here in a spacetrooper sled; he was chilled to the bone; his oxygen was almost gone and they were standing on what was a "hill" for Calabar but which was nevertheless thirty thousand feet. Gun flashes flickered on the distant horizon, a burning city was a patch of pink smudge.

There was a dimly seen figure about fifty feet away, hidden by a rock.

Through his face mask that also had an amplifier speaker, Heller called, "I will have to stand closer to you to give you my message." Thirty blastguns in the ring around him twitched.

The amplified voice came from behind the rock, "You're close enough. I can't believe that the great Jettero Heller, idol of the Fleet, wants to come over to the rebels. I am very well aware of what a combat engineer can do. Give me your message from there."

"I don't even know if I'm talking to Prince Mortiiy," Heller shouted above the shrieking wind.

"I don't even know that you're Jettero Heller!"

"I was introduced to you as a cadet aboard the warship *Illusive* twelve years ago," Heller shouted back. "You were wearing slippers because your feet had gotten burned."

"Anybody could know that. I've met thousands of cadets."

"I have to see your face up close to know it's really you!" shouted Heller. "The message, as I have told you, is for your ears alone."

"That's how you got this far. Men, bind his hands behind him and take any weapons. Only Jettero Heller would be crazy enough to try to penetrate these lines making all this noise."

Two pressure-suited soldiers detached themselves from the ring and moved forward very gingerly. They found no weapons and they tied his hands. They pushed him forward across the intervening gap. Heller found it hard walking: in addition to the wind, the 1.5 gravity of Calabar made him feel like he weighed a ton.

He came to a place behind a rock. A light hit him in the face. A hand pulled away his oxygen mask and then let it drop back. "It looks like Jettero Heller all right," said a gruff voice.

"Turn the light on your own face," said Heller.

"That's nerve. Don't you realize you're talking to a prince?"

"I'm talking to a rebel," said Heller, "and unless you listen to me, you'll go right on being one."

A barking laugh met this. "Gods-blast! What nerve!" Then the light was suddenly reversed and, through the faceplate, Heller saw and recognized the craggy features and thick black beard of Prince Mortiiy.

"All right," said Heller. "I give you my word I am not here to assassinate you or harm you in any way. Send these men back out of earshot. My message really is for your ears alone."

"Comets! I must be crazy. All right, you men, draw back but keep weapons trained on him."

"I have a complete repair crew, five ships coming here. They'll arrive in a few weeks. I think you need them."

"I don't need anything. The people of this planet support me: they're in a livid rage against the Apparatus. Furthermore, Apparatus units are pulling out and the Fleet and Army are inactive. I'm winning this war."

It was a shock to Heller. If the Apparatus was pulling out, they had only one destination: Earth.

Heller glanced around him. The others were now well out of earshot. He leaned closer. "You'll never win this war without something I've brought you."

Mortiiy barked an amused laugh. "There isn't anything in the universe that you could bring that's that important."

Heller said, "I've brought your father."

"WHAT?"

"His Majesty, Cling the Lofty," said Heller.

"Oh, well, if you really have him, bring him in, bring him in so that I can execute him! But, of course, I don't believe you for an instant, as you couldn't possibly have him."

"Your Highness, I do assure you that I have him. I also have the regalia and seal." And he quickly sketched the turn of fate which had brought the Emperor into his hands.

"Then actually he's running from Hisst!" said Mortiiy. "Will he cancel my rebel status?"

"He's unconscious."

"Then he can't declare me his successor."

"Not until he gains consciousness."

"Wait a minute," said Mortiiy. "This is dangerous! If Hisst knows he is here, he will launch all his troops against us! If it gets out that you kidnapped him, the

Fleet and Army will join in. This is EXPLOSIVE! They'd slaughter us!"

"Are there no advantages to having him?" said Heller. "Does the G.C. know he is gone?"

"I came here past Voltar. There's no trace of it in the news. All they're talking about is a man named Gris that I thought was dead."

"Then Hisst is playing this quiet."

"I think so," said Heller.

Mortiiy leaned back against a rock. The wind screamed above them. Finally, he said, "It has just come to me with a shock what must have happened to my brothers and other successors to the throne. It might not have been my father. It could have been Hisst. Heller, do you suppose that man has the incredible effrontery to try to proclaim himself Emperor?"

"He is calling himself a dictator. Emperor is just one step away."

"Well, he can't do it," said Mortiiy. "The G.C. and the Lords of the land have to have positive evidence, a body and the regalia, in order to declare the throne vacant and appoint a successor. If you have the body and the regalia, he has to recover them. Gods-blast it, Heller, all you've brought me is a total assault! Whether he does or does not say you have the Emperor, he won't let anything stand in his way to recovering what you have. You are A LIVING BOMB!"

Heller would have spoken but Mortiiy silenced him with his hand. "I'm trying to think my way through this. Is there any chance my father will recover consciousness long enough to cancel the proclamation that made me a rebel and reinstate me as his successor?"

"That is in the lap of the Gods."

"Heller, if he did or didn't announce it, you're sitting on a shell that is about to explode. I know you have a good reputation but somebody could stir things up to try to find you and Hisst would have the body and regalia. With those, he could make himself Emperor. . . . Oh, I almost wish you'd gone someplace else!"

"Your Highness, how much assault can you withstand here on Calabar?"

"There's two billion population left. The rest have been slaughtered. Most of the cities are rubble. I frankly don't know."

"I got an estimate," said Heller, "while I was looking for you. This war has gone on for five years so you have not done too badly. I think you could stand off the full force of the Apparatus. The rivers are so wide, the mountains so high. . . ."

"We couldn't stand off the Apparatus PLUS the Fleet and the Army."

"How about a gamble?" said Heller. "How about gambling that your father will regain consciousness in a few months and let's gamble again that he will cancel your rebel status and proclaim you successor. And then gamble that the Fleet and Army stay out of it. And then gamble that we put up such a ferocious defense that we cripple the Apparatus."

Mortiiy shook his head. "Please don't use that word 'gamble' again! You're painting the thinnest forlorn hope I ever heard of!"

"I'm not through, Your Highness. Then suppose we secretly tell Hisst that the Emperor is here."

"WHAT?"

"He will know then that we aren't going to make a public announcement."

"We can't anyway! I'm not in line for the throne anymore. It would not do us any good to announce it publicly. It would bring the whole pack down on us! No, the only thing that would save this is for my father to wake up and proclaim Hisst a traitor by Royal proclamation."

"One other possibility. I inform Hisst secretly that that is exactly what will happen if he brings the Fleet and Army into this war."

"He'd read it as a declaration that the Emperor was dead or incapacitated."

"But he wouldn't be sure."

"Royal Officer Heller, you are insane!"

"That may or may not be," said Heller, "but I can hazard that such a message would drive Hisst close to or over the border into insanity. You were an accomplished Fleet officer, Your Highness. You are aware of the principle that unstabilizing enemy command can often get him to do something rash, foolhardy or do nothing at all."

"Don't lecture me on strategy and tactics, Officer Heller. I was fighting battles when you weren't even weaned. There is another principle and that is, when an opportunity presents itself and one does nothing, one is almost certain to lose. Yours is the craziest battle plan I ever heard of. I will adopt it. Go bring my father. I give you my word I will not kill him. We will put him in a nice, safe cave. You can put the rest of the plan into effect. He may, as you say, recover. Until then, we live on hope. You are crazy, Officer Heller. I like you. MEN! UNTIE HIS HANDS!"

Chapter 7

It was dusk and it was raining. Shining rivulets of water ran from the semidead spaceships of Emergency Fleet Reserve.

As the tug *Prince Caucalsia* came to silent rest on its tail, Commander Crup and old Atty stared nervously as Jettero Heller, not waiting for a ladder, slid down from the airlock on a safety line.

"My Gods, Jet!" Commander Crup whispered, "you've got no business here. There's a general warrant out for your arrest!"

"Hello, Commander! Hello, Atty!" said Heller in a loud voice.

"Sh, sh, sh!" they both said in chorus.

"What are you shushing about?" said Heller. "I can't hear you in this rain!"

"Arrest!" said Crup. "Lombar Hisst has had his agents tearing Voltar apart trying to find where you are!"

"Look," said Heller, again in a loud voice, "if a Fleet officer can't land at a Fleet base without worrying about 'drunks,' I don't know what the Confederacy is coming to."

"It's coming to Hell Eight very rapidly," said Crup. "Hisst is calling himself a dictator and the Apparatus is in charge of everything."

"Not in charge of me," said Heller. "Loan me a fast aircar and, Atty, get this ship full of food and things.

Particularly lots of food. Put it on the Exterior Division account I gave you last time."

"He's crazy," said Crup.

"Couldn't agree more," said Heller.

An hour later, the old gray-haired enlisted man who served as clerk at the Fleet Officer's Club was taking advantage of a rainy night to try to balance his accounts. He heard a sound at the counter, he looked up and saw someone in a streaming raincloak standing there. He went over.

"Could I have my room key?"

The old clerk stared. He went white. "Good Gods!" he whispered. "There's a general warrant out for your arrest! Agents have been here three times in the past week checking to see if..."

"First things first," said Heller. "My key! And then send some hot tup and sweetbuns to my room. Did you know it's wet out there?"

"Jet, you're crazy!"

"Always was. Can't take time to reform now. Tell Bis of Fleet Intelligence to come up if he's around and has a moment."

Ten minutes later, a stunned Bis entered Heller's posh suite. He heard Heller in the shower and went to the door.

"Jet!" said Bis in a stage whisper, "there's a general warrant out for your arrest!"

"Speak up!" said Heller in a loud voice. "Hand me that bottle of soap, would you?"

"Oh, Jet, you're crazy!"

"Seems to be a universal opinion. How you been? Winning any bullet ball games lately?"

"Oh, Jet, you're hopeless."

"Maybe, but not quite. He who hath no hope is not long in the spaceways. Hand me a towel, would you?"

Heller, towel wrapped around him, was soon sitting in a living room chair, drinking hot tup.

Bis declined a canister. "I don't think you realize how serious all this is," he said, perched nervously on the edge of a couch.

"Oh, I do," said Heller. "Going out in rain like this could make even the strongest men catch cold."

"Jet! The Apparatus is all over the place! They want your blood! And they're a (bleeped) bloodthirsty lot!"

"I'm glad you brought that up," said Heller. "Remember that fellow Gris I tried to deliver to the Royal prison?"

"I know. The papers are screaming about him."

"Well, listen," said Heller. "Coming in, I heard a news bulletin that he was being brought to trial. Apparently he's even going to have some attorneys defending him. Do you recall those boxes of papers I sent you?"

"The Gris blackmail file on the Apparatus?"

"Right. I want you to hand those over to his attorneys."

"WHAT?" Bis stared at him. "But they'd use those to try to get him off."

"Possibly. But it sure would upset a lot of people in the Apparatus."

Suddenly Bis barked a laugh. "You know, I think it would. I'll do it. But listen, Jet, you've got to get out of here. They have this place watched."

"Oh, I'm leaving very shortly," said Heller. "Just as soon as you get me a mustard-colored Apparatus officer's uniform and an Apparatus airbus."

"WHAT?"

"Don't tell me Fleet Intelligence hasn't collected some to use in espionage on another service."

Bis held his face in his hands. "Now I know why a combat engineer has such short life expectancy. What are you going to do?"

"The less you know about that, the less you can tell the torturers. Get me a false identoplate along with it. You've got lots of time. Shall we say fifteen minutes at the back door?"

Bis stared at him numbly.

Two hours later, Heller landed the Apparatus-marked airbus on the landing target at Camp Kill. The rain had not reached over the mountains into the Great Desert but the airbus bore signs of it: it was suspiciously clean for an Apparatus vehicle.

The guard officer came into the glaring target lights. He looked at the smudgy identoplate that said "Captain Fal."

"I won't be here long," said Heller. "I've come to pay a gambling debt to Captain Snelz."

"Pickings in town must be good lately," said the guard officer.

"Couldn't be better," said Heller.

"Thanks for the tip that he'll have money. He's in those dugouts back under the hill."

Heller got out. He was wearing big sand goggles. He walked at a leisurely pace through the dusty, cluttered camp.

A sentry stood outside a dugout door. Before he could challenge, Heller yelled, "Hey, Snelz, you got any thudder dice for sale?"

There was an instant flurry inside. Then a white face, just a blur in the night, peered out of the low dugout entrance.

Heller walked boldly past the sentry and entered.

In a hoarse whisper, Snelz said, "My Gods, Jet! Don't you know there's a general warrant out for your arrest?"

"You know," said Heller, in a loud voice, "if people keep telling me, sooner or later I'll believe it."

Snelz shuddered. He turned and made a gesture at a prostitute who lay naked on a far bunk. She grabbed her clothes and scuttled out.

Snelz was tucking his shirt in his pants and trying to drop the door curtain at the same time.

"Heller," he said, "you're crazy."

"No, I'm thirsty."

Snelz, both his shirt collar and his hair standing up, tried to find something that hadn't been emptied in the debris on the table and, after upsetting several bottles and canisters, got some sparklewater poured. Heller sat down and sipped it.

The ex-Fleet marine sat nervously across from him. "Jet, there's a whisper out that Hisst will pay a hundred thousand credits cash for clues as to where you are."

"Cheap," said Heller. "The man always was cheap."

"Why are you HERE of all places?"

Heller reached into his Apparatus tunic and pulled out an envelope. He laid it before Snelz. "This," he said, "has got to be delivered to Lombar Hisst."

"I haven't got access to him," said Snelz. "I'm only a captain."

"Well, I wouldn't think it would be healthy to give it to him," said Heller. "If he received it and those seals were disturbed, my guess is that he would very likely execute the bearer just to be sure his mouth stayed shut."

Snelz looked at the outer cover. It said:

TO LOMBAR HISST
FROM JETTERO HELLER
Private. Personal. Secret.

Snelz's hand began to shake. "This could get me killed just looking at it! Heart failure!"

Heller laid down a five-hundred-credit note. "Just so you don't feel too bad being deprived of that hundred thousand."

Snelz was shocked. "I wouldn't ever turn you in. You're my friend! You don't have to pay me anything either!"

"Well, I told the landing guard officer I was here to pay a gambling debt, so he'll be on to you for drinks, so I don't want this to cost you anything personally. Now think, do you know of a way to get this into Hisst's hand?"

Snelz thought about it. Then he suddenly smiled brightly. "Yes, I think I can do that. And without a hitch."

"It's very important that he get it. No slips."

"No slips," said Snelz.

"Good," said Heller. "That completes my business. Would you like to indulge in a few passes with the dice?"

"Oh, Jet, please to the Gods, get out of here. You have both our bodies halfway down into that chasm right this minute. Don't you realize that Hisst comes to the tower office up there almost every day? He might be in this camp right now!"

"Then it will be very easy to get the message to him, won't it?" said Heller. "Well, you seem to have lost your gambling fever, so I guess I'll run along. I'll stop by the canteen. . . ."

"Jet," said Snelz in a tight and urgent voice, "you get . . . get out of here. Honest, my heart won't start again until you've left this camp!"

"The day you're that scared, Snelz," laughed Heller, "that will be the day. Come on and walk with me to the canteen."

Snelz convulsively was climbing into his uniform tunic.

Firmly but carefully looking very casual, he walked Heller straight back to the landing target area and got him into his airbus.

Heller took off.

Two hours later, at Emergency Fleet Reserve, Heller complimented old Atty for restocking the tug, shook hands with a worried Commander Crup and, exhibiting the ship identoplate of the cruiser *Happy Return*, was spaceward ho for Calabar.

Chapter 8

One cannot help but wonder, dear reader, what the course of history might have been if Captain Snelz had not thought of the man he did when asked to design a way to get the message into Lombar's hands. If he had only told Heller the name that had popped into his mind, the fate of Earth might well have been quite different.

For the man Snelz had thought of was J. Walter Madison!

As he stood on the landing target watching Heller's airbus leave, Snelz was putting through his mind exactly how to do this.

Lately Lombar Hisst had been coming to Spiteos almost every day for a brief period, usually in the morning. He was doing something strange down in the storerooms with that weird powder. Snelz himself had escorted in several truckloads of strange things marked Lactose, Epsom Salts, Quinine, Baking Powder, Photo Developer, Insecticide and Strychnine. Hisst had several technicians who would take something called *amphetamine* out of its original capsules, mix the powder with these other things and then, using new capsules, expand the original batch enormously. According to one of the technicians, Hisst seemed to take a lot of pleasure in this strange exercise: he called it "cutting" and seemed to think nobody else could do it as expertly as he.

And Snelz had noted that the Earthman Madison was never kept informed as to where he could find Hisst: that was no real mystery, as Hisst always had the idea that anywhere he went, an assassin would be waiting for him. So, at odd times of the day or night, Madison would show up at Spiteos.

It had become so well known now that Madison was a close creature of Hisst that Madison could come and go as he pleased. The very distinctive Model 99 with its four flying angels was never even challenged in the air. Once landed, Madison had carte blanche. He needed no escort, he didn't even show his plate, he simply trotted over to the zipbuses, went through the tunnel, up the elevator and into the north tower. Often, nowadays, there weren't even clerks up there.

Knowing Madison for a fake and no friend of Heller's, Snelz selected him for a messenger whose message, it seemed, could end in somebody's death.

Accordingly Snelz, despite the hour, paraded his company. He went down the line, looking very closely at his men. Suddenly he stopped and pointed his baton.

"You there. You have just volunteered. Lieutenant, dismiss everyone but this man and Timyjo."

Snelz took the two men aside. Timyjo was the company's best thief. "Timyjo, go into town and get an expensive suit of gray shimmercloth and all those conservative things that go with it. The stores at this hour should be easy to rob. Make sure they fit this man. Be back before dawn."

Snelz whiled away the time by buying the guard officer some drinks and shooting a little dice. He even had an hour for a nap.

Timyjo returned laden. In his dugout, Snelz dressed the volunteer. He stepped back admiringly. Same height, same build, same hair coloring. To all intents and purposes, unless one knew him well, one was looking at Madison.

Not to take any chances, Snelz put a pair of sand goggles on him, a thing he had lately seen Madison wear.

He gave the fellow the envelope. He said, "Now, don't talk to anybody. Just get on a zipbus, go up in the elevator, walk through the clerk's room, enter the office of Lombar Hisst and lay this squarely in the middle of his desk. Then walk out and come back here."

"And if I don't?"

"Then we throw you in the chasm and forget about it."

It was well after dawn. A sleepy camp was recovering from hangovers.

The volunteer, feeling very nervous, pleaded at least for a canister of tup. Then, fortified, he walked out, got

on a zipbus, got off, got in the elevator, went up to tower
level and entered the clerk's outer room. He froze. The
old criminal chief clerk was sitting there, back to the door.

With no choice but the chasm if he did and the
chasm if he didn't, the volunteer walked boldly across
the room.

The old chief clerk glanced up. "He isn't here," he
muttered and went back to his work.

The volunteer pretended he had not heard. He
walked to Hisst's office door and went in. The place
impressed him very unfavorably: one whole wall was
glass, a throne chair that looked like tomb-loot was behind the desk. But the volunteer wasted no time.

He took the envelope out of his coat. He laid it on
the desk and propped it up with a stinger. Anybody who
sat down would be hit with the address.

The volunteer walked out.

The chief clerk muttered, "I told you he wasn't here."

The volunteer got into the hall.

Meanwhile Snelz was experiencing shock and heart
failure. The volunteer had no more than gotten on the
zipbus when the feeling of being smart and clever
turned, in Snelz, to horror.

THE MODEL 99 LANDED!

In a state of acute paralysis he watched Madison get
out, walk through the dust to the barricade before the zipbus. Snelz didn't dare breathe. Would the officer on duty
notice he was logging Madison in TWICE?

Action was the answer to everything with Snelz. He
drew a hand blastgun, fired at the top of a pole and shattered the light. He ducked.

As glass showered down, the guards raced for cover.
Madison put into action his own method of escape. He

swung aboard a zipbus quickly and looked back as it sped away into the tunnel.

Not daring to think what would happen when Madison ran into "Madison" in the elevator or hall, he did something he almost never did: he prayed.

The volunteer, meanwhile, was waiting in the hall for an elevator shaft to signal it was clear. Somebody was coming up!

Not wanting anything like a confrontation, possibly even with Lombar, the volunteer looked hastily around. There was a big box of fresh computer paper in the hall. It was only four feet high but he quickly dived behind it. Peering out, he was horrified to see the real Madison step out of the shaft!

The instant the hall was clear, the volunteer dived headfirst into the shaft to get out of there.

The real Madison walked into the clerk's office.

"What'd you do?" the chief clerk said, after an indifferent glance. "Forget something?"

Madison walked on into Lombar's office, saying, "I'll wait."

He had the newest clippings from the press. They gave a lot of juicy speeches about Hisst wanting law and order and raging about anyone trying to defame the honor of Apparatus officers, and he knew these shots of his angry face would delight Lombar no end. He wanted to make a nice display of them on the desk.

A stinger was propping up a big envelope and he accidentally knocked it down. He set it up once more. But it was in the way of his clipping spread. He decided it should be put further back. He took hold of it once more and moved the stinger and, then, with a double take, suddenly registered what was in his hand.

He stared, stunned.

TO LOMBAR HISST
FROM JETTERO HELLER
Private. Personal. Secret.

How had that gotten there?

It was still sealed.

Lombar hadn't seen it yet.

Not knowing anything about Heller's admonition to Snelz that Lombar would have the messenger killed, particularly if the seals were broken, Madison quivered with greed to know.

What was this? Some secret communication line?

And as it was from the only reason he was doing all he was doing, he could hardly resist.

He broke the seals.

It was all quiet in the outer office.

Madison swiftly read:

Hisst,

> *Greetings and salutations and all that sort of thing, none of them sincere:*

> *You have known for some time the company I've been enjoying as I left you the present of my baton.*

> *As you know—for you keep saying so on Homeview—His Majesty is suffering from an indisposition, and we really do not want to trouble him with such a small matter as signing and sealing a Royal proclamation declaring you a traitor and a menace to the state.*

> *However, we can promise you that in the event you seek to use the Army or the Fleet in attacking Calabar, the proclamation will be*

---

*issued and that will be the end of Hisst. So
my advice to you is simply to fly into a few
rages, shoot some of your own staff and let
nature take its course.*

> *Hoping not to have the
> pleasure of seeing you
> hanging on the gallows,*
>
> *Jettero Heller*

Madison read it again. Suddenly everything began to
click together. Time after time he had told Hisst that all
he had to do was get a Royal proclamation about this
thing or that: Hisst every time had looked extremely
cagey!

Madison abruptly understood.

There was no Emperor back of that Palace City door
Hisst guarded and saw guarded so carefully!

Jettero Heller had kidnapped the Emperor!

So THAT was what this was all about!

Madison glanced around. He did not think that he
was in any way observed.

This was not a communication line. It was a first
time.

Risks were the very thing his profession was made
of. Madison put the envelope and despatch in his own
briefcase. He left no trace of it on the desk.

He arranged his PR display of clippings. He went
into the clerk's office. He said, "Have there been any
urgent messages for Hisst?"

The old clerk shook his head.

A surge of elation coursed through Madison. What

an outlaw! Heller had somehow, unbeknownst to anyone, slipped into this office, maybe from the roof, and had left Hisst this envelope.

Looking very calm, Madison sat down at the console of the computer and, as though to pass the time, began to extract bits of information he might find handy, such as the strength of forces on the planet Calabar. Then he began to tally up the enormous numbers available in the Army and the Fleet.

Obviously, from the message, Heller didn't want these people after him. Madison was trying to work out how he could accomplish just that.

Oh, what headlines all this would eventually make!

Not right now, of course, but later when he had his campaign all worked out and perfect.

If he had had any slightest doubt before, that he would make his goal, he had none now. He would, for sure, return to Earth in glory—if, of course, there was anything left of it.

Hisst came in an hour later. Madison walked with the man into his office. Hisst was very pleased with the press.

"Things are going well," said Hisst.

"Yes, we'll have you Emperor in no time," said Madison.

HE DID NOT SAY ONE SINGLE WORD ABOUT THE HELLER DESPATCH!

Snelz, when the volunteer, sneaking past the barricade, had returned, sighed with relief.

He saw Hisst arrive and go up to the tower.

Neither the chief nor the real Madison came out.

He could only assume that the message had been delivered.

For a second time, a message which would have forestalled an invasion of Earth had been stopped en route.

And not only that, this one had fallen into the hands of a man to whom it gave total power: J. Walter Madison, who could use it in any villainous way he chose and at a moment when he considered it would be the most advantageous in a headline.

KNOWLEDGE WAS POWER! And Madison now knew that he was the only one on Voltar with the vital, pivotal information that the Emperor was on Calabar and Heller was holding him a captive!

WHAT A STORY!

But not for now. No, no, not for now. This one had to be built up to with the biggest BANG this universe had ever heard!

As he returned to Joy City, the glee in Madison threatened to bubble out and explode!

The fate of two empires was truly up for grabs! And J. Warbler Madman was the one who would do the tossing!

PART
EIGHTY-ONE

Chapter 1

The first toss by Madison came the moment Soltan Gris took the stand in the crowded courtroom.

Lord Turn had bowed to the pleas of his own guard captains, the newssheets and the Domestic Police, who all promised they could not prevent riots unless the people were kept informed, minute to minute, on the progress of the proceedings. They pointed out there were no laws or regulations which forbade it: it was simply a new idea. Lord Turn, against his better judgment, had agreed to a public trial.

Madison, who was behind it, could not have asked for more.

The biggest courtroom of the old castle was jammed from the dais to the entrance doors. Even the buttresses had stages clinging to them. The gray stone looked down upon six thousand people crammed in where only four thousand should have been. The high windows let in shafts of dusty sunlight.

The Homeview crews were in ecstasy. They had never been permitted in a courtroom before and they kept racing about jamming cameras into people's faces, hitting mouths with microphones, telling people to look this way and that, colliding all the while with press photographers and stumbling over reporters.

Lord Turn, in vain, was banging his mace of office

on the dais gong. He was nearly in despair: this whole thing was being seen all over Voltar and, on delay, throughout the entire Confederacy. He was certain people were bound to get the impression that he ran a very disorderly court. He wished to blazes those refreshment vendors would stop hawking their wares at the tops of their voices.

Only when his chief clerk brought him an electronic megaphone did hope revive in him that he would be heard. He pointed it at the gong and struck a tremendous blow with his mace. The result was ear-shattering.

"The court is in session!" Lord Turn roared. "If the prisoner Soltan Gris will take the stand, I can read him the charges!"

Instant hush.

Soltan Gris, manacled, was sitting on a bench surrounded by the three attorneys that the Widow Tayl (Mrs. Gris) had provided him. Gris had thought he would be dressed in a General Services officer's gray.

Instead, he was appearing in the black uniform of an Apparatus Death Battalion colonel. He had protested but his attorneys had said he had no choice. He even had to put on the scarlet gloves.

Soltan Gris was scared: in addition to everything else, he had stage fright.

The three attorneys were trying to look reassuring. They were old men; two of them had been Domestic Police judges and the third a Lord's executioner. Gris did not trust them. But it had been explained to him that this was the closest anyone could get to a criminal defense attorney on Voltar, and although he had to accept them, he still did not believe they were on his side: the explanation had been done by Madison.

His evident refusal to walk toward the railed stand

began to elicit a storm of animal sounds from the assembled, and his attorneys gave him a forward shove and two sergeants grabbed him. With a clank and clatter of manacles, Gris was propelled to the raised rail chair: its door was opened and he was slammed into it, the instant center of all eyes. Yells of hate bombarded him like missiles; a shaft of dirty sunlight from a high, round window blinded him. Gris was confused.

Lord Turn, again using the loudspeaker held to the gong, banged for silence. He hitched his scarlet robe around him and leaned from his massive chair toward Gris.

"You are Soltan Gris," said Lord Turn, "officer of the Coordinated Information Apparatus. Verify if correct."

Gris swallowed hard and nodded.

Turn had every hope of getting this over fast. "You are accused," said Turn, "of false and felonious bigamy committed in this prison. You may make any statement you care to before you are sentenced."

Gris drew a long, shuddering breath. The crime carried the death penalty. He couldn't possibly see how he could get out of it. He had not seen Teenie in the court but he suspected she would have papers showing earlier marriages and would have given them to the judge. It looked like he was a goner for sure.

When he didn't answer at once, the animal sounds started up again. The spectators had had all their weapons removed by guards but that didn't include spent chank-pops and sweetsticks. A few missiles came his way. He gathered the idea that he was not popular. His mind was confused.

Lord Turn hit the gong again to bring order. It was

like a shock to Gris. Suddenly, INSPIRATION! He would say what Madison had told him to say.

Gris shouted, "I accuse Jettero Heller! He is the cause of any crimes!"

Whatever the vast audience had expected to hear, it had not been that. Abruptly, one could have heard a dust mote fall.

Lord Turn sat up straight and blinked. Then he said, "Just a minute. Jettero Heller is a Royal officer. You were HIS prisoner in this jail. But this is NOT the trial we're trying. You are being charged with false and felonious marriage committed within these very walls."

Gris took heart. He hadn't been sentenced yet. His attorneys were all nodding at him. He shouted, "I still accuse Heller!"

A buzz of confusion went through the room.

Lord Turn said, in an incredulous voice, "You accuse him of causing you to commit bigamy?"

Gris glanced toward his attorneys. They were all nodding at him. Madison, on the bench behind them, was grinning. Gris said, "Absolutely. He refused to follow orders. He went absolutely wild. Jettero Heller put me in a position where all I could do to defend myself was to get married again."

The buzz in the room rose in volume: it was becoming a roar of confusion.

Lord Turn hit the gong again. "Clerk," he said to his scribe at a lower desk, "this prisoner is being willfully digressive. Strike those remarks from the record."

But Madison's grin widened. They might get struck on the record but they had been carried by Homeview all over Voltar and would be all over the Confederacy.

The eldest Gris attorney, one of the two ex-Domestic Police judges, rose and demanded attention. "Your

Lordship," he said to Turn, "we accept the charge of bigamy in your prison but will seek to prove it was totally justified."

"WHAT?" cried Turn.

The old attorney said, "To clarify the point, we will have to produce a great many witnesses. They will attest to various crimes and situations that give the background nature of this charge and when we come to the end of this trial, I am sure you will agree that the extenuating circumstances are so great that you will be bound to find our client innocent."

Lord Turn roared, "Don't presume to tell me what my findings will be!" Then he saw the Homeview cameras on him. He must not appear unreasonable or prejudiced. "However," he said with a groan, "produce your witnesses and we will get on with this."

Madison's spirits soared into Heaven Number Seven. It was exactly what he had planned and hoped for. He had brought off a PR man's dream. He almost chortled aloud with delight. Miles and miles of headlines stretched before him like a roaring river of the blackest ink.

And all for Heller!

Chapter 2

A trial which, by Voltar standards, should have taken ten minutes was, artfully, due to Madison's careful coaching, being dragged out Earth-style for days and weeks and, he hoped, months.

And it gave headlines every day and provided hours of Homeview.

The two old Domestic Police judges, in their century on the bench, had seen and judged over every stall and circumlocution that prisoners by tens of thousands had ever dreamed up—and those prisoners had lots of time before trial to think. The old Lord's executioner had heard every plea and dodge that terrorized victims and anguished families had ever strained their brains to put forth. Many had worked and they used them all for Gris.

The basic pattern of defense, however, was always more or less the same.

Witnesses, called by Gris's attorneys, would take the stand. Each would detail and produce incontrovertible, horrifying evidence of a Gris crime. Although many of these crimes had already appeared in newspapers before the trial, here they were exhibited and reenacted and dwelt on for hours and hours, each one, until not the most sordid, vicious detail was left to the imagination. Wrecks were found and hauled in. Bodies were even exhumed and filled the courtroom with their stench.

Gris was becoming more confident, even cockier, in the limelight. When, after a day or two or even three was spent upon a crime, he would again be put upon the stand, he would confess that the evidence was true, that he had done it and that as an Apparatus officer he pleaded guilty to it BUT he would qualify the statement by declaring each time, "JETTERO HELLER MADE ME DO IT. IT WAS ALL BECAUSE OF HIM."

Headlines, headlines, headlines, hours and hours of Homeview. Day after day. Week after week. The public outrage against this Apparatus officer was growing to such a pitch that Lord Turn borrowed tanks and stationed them in front of every gate. Not only was the courtroom jammed each day but the whole hill on which the castle stood was a constant jam of spectators. Every Homeview set on Voltar was playing to crowds.

Several times Lord Turn addressed the Gris attorneys. "How in the name of anything holy is this continuous blackening of your client ever going to get him off?"

The attorneys calmly ignored Turn's bafflement. They just continued to produce more crimes. Gris continued to plead guilty to them. Gris continued to assert that Heller had made him do them. And so the show went on.

The Fleet was becoming absolutely livid. These accusations by a "drunk," sitting there and grinning now in his black Apparatus colonel's uniform, continually accusing a Royal officer of the Fleet—and of all people, Jettero Heller—and never explaining for a moment how or why he had made Gris do it was getting to be a lot more than the Fleet could take.

The court was only running mornings, and one afternoon Madison received an urgent summons from Lombar Hisst to come at once to the Apparatus plaza in Government City.

He flew in but was diverted by an Apparatus patrol to an entrance through the cliff below. Even so, he had a glimpse of the plaza: it was packed with Fleet staff cars bearing admirals' pennants.

Lombar Hisst was in a dungeon room under his office. He met Madison the instant the PR man stepped out of the airbus.

"You've got to help me," said the agitated Hisst. "There's a deputation up there. The most senior officers of the Fleet. The Fleet outnumbers the Apparatus ten to one, even more. They're very angry about what Gris is saying! What if they mutiny?"

"Now listen," said Madison, in a calm, reassuring voice, "this is just a problem in PR and we are being very successful. The basics are Coverage, Controversy and Confidence. We surely have Coverage: every paper is giving us front page every day and the Homeview exposure is terrific. This deputation is vital Controversy. We could not possibly do without it. Now all we have to add is maximum Confidence."

"That's what's getting shaky," said Lombar. "Mine."

"Oh, no, no," said Madison, "this is all part of the plan. This is a heaven-sent opportunity for image building. You can raise public confidence to the stars with it! This is just another great chance to be a STRONG MAN! Somebody not to be trifled with! Now give me one of those presigned blanks we got from the Grand Council. I'll send for my camera crew. You just let those admirals cool their heels while I set this up."

Lombar, much reassured, did as he was told.

An hour later, in his cave of an office, before the cameras of Madison's crew, he stood tall in his red uniform and glared at the deputation in powder blue.

In a roaring voice, into the incredulous faces of senior Fleet officers he had not even invited to sit, Lombar Hisst, using the Madison prepared speech, stormed, "You are here to complain about the statements of the prisoner Gris. I shall have you know that he is not representative of the Apparatus. Apparatus officers are honest and upright men, beyond reproach. That is more than I can say for officers of the Fleet. You have dared to question what I, the Dictator of Voltar, have ordered. Therefore, know all, by order of the Grand Council and signed by the Lord of the Fleet, its member, the following regulations are in effect at once:

"A) No officer or personnel of the Fleet may mention the name of Jettero Heller.

"B) No officer or personnel of the Fleet may speak ill of the Apparatus.

"C) No officer or personnel of the Fleet may complain about myself, Lombar Hisst, in any way, or question any order that I issue, no matter how or where.

"D) Fleet officers must salute any officer or personnel of the Apparatus.

"E) Any offender against these regulations shall be docked a year's pay.

"The deputation before me is dismissed. Get out of here at once!"

A senior, gray-haired admiral, the whole front of his uniform gold with decorations, stepped forward. "Hisst, I can see from here that the order you hold in your hand bears no Royal seal. It cannot therefore be enforced, as it has no validity."

Hisst drew himself up like a red thunderstorm. The cameras were rolling. "You, sir, have just violated Section C of this issue twice. You have questioned an order I gave and the deputation which came to me so impudently has not left! Therefore," and he reached down to his desk for another order Madison had just typed in case, "the entire Fleet is restricted to its ships and bases and this order calls upon the Army to enforce it. Now salute and LEAVE!"

They did not salute. They left.

The camera crew went out to show them getting into the airbuses.

Lombar was ecstatic. "They obeyed!" he said to Madison. "Did you see their faces? Almost purple! But they are cowed! Why, I suddenly realize I can use them to relieve the Apparatus on Calabar and begin to organize the invasion of Blito-P3 in earnest!"

"Oh, yes, indeed," said Madison. "Today you've taken a giant step forward to assuming total power and the Crown."

"I certainly have," said Lombar, expanding. "When we capture Rockecenter and put him back on his throne there, I'm going to have to tell him what a truly magnificent aide you are."

Madison grinned.

This was cream on top of cream.

Yes, his homecoming would be glorious.

He just had to make sure that he had finished his job with Heller.

Chapter 3

Madison felt now that it was time to advance his program a notch. According to his notebooks, with this trial, so far, he had been using a PR technique known as "invidious association."

Day after day, as the gruesome testimony ran on, Lord Turn would challenge the Gris attorneys, demanding they inform him exactly what this or that crime could possibly have to do with Jettero Heller. In fact, each time Gris would take the stand again to admit guilt and state that he had done it because of Heller, Lord Turn would lose no chance to again demand an explanation—what did this have to do with the charge against Gris and what did it have to do with Jettero Heller? But the Gris attorneys were old, experienced hands and, with this legal dodge or that, would insist on their rights to present the case IN FULL before giving any explanation of relevance. In due course, they solemnly promised Lord Turn, it would be revealed just how the charge of bigamy was incurred by Gris because of Heller.

The image of Heller was becoming surrounded in mystery. Now it was time to begin to give it more substance. To a master of PR like Madison, it was just child's play. The next move, while the trial continued, was to begin the image remold. It was time to release the musical.

He got Hightee Heller on the viewer-phone. "I understand," he said, "that the play, *The Outlaw*, is all ready to hit the stage."

"That's true," said Hightee. "Sets and costumes, music, all rehearsed and ready to go. But I don't think this is a wise time to do it. It has political connotations and the political scene looks pretty rocky."

"Oh, heavens," said Madison, "is that all? Forget it. I can absolutely guarantee that no harm will come to you. Hisst will do whatever I say."

"I've noticed that," said Hightee.

"Well, come on, then, be a sport. The people hate him anyway and they love you. He wouldn't dare touch you. By the way, you haven't heard from dear Jettero, have you?"

"Oh, when I showed the jewel, a Fleet observer wrote in and said he was certain, from the way an Apparatus fuel dump was blown up, that Jet was on Calabar. But that's impossible. He'd never side with rebels."

Madison knew very well that Heller was on Calabar,

but he said, "Of course not. Well, shall we put the musical on the planks tomorrow night?"

"If you can guarantee nothing will happen to members of the cast. We're dealing with Apparatus thugs, you know, and I don't want my friends knocked around."

The shameless Madison said, "I absolutely guarantee on my honor as a gentleman, nothing at all will happen to the cast and no harm will come to you. Hisst just needs a bit of slowing down, that's all."

"All right," said Hightee, "in front of the cameras she goes, tomorrow night, live. Good viewing."

Madison called the manager of Homeview and dictated some announcement spots to go on the air at once and continuing. They were terrific come-ons. He wanted all Voltar in front of sets tomorrow night and the whole Confederacy right after.

At 6:30 the following evening, he ran down Lombar in his Government City office. Madison walked in looking very worried.

"Chief, in just a few minutes, there is something I have to get your opinion on. I tried to stop it but they are so bullheaded over at Homeview. They wouldn't listen, and furthermore, they wouldn't even tell me what it was all about. You've seen the spot ads?"

Lombar was reading some reports of fights and riots between the Army and the Fleet, occasioned by the Army halfheartedly trying to enforce Fleet quarantine to bases. It was giving him some satisfaction to see them quarrelling with each other instead of him. His confidence was rising. The strong-man image seemed to be very effective. He hardly paid any attention at all when Madison turned on the Homeview.

The spot announcer said, "In just fifteen minutes

now, the new HIGHTEE HELLER musical, *The Outlaw*, will come to you live, live, live. It has a new type of music called *downbeat* that has never been heard before. It has a cast of hundreds. After this one showing on Homeview it will move to the Joy City Amphitheater. So this is your last chance to view it free. Hightee Heller takes her life in her hands to bring it to you. So rush out and get your neighbors and friends and people on the street and get them to your set. It may be your last chance to see Hightee. BE HERE!"

Spot ads themselves weren't usually done on Homeview, so the fact that they had been running now every hour for the last thirty-six was creating something of a sensation. There was hardly anyone who did not know that something was going to happen tonight. That "takes her life in her hands" was not understood at all. Was she going to do death-defying feats on the stage or what? The billions and billions of passionately devoted Hightee Heller fans reacted in a number of different ways. A few of them got physically ill at the idea of anything happening to "their dear Hightee." Alarmed calls had been jamming the circuit boards of Homeview all day from every part of the planet and some from other planets which only had delays measurable in hours.

The news followed. As a lot of day programming was given over to the trial, the news itself could get on with other matters. Mention was made that the fighting on Calabar seemed to be diminishing as Apparatus troops pulled out. Several papers were speculating on the target of some punitive strike, guessing at which of several unconquered planets. One said that a race had developed a new and devastating weapon and needed pre-invasion chastisement and a usually informed source mentioned that it might be Blito-P3. Lombar grinned like a toother at that: Madison had told him that such a leak "prepared the public mind."

Then the musical came on with a roar from the studio audience. The performers were all introduced, as is usual. Then with a fanfare the curtain went up and to the downbeat music, playing in a dirge version of ragtime, the Devils and the beaten people howled and moaned. The show had begun. Hightee stepped out and in a brilliant aria described the scene and the history of her brother and herself.

Madison glanced at Lombar. He seemed to find the antics of the red Devils and the abuse of the people a source of gratification. He hadn't really grasped the import of the play.

The brother went through his duplicity, the sister described it all in song, the choruses and scenery were superb.

Lombar seemed to be musing about something as he watched. He even once or twice tapped his boot toe in time to the music. Such was Lombar's ego that he seemed to be missing the point. But Madison knew that no one else on Voltar was missing it. They all knew that Hightee's brother was Jettero Heller. The lead male star in the piece, by Madison's covert interference, was a handsome blond youth from Manco, six foot two.

Then in the latter part of the play, just before the final scenes, Hightee Heller as the outlaw's sister is seen standing on the *cowcatcher* of an improbable *locomotive* of a *train* that is being robbed. Boxes and bags of loot are being taken off. Another robber comes to her, opens a box and says, "Look, we found some of the Devils' clothes, ha, ha, we found some of the Devils' clothes." And he holds up a scarlet Apparatus general's uniform.

Madison, at that moment, looked at Lombar. The Dictator of Voltar was sitting there stunned.

Hightee, at that point, throws back her head and laughs. Then she draws a *six-gun* and fires it in the air to attract the attention of peasants in the nearby fields. These all run up and Hightee sings them a song.

With the crazy downbeat rhythm and singing as only Hightee could sing, the ballad went:

> *The Devil's going to get you*
> *If you don't watch out.*
> *The Devil's going to cheat you*
> *Before you know he is about.*
> *He's going to hit you,*
> *With a great big stick.*
> *He is going to smash you*
> *With a fist that's quick.*
> *But if you saw the Devil*
> *When he was skinned,*
> *You would really find,*
> *He was just a bag of wind.*
> *For the Devil was bred*
> *In a lowly slum*
> *And every unknown father*
> *Was a gutter bum.*
> *The point of this song*
> *Should not be missed.*
> *I am singing about*
> (mouthed only) _____ _____ !

There is no mistaking the words that Hightee's lips form. They can only be "Lombar Hisst." But in their very silence, they are ten times as loud as if they had been spoken.

Then the robber holding the uniform inflates it with gas and it does a crazy dance as it rises. The stage-play brother rushes up, draws his *six-guns* and shoots the uniform full of holes. The peasants and robbers all go into a wild carnival of dance, stamping on the uniform and finally burning it in effigy.

But that wasn't the only thing that went into wild motion. Lombar was up out of his chair, waving his arms about wildly and leaping. "That's me! That's me she's singing about! I'll kill her! I'll maim her! She is holding me up to ridicule! Oh, Gods, I get the point of this play now! She's telling the people to revolt and tear me to bits!" He shook both fists at the screen and would have lunged into it but he tripped over a stool and began to roll around on the floor, frothing at the mouth.

The convulsions lasted until the burning of the effigy on the screen, and then Hisst lay there in a twisted pile, staring at the set as though in a catatonic stupor.

The rest of the play ran off, the brother and sister were both hanged and their bodies seized down into a grave and the vast cast all sadly sang the last song the sister had sung. Then they chorused *The Outlaw* theme song again, but with celestial overtones, and the face of Hightee and factually the face of Jettero Heller himself looked down from heaven. Madison's last touch had not been known to anybody except the bribed technician.

The studio audience went into yells and applause that Madison thought better than to complete. He turned the set off.

Lombar somehow got himself straightened out and fell into a chair.

"Now you see why I was worried," said Madison.

"It's Heller," said Lombar. "Heller put her up to this. All Voltar knows Jettero Heller is her brother. It didn't take that last picture of his face to drive it home! It's a plot against my life! I'll order a Death Battalion to raid her house and shoot her down at once!"

Madison said, "Lombar, all famous figures have to be able to withstand ridicule. It's one of the rules of the game: ridicule the mighty. But be calm, they have played right into your hands. I am glad that you have seen that. You can get even with her and can get Heller to show up. All you have to do is sign this note."

Lombar looked at it. A savage look replaced the shock that had been dominating him. "That's brilliant!" he said and signed it, stamped it.

Madison took it back to see that it was all in order. It said:

> *ARREST HIGHTEE HELLER AND*
> *HOLD HER. THEN BARGAIN WITH*
> *HER BROTHER AND GET HIM TO*
> *COME IN. THEN KILL THEM BOTH.*
>
> *LOMBAR HISST*

"Make sure you get that executed!" said Lombar with a ferocious snarl. "I've never been so affronted in my life!"

"I knew you'd see your way out of this," said Madison. "You can now ignore the details. Leave the rest up to me."

J. Warbler Madman was about to pull off the PR caper of the age.

Chapter 4

The arrest of Hightee Heller took place in the street before the huge dome studio of Homeview.

She had been told that a group of notables and fans from Mistin wished to present her with that planet's symbolic flower. There were some notables there all right, but they weren't from Mistin. They were Death Battalion men in civilian clothes.

Madison had his own camera crew placed on a ledge that outcropped from the dome: it was thirty feet above and could look down on the whole scene. There was another crew there, on the scene itself, assigned by the manager of Homeview. There were several reporters and photographers from papers.

The street was just a typical Joy City street, lined with shops that sold knickknacks and pretty clothes. The main entrance to the dome, however, was imposing, for the pavement just in front of it appeared to be made of gold. It was there that the deputation stood.

Hightee Heller came out of the building: she was dressed in a white gown and gold gloves. Such presentations were quite ordinary: she would simply go down, accept whatever it was, smile, shake hands, thank them and withdraw. It was a little ceremony that took place several times a week. She was usually only accompanied by a couple Homeview ushers to carry away the present or award or whatever it was. No one would have dreamed of flanking Hightee with security men, for in all her career, no one had ever laid a finger on the Homeview star or even frowned at her in public.

She might have been checked by the fact that the deputation was so silent. Usually such groups were more numerous and gave a little cheer when she appeared. This one just stood there, the man in front holding a bouquet.

She was five feet from the apparent leader. He extended the bouquet toward her stiffly. Still moving forward, she put out a hand toward it.

He dropped the flowers to the pavement.

They had masked the blastgun in his hand!

A whistle screamed.

With a single movement, two hundred men stepped out of the different shops. They wore black uniforms and carried rifles. The street was suddenly totally lined with these troops.

From the back of the deputation, a man strode forward, throwing off a cloak to reveal himself as a colonel of the Death Battalion.

Hightee turned to reenter the building.

Two Death Battalion soldiers blocked her way. She turned back to the "deputation."

The colonel's boot crushed the fallen flowers. "Hightee Heller, I arrest you in the name of Lombar Hisst!"

The two ushers made a sudden rush to protect Hightee.

Two actors, placed there by Madison for that purpose in Apparatus uniforms, smashed blood bags into the faces of her protectors! It looked exactly like they had been killed! They fell.

A member of the "deputation" raised and dropped a black sack over Hightee.

Four Death Battalion troopers grabbed her as though she were a bundle and rushed her into a personnel carrier.

Two hundred Death Battalion troops struck down the people who had stopped, stunned, in the street. They raced for their vehicles.

With a shattering roar of takeoffs, the street was empty except for pedestrians collapsed upon the walks.

Then people began to run out of the building and out of the shops. They looked around. They stared at the sky in horror. A woman began to scream.

Madison had the cameraman fade out on the crushed bouquet. It looked as though the battered flowers bled.

He was grinning. It had been carried live, as a special, over all Homeview.

It was on the streets in an hour:

HIGHTEE ARRESTED BY HISST

Madison had it all scheduled. Later papers would carry that her whereabouts was unknown, later ones would headline the beginning of the riots, tomorrow it would be:

BILLIONS MOURN

Madison now had other things to do.

Chapter 5

For three days, the Gris trial took second place. For all three of those days Madison had been beaming a message to Calabar. The message had been carried on all military wavelengths: these were known to be monitored by the rebels. The message, over and over, had said:

> *JETTERO HELLER. ON THURSDAY*
> *MORNING YOUR SISTER, HIGHTEE*
> *HELLER, WILL BE AT HERO PLAZA,*
> *GOVERNMENT CITY, VOLTAR. IF YOU*
> *DO NOT LAND THERE AND GIVE*
> *YOURSELF UP, AT NOON SHE WILL*
> *BE SHOT. LOMBAR HISST, DICTATOR*
> *OF THE CONFEDERACY.*

On Wednesday night, Madison leaked it to the papers. On Thursday morning it was being carried throughout the Confederacy.

Orders were crackling on every Apparatus, Domestic Police and Army line to control and suppress riots.

Hero Plaza is a circular expanse. It is two hundred yards in diameter. There is nothing there but clear pavement since it is often used for affairs of state. In the exact center is a completely plain circular pillar fifty feet tall and about twenty feet in circumference, led to by three circular steps. The only decoration or inscription is on the front edge of the top step: it says Dedicated to the Heroes of Voltar. Madison had chosen it carefully.

Entering the plaza were eight boulevards, usually crammed with traffic. Today each boulevard, at the plaza's edge, was blocked by an Apparatus tank.

At nine o'clock, Hightee Heller, gowned in white, was taken to the pillar by a Death Battalion squad. She was without her gloves now and the shoulder of the dress was torn. Her golden hair was in disarray but it still looked like a halo.

Her eyes were calm as she looked at the Apparatus general who, in his red uniform, was directing the squad.

A camera crew was close to hand, one of the several on duty at the plaza now. Hightee saw the microphone pointing in her direction.

"Jettero!" she suddenly shouted, "If you are listening, don't come in here! They mean to kill you!"

The general had acted slightly late. He clamped his beefy hand over Hightee's mouth. At a gesture, three of his squad chased the camera crew away. But Madison, hidden by a tank at the plaza edge, saw that other crews were covering. It was all going live to the whole Confederacy.

The Death Battalion took a chain. It was twenty feet long and had big links. They clamped one end of it on Hightee's left wrist; they ran the length around the pillar; they fastened the other end to Hightee's right wrist. They made sure the links were solid. She was chained now with her back to the pillar.

The squad drew back.

The heavy guns of the eight tanks at the boulevard ends trained around on Hightee.

Madison grinned. What a tableau! Beauty chained

to a pillar. A vast clear area of pavement. Eight deadly muzzles, ringing the plaza, poised for destruction.

And then things started to go slightly wrong. Possibly the crowds—which, despite roadblocks, had gotten into the boulevards—had been in the grip of unreality. This couldn't possibly be happening: it was too monstrous. But when the Apparatus general had dared to actually touch Hightee to silence her, a roar and mutter had begun to rise.

There must have been a hundred thousand people in those boulevards. There were only two or three thousand Apparatus troops forming barricades to block them.

The barricades buckled.

There was a roar of Apparatus stunguns.

Missiles flew from the crowd!

Apparatus troops charged them!

The Domestic Police were conspicuously absent. The Apparatus knew very little about crowd control.

For twenty minutes there was hand-to-hand fighting.

The crowd in three boulevards managed to break through the barricades. The tanks at the plaza end had to swivel their turrets about and fire.

Then the boulevards were full of stunned and bleeding bodies, civilians and Apparatus alike.

Two Apparatus relief regiments came in and boxed the mobs in the streets from the far end.

It was not until 10:20 that some kind of order was restored. But it was not very thorough, for people from the rest of the city were now surging up, and it took three more regiments to hold barricades as far away as a mile in each direction.

Madison had his eye on the big clock in a tower a thousand yards away. He supposed that Heller would wait until the last minute. At least he hoped so. He had no slightest notion that Heller would surrender. Besides, it would have wrecked his plans.

That clear space out there, a hundred yards in radius from the pillar where Hightee was chained, was ample for someone like Heller to land troops.

Madison did not think his own safety was at risk at all, for he didn't think that Heller would use artillery—it would endanger Hightee. Madison's greater worry was himself getting into the cameras: accordingly he was wearing a General Services gray uniform and he had altered his features with makeup and masked them with sand glasses. If any action started, he was going to step through the port of this tank.

The digitals of the distant clock were flashing second changes. He looked back at the tanks: their muzzles, freed now from crowd control, were pointed back at Hightee.

She was being pulled against the pillar too tightly by the chain. Her stretched-out arms must be half killing her. Her ripped gown had slid half off her shoulder. But she was looking at the sky.

Then Madison heard it.

A sort of booming sound.

IT WAS DIRECTLY OVERHEAD!

Madison looked up. For an instant, he could see nothing. Then he glimpsed a blur that was travelling high at some ferocious speed. What was it? Some strange kind of racer?

His view was suddenly blocked by a swinging gun. The tank was pointing at the sky.

A cry rose up from the held-back mobs.

It could only be Heller. But the high ship was going right on by!

Eight tanks opened up with a bucking, shattering

roar. The odd space-racer had already passed. They were firing after it.

Their shots were going straight through it!

It must be some sort of an illusion being pushed ahead of a speeding ship!

It was almost gone. Then suddenly a gun must have detected the actual vessel behind it.

THERE WAS A HUGE EXPLOSION IN THE SKY!

A direct hit from a tank!

Fragments of a ship were black against the blue!

A shrieking moan came from the crowd. Before their very eyes, the vessel had been shot down!

Madison glanced across the hundred-yard gap at Hightee. She was weeping.

Somewhere distant, the remains of the ship crashed, apparently into a warehouse, for flames shot skyward.

Madison looked at the tanks. He felt that his plans for great PR were gone. He supposed that Heller had been killed. It would make such brief headlines!

But then he saw a tank officer pointing. The arm was stretched upward.

A thousand small objects were drifting down out of the blue. They were above this whole area and made a mile-diameter circle of their own.

They came lower and lower. A tank suddenly opened up to try to shoot at least some of them out of the sky.

Madison saw a distant one wink.

Then he had a sudden impression that all the world had turned blue. Painfully, unbearably blue!

He went unconscious.

Only because cameras kept running would he find out what happened then.

It was blueflash. A thousand of them in antigravity

holders set to let them drift down. They must have been dropped when the high plane went over and were set to explode a thousand to two hundred feet above the pavement.

Almost every person in a mile diameter was knocked unconscious.

Then behind them came a larger bomb. It went *poof* about a hundred feet above the pillar.

The whole area was swallowed in dense fog.

Nothing could be seen.

Then there was the pulsing sound of spaceship drives. That first ship must have been a drone. Heller's had not been touched. There was the thump of a landing in the mist.

Then the click of airlock latches.

Heller's voice! Very softly, "Oh, I am so sorry I had to knock you out."

Shortly another click of latches. Then a throb of drives.

Half an hour later, Madison came awake.

The mist was gone.

There was nothing in the plaza but two broken chains.

HIGHTEE HAD VANISHED!

Madison looked at the bare pillar. No, there was something else there now. Something hanging from a pin.

Madison groggily stumbled forward. He got a camera crew on its feet. He made them go up and shoot the broken chains and then this strange object on the pin.

It was a cheap excursion ticket. It had been reworked so as to read:

A ONE–WAY TRIP TO HELL NINE
FOR LOMBAR HISST

Madison was ecstatic. He had his headline:

OUTLAW BROTHER RESCUES SISTER

HIGHTEE SAVED

JETTERO HELLER CONSIGNS DICTATOR OF VOLTAR TO PERDITION!

Madison had done it. He had converted Heller into an outlaw that could now be chased by every active unit in the whole Confederacy!

And the incident of Hero Plaza had started his client on the road to immortality.

Chapter 6

"I can't imagine how it happened," said a stunned Lombar in the safety of his dungeon office at Government City. "Heller is still on the loose!"

"It's simply that people don't realize yet," said Madison, "that you mean business. They didn't do the job properly. They let you down."

"That's true," said Hisst. "I have been too weak. I

have tolerated the riffraff too long. Now they are rioting in the streets."

"Things have gotten up to a point of national emergency," said Madison. "You need people around you you can trust."

"Trust somebody?" said Lombar, for this was a brand-new idea.

"I admit that someone like that is pretty rare. But we'll have to do something about these riots before we can get on with our business. I'll be right back."

Madison went into another room. There were some Army officers there, looking very unhappy. They had come to report trouble in trying to confine the Fleet to their bases.

Madison said to an elderly colonel, "Who is the most popular general in the whole Army?"

"That's easy," said the colonel. "General Whip."

The others nodded.

"Is he really, truly popular with the Army?" said Madison.

"Men, officers, everybody," said the colonel. "He wins battles because his troops trust him not to waste their lives. And he's a brilliant strategist. He's over at Army General Staff Headquarters right now. You want to talk to him about this Fleet situation?"

"Have him come over here right away," said Madison.

Twenty minutes later, General Whip arrived. He was a tough old campaigner but he had a nice smile. His high forehead showed lots of brains.

Madison's camera crew took some pictures of him. The two logistics men looked him over very carefully.

Madison then went in and had a word with Lombar.

He beckoned from the door to General Whip, who entered.

"General," said Lombar, "there is a Fleet officer named Jettero Heller. He has been stirring the people up. He is now an outlaw. I want you to run him down."

The general smiled, "If you mean Jettero Heller, I'd like to point out that he is a Royal officer. I heard there is a general warrant out for him but courts just won't accept that. If you will give me a Royal order, I will see what I can do."

Lombar glared at him. "I'll have you know that I am Dictator of Voltar. Heller has forfeited any status he may ever have had. I am ordering you right now to get the entire Army busy and run down this outlaw!"

General Whip looked Lombar up and down. Then he shrugged and left.

"I didn't like that," said Lombar to Madison.

"Be patient. You'll see how this works out. All we have to do is wait for a report from one of my crew."

Two hours later, one of the actors of Madison's crew, dressed as an Army officer, signalled to Madison from the door. Madison went over and they exchanged a few words.

Madison came back to Lombar. "It was just as I suspected. General Whip went back to his headquarters and began to laugh at you."

"WHAT?" cried Lombar.

"I expected that he would," said Madison. "What this requires is a show of force. They will only obey you if you are shown to be a man that cannot be trifled with. Only after that can you trust them. Please sign this order."

Lombar looked at it. It said:

> GENERAL WHIP HAS REFUSED
> ORDERS TO FIND JETTERO HEL-
> LER. BRING ME THE HEAD OF
> GENERAL WHIP.

Hisst grinned like a toother. He grabbed his pen and signed it. He stamped it.

Madison took it. He left.

Madison's camera crew came into Lombar's office and set up. Lombar, agitatedly going over Earth invasion plans, hardly noticed them: camera setups were a common occurrence lately. He was much more concerned that, despite his adulterations, speed supplies were very low.

Suddenly the door opened. Five women dressed as noble ladies—they were the circus girls—came in and knelt before Lombar. They were crying.

One of them, collapsing, was supported by two on either side of her. One of these said, "Forgive her. She is the wife of General Whip. She came to plead for mercy. But she has fainted. I plead in her stead. Please, please, please spare the life of General Whip!"

The cameras were grinding. The angles were such that one could not see the faces of the women, only their backs. What predominated in the scene was the ferocious scowl of the red-uniformed Lombar Hisst.

Suddenly there was a commotion at the door. The two actor officers, dressed in Army uniforms, came in. Between them they bore a platter. And on that platter, sopped in gore, appeared to be the head of General Whip!

The women screamed and fainted dead away.

The two officers knelt. "Sir," said one, "your orders have been followed. General Whip has been executed for failure to take your command to hunt down Heller. Here is the head of General Whip."

Lombar glared with ferocity. "That will teach him! My word is supreme! Remove that carrion and these females at once!"

The whole scene had been shot. The room was cleared. Madison walked back in.

Madison had filled out another blank Grand Council order, ready for the signature, as well, of Hisst.

"I think," said Madison, "that when they see that on Homeview, there isn't a single officer out there who won't obey you. Please sign this."

Hisst read it. It said:

TO ALL OFFICERS OF ARMY AND FLEET: YOU WILL AT ONCE BEGIN TO HUNT FOR AND YOU WILL FIND THE NOTORIOUS OUTLAW JETTERO HELLER.

He signed it with a flourish.

Madison grinned. The manhunt he had envisioned would now take place.

The heat and beat of the elation within his veins was close to ecstasy.

WHAT HEADLINES!

*Will Earth survive
Hisst's final rage?*

***Find out in
the final book of
MISSION EARTH
Volume 10
THE DOOMED PLANET***

About the Author
L. Ron Hubbard

Born in 1911, the son of a U.S. naval officer, the legendary L. Ron Hubbard grew up in the great American West and was acquainted early with a rugged outdoor life before he took to the sea. The cowboys, Indians and mountains of Montana were balanced with an open sea, temples and the throngs of the Orient as Hubbard journeyed through the Far East as a teen-ager. By the time he was nineteen, he had travelled over a quarter of a million sea miles and thousands on land, recording his experiences in a series of diaries, mixed with story ideas.

When Hubbard returned to the U.S., his insatiable curiosity and demand for excitement sent him into the sky as a barnstormer where he quickly earned a reputation for his skill and daring. Then he turned his attention to the sea again. This time it was four-masted schooners and voyages into the Caribbean, where he found the adventure and experience that were to serve him later at the typewriter.

Drawing from his travels, he produced an amazing wealth of stories, from adventure and westerns to mystery and detective.

By 1938, Hubbard was already established and recognized as one of the top-selling authors, when a major new magazine, Street and Smith's *Astounding Science Fiction*, called for new blood. Hubbard was urged to try his hand at science fiction. The red-headed author protested that he did not write about "machines and machinery" but that he wrote about people. "That's just what we want," he was told.

The result was a barrage of stories from Hubbard that expanded the scope and changed the face of the genre, gaining Hubbard a repute, along with Robert Heinlein, as one of the "founding fathers" of the great Golden Age of Science Fiction.

Then as now he excited intense critical comparison with the best of H. G. Wells and Edgar Allan Poe. His prodigious creative output of more than a hundred novels and novelettes and more than two hundred short stories, with over twenty-two million copies of fiction in a dozen languages sold throughout the world, is a true publishing phenomenon.

But perhaps most important is that as time went on, Hubbard's work and style developed to masterful proportions. The 1982 blockbuster *Battlefield Earth,* celebrating Hubbard's 50th year as a professional writer, remained for 32 weeks on the nation's bestseller lists and received the highest critical acclaim.

"A superlative storyteller with total mastery of plot and pacing."—*Publishers Weekly*

"A huge (800+ pages) slugfest. Mr. Hubbard celebrates fifty years as a pro writer with tight plotting, furious action, and have-at-'em entertainment."—*Kirkus Review*

But the final *magnum opus* was yet to come. L. Ron Hubbard, after completing *Battlefield Earth,* sat down and did what few writers have dared contemplate—let alone achieve. He wrote the ten-volume space adventure satire *Mission Earth.*

Filled with a dazzling array of other-world weaponry and systems, *Mission Earth* is a spectacular cavalcade of battles, of stunning plot reversals, with heroes and heroines, villains and villainesses, caught up in a superbly imaginative, intricately plotted invasion of Earth—as seen entirely and uniquely through the eyes of the aliens that already walk among us.

With the distinctive pace, artistry and humor that is the inimitable hallmark of L. Ron Hubbard, *Mission Earth* weaves a hilarious, fast-paced adventure tale of ingenious alien intrigue, told with biting social commentary in the great classic tradition of Swift, Wells and Orwell.

So unprecedented is this work that a new term—dekalogy (meaning ten books)—had to be coined just to describe its breadth and scope.

With the manuscript completed and in the hands of the publisher and all of his other work done, L. Ron Hubbard departed his body on January 24, 1986. He left behind a timeless legacy of unparalleled story-telling richness for you the reader to enjoy, as other readers have, time and again, over the past half century.

We the publishers are proud to present L. Ron Hubbard's dazzling tour de force: the *Mission Earth* dekalogy.

"I am always happy to hear from my readers."

L. Ron Hubbard

These were the words of L. Ron Hubbard, who was always very interested in hearing from his friends and readers. He made a point of staying in communication with everyone he came in contact with over his fifty-year career as a professional writer, and he had thousands of fans and friends that he corresponded with all over the world.

The publishers of L. Ron Hubbard's literary works wish to continue this tradition and would very much welcome letters and comments from you, his readers, both old and new.

Any message addressed to the Author's Affairs Director at Bridge Publications will be given prompt and full attention.

BRIDGE PUBLICATIONS, INC.
4751 Fountain Avenue
Los Angeles, California 90029

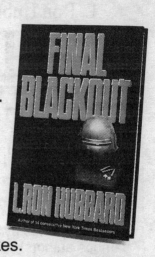